AN HONEST MAN

ALSO BY MICHAEL KORYTA

Never Far Away

If She Wakes

How It Happened

Rise the Dark

Last Words

Those Who Wish Me Dead

The Prophet

The Ridge

The Cypress House

So Cold the River

The Silent Hour

Envy the Night

A Welcome Grave

Sorrow's Anthem

Tonight I Said Goodbye

AN HONEST MAN

MICHAEL KORYTA

MULHOLLAND
BOOKS

Little, Brown and Company
New York Boston London

Mulholland Books / Little, Brown and Company
Hachette Book Group
1290 Avenue of the Americas, New York, NY 10104
mulhollandbooks.com

First Edition: July 2023

Mulholland Books is an imprint of Little, Brown and Company, a division of Hachette Book Group, Inc. The Mulholland Books name and logo are trademarks of Hachette Book Group, Inc.

The publisher is not responsible for websites (or their content) that are not owned by the publisher.

The Hachette Speakers Bureau provides a wide range of authors for speaking events. To find out more, go to hachettespeakersbureau.com or email hachettespeakers@hbgusa.com.

Little, Brown and Company books may be purchased in bulk for business, educational, or promotional use. For information, please contact your local bookseller or the Hachette Book Group Special Markets Department at special.markets@hbgusa.com.

ISBN 9780316535946
LCCN 2022943879

Printing 1, 2023

LSC-C

Printed in the United States of America

For Richard Pine and his family, with gratitude

Acting is all about honesty. If you can fake that, you've got it made.

—George Burns

When we're all gone at last then there'll be nobody here but death and his days will be numbered too.

—Cormac McCarthy, *The Road*

Part One

EXTINCTION LEVEL EVENTS

I

The yacht appeared nine weeks after Israel returned to his father's house, and even from a distance and under the squeezed red sun of dawn, he could see that the vessel was in trouble. Adrift, rudderless, a possession of the sea rather than a partner of it.

Like anyone who'd grown up on an island off the coast of Maine, he'd seen boats adrift before—five of them, he would later recall for investigators—and in four of those circumstances, the boats had been empty. In the fifth, a child had been aboard, alone after cutting the lines at a dock and letting the tide take him. The boy's goal had been to teach his parents a lesson, and Israel supposed he'd succeeded, because the boat was in the rocks before they got to it.

So five times he had watched the meandering, listless behavior of a boat without a human hand to direct it, that drunkard's drift, and five times no one had been hurt. The sixth time would be different.

Why? What was so different about this one? the investigators would ask.

He told them the obvious things—the size of the craft, the knowledge that there would be a crew aboard, the lack of response to his shouts. What he didn't tell them was the way the stillness of the yacht contrasted with the ceaseless energy of the sea and made him think of stories his grandfather had told him in the old Pike and Sons Shipyard, cigar tucked in his mouth, twinkle in his eyes, tales of ghost ships, of frigates washed ashore with skeletons in the hold. Israel spoke instead of the ship's path toward the rocks that ringed Salvation Point and how he felt like he needed to get out there in a hurry or the damage would be swift and severe.

He crossed the channel in his skiff. He'd had two months of daily rowing by then, and he could make the little boat move when he needed to. That morning, he put everything he had into it.

The yacht was at least a hundred feet long, maybe a hundred and twenty-five, and it was hard to anticipate the rudderless craft's motions. Israel came in from the port side, where he had protection from the wind. The yacht had turned in almost a full circle, as if fighting to point south again, to head back home. He put fenders off the sides of the skiff, aligned his path with the yacht's stern, then rode the waves down and into the stern, the contact jarring even with the fenders down. He got hold of a stanchion and tied the skiff off. When he stood, the yacht's superstructure towered above him, its bulbous radar antennas reaching skyward. The vessel's name was scripted in gold across deep blue paint on the stern: *Mereo.*

It was not a pretty name. The word felt harsh, sharp-edged.

Mereo.

He waited out another wave and then stepped off the skiff and onto the ladder. He was halfway up to the deck when it occurred to him that he hadn't even attempted to call out or get the attention of anyone aboard.

Sometimes you knew.

He shouted a "Hello" then. Got nothing back. He hoped, all the way up the ladder and over the stern rail onto the deck, that they'd abandoned ship, although he could not imagine why they would have. He kept that hope even though the yacht tender that would have been used for shore transport still hung from its lift and the gulls rode the wind at a distance. Later that day he asked people about the birds—tentatively, because he didn't wish to describe the scene yet again, but diligently, because he needed to know. No one could explain it. Gulls were not repelled by blood, the detectives told him. They should have been drawn to it.

All Israel Pike knew was that on the morning he'd boarded the *Mereo,* they had not been.

The yacht was a Ferretti 1000, which meant nothing to him. There were stairs with glass-and-steel railings leading up to the raised pilothouse with a flybridge to his left, and just beyond them, the door to the salon, its interior murky behind tinted windows. He should have gone up to the pilothouse first, but the door to the salon was open, so he did what you do when confronted with an open door—he walked right on through.

Sometimes, the person who benefits most from a closed door is the one outside it.

Inside the salon was a full bar flanked by U-shaped settees in white leather. The mahogany accents gleamed. When the investigators asked him what he was thinking in this moment, he answered honestly: He was thinking that he had seen wood like that only once in his life, when he'd helped prep a vacation home on Islesboro for painting. The wood in that house had been cherry, not mahogany, but it had shone like a bride on her wedding day. He'd never seen anything like it before and had not again until he entered the salon in the yacht called *Mereo.*

The first body was slumped beside the dining table—a man in a black polo shirt and olive pants, shot in the head. The corpse should have commanded Israel's attention instantly, but instead he focused on the white carpet, once bright as fresh snow, now ruined by blood. Ruby sprinkles mixed with jets so dark they looked like motor oil. There would be no fixing that rug. People had died here, and yet for one long moment the only question in Israel's mind was: *Who in the hell put a white rug on a boat?* Then reality rode in on the red tide of shock and he focused on the dead man.

He was muscular, with close-cropped blond hair, probably about forty. Hard to tell with so much of his head missing. The bullet that had killed him had been fired at close range.

Beyond him, across that ruined carpet, armchairs and couches sat beside marble end tables, each with a drawer pull shaped like a lion holding a chrome ring in its jaws. High-backed chairs bordered a table set with china and crystal, four glasses at each place. Israel asked about this later. For water and three wines, he was told—white, red, and champagne.

The glasses were all different shapes, he said.

That's right, sir. They are.

Who knew?

He stepped over the body. At the far end of the opulent salon were stairs with polished railings above mahogany steps leading down to the staterooms belowdecks. He crossed the salon, walking on the white portions of the rug and avoiding the blood, like a child determined not to step on a crack in a sidewalk.

Why did you proceed after you saw the first corpse? the investigators asked him.

To count, he answered.

They'd been puzzled by that. They'd been thinking that he'd say something like *To search for survivors* or simply *Because I was in shock.*

The latter might have been true, but the former was not. His mind had accepted what his body already knew: There was no one alive on the *Mereo.*

He'd come to count the dead.

He found two murdered men in a stateroom; given the blood trails, Israel thought they'd been killed somewhere else and dragged there. They were naked, their flaccid cocks pale against blood-stained thighs. Gutshot, both of them. A man wearing a pale pink polo shirt, pants at his ankles, lay in a hallway. He'd been shot in the chest. Streaks of dried blood meandered across the floor like lazy mop strokes.

Four dead men.

So far.

Israel thought most of the shooting had happened between the salon and the stairs. It was hard to tell for sure. It was hard to breathe, let alone think about how the place had looked when the men were among the living. Even with the spaciousness and the wide windows granting the view of the bright blue sea, Israel felt claustrophobic, trapped, a sensation he hadn't known since he'd left prison. That was probably why it took him some time to find the dead man in the shower; he hadn't anticipated how the rooms wound on, with curves and corridors, all of this in a boat.

The man in the shower had been shot in the head, the tiled walls now rinsed in red. He was fully clothed. Hiding in the shower, probably. It hadn't worked.

Five dead.

He found the crew's cabins—small, spartan, with bunks instead of king-size beds—but they were empty. He went out to the deck and saw another victim slumped against a stanchion. No more than thirty, dark-skinned and dressed in a crew member's uniform, he'd been shot in the ribs and back. His blood trail suggested that he'd been fleeing from the salon.

Six dead.

Israel went up to the raised pilothouse. There he found one more, this man also in uniform, shot in the side of the neck, the wound drained of blood so that it showed white ribbons of tendons. The radio microphone was still in his hand.

Seven dead.

He walked through once more to make sure. *One, two, three, four, five, six, seven.*

So much death.

The gulls circled high and at a distance. They didn't even shriek or caw. The first sound he heard other than the water on the hull was the bullhorn from the Coast Guard boat. He hadn't heard the engine as it approached. They asked him about that: *How did you not hear a boat arriving on a calm morning?*

Israel Pike didn't have an answer for that one.

They kept him all that day. Moved him from ship to shore to town police station to state police station. So many questions, so few answers. As he was waiting on the arrival of an FBI agent, he asked the desk sergeant if he could borrow her computer for one minute, one Google search. She had declined to let him sit at the desk and use the police computer but offered to search for whatever he needed so badly.

He told her that he wanted to know what that name meant. *Mereo*.

It was Latin, according to Google, and meant "something earned, deserved, or won, usually by a soldier." The word probably derived from ancient Greek, from an idea of receiving a due portion or allocation from service. It was also related to a Hittite word meaning "to divide a sacrifice."

Before the FBI agent arrived, Israel Pike decided that the Hittites had it right. He did not tell this to the FBI agent, of course. It was not his role to volunteer information. All he had to do was answer questions honestly. He did that.

He would tell them no lies.

It was not up to him to make sure they asked the right questions.

2

They released him that evening and returned to talk to him again the next morning. This time it was a cop Israel knew—Sterling Pike had been the lone sheriff's deputy assigned to Salvation Point Island for more than twenty years.

He was also Israel's late father's brother.

They were not close.

Sterling was accompanied by a woman who looked like she ran marathons without breaking a sweat. She had raven-dark hair and wore jeans and a charcoal waist-length jacket over a startlingly bright white shirt, no uniform, no insignia. Whipcord build, dark eyes that fixed on you like interrogation lamps. Israel's uncle Sterling was a tall man, well over six feet, but stooped, his back bowed and his head cocked forward as if he were always facing a strong headwind. Not an ounce of fat, all lean muscle, weather-lined skin, gray hair, gray eyes, a perpetual squint.

"Hello, Iz," Sterling said. "This is Jenn Salazar. State police, major crimes. Lieutenant."

It was a backward way of identifying his superior, but that was Sterling. Rank didn't matter to him. Sterling didn't see himself as the community's deputy so much as its emperor. He made friends and cut them deals or he made enemies and didn't. You fell in line or you were lined up in the crosshairs. Either way, Sterling was used to deciding how the law was enforced—or ignored—on the handful of tiny islands he policed off the coast of Maine, and the presence of a detective from Augusta wasn't going to rattle him.

"Hello, Lieutenant," Israel said, looking at Salazar as if he'd never met her before. She did the same to him. Even as they gazed at each other without recognition, he thought of the prison-visitation logs. Nobody would check those, would they? Surely not. Surely Israel Pike's prison visitors would be of no interest in this case.

"Mr. Pike," she said.

"Jenn is helping out," Sterling said. "A task force is coming together, you know, get everyone rowing in the same direction here. We got county, state, feds, friggin' Coast Guard involved. I'm kind of running point on the island because of my familiarity."

"Your familiarity," Israel echoed, and smiled. "Right."

Sterling Pike did not smile. "I've briefed Jenn on my conflict of interest."

"Then why are you here?"

"As a liaison."

"A liaison. That's a good one, Uncle."

"You can call me Deputy or you can call me Sterling."

"Sure thing." Israel looked at Salazar. "You're comfortable with his conflicted old ass being here? Seems like trouble to me."

"I'm comfortable," she said. "You'll know if I'm not. You want him to leave, say so."

"He can stay. Been a while since I had a family reunion. Mind my asking why you're here to see me, though? I explained myself about six times yesterday, on the record. I didn't suddenly remember new things overnight."

Sterling said, "You're the witness, Iz."

"That's *Israel*."

"You're the witness, Israel."

"I don't think that's the right term," Israel said. "A witness is someone who sees what happened. I am not that person. I found the bodies, is all. What happened was already done. If anyone witnessed that, it wasn't me."

"You were the first on scene, let's call it that."

"Are you familiar with the victims?" Salazar asked.

Israel knew the lineup by then, just as most of America did—it was not common for two candidates competing for one of the only swing seats in the Senate to share a pleasure cruise together, let alone die on it. Richard Hosmer, a federal judge who'd had the misfortune of boarding the *Mereo* on its last voyage, was a popular candidate everywhere except on Salvation Point Island. One of his signature rulings had had an enormous impact on the island—he'd upheld a federal ban on commercial lobster fishing in a thousand-square-mile area now called the Lost Zone, waters that had been subject to countless lawsuits, ranging from territorial disputes to endangered-species protection, before being closed in a bilateral agreement with Canada. Hosmer hadn't made the decision, but he'd been one of three judges who'd upheld it, and he was from Maine, so he received both credit and blame in his home state. His level of popularity in Kennebunkport was very different than it was in Salvation Point.

Hosmer's private security consultant, a man named Jay Nash, had been murdered too. Why a bodyguard had been on board was not clear. Considering that everyone on the yacht had been killed, the bodyguard's résumé would have taken a hit even if he'd survived.

The second Senate candidate on the yacht was Paul Gardner, the attorney general of the state of Maine. With him had been Morgan West, a division chief within the AG's office, currently one of Gardner's top lieutenants, formerly a law-school classmate.

Drew Gardner, Paul's older brother, had owned the yacht. He was a hedge-fund guy who also liked to dabble in movies. Although his cinematic efforts had been disasters, he'd backed a sitcom about cowboy brothers in Montana who'd patented a meatless burger, and that show practically printed its own currency.

There had been a captain and a crew member killed in the slaughter as well, but nobody talked much about them, not with all the lawyers and politics and money in the mix.

"I know the names," Israel said, "and what they all did. The basics, I guess."

"How'd you come by that information?" Sterling asked, as if the story were not national news, as if the victims' identities were secrets.

"I learned about them from Steve Inskeep this morning."

Sterling frowned. "Inskeep. Is he the guy who owns the lumberyard west of Rockland?"

"He's a radio host," Salazar said, sounding faintly exhausted. "On NPR."

Sterling grunted with what might have been disapproval.

"Steve explained most of it to me," Israel said, "and Rachel Martin filled in the blanks."

Sterling looked at Salazar. She nodded. "Another one," she said. "Same show."

Sterling turned to Israel. "So the point you're trying to make is that you didn't know the victims personally?"

"Not trying to make any point. Just answering the question."

"Uh-huh. Look, may we come inside, Iz—Israel?" Sterling said. "Get out of this wind?"

This wind was a lovely light summer breeze.

"Sure," Israel said. "Out of this wind."

They came in. Israel closed the door, walked into the kitchen, sat at the table. Sterling and Salazar took chairs across from him. Sterling got out a digital recorder and set it on the table, and Salazar got out a notebook and a pen. Israel Pike looked at the recorder and the notebook and reminded himself that he'd done nothing wrong—not on that yacht, at least. That was the only thing that mattered. There was no one on God's green earth who would believe that

Israel Pike had ventured out to a luxury yacht and gunned down seven men. Still, his heart was hammering.

"Don't want to make you do this on a loop, telling the same story over and over, like yesterday," Salazar said.

"I think you've already got it all on video, but I guess I will tell it again."

"This guy, he's a pro with police," Sterling said to Salazar.

Israel kept his eyes on Salazar. "What he probably means by that is that I did fifteen years at the state prison. I was charged with murder, pleaded guilty to manslaughter. I suspect you're aware of all that."

"Fifteen years is a lot for manslaughter."

"Felt like it."

"What added the time?"

"Had a few fights," Israel said. "Those things happen in prison."

"Happen more frequently to people with anger-management problems," Sterling said. "I heard you broke one man's leg in three places. Hell of a way to fight."

Israel didn't bother to look at him, didn't bother to say that three men had come at him that night, one armed with a knife, the other two with pieces of an aluminum mop handle that they'd sharpened into spears.

"Who did you kill?" Salazar asked, looking at him with a steady gaze as if she didn't know the answer.

"My father. Sterling's brother. That's the tiny *conflict of interest* he referenced. In a community with more than one cop, he probably wouldn't be allowed to play liaison."

Salazar didn't react. "Did you grow up here?"

"I did. My mother died the year I was born. I didn't know her. My grandparents did the work of raising me because my father was on the water so much. I basically grew up around my grandfather's boatyard. That was a big industry on this island once.

Boatyard's closed now, like most things here, but you can still see the building."

"When did you leave?"

"Moved to the mainland when I was eighteen."

"Why?"

"They'd closed the Lost Zone up here, and that meant the fishing as an industry was dying out. Then my grandfather died…after that, I wanted to see a different lifestyle, I guess."

"And how did that go?" Sterling asked.

Israel looked at him. "What's the point of that question?"

"Answer it and I'll tell you."

Israel turned back to Salazar. "I struggled with some things. Drinking, drugs. I didn't want to be on the island but I didn't know how to be anywhere else. I'd been raised in a different culture, and—"

"Culture," Sterling interrupted. "So that was the problem. I never knew who to blame. Turns out it was the culture. Fascinating."

Israel did not take his eyes off Salazar. "I came back here with my father for a summer alone and then we had a fight and I hit him and he died. Sterling arrested me and I went to prison. I guess he thinks it's fun to make me go through all that again, but I don't see how it will help you find out what happened to those people on the yacht."

Salazar tapped her pen on the notepad. Studied him. Said, "Mind if I turn on a light?"

The kitchen window faced west, missing the morning sun, leaving the room dimly lit. "I don't have one," Israel said.

"You haven't turned the electricity on?" Sterling asked, incredulous.

"Not yet."

"You've been back, what, three months?"

"Close to it."

"Thought you were listening to the radio this morning, though." Sterling looked like a cat who'd just pounced.

"There are these things that hold electricity right inside their own little compartments," Israel said, outlining a small square with his hands. "Called batteries. Keep your ear to the ground on those, they're going to catch on."

"Witty guy."

Israel rose, removed the globe from a kerosene lamp, lit the wick with a match, then replaced the glass globe over the wick. It threw bright but unsteady light.

"You got heat out here?" Sterling asked.

"It's July. You cold?"

Sterling gazed around the house with fresh eyes, taking inventory of Israel's life. It was the look of a cocky bull searching your cell, a sense of authority so absolute that it was dehumanizing, and Israel had to take a breath and glance away as the urge to slap his uncle out of his chair rose in him.

"Thank you for the light," Jenn Salazar said. "I didn't realize you were off the grid." Saying it in a neutral tone, as if it didn't matter to her one way or the other. She was very good, and Israel needed to be as good. That would have been easier if she'd come here with anyone other than Sterling. That wasn't her choice, of course.

"Not really off the grid," he said. "The boatyard has power, has a shower, has a galley kitchen. I don't intend to keep the electricity off forever. I don't have much need for it in the summer, that's all. I thought you came out here to ask about the *Mereo,* not my utility bill."

"That's right," Salazar said. "I'd appreciate hearing how you found them."

"Have you heard it already?"

She didn't blink. "Yes."

"Watched the video or listened to it?"

"Both."

Israel nodded.

"One of the police you talked to mentioned you were out taking pictures yesterday morning," Sterling said. "Is that right?"

"That's right."

"You do that often? Take pictures?"

"Yes. I'm a photographer. Amateur, but…" He shrugged.

"Good deal," Sterling said as if he were truly impressed. "That's a real skill. Where'd you pick that up?"

"In prison."

"Oh yeah? They offer photography classes?"

"Yes. I earned college credits."

"That's great. Really, the opportunities in a modern prison, they're bountiful."

"Bountiful," Israel echoed. "Sure. How about you turn the recorder on, because I'd like to tell this story just once more and get on with my day."

Sterling hesitated, spoiling for a fight, then punched a button on the recorder. Israel waited until he saw the red LED light that promised the device was recording and then said, "Should I have a lawyer here, guys?"

Nobody spoke for a moment. Then Sterling said, "You've obviously got the right to counsel, you know that, but do you feel a need for one? As you said, you just found the bodies."

Do you feel a need for one? There was no winning answer to that question. There was a right answer, and that was probably *Yes, I do,* but there was no winning answer. No matter which one you picked, you could get in trouble.

"I'm fine," Israel said. "Let's get to it."

His eyes stayed on the tiny red LED light on Sterling's recorder when he began to explain how he had found himself on the yacht, counting the dead.

3

Israel said it all again, said it the way he'd said it before.

They let him speak, watching him with those matching squints. Sometimes Salazar tapped the pen against the notepad and sometimes she didn't. She never wrote anything on the pad. The red light on the recorder always glowed.

When he was done, and only when he was done, Salazar asked her first question.

"You rowed out to the yacht?"

"Yeah."

"But you've got a boat with a motor, yes?"

"The skiff's easier."

Salazar looked at Sterling, then leaned forward, bracing her slim arms on Israel's kitchen table. She wore one simple silver bracelet that glinted against her olive skin. It slid down her forearm and jingled against the table and reminded Israel of a handcuff.

"How often do you use the big boat, Mr. Pike?" Her eyes shone in the lamplight.

"Not much," he said. "It runs, though. It was an option, if that's what you're driving at."

"No," Salazar said. "That's not it. I'm just curious…you're a lobsterman by trade, but you don't use your own lobster boat. Why not use a boat that has power?"

"I don't like the sound of engines."

"When did this start?"

"I can't say I ever liked the sound of an engine," Israel said. "I like the sound of an ocean. One gets in the way of the other."

Sterling said, "As for her question, though, about when it started, I don't think she was asking when you decided you liked the sound of the water better than the motor. I think she meant when did you start fishing that way, out of the rowboat? Is that fair, Jenn?"

"That's fair."

Israel looked at Sterling with flat eyes and said, "With my father."

"Charlie used the big boat most of the time."

"Sure. It made sense then. You could still fish in the Lost Zone."

Sterling's eyes brightened. "Did that matter to you? The law change?"

"No."

"Why not? In this community, it mattered to everyone."

"You telling me or asking me?"

"Asking."

"Same answer: It did not matter to me."

"Same question: Why not?"

"Because it felt inevitable."

"Not to everyone."

"Thought you were asking me specifically."

"What's the goal with the rowboat?" Salazar interjected.

Israel turned to her. "The goal?"

"You really just trying to avoid the sound of an engine?"

Israel took a breath, tried to keep his attention on her, tried to forget Sterling was in the room. "The goal was to connect with a way of life that existed out here once. How my grandfather lived. It was a hard way but it was a clean way. It was just you and the sea and your body and the world's body. And we're killing that world…" He paused, thinking that *killing* was the wrong word. "We invent all kinds of poison and we call that progress, and some of it is good, sure, but all of it comes with a cost, right? Maybe the worst of those poisons is distraction. A lack of attention to the right things. When I came out of prison, I wanted the peace out here."

"You needed to find that calm," Sterling threw in. "Sure."

Needed to find that calm. As if Israel usually didn't have it. What was the opposite of calm? Tumultuous, wild, enraged. Crazy.

How someone would have to be in order to gun down seven men on a yacht.

He watched Salazar. Tried to breathe in her calm, her confidence. How was she doing it? How did you look that steady when seven people were dead?

"But you keep the big boat," Salazar said. "Why not sell it?"

"These answers are going to tell you who killed those seven people on that yacht?"

There was a beat, Sterling squinting at him and Salazar leaning back, that silver bracelet like a handcuff sliding from her wrist up her forearm, the blank notepad sitting before her. The red light on the recorder glowed.

"My grandfather built that boat," Israel said. "One of the last ones he made at a boatyard that was pretty famous in its day. It belonged in the family."

His uncle's jaw tightened at that.

"For the memories?" Salazar asked.

There was a pulse behind Israel's eyes. He made himself flatten his hands, pressed his palms against his knees. "Sure. The memories."

"So you got out, came back to the island, and you wanted the quiet," Salazar said. "The calm."

Israel looked at the red light. "You don't have much to go on, do you?"

"What's that?"

"Seven people butchered on that yacht like the friggin' Manson

Family stopped by, and..." Israel spread his hands. "You're talking to a lobsterman."

"We've got hundreds of leads," Sterling told him. "From around the whole country—the whole world, literally. We got plenty. Just talking to you because—"

"First one on the scene," Israel said.

"Exactly." Sterling rolled his crisp sleeves up his sinewy forearms. Did it slowly, precisely. Then he said, "First few times you talked through this yesterday, you said you thought one of the dead men looked familiar, but you couldn't place him."

"One of the guys running for Senate."

"Which one? Gardner or Hosmer?"

"I didn't recognize Hosmer. Gardner was the one who seemed familiar."

"How'd you come to know Paul Gardner's face?"

"Same way as anyone, I suspect. Newspapers and television."

"You got a battery-operated TV out here?"

"No."

"But you've seen—"

"There are other televisions in the world," Israel said. "I've seen a few. Go into those places, serve you food that you don't have to cook? What do they call them? Roost-a-rants?"

"Okay, Iz. No need to—"

"Israel."

Sterling's lips pursed as he worked at his front teeth, sucking at them like he had a seed stuck between them. "That's where you'd seen Paul Gardner, then? Newspapers and television?"

"Correct."

"Never had any personal interactions."

"Nope." Israel glanced at Salazar again, saw a question in her eyes, and a cold tingle came alive at the base of his neck. She didn't know where Sterling was going with this. Israel did not like that at all.

"You don't know what he did before he ran for attorney general?" Sterling said.

"I don't."

"Really?" Acting surprised.

"I assume he went to some good school or another. Harvard or Yale or whatever. Law school. I don't know what in the hell he did."

Sterling smoothed the crisply folded sleeves of his shirt. "He was a prosecutor."

"Okay."

Sterling looked up. "He was *your* prosecutor. Paul Gardner sent you to prison. You don't recall that?"

4

The cold tingle in Israel's neck spread to his gut.

"The hell he was," Israel said. "Guy in my case was Hammond. What was his first name? John or Jim."

Israel could see that man, a big-bellied bald guy with a goatee. Nice enough, respectful even to the people he was trying to see jailed. Hammond, sure, that was it. John Hammond.

"That was his deputy," Sterling said. "But it was Gardner's office. Gardner's case."

"I didn't know that. I knew the one from the courtroom."

"Gardner came into the courtroom."

"Bullshit."

"True shit."

Israel thought, *Motive. Son of a bitch, he thinks he's got a motive.* The cold tingle turned into a hot flash of fear, flaring bright, like that red light on the recorder. He could no longer look at Salazar.

He said, "I think we are done here."

"Now, why would that be?" Sterling said. "You're the one who told us that you wanted to help."

"I have helped. More than enough. What I remember or do not remember about Paul Gardner is not helping you, and it's damn sure not helping those families."

"Lot of law enforcement died out there," Sterling said. "An attorney general, one of his top men, and a federal judge."

"I know it. I suspect their families would like you to make some progress on the case. You're not doing that right now."

"Do you own any firearms, Iz?"

"Stop calling me Iz. I'm not nine years old sitting around the fucking Christmas tree, Uncle."

"Don't I know it. And don't call me Uncle. I'm your father's brother. After what you did, those became different things."

"Agreed," Israel said.

Silence. Salazar watching them. She was so damn cool, perfectly willing to give it time, to let things simmer, boil, and maybe burn.

"Do you own any firearms?" Sterling repeated.

"No, I don't, because I'm a convicted felon. It would be illegal for me to possess one."

"Good to know. Of course, you didn't own a gun the first time you killed a man either."

"It's time for you to go," Israel said. "Past time, actually."

Salazar stood. Sterling didn't seem happy about that, seemed ready to push ahead with the building conflict.

"She's your superior, no?" Israel said. "Follow her lead, Sterling."

His uncle gave a low dark laugh, like the sound of rising storm wind, but he stood. "We appreciate your time."

"Uh-huh."

"And we'll probably need a bit more of it in the future," Sterling said. "You understand."

"Close the door behind you," Israel said.

Sterling left it wide open, naturally. Israel sat for a moment, then went to the door and saw that Salazar was still on his front porch. Sterling was continuing down to the dock, where the police launch was tied up beside Israel's skiff, but Salazar had stopped and was making a show of struggling to light a cigarette in the breeze.

Israel stepped out.

"You didn't know he was your prosecutor?" she said without looking at him. "How could you not know?"

"I'm wondering the same thing, only I'm thinking how could *we* not know?"

She lit the cigarette. Inhaled and blew smoke theatrically, lips too pursed. She wasn't great at pretending to be a smoker. Not natural. A problem, considering she'd come up with the idea of having smoke breaks so they could speak privately when listeners were a concern. As good as she'd been during the interview, she was rattled now. They couldn't let Sterling see that. He had reached the dock but hadn't looked back. Not yet.

"This is bad," Israel said.

"We're fine."

"It's motive. It's a reason to look at me harder."

"Nobody's looking at you. Sterling wants to make you sweat, that's all."

"The man wants to bury me. And you know better than anyone that he can. What starts on this island doesn't end on it, not where he's concerned. He can reach farther than that. If he sees an opportunity, he'll take it. If he feels threatened? Well, then I'm fucked."

Sterling was looking at his cell phone, head down. Salazar took another drag, coughed. The sound caught Sterling's attention, made him look up from his phone. Israel wanted to take the cigarette from Salazar and stub it out. He turned away, rubbed his temple to shield his face from view, and whispered, "What happened on that boat?"

Salazar turned to him, the cigarette pinched awkwardly in her fingers. "You really don't know," she said.

"Absolutely not. I thought you—"

But she was shaking her head. The two of them stood there with smoke and secrets between them, Sterling Pike watching them from the dock.

"We're fine," Salazar said again. "You'll be fine."

"Sure," Israel said, his mouth dry. "Where are the women, Jenn? Do you know?"

Her eyes told him that she had no idea.

Israel had to grip the porch railing to keep his hands from shaking.

"Was the yacht under task-force surveillance?" he asked.

"I can't talk about—"

"I need to know if there's anyone alive who can verify that I wasn't on that ship when people were murdered!"

"I don't know."

Three soft words that hit him like jabs from a professional fighter—*pop, pop, pop*—impacts to the head that also weakened the legs and the core.

He had always believed she understood more than she was telling him. Now she didn't know? When you agreed to work as an informant for a cop, you trusted that the cop was in control.

"No one was watching the yacht?" he whispered.

She shook her head. Her eyes were on Sterling, who had pocketed his cell phone and was looking back at them.

"What *happened* out there?" Israel asked again.

"I'm going to find out."

"Anyone learns I've been working with you, I'm going to get killed. You understand that? It's not about a prison cell, not out here, it's—"

"I'll keep you clean."

"Salazar—"

"I gotta go," Salazar said. "You just keep telling the truth about the yacht. That is your only job."

"I'm doing it."

"Then you'll be fine," she repeated, and she stubbed the cigarette out on his porch railing, flicked the butt into the grass, and stalked off to join Sterling, trying her damnedest to look like a suspicious cop. All Israel had to look was scared.

It was not hard.

5

In the first five months after he and his father had become the sole residents of Little Herring Ledge, Lyman Rankin had heard a helicopter three times. Each time it had been a Coast Guard chopper, but he always came out of the house to gaze at the sky and wave. He always hoped that one might land.

They didn't, of course. No one visited the Ledge.

Until the yacht broke down just offshore.

At least, Lyman assumed it had broken down. He couldn't imagine another reason for all the helicopters and excitement. Coast Guard helicopters, police boats, news choppers—it was without a doubt the single most fascinating event Lyman had ever witnessed on the Ledge, and despite that, or maybe because of it, his father grew enraged at Lyman's interest.

"Stay in the house, damn it," Corey Rankin barked.

"I wonder what it's all about," Lyman said.

"Rich people," Corey responded, scarcely bothering to remove the PBR from his mouth. "Somethin' to do with that friggin' yacht, and I can tell you exactly how many shits I give about anything to do with rich people. So stay in the house and get your work done."

Get his work done. This was interesting instruction, seeing as how it was summer vacation, so no schoolwork, and the words came from an unemployed man. There was nothing to do on Little Herring Ledge, which was just a chunk of rock that had drawn human inhabitants only because of the rock itself. First people came to put up a lighthouse to warn sailors, then to dig quarries. The quarries had closed years ago, and the lighthouse was automated. There was no need for a human presence on the Ledge, and certainly there was nothing to do on it. There weren't even chores for Lyman to do in the house; if he attempted to clean, his father complained that Lyman's mother should be doing that. Never mind that Lyman's mother had been gone for years—cleaning the house was, evidently, still her responsibility.

So, as the helicopters cut through the air and the boats churned through the water, Lyman stayed inside and read a book, *Cujo*, by Stephen King, while his father drank and threw darts. Corey Rankin was a hell of a darts player. He could throw a bull's-eye with his right hand until he'd had a twelve-pack or so, and he could usually throw one with his left hand through the first six-pack. He was ambidextrous, which was major-league cool for throwing darts and major-league trouble for the kid he smacked around when he got drunk and angry.

Sometimes they would play together. Corey's mood darkened with the increasing activity offshore, though, so Lyman kept his head down, eyes on the book. *Cujo* probably wasn't on your average sixth-grade reading list, but Corey Rankin had no interest in his son's media diet, and reading books was the one thing Lyman could do on the Ledge. There was no cell phone signal, no internet, no trace of the world he'd known in Framingham and Gloucester and Portland and the other various stops they'd made in his twelve years of life before spiraling back to Little Herring Ledge. The television out here got three channels—unless there was a storm. Lyman wasn't allowed to touch the television. Those three channels were his father's domain.

For a full forty-eight hours after the excitement offshore with the yacht, Corey Rankin stayed in the house and kept his son inside with him. By the second day, Lyman was beyond stir-crazy, and when Corey Rankin passed out in his armchair just after sunset, a beer in one hand, a dart in the other, Lyman knew it was time to move. He gave it a minute, listening to the grunting snores, then rose and crept to the front door.

He hadn't waited long enough. The creak of the floorboards woke Corey, who burst upright like a shark breaking water in pursuit of a seal.

"I'll be damned if you're runnin' outta here again! I will be *damned*! There's already been enough runnin' out on me thanks to your mother, I'll guaran-fuckin'-tee you that!"

But he was slow rising from his chair, and the beer can he threw was almost empty, light enough that it didn't track right, smacking off the wall beside Lyman and sprinkling him with that pungent odor of Pabst Blue Ribbon. The beer was cold and sticky on his cheek and it stunk but it did not hurt and then he was out the door and running through the rough grass and into the sea breeze.

As he ran, he thought of his mother, of a night in Framingham when she had pushed open the screen door and shouted at Lyman to run from his father and he had listened. He ran and she stayed and when he finally came home, her nose was broken and her eyes were black. She held him and wiped his tears and told him that he had done the right thing, but the truth was that she'd been left alone to take the punishment. His father was cruel to him, yes, but never as brutal as he was to her. On the night that Lyman had run and she had stayed, she had been beaten, and he was untouched. He thought that he remembered her gazing out the open door, escape ahead, agony behind, looking like she was wondering if she'd made the wrong choice.

He wasn't sure if the memory was real. She had been gone for so long, it was hard to say what was real and what he'd invented to make sense of it all, like writing a story and pretending it was about other people when it was really about you.

Either way, when she'd run, she did not come home.

It had been just Lyman and his father ever since, going from town to town, crappy apartment to tumbledown trailers, one house with plastic sheeting for windows, and eventually right back to the Ledge. Lyman kept running, but unlike his mother, he kept coming back. He didn't have another choice. In Framingham, he'd had places to run *to*—friends' homes, parks, the library. On the Ledge, though, he was a prisoner, unable to get off the rock unless it was low tide and the breakwater across the strait to Salvation Point Island was passable. And even if he made it to SPI, it was just another island.

His savior turned out to be a dead man.

Dwayne Purcell had been the Rankins' landlord in the years when Lyman was a small child and his mother was still around, their first stint on Little Herring Ledge, before Corey moved them south. Corey had been born and raised on Salvation Point and had ended up on the Ledge not once but twice because he was terrible at making money and worse at keeping it.

Lyman had only vague memories of Mr. Purcell. There was a grand total of four houses on the desolate Ledge and he'd occupied one of them. Then he died and no one was interested in buying the property because no one was interested in living on the Ledge. Eventually, a local cop named Sterling Pike bought it for pennies on the dollar. That was Lyman's father's phrase, *pennies on the dollar,* always said with disgust, as if it had been a bargain. Lyman thought that was what the place was worth, pennies, pure and simple.

Dwayne Purcell's former house decayed. When Lyman and his father returned to the Ledge in March, Corey spotted the buckling doorframe and said that it just wasn't right, letting snow blow into the old man's house, never mind that the old man was dead. He grabbed a sheet of plywood and a screw gun. That had been a good night. They'd worked together, Lyman holding the plywood in place while his father zipped home the screws and explained that the frame was starting to rot, so a short screw wouldn't find purchase.

"What do you mean, *purchase?*" Lyman asked, thinking of money, of buying things.

Corey spoke around a deck screw held between his teeth. "Something it can hold on to, to keep it at home. Keep everything from falling apart."

Lyman had liked that old word used in a new way, *purchase,* and it stuck in his head and was still there the first time he'd removed the screws in the plywood so he could sneak into the dead man's house and hide from his father. That had been April. Removing the screws with his Leatherman had been hard work. He'd gotten it done, though, and when he put them back in, he didn't tighten them down so far. By the third night, he tightened only one on each of the corners. By summer, he settled for one beside the handle, like a latch. Something he could open quickly.

There were three abandoned properties on the Ledge, and Lyman had hidden in each of them at one point or another, keeping his father guessing, distracting him from the Purcell house. Lately, his father didn't bother with pursuit. Tonight was no different. There wasn't so much as the smacking of the screen door or a shout. Lyman knew why: Corey had thrown his beer and was distracted by replenishing. He was probably down on his hands and knees in the kitchen right now, counting the precious cans in the fridge.

Lyman crossed the overgrown yard silently. Drew the Leatherman from its holster on his belt and flicked the Phillips screwdriver tip open. He loved that Leatherman. It had been a Christmas gift from his mother before she ran away. Somehow, it felt appropriate that it now functioned like a key in a lock to the only safe place he knew.

The Purcell house offered true privacy and even a little excitement, like a clubhouse. Most of Mr. Purcell's furniture remained, and while Lyman didn't feel comfortable sleeping in the dead man's bed—it wasn't like he believed in ghosts or anything; it was just the idea of it that was troubling—he snuck his sleeping bag down and put it on the floor in front of the telescope. The telescope looked due west, and on a clear day you could see the mainland. The house smelled better than Lyman's own home. It did not take much Pine-Sol and elbow grease to make a big difference. It was a good feeling, setting things in order.

He stepped from the ground up to the floorboard above the joist and walked to the plywood door he'd hung with his father. Felt with his fingertip for the single screw he'd left in the plywood.

It was not there.

He could feel the hole where it had bored through the wood, but not the screw. He frowned, thinking of how carefully he'd driven it in, righty-tighty, ten turns. The screw had been secured but now it was gone. It had lost its purchase.

He had a camping headlamp in his pocket but he wasn't willing to risk the light out here where his father might spot it. He would find the screw tomorrow. He lifted the plywood, ducked through, then let it drop into place behind him like a trapdoor.

He smelled the trouble before he saw it. A new scent was in the dark house, one that overrode his diligent Pine-Sol efforts, one that made him think of salt water and copper. He fumbled for his headlamp, clicked it on. The first click brought on the dim red glow that was supposed to save your battery and protect your night vision. Tonight, it spread a crimson shine over the woman in the swimsuit. She was standing no more than five feet from him, and the hatchet in her hand gleamed.

When she said, "Make a sound and I will kill you," Lyman Rankin believed her.

6

Five seconds passed, maybe ten. Hard to track because Lyman's heart and lungs were no longer in agreement. He couldn't slow his heart down but he couldn't force a breath out either. The woman stood there bathed in the red light, looking at him, the hatchet in her hand. She was not much taller than him, and she was thin, but every muscle in her body pressed taut against her skin and he thought that she would be able to overpower him even if she didn't have the hatchet.

She was wearing nothing but the swimsuit, and the smell of salt water was heavy. Salt water and copper. No, not copper.

Blood. She smelled of salt water and blood and she seemed to have come from the sea itself.

Lyman's hand began to shake, making the light shudder across the woman.

She said, "Down."

Down, like he was a dog. He obeyed like one. Sat on his butt on the floor, almost gratefully. The shaking that was in his hand was going to move to his legs sooner or later. The woman looked disappointed with him, though, as if he'd done the wrong thing, so he started to get back to his feet but she made a small motion with the hatchet and he decided to stick with what he'd been doing and kept his butt on the floor.

She said, "The light. Down." She had a heavy accent, vaguely familiar. He was scared of her when she spoke but even more scared of her when she didn't, when she just stood there holding the hatchet and looking at him.

He set the headlamp down on the floor. That moved the red glow from her face to her feet. She wasn't wearing shoes, and for a moment he thought that the dark ribbons that lined her feet were tangles of grass or seaweed. Then he realized they were cuts.

So many cuts. All of the dark lines were blood lines, some darker—which meant deeper—than others, but so many that it was hard to tell where the blood stopped and skin began. The blood was dry, but the cuts were not old. Now that the light was lower, he could see footprints leading across the old wooden floor, each step inked with her blood.

If he hadn't been sitting down, he would have fainted. As it was, he just curled up, his knees tight against his chest, and turned his face away from her.

She said, "No sound. No sound."

"Okay," he said aloud, screwing up even when trying to go along. She made a soft hiss and he nodded and lifted his hand to show that he understood his error and wouldn't repeat it.

He kept his face turned away from her and his knees tight to his chest and he held his breath, even though he felt like he was drowning. When he finally heard her move, he envisioned her coming toward him, lifting that hatchet, and whistling it down at his skull.

She stepped away. Walked out of the room and down the hall. Left him there.

Run, his brain screamed at him, but he couldn't force himself to move. He looked at the plywood over the door. All he had to do was hit it running, knock the board down, and keep running, straight into the ocean if he had to.

But she came from the ocean, he thought, and running didn't seem like a very good idea.

He was still on the floor when she returned. He chanced a glance in her direction and saw the bare legs and bloody feet. He looked up, fearing the hatchet, and saw that she was carrying blankets.

And his sleeping bag.

She lowered one of the blankets. "Take it," she said, and, when he hesitated, she uttered a word under her breath that wasn't English. While he did not know the word, it felt like a cussword, and he understood why her accent was familiar: It was French. He knew a little French, bits and pieces. His mother had grown up in Quebec, where they still spoke French. He wasn't cold, but if the woman with the hatchet wanted him to take the blanket, he was going to take it.

She went into Dwayne Purcell's kitchen and picked up one of the straight-backed wooden chairs and carried it out, the chair in one hand and the hatchet in the other, Lyman's sleeping bag draped over her arm. She set the chair in front of Lyman, sat down, and spread the sleeping bag over her lap and tucked it under her arms, making a sort of cocoon out of it. Then she rested the hatchet on her knee, her fingers curled tight around the handle.

"Brighter light," she said.

Lyman shook his head.

"Make…it…brighter," she said.

"No," Lyman said. Then, hurrying: "I can't let my dad find me."

Silence. Then she leaned forward, reaching for him. He scrambled backward and smacked against the wall as she picked up the headlamp.

"Stay," she said, again like he was a dog.

Lyman stayed.

She looked the headlamp over, clicked the button, and in the brighter light, he saw a dark line along her neck, leading away from what looked like a hole above her breastbone, and for an instant he was certain that someone had tried to cut her throat. Then she moved, and the line moved with her, and he realized it was a necklace, a simple, thin chain with a small pendant. She twisted the headlamp and fixed the beam on him. He lifted a hand to shield his eyes. She moved the beam, studying him from head to toe, then turned the light off.

They sat together in the darkness. Lyman could hear his heartbeat. He thought she had to hear it too.

"What is your name?" she said.

"Lyman. Lyman Rankin."

"Where did you come from?"

He pointed. "The house next door. You can't see it from here, but it's there. Behind the pines, there's—"

"Shh." In the dim moonlight, he could see her making a patting gesture with her free hand, telling him to keep it down. He tried again, this time in a whisper.

"I need to hide here. My dad can't find me. Okay? Please. This is the place where I hide."

"You hide."

"I *need* to hide!"

"*You* need to hide."

"Yes."

She started to laugh. It was quiet but it was definitely a laugh, and yet it was the single most frightening sound he had ever heard.

"Okay," the woman with the bloody feet and the hatchet said. "We will hide, Lyman Rankin. We will hide."

7

Israel Pike slept poorly, dreaming of bright red blood on bright white carpet, and woke with a headache of the sort he hadn't experienced since his drinking days. His mouth was even dry, the way it had been after a bad whiskey night. He found his water bottle, drank, and still felt dehydrated, his tongue thick, mouth chalky. He turned on the radio to listen to NPR's *Morning Edition,* thinking it would help to hear global news, to exist outside of the island, outside of himself. His grandparents had always made him listen to the news on the radio, reminding him that there was a big world out there and it was important to think about perspectives from other places. Josiah and Miriam Pike had no use for TV news. Their sons, Charlie and Sterling, had no use for any news that wasn't delivered in person. *There's enough drama on the island,* Charlie would say when his parents turned on the radio. *Why do you have to worry about Bangladesh?* Always his example, Bangladesh. He wouldn't have been able to point to it on a globe if you'd spotted him the continent.

The radio that sat on the kitchen counter was almost as old as Israel, burning through its bulky D batteries, and it had a red power light that reminded him of Sterling's recorder. He had turned it on looking for escape, but he instead heard Rachel Martin's familiar voice saying his name: "The bodies were discovered by a Salvation Point Island native, Israel Pike," she said.

It felt intimate, personal, because he'd spent so many mornings in prison listening to her explain the outside world to him. Now he listened as she explained his own life story. She got it right. He appreciated that. No editorializing, no innuendo, just a nice accurate summary; her tone remained neutral even as she noted that he'd killed his father. She then moved on to describe those who'd been found on the yacht. He'd seen their faces in photographs provided by the police and the FBI and now he couldn't help picturing them as he'd found them, seeing them in death even as she described who they'd been in life.

Paul Gardner, forty-nine, attorney general of the state of Maine, freshly minted Senate candidate, married, two children.

Drew Gardner, fifty-six, hedge-fund founder and television financier. Owner of the *Mereo*. Divorced twice, no children.

Richard Hosmer, sixty-two, U.S. district court judge, had been opposing Paul Gardner for Senate. Unpopular on Salvation Point due to his vote to uphold the ban on lobster fishing in the hotly contested Lost Zone between Maine and Canada.

Morgan West, fifty-two, chief of the investigation division, Office of the Maine Attorney General. Married, three children.

Jay Nash, forty-nine, Indiana native, Marine captain, Afghanistan veteran, founder of a private security company. Worked for Judge Hosmer as campaign security chief.

Manuel Correa, thirty-three, crew member of the *Mereo,* native of Miami, single, no children.

Tony Winslow, forty-five, captain of the *Mereo* for all six years that it had been owned by Drew Gardner. Two decades of work around the world in the yachting industry. Divorced, one child. Resident of St. Augustine when he wasn't at sea.

Rachel Martin reported that police had not yet offered a theory as to why two rival candidates had met aboard a yacht in a remote location. The campaign had been so contentious that Hosmer and Gardner hadn't even agreed to debate, so the two of them taking a pleasure cruise seemed unlikely. Obviously, she said, there were many more questions than answers at this time. Then her voice was gone, and a local voice was reminding Israel to support Maine public radio, saying that he could become an evergreen sustaining member for the cost equivalent of a cup of coffee per week.

There had been no mention of any women aboard the yacht.

Where the hell did they go? he wondered, his heart rate rising. Because he knew they had been there. He was sure of it.

Wasn't he?

He needed to speak to Jenn Salazar. Privately. He closed his eyes, saw the blood on the shower tile again, blood on the carpet, blood on glass and stainless steel and teak decking. So much blood, so many wounds, holes punctured in flesh and bone and ligaments, punctured by bullets. Whose bullets?

The house felt cold but he didn't want to start a fire. He knew he should eat but he had no appetite. He needed to clear his head. Should he head out on the water to fish? Would that look like an innocent man returning to normalcy or a merciless killer indifferent to the tragedy?

He hadn't killed anybody, damn it.

Not this time.

The radio returned from a support-public-broadcasting plea but instead of moving on to the next news segment, Rachel Martin said Israel's name again.

"The *Portland Press Herald* is reporting that Josiah Pike, Israel Pike's grandfather, referenced Richard Hosmer in a letter to the editor written years ago. We have the *Press Herald*'s managing editor, Kathryn Skelton, on the line with us now. Good morning, Kathryn."

"Good morning."

"Can you explain this letter to our listeners?"

"Yes. Josiah Pike was addressing Hosmer's vote in support of the closure of commercial lobster fishing in nearly one thousand square miles of water in the Gulf of Maine. It was a federal ban enacted to preserve endangered species, such as the North Atlantic right whale, and end territorial disputes between American and Canadian fishermen that had sometimes escalated to violence. It was a highly contentious decision, as it affected an area of enormous economic importance to Maine's fishing industry.

"Josiah Pike wrote, 'Hosmer's ruling failed to appreciate the inevitable: The whales will continue to die; the lobsters will continue to move to colder waters; the fishing communities will die. What will replace the fishing community is the only question. We already know this. Hosmer had a choice to make—to give an island community a swift death sentence, or to let nature take its course in its own time. Judge Hosmer is among those who would like to pretend that humanity can dictate extinction-level events. We cannot. We can only affect the timeline.'"

"Has Israel Pike commented on his grandfather's letter?" Rachel Martin asked.

Israel turned off the radio before the newspaper editor could respond.

He had not known of the letter, but he wasn't surprised by it. His grandparents considered political advocacy more a requirement than a choice. The letter had been written years before Richard Hosmer had been murdered on the *Mereo*. It was insignificant.

He had a sense that the rest of the world might not agree. It was eerie, the way he'd begun to feel as if he belonged with the group on the yacht. Both Gardners, Hosmer, Nash, West, Winslow, Correa, and Israel Pike—all lost to the *Mereo*.

He had to find a way to talk to Salazar. Nothing could begin until they'd spoken—spoken alone, without any recorders on the table.

When he heard the footsteps on his front porch, he thought it might be her, as if he'd conjured her through forceful wishing.

It was not Salazar.

It was a reporter with a microphone, a cameraman behind her.

8

A blond woman in an L. L. Bean fleece with a *PenBay News* logo smiled at Israel. She was nearly as tall as he was, her face youthful and tan, her blue eyes bright, her mouth full of perfect teeth. Behind her was a young guy dressed in khaki from his boots to a Tilley hat, like he was going on a safari. He held the TV camera.

"Mr. Pike?" the blond woman said. "Good morning. I'm Madison Cooper, with *PenBay News*. Usually local, but today we're on a national assignment. Big deal, right?"

Like it was all a joke, smiling, her teeth as white as that rug on the *Mereo,* her lips as red as the blood.

The camera was recording. Israel could tell from the red light. Why was it always a red light on a recorder? Like a last warning for the fools who spoke into them. *Stop,* the red recording light warned, and that was precisely when most people started to talk.

"We do not want to intrude or take up any more of your time than necessary, I promise," Madison Cooper said, "but I understand you were the man who discovered the terrible scene on the—"

"I can't talk about that," Israel said, trying to look at her and not the camera.

"Completely understand. Can you do me the favor of a 'No comment' for the camera, at least? It's a long trip out here."

Still with that bright smile.

"That's all you want?" he said. "For me to say 'No comment'?"

"I'd be grateful if you could offer more than that."

"I can't. It's for the police to discuss."

"Absolutely. Save my job, though, and just say a little on camera?"

He was already on camera. He looked out at the water and tried to feel as if he were riding the swells. *Stay calm. Don't give her anything, but don't provoke either. Attract no attention.* It was just like being in prison. *Float beneath the radar. Keep your head down. Survive.*

"I'll give you that one sentence," he said. "No more."

"Thank you." She touched his arm lightly with her fingertips, turned to the camera, shook her hair out, pulled her shoulders back, and blasted that smile at the cameraman. Maybe that was why he was dressed for a safari—protection for the scorching sun of Madison Cooper's smile.

"I'm here on Salvation Point Island today with Israel Pike, the man who discovered the grisly scene."

She managed to shut the smile off with the words *grisly scene*. Looking properly grave, she turned to Israel. "Mr. Pike, I can only imagine how difficult that experience was. What was your night like—were you able to get any sleep, or has this been nonstop horror?"

He'd underestimated her. He'd expected her to ask about the scene, and then he'd say, "No comment. Only the police can answer that question." But the police couldn't vouch for his sleep, and saying "No comment" to such an empathetic question would make him seem harsh, angry.

"It is a tragedy," he said.

"A terrible tragedy," she agreed solemnly. "And we know, of course, that you want any description of what you saw aboard the *Mereo* to come from the police, but I'm curious, on a human level, if this experience hits harder when you've known the painful price of a violent crime in your own life?"

He parted his lips to ask her what kind of trick question that was, then remembered the damnable red recording light on the camera. He looked into her eyes and saw the glimmer of pleasure in them. A look that said *You saw the blond hair and the tan skin and the white teeth and you underestimated me, didn't you? Well, smile for the camera, fella, because I've got your nuts in a vise now and the whole world is watching.*

"Mr. Pike?" she prompted.

He looked from her to the camera. Wet his lips. Said, "My story is of no significance today. I hope your thoughts are with the families of those victims. That's where they belong."

Pretty good. Not taking the bait, not showing his anger.

"And you've experienced what those families are going through right now. Your grandfather's boatyard was a local landmark on the wharf here for decades, and your father was a beloved member of the Salvation Point lobstering scene. I—"

"No," Israel said. Snapped, really, the word coming out harshly enough that Madison was able to give wide eyes for the camera. Which was what she'd wanted.

"Pardon me, Mr. Pike?"

He lifted his hands, palms out, a gesture that was supposed to convey helplessness, show that he was giving up. Madison Cooper took a fast step backward, though, as if it were an act of aggression.

"Mr. Pike, calm down, I'm just doing my job. Your own conviction is not at issue."

Israel lowered his hands, put them in his pockets, and looked directly into the camera. Said, "My thoughts are with the families of the victims."

"I'm sure they are. Now, law enforcement on this island is minimal, and I understand that your uncle is the deputy in charge. He was kind enough to grant me an interview, and he mentioned—"

"I don't speak to my uncle, and I'm done here."

Israel turned and left. Didn't hear the rest of her words because the red tide of rage at the idea of his uncle commenting about him on camera made his blood thunder in his ears. Kind enough to grant her an interview. That was Sterling, bless his benevolent black heart.

He crossed the yard and walked down to the dock. Only when he reached the skiff did he look back.

They were still filming. Following him.

He untied his skiff and pushed away from the dock while they filmed him from above. Madison Cooper shouted a question. Israel did not look in her direction. He dipped the oars into the water and pulled, a circular motion, forward and back and up and down in a smooth churn, so practiced now that he was hardly aware of the technique of it, could ride on nothing but muscle memory. It was hard work, but that was important; in the work and the repetition, he cleared his mind, cleansed his heart.

That was how it felt most days, at least.

Not today.

He rowed and he rowed, out of the channel and then north as the swells rocked him, his body shifting with the unconscious expertise that came from practice.

The sun climbed while he pulled the traps that he'd already set, checked the catch. Shorts, mostly, so small that he didn't even need to measure. The waters just off Salvation Point rarely delivered; all the value was out there in the Lost Zone, below the thermocline. The last string had some decent one-and-a-half-pounders, soft-shells. Not a great haul, but enough to make some money. Maybe enough for fifteen minutes of a good lawyer's time. Maybe five.

He shouldn't need a lawyer, though. Israel Pike was a killer, and he was an honest man. They were not mutually exclusive. Even with his uncle, whom he hated more than anyone alive, he hadn't lied. He wasn't an unreliable narrator. He was a withholder.

It was different.

Wasn't it?

An informant was nothing but a storyteller. A good informant told the truth. A smart informant told the truth as needed.

There were a lot of foolish informants in prison cells and burial plots.

And maybe some smart ones.

He worked hard and fast and tried not to think of the *Mereo*, but the sun on the water reminded him of the morning when he'd taken the skiff out and climbed aboard. He could see the white carpet with the crimson stains.

My prosecutor.

He should have recognized the face, he supposed, but it wasn't as if Gardner had actively prosecuted him. He'd had a deputy handling it, and Israel had had a public defender, and he hadn't gone to trial. Israel had not had a lot of one-on-one time with any prosecutor. It would be easy to prove that. Nobody would believe that Israel was so enraged over ten minutes of a prosecutor's time that he'd nursed a grudge through fifteen years in prison, then tracked the man down and butchered him along with six innocent people on a yacht.

Right?

A wave caught him by surprise then and knocked him down, his knee banging off the hull.

He counted his strokes from then on, making conscious what had been unconscious, reminding himself of the rhythm, of a thing taken for granted that suddenly was hard to find. Pulling forward, not drifting backward.

He rowed, and he ached, and he remembered the day he had committed murder.

9

Israel had been on the island with his father for five weeks before the fight happened. It was a very different island than it had been when he was a boy, when his father had been a fisherman in lucrative grounds and his grandfather had run Pike and Sons Shipyard, where most of the working craft in the harbor had been built. There was a summer population, of course—this was Maine, after all—but for the most part the island belonged to year-rounders, with a legacy built by hard people who made a living in a hard place. It was a legacy that meant a lot to those who lived there, particularly the multigeneration families, of which there were many.

Or *had* been many.

The population had cratered after the Lost Zone was closed to commercial fishing. The waters closer to the island could support a few fishermen, but not a village of them. Families had left. A few private estates went up, but not as many as everyone had predicted. The island was too far out, too hard to reach, too rugged. Tourists stayed in Bar Harbor, Camden, Boothbay, Ogunquit, Kennebunkport. Even the ones who wanted the island life had Islesboro or Vinalhaven or Monhegan. Salvation Point was just too far north and east for the vacation set—also, although no one wanted to admit it, too depressing. As the fishermen moved in new directions or entered new trades following the closure of the Lost Zone, houses emptied and businesses closed. With no clear plan for a reinvention of itself, the idyllic fishing village edged toward ghost-town territory, a smaller, more isolated version of so many manufacturing towns in the Northeast and Midwest, more of a memorial than a community.

Israel wanted to return, though. For many reasons. Some of them were about his father, others were about himself. Israel felt what any addict did in private moments: a desperate desire for a helping hand, a way out. The island, especially in summer, struck him as a more palatable option than any other. He could help his father, and his father could help him. They would do this, he thought, by working together and working with their hands. A return to the old ways. Restorative.

The thing Israel had not counted on was his father's perception of the past. To Israel, going to the island was a chance to discuss what could still be saved. To Charlie, it was an opportunity to discuss what had already been lost. What was beyond recovery or redemption.

He spoke endlessly of what he saw as the sad demise of not simply the Pike family or even Salvation Point Island but of the entire country, the loss of America's morality, work ethic, and compassion. He saw Salvation Point as a symbol, a place of opportunity and gumption that had once teemed with loving neighbors and stern but benevolent authority figures, a place of patient lessons and collective wisdom, *Happy Days* rebooted on an island. The more he talked of the past, the more idealized it became, and Israel's struggles seemed to strike Charlie as an insult to the place itself.

The fight on the dock had been born of this friction. The destruction of the future had boiled right out of the past.

Israel and Charlie had spent ten hours on the water in rough weather, a series of cold, pelting rain squalls that belonged more to November than June, and when they got back to the wharf, Israel wanted a drink so badly that he'd have handed his wallet over for a single cold beer. He tied the skiff to the pier and began carrying their pittance of traps up the ladder by hand. Charlie sat watching his fellow lobstermen load massive piles of traps with winches. His own powerboat sat beside them, idle. Wasted. Because of his son.

"Your grandfather," he began. This was the way so many of his sentences that summer had opened. Sometimes it would lead to a pleasant memory, an amusing anecdote, or a practical skill. But in that moment, on that day, in that weather, it did not.

"Your grandfather," Charlie had said, sitting there in his orange oilskins with his eyes on his idled boat, "worked this way when he was a kid. This was nothing. He was only sixteen when he built his first real boat. I'll tell you exactly how many days of work he missed because of booze."

Israel was climbing into and out of the skiff, moving their sorry stack of traps onto the pier, well aware of the other men on the wharf who were listening, all of them ready to go home and tell their wives and children what they'd overheard Charlie Pike telling his ne'er-do-well addict son. Charlie sat in the stern of the skiff down below the pier while Israel unloaded the traps in the rain. He kept his voice loud to make sure that Israel couldn't easily walk out of earshot of the talking-to.

"Your grandfather was a different breed. They don't make 'em like that anymore, son, and I'm sorry as hell to have to say that. I truly am. But there isn't a one of your generation that understands this world like your grandfathers did. Your uncle and I, we know. We saw it. But people your age? No appreciation. No grasp."

To this day, Israel wasn't sure if he'd have done what he did next had they been alone on the pier and not had the audience of fishermen observing like a jury who'd already reached their verdict. He was standing on the pier with his back to the skiff, a busted wire trap in his wet hands, the rain still coming down, trying not to listen, trying to focus on the rain and the wind, when he saw his uncle among the onlookers. Sterling was alone—he always seemed to be alone, despite two marriages and two children. The marriages ended in divorce and the ex-wives left the island, and Sterling's sons, one from each marriage, went with the wives, and none of them returned. His sons were a few years older than Israel, but Israel had only the dimmest of memories of his cousins. Family get-togethers hadn't been a part of his childhood. For many years, the Pike brothers had been estranged. Sterling Pike had seen his deputy's badge as a symbol of leverage rather than leadership, viewed bribes as a revenue stream. Israel's father kept him at a distance; Josiah and Miriam Pike had nothing to do with their younger son at all. On an island, such a silence was thunderous.

So were reunions. The day Charlie Pike returned to his brother's side, everyone on Salvation Point knew what it meant—he'd lost, plain and simple. Traded honesty for money. It was only after the Lost Zone had closed and money got tight that the Pike brothers made their peace with each other. The locals all saw it for what it was, but they expected his devil's bargain was about more than a mortgage.

It was about his son.

By then he'd bailed Israel out of jail three times and put him through rehab once. Costly endeavors. Combine one ne'er-do-well child with the closure of the fishery that had sustained Charlie all these years, and you could almost understand why he'd darkened his brother's door with a request for help. What else could you do? People blamed the son for the father's sins.

So did the son, most days. It was one of the reasons he had returned, determined to sort things out. He had come back to the island to fix things not only for himself, but for his father.

It might have been possible if not for his uncle's presence. He'd never know for sure now, but he believed that was true. On the day of the killing, Israel had just spotted Deputy Sterling Pike when his father burst out with another verbal volley.

"I'm glad your grandfather is dead," Charlie barked at Israel.

"I swear I am, because if he'd had to see his own grandson turn junkie, it would've destroyed him. If he'd had to watch you bring your carnival act of a life onto the very wharf where he worked to provide for his family, it would have *destroyed* him! To think he left this property to *you,* to think he had that much hope in *you,* well, it's friggin' embarrassing. That's all I can say about it. I'm glad he's not here to feel the shame."

This was audible all down the wharf, and Israel saw the pleasure on his uncle's face. Rage hit him like the prick of a needle and the depression of the plunger, the vein of fury found, then flooded. He whirled to fling the busted trap in his hands down into his father's skiff, envisioning it as an explosion of noise and rage, but a harmless one. A show of anger, nothing more.

The problem was that Israel hadn't heard his father move.

In the driving rain and over the hum and creak of the winches and the clatter of traps, he'd heard only the words; he had no idea that his father had bolted from his seat in the stern of the skiff and up the ladder to the pier while he shouted. When Israel whirled with the trap in his hands, the torn wire ends jutting out like nails in a broken board, he believed his father was seated down below, expected that he could smash the trap down into the boat or whistle it over his father's head and into the sea—furious but ultimately harmless.

Instead, he saw his father's fuming face, right there at the top of the ladder, his stained GRAFFAM BROS. SEAFOOD cap dripping with rain, his eyes lit with righteous rage.

So many things had gone wrong so fast. For countless nights in prison, he'd lain awake wondering what might have changed with a single detail. If he'd heard his father on the ladder; if he'd had an intact trap in his hand instead of the jagged, busted one; if it had been dry instead of raining; if the tide had been higher. Inconsequential things in the eyes of anyone who'd watched him smash the broken lobster trap into his father's face, but so crucial to the result.

The tide was out, which meant there was a longer distance between the pier and the skiff for his father to fall. The wood was slick with rain, which meant his father's last attempt at grasping the ladder was futile. The trap was broken, which meant those jagged ends of wire punctured his face and ripped through his flesh, presenting blinding pain instead of a stunning blow. And his father was standing right there when Israel thought he was still sitting down below, a target that couldn't be missed.

Charlie Pike fell from the top of the ladder down into the skiff and landed awkwardly, his skull smacking the oarlock with the sound of a flat clap but the echoing resonance of a rung bell.

Now, fifteen years later, Israel had served his sentence, and the sun was shining. It was a new day in a different world. So why did he feel as if he'd once again missed something crucial when his back was turned?

Keep telling the truth, Salazar had said. *Your only job.*

What she hadn't known, or hadn't acknowledged, was that the world might not care if he was telling the truth. The public was less interested in real justice than in the clean, self-righteous satisfaction of immediate blame. They didn't want the truth. The truth was complicated, messy, required something of them, maybe even an admission of their own fallibility. All the questioning and the listening and the thinking, so exhausting, who had the time?

They just needed someone to hang.

I O

Before the first dawn light reached the easternmost shore of the United States, Lyman Rankin fell asleep in a dead man's house while a strange woman sat beside him holding a hatchet.

He hadn't thought sleep was possible, but eventually he got tired. Besides, he figured if she'd intended to use the hatchet on him, she already would have.

She'd sat there and stared at the door and listened. Listened in a way Lyman understood, different from the way most people did it and closer to the way an animal did. She listened as if there might be a predator out there. Listened as if her very life depended on it.

In a strange way, he began to feel comforted by her presence because she *was* so alert. Nobody was sneaking up on them, that was for sure.

So he slept.

When he woke, it was full daylight and she was still in the chair. She had dark hair and dark features and dark eyes, the delicate bones of a bird, wrists as thin as Lyman's. She wouldn't have been the tallest girl in his class. She would have been the strongest person in his class, though. Her arms were lined with lean, taut muscles.

And bruises. Dark ribbons of black and blue. Her arms looked better than her feet, though. Her feet looked as if they'd been pummeled with a hammer and then scraped with sandpaper. The sight was enough to make him physically uncomfortable, and he shifted away. That was when she realized he was awake.

She fixed her dark eyes on him. "Hello, Lye-man." His name broken into careful syllables.

Should he answer? Why not? "Hi." Then, after a pause, "What is your name? I should know it."

She shook her head.

Lyman stood up slowly. She watched him but did not move to stop him. He went to the window, watching her out of the corner of his eye, waiting for a rush of motion but not really expecting it. Not anymore. If he tried to leave, though...

Maybe then.

His stomach growled. They both heard it, loud in the empty room. He hesitated, then went to the cupboard where he had his stash of food. If she hadn't found it yet, she would soon.

"I have cereal but no milk," he said. "And two granola bars. Peanut butter chocolate chip."

She didn't answer. He took the granola bars out of the cupboard and crossed the room and held one out to her and used his teeth to tear open the packaging of the other one. It was the closest he had stood to her. He could smell the sea again. And the blood.

She reached up, the sleeping bag falling away from her slim, strong arm, and took the granola bar. She opened it the way he had, using her teeth to tear the wrapper, but she did that only because she did not want to let go of the hatchet. In the daylight, he could see that the center of the blade was chipped, a V-shaped nick torn out of its heart. The blade had to have struck something very hard with a lot of force to get that nick.

They ate and looked at each other and Lyman had the sense that she was as puzzled by him as he was by her, that she was wondering why he had food here, why no one had come looking for him.

"He only looks for me if he's angry," Lyman said, as if she'd voiced the question.

She cocked her head.

"My father," he said. "During the day, he's usually okay. He either sleeps or works if he can find some part-time thing, you know, a pick-up-change job."

She frowned.

"Cash," he said. "Cash only."

She nodded.

"He has one now," Lyman said. "For a few days, anyhow. Painting, I think. But I need to let him see me. It's only when I'm gone for a long time that he gets angry enough to look."

"You cannot go," she said.

Lyman finished the last of his granola bar, licked the wrapper, then crumpled it and put it in the plastic bag where he kept his garbage. "I have to. Otherwise he *will* look for me."

"We hide," she said.

Lyman understood—she didn't want to risk losing a good hiding spot. "You're preaching to the choir," he said. Another frown. He tried again. "Pot to kettle. No, that's not right. We're in the same boat, is what I mean. You don't know any of those?"

She didn't answer. He thought she understood him fine, though.

"You get the point," he said. "Right now, my dad isn't looking for me, so he won't find you. But if I stay here? He'll come looking for me. And find you."

She glanced at the hatchet. He didn't like the calm in her eyes.

"Were you on that ship?" he asked. "The big yacht, the one that all of the helicopters came out for, and the police and the Coast Guard?"

When she turned her attention back to him, he wished he hadn't asked. There was a danger to her that he hadn't felt since the sun rose.

"Are you kidnapping me?" he said, thinking that it wouldn't be so bad if she did, because she seemed less violent than his father, and being kidnapped by someone who wouldn't hurt you sounded like an adventure.

"No," she said. "I must hide. That is all."

"I get it," he said, and he really did get that part. "But for you to hide well, I need to leave. It's the only way it works. If I go, I will come back and bring you more food. And something for your feet. Ice, at least."

When he said *ice,* she got a look on her face like he'd offered her water in the desert.

"They hurt bad, don't they?" he said.

She glared at him. Tightened her grip on the hatchet handle.

"I can bring ice and some Anacin. My dad always has that crap around. He couldn't get his motor running without it."

She looked from him to the door. Weighing the risks.

"Look," Lyman said, "you're in *my* hiding place. Trust me, I don't want people to find this spot. I need it more than you do."

She laughed, a sound that made the back of Lyman's neck prickle. But at least she was following along.

"If they find me, they will find you," he said. "But I can come back. I won't tell."

Dark, flat eyes fixed on his. She wet her lips. Looked at the door. Considering.

"One hour," Lyman said. "I will come back with ice for your feet in one hour."

Still no answer.

"Look," he said, "I will hide you. I am honest. I promise."

It was one thing to say it, but why should she believe it? Anyone could *say* they were honest. Lyman reached in his pocket and withdrew his Leatherman, his most prized possession. She saw it and straightened, and the corded muscles in her arm stood out again as she gripped the hatchet even tighter. He extended the Leatherman to her. She stared, confused.

"It's special to me," he said. "So you take it, and I'll come back for it. That's proof."

The look she gave him then was almost more frightening than the hatchet. There was a tenderness to her eyes that reminded him of the way his mother had looked at him long ago. She put her hand on his and pushed the Leatherman away. Gently, as if she weren't holding a hatchet in the other hand.

"One hour," she said.

Lyman exhaled from deep in his belly. "One hour," he promised.

When he slipped out from behind the plywood that covered the door and into fresh air, he should have felt elation at his escape. Why on earth would he actually consider going back?

Her feet, he realized as he jogged toward home.

He felt terrible about her feet. He knew the experience of hiding, and he knew the experience of hurting. The least he could do was offer her ice.

His father was at the kitchen table, drinking a can of Monster Energy Rehab tea. He regarded Lyman with pale blue eyes that seemed like chips of late-season ice. His face was lean, but the drinking had sharpened the bones around his eyes and cheeks while pooling soft flesh beneath his chin, like something melting. His broad shoulders and muscled chest sagged and a pooch of beer gut had emerged above his belt. Cruelty, like gravity, pulled you down.

"Fuck you been all night?" he said, sounding as if his vocal cords had been burned out. He was mean in the mornings, but never fighting mean. There were rare times when he seemed almost re-morseful, a sheen of sorrow showing beneath the nastiness. Though Lyman figured that any regret was due more to his headache and sour stomach than to any fear—or bruises—he'd imprinted on his son.

"Upstairs. In my room."

"Bullshit. You ran out last night, didn't come back. Where were you?"

"My room," Lyman said again, looking him dead in the eye. "I stayed out in the yard until you passed—" Corey straightened in the chair. "Until you were asleep. Then I came in and went upstairs."

"Oh yeah? Where was I sleeping, wiseass?"

"On the floor," Lyman said, not missing a beat and not looking away.

His father made a soft grunt and *did* look away, and Lyman realized with a mix of relief and disgust that the lie had been believed.

"You have your wise ass planted right here in this kitchen when I come home," his father said. "I'm working today for that old prick Larry Toland, laying caulk in some rich asshole's house, and I'll be damned if I'm gonna make your dinner when I've done a day of work for a son of a bitch like that. You need to pull your own weight around here."

Lyman looked at the stain on the wall beside the door where the beer can had just missed his head last night. Thought of the inside of Dwayne Purcell's house, where the old, worn trim shone and the window was so clear, you almost had to know the glass was there. All it took was effort.

"I'll make sandwiches," he said.

Corey Rankin grunted.

"I will. Good ones," Lyman said, putting enough of a plaintive whine in his voice to sell it. The way he'd sounded back in the days when he'd hoped there was a case to win, some approach or argument or expression he might make that would bring his father out of his shell and reanimate him, like Dr. Frankenstein's alcoholism cure. "I'll make sandwiches and have them ready for you so you can just relax after dealing with Mr. Toland all day."

A familiar speech. Had he heard his mother say words like those? Probably.

His father made that grunt again, but he nodded, and Lyman knew why: He was already hungry, but he was hurting too bad to go through the motions of making food. Also, there wasn't much food in the house to be made. Which led to the next step.

"I just need a little money to run down to the store and get some meat and bread."

"Shit, you and needing money. Like your whore mother."

Yes, Lyman wanted to say, *that's exactly right, I am asking you for money for meat and bread to feed* you *and that makes me just like my whore mother.* He took a breath. "I can't make the sandwiches without meat and bread."

The previous evening, that remark would have sent Corey Rankin bursting to his feet and balling up his fists, but in the morning, with the sunlight hurting his eyes, he couldn't muster the effort. Besides, he wanted the sandwiches. He dug a five and four singles out of the back pocket of his jeans, looked at them forlornly, and tossed them on the table.

"You best set the change right down there when you're back. All of it."

"I will," Lyman said, and he always did. Always had, at least. Today...well, today he wasn't so sure.

"A 'Thank you' would be nice." The pool of soft flesh under his chin thickened as Corey Rankin dipped his head like a dog that wanted to fight.

"Thank you," Lyman said, and then he walked upstairs and went into his room and closed the door. Sat on the bed and checked the clock on the microwave that sat on the floor beside his mattress. The microwave didn't work but the clock on it did, and it could be used like an alarm if you subtracted the hours right and pressed Start. Nothing would heat and the plate wouldn't turn but the clock would still tick down and eventually beep. It was how he'd managed to get to school on time after his father had pawned his phone.

Lyman set the microwave for twenty minutes, pressed Start, stretched out on the mattress on the floor, closed his eyes, and went to sleep.

I I

When the microwave timer beeped, Lyman woke slowly, rubbed his eyes, and punched the button to shut it off. Half an hour of his deadline was gone, but that meant his father was too. All that mattered.

He got up and brushed his teeth and rinsed his face with cold water, then went downstairs. The nine dollars sat on the table. He pocketed it, but he had no intention of going to the store. Not just yet. Instead, he found the Anacin bottle on the counter and shook out eight tablets. Hesitated, thinking of the woman's feet, then shook out six more. He found a clean garbage bag and went to the freezer and filled it with ice, which was the one thing Corey Rankin always kept well stocked.

In the bathroom, Lyman found a bottle of hydrogen peroxide and an expired bottle of Bactine and a roll of gauze. He filled the cargo pockets of his shorts with the first-aid equipment, then grabbed his garbage bag full of ice and left the house.

It was a bright day with a high cloudless sky and the ocean sparkled like broken glass. Calm seas, everything bright and glittering. He wondered if his father was actually down at Larry Toland's or if he'd gotten on the ferry and headed to Rockland. He did that sometimes. Didn't think Lyman knew, but this was an island; secrets were hard to keep. Whatever Corey found in Rockland did more damage than the booze. When he came home, he wasn't fighting mad but hollowed out, a zombie who regarded Lyman with confusion, not anger. Somehow, that was worse.

Lyman jogged across the yard and down behind the firs toward the Purcell house. It looked like the worst of the three abandoned homes on the Ledge, but it was the cleanest and strongest on the inside. You could never trust the outside.

The woman with the hatchet opened the door before he did. Or, rather, pushed back the plywood plank, but it had the same effect. He was back with ten minutes to spare.

"Lye-man," she said. She still said it stiffly, as if the name were two words: *Lye. Man.*

"Hey. I came back." He held up the garbage bag. The ice sloshed around. "With ice."

She looked at the bag, then at him, then pushed the plywood sheet farther from the frame to grant him access. She took the bag of ice. He fished out the Bactine and the gauze and then took out the Anacin tablets and put them on the counter.

"It's a start," he said. "I got money too. I can buy some food. It's not much money, but I'll get something better than the granola bars."

"Money," she echoed. "You need money." She did that almost-smile thing, a tensing of her face that wasn't unfriendly, and then she limped past him over to the old couch and lifted one of the cushions up. He saw that the layer of fabric on which the cushions rested had been cut out. The hole was neat and square and small enough that the cushion wouldn't fall right through. She was, he realized, pretty accurate with that hatchet.

She set the hatchet down on the middle cushion. Then she bent over, and the blanket she'd knotted around her waist parted and he saw her bare legs and the curve of her butt and he looked away, embarrassed. He felt something, some flush of emotion that felt good and bad at once. Like it was both natural to want to look and awful to want to look.

He faced the window and watched the sea.

She said, "Money, Lye-man."

"I have nine dollars," he said, still looking away.

"Money," she repeated, and he turned back.

She was facing him, the blanket covering her legs again, and she had thick folds of bills in her hands. Even one hand held more bills than he'd ever seen in one place in his life.

He said, "Holy shit." Couldn't help himself.

She crossed the room and offered him the money. He didn't know what he was supposed to do with all that money, and it made him nervous, so when he took the cash and began to stuff it into his cargo pockets, his hands were shaking a little and several of the bills tumbled free and floated down to the floor.

"Sorry!" He knelt and reached for them and then he froze. There were rust-colored streaks across some of the bills. Thick and dark.

Blood.

He looked up at the woman, and the woman looked down at him. She didn't speak. Lyman parted his lips but he didn't know what to say. Finally, he ducked his head again and put the bloody money in his pockets as fast as he could.

12

Israel was rowing back to his dock when he saw the ATV parked in his yard.

A Kawasaki four-wheeler with knobby tires and a grille guard, the driver's seat empty. The man who'd come in on it was standing on the dock, the sun throwing his shadow across the water. He wore jeans and a tan blazer over a pale blue shirt and expensive boots gleaming with fresh polish. They were not boots that anyone should wear on an ATV.

The man knelt without a word, grabbed the bow cleat, pulled Israel's skiff up to the dock, and tied it with smooth, familiar motions. He had a lantern jaw, a deep tan, and dark hair that was cut short and brushed back from a receding hairline. Sunglasses reflected the scene and hid his eyes.

"Hello, Mr. Pike. I'm J. R. Caruso."

"Which network are you from? The answer will still be 'No comment.'"

"No network."

"Just trespassing for the thrill of it, then?" Israel climbed out of his skiff and onto the dock and stood before the man. Caruso was exactly his height, a shade over six one, his shoulders just as broad, his frame seeming to mirror Israel's 185 lean pounds almost ounce for ounce, like a boxer picked specifically to match another fighter.

"Hoping to speak with you for your own benefit," Caruso said.

"Oh, boy."

"I applaud your skepticism. A man in your position should not assume he has friends."

Israel gazed down at the dock. Caruso's polished boots looked like coffee, a liquid sheen. "How much did those boots cost?" he asked.

"I don't recall the price." Caruso seemed mildly amused by the question.

"Who makes them?"

"They're Vibergs."

"Never heard of it."

"Canadian company."

"They're the most beautiful boots I've ever seen," Israel told him, "so you aren't a cop."

Caruso grinned. He had bright white teeth to match the bright boots. Everything about the man seemed to shine, and yet Israel watched his body language, the way he stayed still as the dock swayed and how he kept his shoulders back and his feet balanced, and knew not to underestimate the man. He might be pretty but he was not soft.

"Not a cop today," Caruso said. "I was once, though."

"What are you today?"

"Private investigator."

"So no authority is what you mean. And again, we've got the trespassing issue."

"I was with the North Carolina State Police for four years."

"Shame we're not in North Carolina."

"Then I joined the army, got a job as an MP," Caruso said as if Israel hadn't spoken. "Did that for six years, got out, and went back to school."

"I don't remember asking for—"

"Graduate degree in forensic sciences from George Washington

University, took some specialized courses with the FBI, the Secret Service, the Armed Forces Institute of Pathology, Northwestern University's medical school, the Smithsonian Institution, the Cleveland Clinic, and Scotland Yard."

Israel said, "The Smithsonian?"

"That's right."

"The museum?"

"They do other things."

"I never knew that."

"Forensic anthropology," Caruso said. "They're the best in the world at it."

"The things you learn," Israel said, thinking, *Cop, soldier, forensic scholar—this is not an encouraging blend*. "I expect there's a reason you just ran through your résumé."

"There is. My specialty is crime scene reconstruction."

"Sounds like interesting work. I don't have a crime scene that needs to be reconstructed, though."

"I think you do," Caruso said. He still hadn't moved. Stood there on the swaying dock facing the wind and looking so calm that it was unsettling. "I recommend you take a ride with me, hear me out."

"Take a ride with you."

"Yes. Because the police will be here soon, and then you're not going to have time to hear other options."

Israel looked from Caruso to the house. The yard was empty. He didn't like how confidently Caruso had predicted the imminent arrival of the police.

"They will have a warrant," Caruso said. "You will have to deal with that. I advise you to listen to what I have to say before things get chaotic."

"A warrant for what?"

"To search your home. You have two options: One, you hurry up to the house and deal with whatever needs to be dealt with before they arrive. Two, you take a ride with me and hear me out."

"Or three," Israel said, "I tell you to fuck off and I go take a nap because I've got nothing to fear from the police."

Caruso waited.

Israel wanted so badly to tell him to fuck off. Wanted so badly to walk up the hill to his house with the carefree stride of a man who had nothing to fear.

He couldn't.

"Fifteen minutes of your time," Caruso said. "We'll sit on the plane and talk and I'll bring you right back down to deal with everything that's headed to your door."

"The plane."

"That's right."

Salvation Point had an airstrip, not an airport. You couldn't land anything large on it, which meant that it was used only by private planes and medevac choppers—summer money and dying locals.

"If you're a private investigator, who's your client?"

"A victim's family."

"Which one?"

"I can't disclose the family. Confidentiality issues. You understand."

"Sure."

Caruso looked at his watch. It was styled like a tactical aviator's watch but gleamed and glistened in the way only real jewelry did.

"Fifteen minutes," he said. "Or you can wait on the police."

The wind whipped the water, and the dock swayed, and Caruso stood with his impeccable balance.

"Been a while since I was on an airplane," Israel said.

Caruso showed his white teeth again.

They walked up to the ATV and Israel sat down in the shotgun seat and Caruso fired up the motor and pulled out. He drove fast and held the wheel with one hand while his other floated near his right hip. He wasn't wearing a gun under the blazer but his gun hand still drifted there. Habit.

The airstrip was in the middle of the island, a slash of asphalt surrounded by low grass and metal fencing. Israel remembered the outcry from year-round residents when it was expanded. It would change the culture of the place, they said, if people didn't need to come by boat. The outcry didn't mean much. The airstrip had been put in and in the summer months, personal planes came and went. A few in the fall. None in the winter. Today there were four planes parked beside the single hangar, three prop planes and one small, sleek jet.

Caruso drove to the jet.

He parked in the shadows behind the lowered stairs, hopped off the ATV, and motioned to the steps. Israel walked up them and ducked to go through the doorway and then he was inside a private jet for the first time in his life. It felt strangely similar to entering his first prison cell—a prickle up the spine, a warning that he'd be wise to run if he could.

"Take a seat," Caruso said. "Want something to drink?" He went over to the minibar near the front of the plane. There were wine bottles and a decanter of whiskey and an ice bucket.

"No, thanks."

The door to the cockpit was closed. The rear of the plane wasn't opulent, exactly, just nice. Elegant. A pair of white leather couches at the rear, in front of the lavatory, and then four white leather reclining seats closer to the cockpit. Wood trim that shone like Caruso's boots. Gold accents. It reminded Israel of the *Mereo*. He didn't care for that.

He sat on one of the couches and Caruso took the other,

spreading his arms out to rest on either side and crossing one foot over his knee. He kept the sunglasses on. "You know who the most useful person in the Kennedy-assassination conspiracy theory was?" he said.

"Excuse me?"

"Consider the conspiracy theorists. Who helped them the most?"

"Oswald, I guess."

Caruso shook his head. "Jack Ruby. Without him, Oswald stands trial, speaks, and people can decide things for themselves, right? But then Ruby pops him and we get sixty years of crazy theories with another hundred to come. Thanks to Ruby, the doubters never sound completely crazy. The prosecutors got to blame a dead man, but the conspiracy theorists will forever remain unsatisfied."

Israel stared at him. He wished he'd asked for a drink now.

"What you need," Caruso said, "is a story that sells. Something the media can believe, the prosecutors can believe, the police can believe. I'm not saying that we need a story without any question marks. Only a fairy tale wraps it all up. We don't want to tell a fairy tale about how those men on the *Mereo* were murdered."

Israel looked at the man's tan face and found himself thinking, *The Smithsonian teaches forensics.* All the shit he should be considering, and that was the one thing that stuck in his mind.

"This is where I come in," Caruso said. "I can benefit your cause."

"I don't have a cause."

"You are the cause. You don't want to die for a crime you didn't commit. Or at least, didn't commit alone."

"They don't have the death penalty in Maine," Israel said. "Good news for me, right?"

"Again," Caruso said, "I think of Jack Ruby."

"Now, that remark isn't designed to make me feel good."

Caruso sat up and leaned forward, matching Israel's posture, the two of them hunched together like coaches working on a game plan.

"Presenting an acceptable story of the crime that occurred aboard the *Mereo* will benefit my client. It will benefit you as well."

"I've presented my story. It's called the truth."

"Your uncle might disagree, and I'm not sure Sterling is a good man. We'll find out. If I were you, I'd rather not find out on the sharp end of his stick."

Of all the people Caruso could have mentioned as a threat, he'd chosen the island deputy, a man so far down the chain of command that he shouldn't even have been on Caruso's radar.

"Sterling?" Israel said, doing his best to sound scornful. "Try harder to scare me, man. My uncle doesn't have any power."

"He might be given it."

"Given it?"

"It's possible, right? Competing powers, competing agendas—this is a complex thing."

"Speak English."

Caruso sighed. "You understand who died on that yacht, who these people were, what they did, what circles they moved in. But do you understand that their deaths might have very damaging consequences for those they left behind?"

Israel stared at him.

"The crime needs to be investigated," Caruso said. "The victims' families do not need to be. Follow?"

Israel followed. Someone wanted to avoid a scandal.

"Who's running the preemptive strike?" he asked.

"When you have competing interests," Caruso continued as if he hadn't heard the question, "and competing powers, you'll have a rush to explain what happened on the *Mereo*. You will be a star player in those stories. I could help you tell one, or someone else could use you in theirs. One way, you get control. The other, you get only consequences."

"Or I tell the police what you just said and watch them put you in handcuffs."

Caruso grinned at him. It was such a calm, fearless smile that Israel's gut clenched. What would it feel like, he wondered, to fear nothing? "The media, then," Israel said. "They'd love to hear it from me."

Caruso turned his hands palms up, a *Go for it, buddy* gesture, smiling all the while. Israel fell silent, out of impotent threats.

"I want you to think about plausibility," Caruso said. "I want you to think about Oswald and Ruby and quiet closure."

"The Kennedy assassination was *quiet*? They're still writing books and making movies about it."

"Not pressing fresh charges, though, are they?"

"I'm confused," Israel said. "Do you think Oswald killed Kennedy or not?"

"I don't care," Caruso said. "The story was told and most of the world moved on. It's settled. That, Mr. Pike, is what you need to remember."

"Damn. I thought you'd solved it and I was about to be the first to know."

Caruso stopped smiling, and again Israel saw the hardness, the thing inside this man that no crisp shirt or thousand-dollar boots could hide.

"You were prosecuted by Paul Gardner," Caruso said. "Your grandfather wrote a hostile letter about Richard Hosmer."

"Hostile." Israel snorted. "He was more polite than most people on this island when they shut down fishing in the Lost Zone. If Hosmer had shown up here back then, he'd have—"

He stopped, and Caruso smiled.

"He'd have been killed? Is that what you were going to say?"

"What I was going to say was that you're a fool for thinking the letter matters."

"Hang on, hang on, let me finish spinning it," Caruso said. "You have a vendetta against this man Hosmer, who's running for Senate, and against Gardner, who's also running for Senate. I need only one of them for the case against you to work, and I've got two. You have an irrational hatred, and you've had time to nurse your grudges, with all those years in prison, and you've clearly got a temper problem, having killed your father in front of a dozen witnesses and then added more years to your prison sentence because you couldn't stop fighting."

"I wasn't starting fights. That's important."

"What's coming your way now is not some meth-head with a broom handle, Mr. Pike. It's a very different game." Caruso sighed and rubbed the bridge of his nose, his patience clearly waning. "Do you at least trust the state cop?"

Israel felt his breath catch. He tried to look surprised. "Salzazar?" Intentionally mispronouncing it.

Caruso cocked his head slightly, frowning. Israel knew he was overplaying it.

"She showed up at my door with Sterling," Israel said. "What do you think?"

Caruso nodded slowly but didn't speak. Israel did not want it to go in this direction.

"*Should* I trust her?" he asked, hoping it sounded like a fresh question and not one he'd spent months considering.

"You should trust no one, Pike. But you've got better odds with me than with most."

"I'll keep that in mind."

"I hope so. I know you're not entirely without power, though. You've got some friends in high places."

Israel laughed.

"No," Caruso said, unsmiling, "you really do. The parole board reconsidered you earlier than they should have. In my experience, that requires an advocate with clout. Who was yours?"

Israel stood. "You don't need to worry about my friends in high places, Caruso. And I need to be on my way."

"Sit down."

"Nope. I'm done."

"Here, take this." Caruso extended a business card. "Call me. We can do some spitballing."

"Seven people murdered and you want to spitball ideas on how to lie about it?"

Caruso pressed the card into Israel's palm. Israel took the card by the edges and tore it in half.

Caruso wasn't watching him, though. He walked past Israel and tapped on the cockpit door. It opened a crack, and Israel could see the two pilots inside. They were in military uniforms.

"We'll be heading out momentarily," Caruso told them. The door closed again. He turned back to Israel. "Do some thinking, Mr. Pike. I hope to hear from you."

Israel meant to drop the pieces of the torn card on the floor. He really did. Instead, he put the two halves in his pocket and left the plane. Caruso didn't call after him. The sun seemed impossibly bright on the tarmac. Israel walked to the end of the runway, through the fence, and out into the grass. Behind him, the jet engine engaged, a muscular hum that throbbed the earth. He didn't look back. Kept his head down and tried not to think of that famous photograph of Jack Ruby firing the pistol into Lee Harvey Oswald's chest while the police stood all around them.

Caruso had given an impressive performance. All that talk about Jack Ruby, all the bullshit about his own expertise, the courses at the friggin' Smithsonian. Quite the thespian, J. R. Caruso.

I saw those pilots, he thought. *Their uniforms weren't from the wardrobe department.*

Or maybe they were. How would he know? One of the murdered men on the *Mereo* had been a movie producer, after all. Israel couldn't let Caruso get into his head. The man had no authority. Caruso was simply another asshole trying to put the squeeze on him.

Israel crested the low rise above his house, looked down, and saw the only person in the world he wanted to see: Jenn Salazar.

But she was not alone. Sterling and two uniformed cops were with her, waiting at Israel's front door.

13

Morning, Iz," Sterling called as Israel came down the hill. "Israel."

"My mistake."

Israel didn't know the two uniformed cops, both male, both with the Maine State Police, who were beside Sterling. Jenn Salazar stood behind them, hands jammed in the pockets of a state police jacket. She avoided Israel's eyes, but she looked troubled. Sterling looked hungry.

"What's up, Sterling?" Israel asked.

"Deputy."

"Excuse me?"

"You can call me Deputy or sir."

Israel repeated, "What's up?" and left it at that.

Sterling held up a piece of paper that had been rolled up tight. "Search warrant," he said.

Caruso had been right.

"You gotta be kidding me," Israel said.

"Sorry."

"I bet." Israel ran a hand over the stubble along his jaw. Looked at the two cops behind Sterling and then at Salazar. He held her gaze for a brief moment, looking for some insight that she couldn't communicate to him with the others around.

"There are some things missing from the yacht," she said. "You were on board. We have to check."

"I went directly from the *Mereo* into a police boat," Israel said. "Didn't have any opportunity to abscond with one of the wineglasses."

"There were no security cameras on the yacht," Salazar said.

"So you've got only my version?"

She nodded. Trying to look hard and suspicious, but Israel saw the fear in her eyes. They would need to talk alone soon, risks be damned. Too much had changed too quickly.

"And we trust you," Sterling said with his best *I'm on your side* bullshit. "That's why we want to clear it out of the way. Just a walk-through, make it fast."

Israel turned to him. "You got a list, right?"

"List?" Sterling started toward the house, forcing Israel to follow him or be left behind.

"A search warrant is not a wide-open thing," Israel said. "If there's shit missing from that boat—or if someone is pretending there is—you've got to look for those things. You don't get to just pick and choose. The search has to be specific, narrow."

"Been talking to lawyers, I see."

"Been reading Michael Connelly books in a prison cell. But the point stands. The search needs to be limited."

Sterling smiled. Handed Israel the rolled-up paperwork. "It's all there in black and white for you, but, yeah, we've got a narrow list. Shouldn't take long."

"What's missing from the yacht?" Israel asked.

"Seven lives, for one thing."

"What is missing from—"

"Money," Sterling said. "Cash dollars."

"I've got forty in my wallet. You're welcome to them. I'll just need a receipt."

"And photographs," Salazar said from behind them.

Sterling scowled at her like she'd stolen his punch line. She ignored him, watched Israel. She stood with her shoulders back and her chin lifted, like a cocky boxer confident nobody in the ring could lay a glove on her. Israel knew what she had to be feeling, though. Some version of the same cold clench that had hold of his lungs.

"Photographs of what?" he said, thinking of how Caruso had known about the search warrant before it was served, thinking of that iconic shot of Ruby murdering Oswald while the police looked on.

Sterling clapped him on the shoulder. "Let's make it easy on each other. I don't have any time to waste dropping hooks where there aren't any fish, you know? Same as you."

"Same as me," Israel said, shrugging off Sterling's hand. He could feel his heart knocking hard on his chest, as if it wanted out.

"Yes. We'll go through the house, go through the boatyard, and get out of your hair."

Israel's hammering heart seemed to stop altogether.

"The boatyard."

"That's right." His uncle looked at him with a glimmer of pleasure. "We're required to search any property you own."

The boatyard had been willed to him, leapfrogging a generation because his grandfather had not wanted his sons to own it. Sterling had been livid when he found out about the trust. The soul of the community had once been headquartered down at the Pike and Sons Shipyard. It dominated the wharf, the first building visible from the ferry, and its long barn-red structure had been photo-graphed and painted by some of the finest landscape artists in the world. It was empty now, and it would stay empty, its days as a moneymaking, power-brokering center long gone—but it would not belong to Sterling Pike. Not ever.

"This is bullshit," Israel said. "You know it is. What the hell are you trying to prove?"

"Recidivism is a risk, nephew. You want that I should take

you at your word that you're a changed man, that fifteen years in a cell made you ready to return to society without all the temper that put you into that cell. Statistics tell me it's not that likely."

"You know damn well I didn't kill anyone on that yacht."

"I'm not sure where you've done your killing other than the one I saw."

His smirk made Israel ball his hand into a fist.

"Easy," Salazar warned Israel.

"He's fine," Sterling said. "Aren't you, Iz? Prison touched his soul, Salazar, turned him into a pussycat, sweet as can be. No fight left in him. You can see it in his eyes, no? Isn't that the look of a reformed man?"

Baiting him. Trying to get a response, trying for an excuse to cuff him. Israel unclenched his fist and looked at the ocean and remembered his grandfather's face—the white beard, the blue eyes, the curl of an amused grin at the corner of his mouth. A kind man. A calm one. That was why he'd been beloved on his island. He was kind and he was calm and he was nothing like his sons. What they'd become, he had never understood. It had haunted him until death. Israel thought it had actually *caused* his death. The coroner called it a heart attack, but it had really been heartbreak. Josiah could not understand how he'd raised two men who'd become so corrupt so easily. He couldn't bear the knowledge.

And he didn't even know the worst of it, Israel thought. *He had no idea how deep the rot went.*

He looked his uncle in the eye and said, "Search whatever you need to search, Deputy. It's no trouble to me."

Sterling was disappointed. He'd wanted to find the rage that he remembered.

"Open the door," he said.

Walking up to his father's door with trouble chasing him felt strangely inevitable. Everything old becomes new again. The past chases the present. Tide rolls out, tide rolls in.

"Go find your missing money," Israel said after he opened the door. "I don't have to stand here and watch you search. I'm gonna go have a smoke."

14

Israel went over to the porch railing. He heard Salazar speaking in low tones to his uncle.

"I'll watch him, make sure he's not hiding anything, keep him on the property."

Make sure he wasn't hiding anything. Salazar, of all people, saying that.

She stepped out, closed the door behind her, and joined him at the railing, facing the ocean in the shadows of the tall spruce trees that flanked the house.

"How'd I end up alone on the gallows, Salazar?"

"Shhh."

"Fuck you, shhh. Give me a cigarette. I've got to do what I say I'm doing, isn't that the whole idea? We keep the little act up even while that son of a bitch in there is *not* pretending?"

She took out a pack, handed it to him, and laid the lighter on the porch rail. He lit the cigarette and smoked and listened to the sounds of the police searching his father's house.

"We *have* to talk," he said, voice low, hand shielding his mouth.

"I know. Not here. But soon."

"If it's *not* soon, it'll be in a jail visitation room, this time with a camera on. Why is Sterling leading this thing, anyhow? You can pull rank."

"That would be a risk."

"Maybe it's one worth taking!" His whisper almost a hiss.

She leaned in close to take the lighter from him. He could smell her shampoo, or maybe it was lotion, something with a hint of juniper to it.

"Is the boatyard clean?" she whispered.

A simple question without a simple answer.

"He won't find anything you're worried about," Israel said.

She frowned, not following him. She would understand soon enough.

"I need an actual conversation," he said. "Not whispers. This is… unraveling. Fast."

She checked the house again, making sure she wasn't being studied by Sterling. In all the time Israel had known her, she'd always arrived with the next moves in mind, and he'd taken solace in how well she planned.

"When the search is over, take the ferry into Rockland," she said.

"Rockland? The hell do I need to go that far for?"

Her eyes told him that was a fool's question. Anywhere closer than Rockland, he'd probably be recognized.

He nodded grudgingly. "Will they let me get on the ferry?"

"I think so."

"*Think.*"

"Yeah. It's a search warrant, not an arrest warrant. Pretend you're looking for a lawyer in Rockland. Walk around a little, knock on doors, get a couple business cards, whatever. Then go to the bar down there, what is it, the Eclipse? No, the brewery, Rock Harbor. That's better."

"I'm not allowed to drink. It's a parole violation."

She met his eyes. "Exactly. So when I go in to bust your balls, it'll make sense. It'll play."

It'll play. He'd heard her say that back before seven people were murdered, back when she'd dangled freedom for favors.

The front door banged open. Salazar stepped away from him as Sterling and the two uniformed cops came out.

"All clear," Sterling said. "Let's walk on down to the boatyard, shall we?"

It had been a hell of a fast search of the house. Sterling wanted to get to the boatyard. Israel's mouth was dry as he thought of what waited for them there. It was not evidence of a crime, but it was not something he could easily explain either.

"You don't need to search the fucking boatyard, and you know it. You shouldn't even be here. It's a conflict of interest. We're family."

"We're not family. We share blood, that's all. And you can make any conflict-of-interest complaint you want to, but I'm still searching that boatyard. You want to go with us or you want to give me the keys? Might be easier on you if you stayed here. Whole damn island will be watching down there, you know. I don't want them to get the wrong idea, think I'm perp-walking you all over the island."

He was smiling now. The son of a bitch was openly smiling.

"I'll walk with you," Israel said. "Let them think what they want."

15

It went exactly as Sterling had predicted. Israel walked up the island's main road flanked by police, and every person they passed by paused to watch. By the time they reached the harbor, they'd picked up an audience, people trailing behind, curious eyes, suspicious eyes. There was a camera crew at the wharf. They looked like they'd been expecting this. Israel suspected his uncle had prepped them, same as he had with the reporter who'd arrived at Israel's door that morning.

He wants to see me break. Same way I did before, in the same place.

It wasn't going to happen. Not this time.

He led them past Dar Trenchard's market and across the parking lot to where a high chain-link fence guarded the boatyard. He'd paid for the fence from prison, a man trapped behind walls adding another one out in the free world, after Dar told him a few of the windows had been broken. There hadn't been any more vandalism, but there wasn't much to interest a vandal. The cavernous old building was empty, nothing left of its magic but the memories.

I will testify on your behalf, Sterling had told Israel once, sitting across from him in the jail visitation room. *I'll put you with the right lawyers, the right judge. It will be wrongful death, two years maximum, easy time. All you have to do is sign that boatyard over to me, Iz.*

Israel had done fifteen years, and none of it was easy time. His uncle had seen to that.

But he still had the boatyard.

The gate was fastened with a heavy padlock on a looped steel chain. Israel unlocked it and pulled the gate open, the aluminum scraping over the asphalt. Ahead of them was the empty parking lot, the vacant office building, and the towering shed. His father's boat floated at the dock, alone. It was the last boat that had ever been made at Pike and Sons Shipyard. Israel's grandfather had named it the *N'ver Done,* the spelling tweaked with that apostrophe so that it sounded the way his wife had said it, a simple, gusting phrase that suggested work was a storm that had to be ridden out, accepted, and endured, that work was *N'ver Done,* the way nor'easters were guaranteed, part and parcel of existence in this place. The sentiment had been one of pride, not exhaustion. Of endurance.

The *N'ver Done* was the only boat at the dock. The shipyard was barely more than a cratered asphalt patch surrounded by chain-link fence, all the equipment removed, the old buildings where a dozen men had once been employed nothing but gutted pole barns. Israel supposed that employing a dozen men was nothing to brag about in a world of billions, but it had been once.

He swore he could still smell the sawdust.

"Good memories down here," Sterling said cheerfully. "I remember your first Trap Day. You probably don't, but I do."

Trap Day was an island tradition—the launching of the fleet for a new season of fishing. Instead of leaving each fisherman to load up his own traps, the whole community joined in, forming a bucket brigade of sorts, handing lobster traps instead of pails of water, hustling and laughing, filled with the promise of a new season. And the fear, of course. There was always an undercurrent of fear. Every few years a boat went out and didn't come back. The water off Salvation Point was unforgiving.

Israel had loved Trap Day as a boy. His father carried him on his shoulders, booming out jokes, and his grandfather held court from his bench outside the boatyard office, smoking a cigar and telling old stories in a low, soft voice. Salvation Point had been a beautiful place to live when Israel was too young to understand that it was already dying.

Sterling said, "I thought you'd turn out to be a fisherman, of course. Like Charlie. Or maybe a boatbuilder. I guess I wasn't too good of a detective back then, was I?"

"Some things never change."

Sterling was looking up at the weathered red wall where the company name was painted in neat block letters: PIKE BOATYARD. You had to look closely to see the fresh red paint that Israel had applied to cover the AND SONS that had followed PIKE. He would've smiled, watching Sterling take this in, if not for the search warrant.

"You in here much?" Salazar asked Israel. He knew she was trying to think of any way to redirect this search, and she wasn't coming up with one.

"No," he said. "Not too much."

He came to the boatyard daily. The electricity was on here, and he used the shower and the little galley kitchen and he developed his pictures in the homemade darkroom in what had once been the mechanic's bay. Most of the pictures were for Salazar. Those were gone. Some were for Israel. Those remained.

"Open it up," Sterling said.

Israel headed for the office, which was a small, trim building that stood in front of the expansive barn structure. Signs for diesel and gas and ice still hung on the walls, although the pumps had been pulled years ago and the ice bins were warm and dry. A wrought-iron bench sat beside the door, facing the wharf. Israel's grandparents had spent almost every nice evening down there, watching the sun set. On a clear night, you could see nine lighthouses from that spot.

Israel had the key in the lock before Sterling said, "Tell you what—let's start in the shed."

That was when Israel realized that Sterling already knew what waited there. He looked from his uncle to Salazar, hoping she could help. Her face told him that she couldn't.

"There are photographs in there," Israel said in a low, tight voice. "But not a single damn one of them came from the *Mereo,* and you know it."

"Terrific," Sterling said. "Shouldn't take us long, then."

There was no way to avoid it.

Israel led Sterling past the old office building and on to the shed. Unlocked one of the massive barn doors and slid it back. There was no protesting shriek of rusting metal here; he'd straightened the track and oiled it carefully when he returned. He wanted to come and go from this place in silence and solitude. It hadn't worked.

Sterling reached past him and hit the light switch. The old fluorescent fixtures buzzed, flickered, and lit.

One of the uniformed cops said, "What the fuck is this?"

No one else spoke. Even Salazar was staring around the room with wide eyes.

The space was empty save for a stack of battered lobster traps in the center of the room, carefully arranged in stair steps, twenty feet high at the peak, like a monument. There were nearly a hundred traps in the towering stack, and ten-by-twelve photographs hung from half of them. All the photographs were in black-and-white.

All the photographs were of children.

Leaning against the center of the trap-stack tower was the stern from an old fishing boat. Crisp, clean white, the name INNOCENTS painted across it in black script.

Israel's mouth was so dry he didn't think he'd be able to speak. Then his uncle started across the room, head tilted, one hand drifting for his cell phone, and Israel's explanation came before the question.

"It's all one piece," he said. "Like a gallery exhibit."

Salazar looked at him then. Her eyes were frightened and

searching and deeply confused. He could explain it to her if they were alone.

But they weren't.

Sterling drew his phone, snapped a few pictures, then lowered it. Leaned closer. Israel could see over his shoulder. The photograph he was looking at was of a kid running the riprap between Salvation Point and Little Herring Ledge. The boy was in midair, leaping from one rock to the next, neither foot touching the ground, and the sun was on him but a dark thunderhead loomed on the horizon. Israel loved that picture.

Sterling sidestepped it, looked at another shot, and his whole body went still. He pointed at a picture of a smiling girl in a tank top.

"What's this about?"

The tip of his index finger indicated the girl's cleavage, and that was wrong, so wrong. Sterling was missing her smile. The smile was the point. It was authentic, the smile of someone who had not yet known heartbreak. Sterling couldn't see that, though. He saw that her tank top was cut low and she was leaning on the railing of the dock, so her breasts were pushed high. That was the problem. No. That was *not* the problem, damn it. She could dress however the hell she wanted. The problem was Sterling's frame of reference, Sterling's gaze, Sterling's worldview. He couldn't let her just be there, a human with a smile.

"Israel?" he said. "Who is this girl?"

"I don't know her," Israel said quietly. The uniformed cops were staring at him. Salazar had looked away.

Sterling moved to the next trap. Stopped in front of another girl, a different girl. "You don't get names, eh? Just...take their pictures? Do you get permission?"

"They're not posing," Israel said. "That's the point. They're real. They're alive."

What a poor word choice.

"This is what you learned in prison?" Sterling said. "How to take pictures of kids?"

"It's not pornography, damn it."

Sterling ignored him, shifted to his right again, studying another picture, another girl. This girl was hanging upside down from the branch of an apple tree, her knees folded around the branch, her hair cascading down, her hands outstretched and reaching but not quite grazing the ground. She seemed to be straining for the earth, but it remained just out of reach, and that was the point.

"This is Melody Osgood," he said. "She just got her driver's license. She's sixteen."

Israel didn't respond.

"She know you took the photo?" Sterling asked.

Silence.

"Does Oz know?" Sterling said, meaning her father, Matt Osgood, who was known only as Oz to anyone on the island. Oz was a fifth-generation islander, one of the few fishermen who'd refused to leave in search of better ground when the Lost Zone was closed. Oz had a hell of a temper.

"Answer me," Sterling said.

"The point of the picture is—"

"I heard you, the point is that they're not posing. The point is that they don't even know you're taking pictures of them, in other words."

He said this last part as if Israel was completely clear to him now, a piece that fit neatly into the puzzle.

"Find a picture that was on the *Mereo*," Israel said. "That's all you're here to do. Go on and look for something that was on that yacht, and when you don't find it, get the hell out."

Sterling lifted a finger, about to point at Israel and issue a warning or assert his authority, but stopped. A glimmer of some pleasing idea flickered over his face, and he nodded.

"Sure," he said. "You're right. That's all I'm allowed to do. Search and seize."

"You can't take anything that wasn't on that boat."

"No, I can't. But I can compare these photographs with the ones that went missing. There are other police agencies involved. They'll need time with your...collection."

"Why aren't those agencies here?"

"Because it's my island," Sterling said. "But you want more police? You can have 'em." He eyed the lobster-trap photo tower. "I won't have any trouble doing that."

"Maybe someone you don't know would be good. Speaking of which, you knew Paul Gardner, didn't you? Asked a lot of questions about my memories of the man, but you would have worked with him over the years yourself."

Israel saw Salazar blanch, could almost feel the urgency of her stare, begging him to shut up.

"You asking me if I knew one of the prosecutors in my county?" Sterling said, voice low and dark. "Or are you trying to intimate something even more stupid than that?"

Israel looked at Salazar and then away. "Point is, it's a small community, we all bump into one another, and yet I'm the only one being harassed because of this."

"Harassed. Always the victim."

Salazar cleared her throat. "Speaking for the state police, with jurisdiction that extends well beyond this island, I can assure you that either we're removing every one of the pictures now or we retain access to the property for a longer duration, Mr. Pike. That's the only way this ends."

She said it like a hard-ass to please Sterling, but Israel heard the message within the message: *Pick your poison. Either the doors stay open for him, or he takes the photographs.*

"I'm locking that door tonight," Israel said. "There's no evidence in this building, and I'll be damned if I let you keep coming inside."

"All right," Sterling said, pleased. "We'll go ahead and carry the pictures out. Salazar, you want to make an inventory?"

"None of them were on that yacht," Israel said. "You're wasting time and don't even care. Don't even want to pretend to be a real cop."

"Why do you take so many pictures of kids, Iz?"

Israel looked away. "I want a lawyer. Now."

"Why?"

"Because it's my right."

"Sure it is. And when you get one, you let them know that we'll have these photographs. Because that is *our* right. I'll also have to notify the parents, of course. Those kids are minors, and I've come into possession of the pictures during a homicide investigation."

Israel stared at him. "You want me to be chased out of my home, is that it? Send the villagers my way with their pitchforks and torches?"

"It's not your home," Sterling said in a low voice. "And nobody encouraged you to come back to it."

With that, he turned away and began to instruct the uniformed officers on how to remove the photographs.

They passed the traps from gloved hand to gloved hand and then stacked them outside the building as a larger crowd gathered to watch, and in a terrible way it was almost like Trap Day, except instead of loading boats for launch, they were building walls around Israel, building them tall and tight.

16

Lyman Rankin had to wait an hour before the tide receded enough to let him cross from the Ledge to Salvation Point. He covered the half-mile expanse at a jog, leaping expertly from wet rock to wet rock, his practiced feet knowing exactly where to find the flat landing zones. Although most of the rock between Little Herring Ledge and Salvation Point was natural, a top layer had been added in the days when the Ledge was a quarry. A breakwater had been made of giant slabs of riprap.

Running the rip was what everyone called making the crossing by foot. Lyman Rankin could run the rip better than anyone. It wasn't as easy as it looked. The slabs of stone were uneven and slick. Sometimes he'd watch tourists try to make the same crossing, and he'd laugh quietly as they slipped and scrambled and held hands.

As the water receded, tilted stone slabs broke the surface. He usually waited for the second layer of stones to show, giving the top a longer time to dry, but today he was in a hurry, so as soon as he had a clear path, he went for it. There was no need to run other than for practice.

And joy. Lyman *loved* running the rip.

The first steps were easy, the way things tended to be when retreat was still an option. When you got about thirty strides out, though, the stone slabs took on a steeper pitch and suddenly you were more aware of how slick they were underfoot. Tendrils of rockweed loomed like land mines; plant your foot on one of those and you were going ass over teakettle. When you got fifty strides out, the land disappeared from your peripheral vision and the ocean seemed to get bigger. This was where Lyman would see visitors turn around and go back, as if they'd forgotten some appointment. He understood it. The ocean did not seem intimidating when you had other options. As soon as it surrounded you, though, a primal awareness crept into your brain, and even the calm swells seemed to carry a greater power, a reminder of all the lives that had ended underwater. A reminder that yours could be one of them.

He sped up at this point. He was wearing Salomon shoes that someone had donated to the Goodwill in Rockland in almost-new condition. They had a great, sticky tread, perfect for wet rocks, much better than the beat-up Nikes he'd been wearing since they lived in Framingham and that were like drag slicks. The first day he'd run the rip in the Salomons, he felt like a different person— stronger, faster, more surefooted. *Better,* period. He thought that most people didn't appreciate the difference a shoe could make because most people didn't *have* to run. They got to pick their time and their place if they ran. Send Corey Rankin out behind them, and they'd understand just how special the tread on a good shoe was.

He tried to remember what shoes his mother had been wearing when she finally ran. He couldn't picture them. They would not have been nice shoes.

In the spring, Lyman's class had been instructed to write an essay about something they loved. The teacher didn't tell them that they would need to read parts of it out loud. Lyman was embarrassed after listening to classmate after classmate read about their parents or their grandparents or maybe Christmas morning and he had to get up and read his first sentences: *I love traction. Strong rubber that grips the wet rock and lets walking become running and running become flying.*

Kids had started laughing, so Lyman hammered it up, acting as if it were a joke to him too. He was new to the school; being a clown was a survival mechanism—it allowed you to fit in, maybe even make a friend or two. He'd ad-libbed a line about jumping over dumb homework, figuring it was worth whatever trouble he got in with Mrs. Robinson just to save face. Mrs. Robinson didn't give him extra work or detention or a note to take home, though. She gave him a book. It was called *Maniac Magee,* and it was about a homeless kid who wanted to be friends with everyone and didn't always succeed. The kid could run on the rail of a train track. It was the best book Lyman had ever read, the only one that seemed to get the world right.

On a normal day, he would finish the run with a flourish, leaping up onto the highest rock on the Salvation Point side so he could make a longer jump down, bringing his knees up to his chest and stretching his arms wide, like a skateboarder. Today, though, he just ran straight through. There was no time to fool around. Groceries had never felt so exciting.

There was only one year-round store on the island, a market called Dar's that was sited just above the wharf. In the summer, a few others opened, but they catered to tourists, selling ice cream and an unholy number of things shaped like lobsters. Dar's was the only place to go for essentials. Lyman loved the way such a small store could have so much, and he liked Dar herself—a pretty, kind woman who had gray hair but a girl's smile and who could look at Lyman and his father and see two different humans. A lot of adults figured bad dad equaled bad kid. Dar wasn't like that.

"Morning, Captain," she said as soon as Lyman entered. That was what Dar always called him. The first time she'd done it, not long after Lyman had arrived on Little Herring, he mumbled that you needed a boat to be a captain. Dar pulled him aside, out of range of listening ears, and told him that all he needed to do was go to the library and read a few books about the sea. *You do that, read about any sailor of any era you like, and come back and tell me which one of them never lost a ship. If you find one, I'll call you whatever you like, and you can call me a horse's ass. But until you do? You're Captain to me.*

He'd had to smile at the idea of looking at the woman and calling her a horse's ass. So the nickname had stuck, and Lyman had actually read a few books about sailors too. Not to prove Dar wrong but to reassure himself that the storekeeper was right. He never did come across a famous sailor who hadn't lost a ship, either. It happened to the best of them.

"Good morning," Lyman said, although he wanted to avoid Dar's gaze, which always seemed impossible. He had also been worried about being observed by one of the crew of nosy old-timers who seemed to spend half their days sitting at the lunch counter, but they were all standing by the window, watching some activity on the wharf. Usually, Lyman would have been curious and gone to join them, but today he appreciated their distraction. He grabbed one of the little baskets that were stacked by the front door and headed for the produce cooler. It was small, not much larger than two household refrigerators set side by side, and yet it held anything you needed for a decent meal. He got turkey and salami and sliced cheddar cheese and a loaf of bread for the sandwiches he'd promised his father. Hesitated, then added a container of Raye's mustard. That knocked the price tag up, but his father loved Raye's mustard…and today, Lyman could cover the cost and still leave plenty of change on the table.

With the Rankin house settled, he turned his attention to the needs of the Purcell house. He got English muffins and peanut butter. Added some more cheese. A box of Triscuits seemed smart; she could use them with the cheese, but what if she didn't like cheese? There was smoked-salmon spread in the cooler. He'd never had it—it was expensive—but he added it to the basket, which was growing heavy. The woman in the Purcell house wasn't the picture of health, so he added two cans of ginger ale and a bottle of Advil. When he was little, his mother got him Orangina when he was sick, which had a flavor like orange juice but with extra sparkle and fizz. *Champagne for the young brain,* she would call it, touching his face with the back of her hand, feeling for fever.

It had been a long time since anyone had touched Lyman Rankin's face with kindness. He went back to the cooler and took out two bottles of Orangina and added them to the basket.

"Son of a bitch hasn't even been back three months and already the police are up his ass," someone at the window said, and Lyman glanced up, curious. Dar looked over too, and she seemed sad.

"Born for trouble, that one. What the hell are they carrying out?" another man asked.

"Old traps."

"Nah, look at the traps, you blind bastard. There's somethin' on 'em."

The old men squinted.

"Come on, let's walk down and get a clear look."

They passed Lyman without a glance. He moved for the rack of Salvation Point Island T-shirts. It was Dar's only concession to tourist-trap junk, and he thought he remembered seeing some fuzzy socks in the mix. They had to be more comfortable than gauze.

He couldn't find the socks, but there was a zip-up hoodie on sale, the cotton soft against his palm, and he thought of her wearing nothing but that swimsuit and covering herself with the blanket, and he added the hoodie to the top of the basket. Then he started for the cash register.

That was when he saw the socks. Big and fuzzy, just like he remembered. He grabbed them without pausing, wanting to get to the register because the basket was heavy and awkward and he didn't want anyone looking too close at what he got or how he paid for it. He set it all down on the counter and Dar regarded it with curiosity.

"Big shopping day."

"Yeah," Lyman said. He didn't want to talk too much, didn't want to stand out in Dar's memory today. Then he saw her eyebrows go up and he thought, *Uh-oh.* Dar lifted the fuzzy socks, turned them around, and presented them to Lyman without a word.

Lyman had grabbed them so fast, he'd missed the writing stitched across the bottom of the tourist-trap socks: IF YOU CAN READ THIS on the right, BRING ME MORE WINE on the left.

Lyman said, "Uh…"

Dar waited. Lyman frantically tried to come up with an excuse.

"It's better if he laughs," Lyman said at last.

Dar's eyes softened. "This'll make him laugh?"

"Maybe."

"But if not…"

"Then the joke's on him," Lyman said.

She let out a harsh breath that might've been a stifled laugh. Studied Lyman and studied the socks as if she weren't sure what to do. Then, finally, she scanned the socks and put them in a paper grocery bag and then looked around to be sure they were alone before she motioned Lyman closer. When he stepped up, Dar squatted so they were eye to eye.

"You doin' okay, Captain? Or you need someone…to talk to, maybe?"

Lyman shook his head. "He's working now. So it's okay. He's okay."

Dar watched him like a seagull scouting a picnic, waiting to swoop in.

"Today he'll think they're funny," Lyman said. "Maybe not tomorrow."

"That's good, Captain. I just want to be sure. And I'm glad he's working. Larry Toland isn't much fun, but he'll give an honest reference for anyone who did good work for him."

Lyman didn't think to ask how she knew his father was working for Larry Toland; Dar seemed to know everything that happened on the island. When she read off the total—$68.74—Lyman offered four twenties. They were the cleanest of the bills, with only minimal rust-colored stains, none of them soaked through with blood. He held his breath, but Dar didn't give the bills much of a glance, just made the change and handed it to Lyman and then passed him the bag.

"You take care of yourself, okay, Captain?"

"I will."

Dar nodded and watched him go with a look that had grown familiar to Lyman—pity. He felt that pang again, something not right in his heart, even though he was doing the right thing. He ignored it, though, pushed through the door and walked out into the sunlit day with his bag of supplies. A tourist was coming in, dressed in khaki shorts and a pale blue polo shirt and wearing a fancy watch, and he stepped aside with a smile.

"A man on a mission," the tourist said.

"Yeah," Lyman mumbled. "Thanks."

As he walked on, he realized that's exactly what he was today— a man on a mission.

It felt good, having someone who'd accept help.

17

He couldn't see her when he pushed back the plywood and slipped inside. The living room was empty, the chair she'd sat on while she watched him in the night was gone, and the bloody footprints had been scrubbed away.

For a moment, he thought he might have imagined the whole thing. Maybe that was the price of a summer of beatings and running and hiding. Maybe you just went crazy at some point.

Then, from the dark hallway: "Lye-man is back."

Lye-man. As if she were learning it each time she said it.

"I'm back," he announced, and she emerged slowly from down the hall. She was limping but trying not to show it. The gauze was wrapped around her feet now. She also wasn't holding the hatchet. And, he realized, he couldn't smell her. Instead, he smelled the Pine-Sol. She must have used that on the floors, removing her footprints. She still wore the blanket over her shoulders, though, head held high and chin tilted slightly upward, as if daring him to fight her. He knew better than that. He also knew enough to realize that she was tired of having nothing but the swimsuit and the blanket.

"Here," he said, and he set the grocery bag down and pulled the hoodie from it. "Keep warm."

She took it gratefully, more hungrily than she'd taken the food or even the gauze for her feet. Something about that made him uncomfortable in a way he couldn't quite define. But she was happy with it, and that was good. She put the hoodie on over the swimsuit top, zipped it up, and ran her hands through her hair several times before pulling the hood up too. Then she wrapped the blanket around her legs and knotted it expertly so it hung like a long skirt.

"Thank you, Lye-man," she said.

"Sure. There's more." He dug through the food and found the socks and offered them. She took them from his hand and regarded the writing on the bottom and cocked an eyebrow, looked at him with an expression that could be described only as *What the hell?*

"All they had," he said. "It's supposed to be a joke."

She studied him, nodded once, and sat down on the old couch. He watched her separate the socks from the plastic clip that held them and tug them on, gingerly, over her gauze-wrapped feet. When they were on, she closed her eyes. It was just for a second, but her expression told him how bad her feet had been hurting. She opened her eyes, and he felt as if he'd been caught staring, so he got up fast and took the grocery bag into the kitchen.

"I can get more, but I didn't want to get *too* much. Not right away. Because you need to hide."

He was not sure how much of this she followed, but she seemed to understand English better than she could speak it. He thought about her reaction to the socks then, the way she'd looked at him as if he were insane, and he turned back to her.

"You can read English," he said.

Her face was shaded by the sweatshirt's hood but he could still see the darkness pass over it. She did not want him to know that she could read. But she'd looked at the socks and reacted immediately, not pausing the way she did when trying to talk to him.

She said, "What?" as if she had not understood him, but her face told him that she had.

Lyman stacked most of the groceries in the fridge, left the crackers out, and turned to face her. She was still sitting on the couch, her feet stretched out in front of her. IF YOU CAN READ THIS, BRING ME MORE WINE.

"I don't have wine," Lyman said, "but I have this."

He brought the two bottles of Orangina over. Opened one, heard the satisfying hiss of fizz when the seal broke. He smiled and handed it to her.

"Champagne for the young brain," he said.

Her eyebrow lifted again.

"It was something my mom would say," he explained. "You're not young, though…I mean, you're not old either—not, like, really old, at least."

She almost smiled, he thought. Her eyes did, anyhow.

"I do not have a young brain," she said. "I should, but I don't."

He thought that it was the first real thing she'd shared with him.

"I know," he said. "I don't either. Not anymore."

She lifted the bottle and took a sip of Orangina, then pulled back as if surprised by the carbonation or the taste and gave the bottle an appraising look—but not a dissatisfied one.

"Good stuff, right?" Lyman said. He opened his own bottle and drank. The taste, with the combination of sweetness and effervescence—that was the big word for *fizz*—was perfect. Absolutely perfect. For a moment he wanted to close his eyes and picture his mother leaning over him and touching his face. He saw the woman watching him with interest, though, so he simply smiled and took another swallow, a longer one this time.

"Pain brain," he said. "For you and me, it is champagne for the pain brain."

For a long time, he thought she wasn't going to respond. She preferred to keep everything silent. Then she leaned forward and extended her bottle of Orangina. Lyman knew the gesture well— his father would frequently lift his glass in a toast to no one at all. Or to someone only he could see.

Lyman extended his own Orangina, and they clinked bottles, then sipped their drinks, silent. He watched her and reminded himself that there was one heck of a lot of bloodstained money in the couch. That should scare him, and yet it didn't. She was nice. He was sure of that. She could have hit him—could have *killed* him—but she had not. The money, he figured, was not his business. He was very tired of everyone on the island knowing everyone else's business.

"I respect privacy," he said.

She gave him another one of those raised-eyebrow looks, which seemed to be her default expression. She had very thin eyebrows, artistic, as if someone had drawn them on. She was pretty, he realized, if you overlooked the blood and the bruises and the torn-up feet. And the hatchet, of course. That would be hard to get past for a lot of people.

"I won't tell on you is what I mean," he said.

"Thank you."

"But it is hard to hide on an island," he said. "This is the best place to do it, but you still need to be good at it. Hide smart."

That wasn't good grammar, but she understood.

She said, "I will hide smart, Lye-man."

He started to explain it was just *Lyman,* but there was something funny about the way she said it, like it was a nickname, an inside joke. The way a friend would refer to another friend.

He no longer minded her invasion of his sacred place. It was nice to have some company. And no matter what her socks said, she wasn't a drunk. That was a pleasant change.

"I need something to call you," he said.

Silence.

"Not your *real* name. Just something to say. If I'm Lye-man"— he said it like she did—"who are you?"

Still nothing.

"Okay," Lyman said. "Then I get to pick. I'll call you Hatchet."

She pulled the hood back, which let the light fall across her face. Then she smiled. A real, honest-to-goodness smile.

"Hatchet," she said. "That will do."

"Where are you from?"

A pause. "Canada."

"I knew it!" He leaned forward, almost sloshed the Orangina out of the bottle. "You speak French, don't you?"

She looked alarmed, as if she was surprised that he'd picked it up.

"Don't worry, I don't know French," he said. "Just the sound, really. My mom spoke French." A wave of excitement hit him then. "She was from Canada too. A town north of Quebec City." He wasn't sure where, specifically—Canada was huge, dauntingly large. He'd scoured the map before, looking for a clue, something that might remind him of places his mother had mentioned and he'd forgotten. Something that might tell him where she had gone when she ran.

"Her name was Anna Lafortune. She never went by Rankin. Did you know anyone named Lafortune?"

She seemed unsettled now.

"It's not a big deal," he said, though of course it was the biggest of deals.

"I have met a Lafortune, maybe," she allowed. "No Anna."

"It's a big family," Lyman said. "There were lots of cousins." He had not met anyone from a French-speaking part of Canada since his mother left, and the potential of it excited him more than it should. He knew it wasn't likely that his mother and this woman had crossed paths, but hope was a powerful thing.

"You don't want to tell me your last name, do you?"

She shook her head.

"You should, though. Maybe she knew you. Maybe you're family, I don't know."

She kept shaking her head.

"It's not impossible," Lyman snapped, feeling exposed now, vulnerable. She was from a massive country with millions of people and there was no chance that she'd met his mother. He didn't care if she had. His mother had left. She was gone and she wasn't coming back and Lyman didn't need to act like a baby about it.

"Forget it," he muttered and took a sip of the Orangina. The bubbles were still there but without the same fresh burst. He was looking at the floor when she spoke again.

"Never impossible," she said in the gentlest tone he'd heard from her, a voice so soothing that it made him look back up despite himself. She watched him with kind and knowing eyes.

"Right," he said. "That's all I meant. It's not real but it *could* be."

She nodded.

Lyman lifted the bottle in a toast. "Never impossible, right, Hatchet?"

That ghost of a smile passed over her face again, and Lyman felt better, no longer embarrassed. When she smiled and spoke in that soft, kind voice, it was so very easy to forget that there was a pile of bloody money beneath her.

18

The ferry arrived while the police were stacking Israel's photographs outside the boatyard. A small crowd had gathered, more than a few pictures had been taken, and Sterling enjoyed it all. Israel watched. He was good at being still, at being observed. Prison life.

He could hide the rage, but he couldn't extinguish it.

His uncle didn't speak until Israel left the boatyard and walked toward the wharf.

"Hell are you going?" Sterling snapped.

"Getting on that ferry."

"You kidding me?"

Israel turned and looked at him. "Thought that was a search warrant. Did I miss the arrest warrant?"

There was a beat of silence.

"Be a dumb mistake to run," Sterling said finally. "Pinnacle of stupidity."

"I don't run."

"I guess I remember that. You stood pretty calm the day you killed my brother." Sterling looked from Israel to the stacked traps. "A long stretch in prison can screw with a man's mind. Yours was never particularly strong to begin with. What happened in there? You want to tell me? Be better for you to tell me now. Certain kinds of abuse, they can alter a man. People know that. People will understand that."

He wanted Israel to snap so badly, it was inked on his face like a tattoo.

Israel said, "Be sure to lock up when you're done. It's my boatyard."

"My fuckin' island."

"No," Israel said. "It's actually not."

He left, and Sterling didn't stop him. When he passed Salazar, she didn't look up. He carried on across the parking lot and down to the wharf, and his neighbors parted around him to give him a leper's distance. They were curious and suspicious now. Once Sterling started talking, that would turn into something darker. Island justice.

He couldn't bring himself to look back, but it wasn't because he was afraid of eye contact with anyone. He couldn't handle watching them take his photographs away. There were some beautiful pictures in the mix. His finest work, and no one understood.

Innocents.

What he was building in the empty shell of the shuttered business on the dying island was something beautiful. He could not explain it if he tried, and he thought that he knew better than to try, but he would at least once. With Salazar, and no one else.

He remembered the way she'd looked from the photographs to him, though, the troubled expression in her eyes.

I have done nothing wrong, he told himself, and it was true.

But you could still make a mistake doing the right thing. That was what he had done. He'd cared too much about the art of it. He'd needed the art of it, needed that burst of bright light in his soul while he did the dark work that Salazar wanted him to do.

He hadn't killed anyone, at least. The yacht killings were all that people cared about. He was clean and they couldn't prove otherwise.

So walk like it, he told himself, and he took care to look everyone he passed in the eye as he made his way up to the market that sold every essential good on the island and provided the essential gossip for free. Let them all get a good look; let them all listen; let them all go home and tell their families that he wasn't scared.

Dar Trenchard was working the register. He was relieved by that. There were other friendly faces on the island, but nobody like Dar. Nobody who knew him, not really. They all knew *of* him. Very different thing. Dar, on the other hand, knew *him.* They were cousins, although it had never felt much like that, with the age difference and the lack of family interaction. Their grandmothers had been sisters. She had visited him in prison every year on his birthday. She brought blueberry pies and spoke only of his grandfather and grandmother.

You didn't forget a thing like that.

Dar was about fifty-five—or maybe sixty now?—but she still looked forty. Had an easy smile and that kind of earnest enthusiasm that suggested the world had treated her only with kindness. Strangers would never guess that she'd buried both of her parents before she turned twenty, then taken over their business and run it single-handedly, teaching herself everything from accounting to boiler repair to how to evict a drunk.

Israel walked through the crowded aisles to the cooler that stood across from the register, pulled open the door, and grabbed a Diet Moxie, that unique cola that was a Maine staple but almost unknown in the rest of the world. He tried not to let his eyes linger on the beers beside it. Lagers and IPAs and session ales and saisons, so many types of beer being produced now that it made his head spin. How was it possible to look at a tallboy can of PBR and, knowing that it had brought him nothing but trouble in his life, still feel an immediate fondness? He took the Diet Moxie back up to the register. Dar searched his eyes.

"What's going on down there?" she asked, genuine concern in her voice, not merely fishing for gossip.

"Police are pretending they have some real leads."

He braced himself for another question.

"You okay?" she said. It wasn't the question he'd anticipated, and Israel loved her for asking it so clearly, in earshot of everyone in the place.

"Hanging in there. Like I said, they're wasting time. Doesn't bother me, just sad that they're not any closer to something real, you know?"

"People are saying there were a lot of bodies on that yacht."

He didn't know how to act for a minute, was too aware of the watchers. One thing you learned fast in prison: Peripheral vision was crucial for survival. He wished he could block that skill out, learn how to focus only on the person in front of him. There were three men and two women sitting at the lunch counter, everyone watching him with undisguised interest. None of them had spoken to him since his return, but all of them would listen happily now.

"Seven," he said, loud enough for the room. "There were seven."

"You saw them all?"

He cracked open the soda and took a sip, crisp bubbles bursting on his dry tongue with that strange Moxie taste, like bitter licorice.

"Sorry," Dar said. "Last thing you need is an interrogation."

He wished she'd picked a different word. "I saw them all," he said. "Hey, I had ordered some film?"

"Right. I love that. First time you asked me if I could get film, I thought you were talking about some new product I wasn't hip enough to know about, some new vape-pen bullshit or whatever. No, you wanted actual film for a camera. Not as easy to find as you'd think. But you real photographers, you still want it. Leave us amateurs to our iPhones."

He'd heard this from her before and had the sense that she was repeating it for the room, validating his open interest in photography before the rumor mill pushed it darker. He appreciated it but wasn't sure how much help it would be.

"I love taking pictures of this place and these people," he said, and that was true.

She ducked below the counter, searching for the film, her gray-blond hair falling forward, exposing the burn scars on the back of her neck. Israel had heard the stories of how her father had gotten so drunk that he'd set his own deck on fire. Dar had run out and beaten the flames off him with one of the ridiculous palm fronds he'd hung up over the charcoal grill. Every time Israel's father told that story, he told it like a joke. Israel's grandfather had been the one who told him, very softly, that you could still see the burns on Dar's neck all these years later.

She popped back up, film canister in hand. "Why is Sterling searching the boatyard?" she asked.

Israel shrugged. "My bet is the feds left him on the island trying to look busy."

He forced a laugh; she forced a smile. Out in the bay, the ferry sounded its horn.

"They're playing my song," he said. "Thanks again, Dar."

"Sure. Take care, Israel."

"You too." He paid for his film and soda and started to go.

"Say, Israel?" She waited until he turned back, then said, "I'm sorry. That you found them."

She had blue eyes that only color film could do justice to. That was a shame, because he did not work with color. He liked black-and-white, light and shadow, no filters or bullshit. If you needed to shine it up to sell it, you never understood the story to begin with.

"Thank you," he said, then he nodded to the watchers at the lunch counter, left the store, and walked down to the ferry, wishing that he had not allowed Salazar to take advantage of his photography.

It was the one pure thing he'd brought to the island with him, and now even that was corrupted. He wanted to run back into the market and explain, tell them that he was an honest man and he had returned to this place to do the right thing for all of them.

The image of the red blood on the white rug assaulted him once more.

The right thing had gone so very wrong.

When he held out his ferry ticket, his hand was shaking.

He walked to the bow and kept his hands in his pockets so no one would see if they trembled. He stood there the entire way across, watching the white sea foam churn below the hand-painted sign that said EMERGENCY ESCAPE.

He did not throw the film overboard until they were in very deep water.

19

Rockland was a long ferry ride away, which was precisely why Salazar had picked it. No camera crews on the wharf. No police at the ready. Israel left the ferry walking fast and with his eyes down, heading up the hill toward town. Franklin D. Roosevelt had been at this boat landing once. The streets had been packed with onlookers, all the people applauding and cheering and not a one of them aware of the fact that the president was visiting Maine because of a secret meeting at sea with Winston Churchill. In Rockland, FDR had taken off his hat and waved to the crowd and grinned calmly, knowing all the while that his country was headed to war.

Today, Israel Pike felt about like that, sure that a war was coming and that he was the only one on the street who knew.

Pretend you're looking for a lawyer, Salazar had advised him. Was it time to stop pretending? No, not yet. There were probably fifty evidence technicians working that yacht right now, pulling hairs and fibers and scanning floors with black lights and doing whatever the hell else they did. Finding evidence that would show how the men on that boat had died, and it hadn't been at Israel Pike's hand.

Not exactly, anyhow.

Not quite.

Or...

He felt light-headed suddenly and almost sat down on the sidewalk, he was so sure his legs were about to go out from under him. Instead, he stopped and squeezed the bridge of his nose and waited for his vision to clear. The sun was too bright today. It reminded him of the *Mereo*'s glass and steel, and white rugs. Of the blood.

Seven...

Murdered...

Men.

He got his feet moving again. One thing about prison—you learned that time marched along with or without you.

He knew one attorney in Rockland by name. Pete Gibbons. He'd handled the probate issues when Israel's grandparents died, and he'd acquired Charlie Pike's old lobster boat for Israel when Israel told him to. Hadn't asked why a man in a cell wanted a boat. Later, he'd helped Israel spend the last of his money to put the new fence up around the old boatyard. Hadn't asked about that either. He had known Israel's grandfather, and that was enough for him.

Gibbons's office was nine blocks from the ferry terminal. Israel went in, and the woman behind the desk looked up at him and smiled and asked did he have an appointment.

"No, it's a last-minute deal."

"Well, I'm sorry, but Mr. Gibbons won't be able to do that. I can look at his schedule and get something set up. How's Thursday for you?"

"It's an urgent matter, actually."

"Oh?" She looked at him, waiting for more.

"With the police, I mean." He didn't want to say anything about this to the receptionist, but you couldn't talk to the lawyer without dealing with the receptionist.

When she said, "Is there an arrest warrant?" without batting an eye, as if it were the most natural question in the world, he felt relieved.

"No. A search warrant."

"When will it be executed?"

"It already was."

She was typing notes, calm. "Today?"

"Yes."

"Do you have the paperwork?"

"No. I mean, yeah, they gave me some, but I left it at the house." Realizing now how moronic that had been. Where had he put it? He didn't know. He remembered it in Sterling's hand, that was all.

"Do you know what they were searching for?"

"Uh, evidence is what they said."

"Yes, sir. I mean were they searching for drugs or paraphernalia or—"

"Pictures. And money."

She kept on typing, but her face seemed to tighten up. She was used to dealing with criminal offenders but she did not like hearing the word *pictures*.

"All right. And your name is?"

"Israel Pike."

The keys clicked a few times before the sound stopped and she looked up at him again, a half-light of recognition in her eyes.

"Are you the one that—"

"Found the people on the boat," Israel said. "Yes."

She held his gaze and looked at him appraisingly, as if she were trying to determine his guilt before he met with her boss.

"Mr. Gibbons is in court today," she said, "so I'll get him the message, but it will be a few hours before you hear from him."

I only went back to that island to help people who needed it, he wanted to shout in her face. *Why don't you tell Mr. Gibbons that! Just because I can't tell the truth does not mean I'm a liar! Tell him that!*

He walked back out to the sidewalk. Looked up the street, saw the sign for the Rock Harbor Brewing Company, and wondered if Jenn Salazar was on her way yet. She wanted him to put on a show, but what exactly did that mean? Just sit there? Or should he have a beer?

Wouldn't do any harm to blend in, he decided.

20

Hatchet was afraid to leave the house, but Lyman Rankin made a compelling argument as the day wore on.

"Look," he said, "if there's any trouble, you'll need to know where you're going, right? You came in here in the dark. I'm not sure where you came *from,* but you didn't see much of the place, did you?"

She shook her head.

"Well," he said, "it would be smart to get the lay of the land."

She looked at her feet, and he knew what she was thinking. The gauze and the socks helped but not enough that she felt good about scrambling around the rocks.

"Hang on," he said. "I've got just the thing." She tensed when he went to the door. "I'll be right back," he said, and then, when she looked uncertain, "Hatchet, you've got to trust me, remember?"

That almost-smile, so at odds with her sorrowful eyes, flickered and she nodded once and made a little *Get out of here* wave. Lyman pushed the plywood sheet back and peered out, taking his time to check in all directions, not so much because he feared a watcher but because he wanted to assure her that he was a diligent accomplice. Then he slipped out and ran across the yard, up the rocks, and through the thick copse of pines that screened the Purcell place from his own house.

"Dad?" he called tentatively from the porch. It was noon and his father shouldn't be home yet, but he'd been fired from jobs midday before, so Lyman exercised caution as he entered. The house was empty. He went upstairs and entered his father's bedroom for the first time in months. It stank of stale beer and sweat, stank of sadness. The plastic tub where they stored old clothes was under the bed, and he pulled it out. He knew some of his mother's things remained, but all he wanted was her muck boots. They were rubber, calf-high, loose at the top, with thick, grippy soles. Most people on the Maine coast had a pair like them. Before she'd run off, Lyman's mother wore them when she took him clamming. Those had been fun days.

As he pulled the boots from the tub, he discovered two pill bottles. They were the kind of bottles you got from a pharmacy, only these didn't have any labels on them. One had round blue pills; the other, nearly empty, had oblong white pills. Lyman didn't remember seeing them before, but he hadn't looked. His mother's things brought up memories that he could do without. He grabbed the boots, then paused. Thought about Hatchet covering her legs with the blanket, about the way she did not like to have any of herself exposed if she could help it. He moved the pill bottles aside and sorted through the clothes in search of something suitable. His mother had been taller than Hatchet, but not by much. In some ways, they looked similar. He pulled out a pair of old track pants, soft nylon, and jammed them into one of the muck boots, then shoved the old tub back under the bed. He didn't like looking through it. The clothes still smelled vaguely of his mother, which seemed impossible but was true, and there were also garments in there that he didn't want to think of his mother wearing, underwear and bras. Gross.

He was halfway to the door when he realized that what he thought was gross, Hatchet might need. Lyman had bought her socks, but he sure wasn't buying her underwear.

He sighed, went back, slid the tub out from under the bed, took off the lid, and put the boots inside. Then he put the lid back on and carried the tub downstairs.

Outside, he paused again and checked the yard. Open grass, unmowed; empty rocks; empty sea beyond, bright with lines of lobster buoys. No sign of human activity. Hatchet had picked a good spot to hide. But from what?

Blood money. You know that. And you know she has to leave before you both get in trouble.

"Tomorrow," he whispered to himself. He would tell her to leave tomorrow. At least then she'd have boots to walk in.

He carried the plastic storage bin across the yard and through the pines and back down to Purcell's place. Went up on the porch and whispered, "It's Lyman," at the plywood sheet.

She pulled it back, peered out at him from beneath the sweatshirt hood, then stepped aside. She had the hatchet in hand again. He thought she probably always did when he was gone.

He ducked into the house and put the plastic bin down. "Here. Stuff you can use. The boots will be good for walking outside."

She eased down on one knee and pushed back the sweatshirt hood to see clearly. Her dark hair fell across her shoulder as she opened the tub and sorted through the contents. She registered the orange pill bottles but didn't linger on them. She rifled through the clothing, her fingers moving quickly at first, then slower, and finally she stopped and turned back to him, a question in her eyes.

"My mother's stuff," he said. She seemed concerned by that, so he shook his head. "She's gone. She left a long time ago. Nobody will know these are missing."

Her face changed, but it was a subtle shift, like the way the ocean could change colors depending on the sunlight—her concern was still concern, just a different type. He'd seen this kind of concern on other faces. Teachers', neighbors', Dar's at the market. People who felt sorry for him.

"I don't care if you want them or not," he said. "I just thought you were all…" He waved a hand at her. "I don't care," he repeated, then he turned away and went to the telescope and put his attention on the open water. She went down the hall and returned a few minutes later wearing the boots, nylon track pants, and a Celtics T-shirt under the unzipped hoodie. The boots came up almost to her knees, and the track pants that were tucked inside them bulged out like old-fashioned knickers. She looked so silly that he wanted to laugh but there was a gratitude in her eyes that kept him from doing that.

"Better?" he said.

"Better."

"Okay. Can we go outside now?"

She sighed.

"You need to know," he told her. "And my dad will come home soon, and then I won't be around to show you."

When they left, she took the hatchet.

The Purcell property covered a horseshoe-shaped cove with high rocks to the left and right and a steep drop out in front. Only the back of the property, screened from Lyman's house by that dark copse of thick pines, failed to provide a coastal view. It was like the Alamo, he thought. Well protected. Then he remembered what had happened to the people at the Alamo and wished he could think of another fort.

She walked behind him, moving with a limp but at a decent speed, as he pointed out the places where the steep, jagged rocks allowed for easier access to the shore below, with its rounded stones and huge, flattened slabs.

"Nobody can see you down there," he said, pointing at the bowl-shaped basin. "Not unless they come all the way down to where you are." He thought about it, then added, "Or if they're coming in from the water, but that would be a bad place to bring a boat."

Hatchet watched the big, easy waves pound into the cove.

"When there's a storm," Lyman said, "it's a bad place to be. The water hits those rocks, and then it's like a geyser." He made an exploding gesture with his fingers.

"Is there a boat?" she asked.

"No. My dad has a little Zodiac dinghy, but that's all. He took it today."

She nodded, looking troubled, realizing that she was trapped. Lyman knew how that felt. He endured it every day on Little Herring Ledge. "Do you like fishing?" he asked.

She shook her head.

"Do you like fish to eat?"

She nodded.

He hopped down the rocks to a deep notch in the stone where he'd hidden an old surf-casting rod wrapped in a gray plastic tarp he'd found in another one of the abandoned houses on the Ledge. His father had found him in that house. It had not been a good night.

He unwrapped the tarp and withdrew the rod. The reel was old and made a grinding sound, but the rod was good and he'd replaced the line. The line was tipped with a simple silver jig in a pendant shape that sparkled when it sank. Sometimes he tipped it with clam strips or bloodworms, but on a sunny day when the fish were in the cove, all you needed was the jig. A day like this.

"I'll catch the first ones for you." When he looked back, she was picking her way gingerly across the rocks. Every few steps she stopped and looked back to ensure that she wasn't visible from the land above. She didn't look out at the water with the same wariness.

"Watch me," he said.

He cast the jig out over the water in a high, sparkling arc, firing it harder and farther than necessary, as if trying to fling his worries about her away.

The jig sank about ten feet before he felt the first tug. Sharp and firm, no toying around with it like a freshwater fish. In the ocean, it was all business. He lifted the rod tip and set the hook and reeled. The resistance told him it wasn't a big fish, but what the heck, any fish was fun.

It broke the water in a glittering thrash and then hung limp and resigned as he reeled it all the way from the surface to the rock. Hatchet was standing about five feet from Lyman and one rock below. She seemed almost afraid of the fish, and that struck him as funny.

Don't tease her, his better angels warned, but his better angels lost in a swift but resounding debate. He swung the twisting fish toward her.

She ducked and covered her head and snapped something in French—he was pretty sure it was another curse word. He laughed, let the fish swing back toward him, caught it in his left hand and worked the hook out with a quick, practiced twist. Hatchet looked up at him from a half crouch, hands still over her head, and saw him grinning. She straightened.

"You do not amuse, Lye-man."

But her mouth had curled in the slightest smile. He grinned and pulled his arm back as if he were going to toss the fish at her. She shook a fist at him, but the half smile remained, and he thought, *No way she could hurt anyone. No freaking way.*

He dropped the fish back into the water and held out the rod. "You try."

"No."

"Come on."

She sighed and took the rod. He hopped to her rock so he could stand level with her while he showed her how to use the reel. On the first attempt, she didn't release the line properly, so the jig whipped back toward them, its hook spinning, and they both ducked. She got it on her second try, sent the jig sailing out and down into the sea, then looked at him with a questioning eye.

"Just let it sink. It sparkles. They like the sparkle."

When she turned the reel handle to flip the bail, there was an immediate tug on the line, the rod tip dancing. She didn't need to look to him for guidance this time; instinct took over, and she tugged back on the rod and set the hook.

"Nice!" Lyman cried. "You got one! Just reel it in."

She reeled the fish all the way up to their rock, the rod bent nearly double. Lyman reached out, grabbed the line, and brought the flopping fish in, its wet body glistening in the sun. It had a clear lateral line running from jaw to tail, black-green above the line, smoke-colored below. Not as pretty as a trout, but Lyman thought almost any fish was pretty in the sunlight.

"Do you know what kind it is?" he said.

"Yes. It is called bigger-than-your-fish."

He was so surprised that he whipped his head around and stared at her, saw the amusement in her eyes. She was teasing him!

"Not much bigger," he said.

"Still…"

He nodded grudgingly. "Okay, it's a little nicer. You want to take it?"

She flattened her lips in distaste and shook her head, and he smiled and knelt and set to work removing the hook. She'd waited a little too long to set the hook and it was embedded deep in the jaw. He worked it free easily, but a splatter of blood painted the rocks, and he saw her eyes change. The amusement vanished, dark sadness in its place.

"It's okay," he said. "It will be fine." He tossed the fish back into the sea, then dropped the jig so it dangled, ready for another cast. "Good start," he said. "Try again."

There was a rush of movement and shadow and when he looked

back at her, he saw that she was sitting down on the rock as if the strength had gone out of her legs.

"Don't worry," he said, "you didn't hurt it bad."

She was staring past him, and he followed her gaze and realized that she was looking at the bright, ruby-colored drops of blood that dotted the pale stone.

"It'll be fine, I promise—" he started, but he understood that she was not thinking about the fish. The sight of the blood had triggered a memory, or a fear, or both. "Where did you come from?" he asked despite himself.

She looked away from him and toward the sea and let the wind fan across her face. The hood was down and the wind blew her hair back. She wasn't that old at all, Lyman thought. In that stretch between being a girl and a woman, maybe nineteen, twenty? He didn't know.

"Hatchet? What happened to you? How did you get here? Why are—"

She turned back to him. "No, Lye-man. Do not ask me. Please."

"I won't tell anyone. Swear."

She put a finger to her lips and shook her head.

Lyman's frustration rose, fueled by a combustible mix of fear and curiosity. "You don't trust me? That's crap! I brought you food. I bought you socks!" The last words, said too loud, made her immediately look up at the ledge above them to see if he'd drawn anyone's attention.

"Nobody can hear," he said sullenly. "People don't come here. Except for my dad."

"He is mean?" she asked, and her accented voice was tender in that way he both loved and hated. It reminded him of his mother's voice, or at least her tone.

"Yeah," Lyman said softly. "He's mean. He doesn't explore the Ledge much. You won't see him." And then he blurted out: "How long will you stay?"

She didn't answer. She stared out at the endless sea as if the question weighed heavily on her mind. He had no idea how she'd arrived on the Ledge, but he was sure she didn't have a plan for leaving it.

"There's no rush," he said. "I won't tell, and people won't show up."

"People might show up," she said carefully. She looked at him, brushing her hair out of her eyes, and her face was grave. "If they do, you hide."

"I told you, you can trust me."

"No! You *hide* from them. They might hurt you."

He felt the wind colder then, although the sun was still high and warm. "Why?" he asked. "Why would they hurt me?"

"They are bad men," she said simply.

"Why are they looking for you?"

She didn't answer for a while. At length, she said, "If they find me, they will kill. If you see them, you hide."

"Okay. But I'll tell you they're here first. Warn you."

She shook her head emphatically. "*No.* You hide, Lye-man. Fast."

He felt very afraid then. For himself, yes, but mostly for her. She wasn't that much older than him and she was hurt and she was running from bad men. Those were all things that Lyman Rankin understood all too well. Wherever Hatchet had come from and whatever she'd done, Lyman Rankin was sure she needed a friend.

That was when his father's voice cut the air.

"Lyman! Where are you? Get up here!"

2 1

Hatchet ducked, looking left to right with wild eyes. There was nowhere to run, but they were below the surface of the yard, out of sight of anyone who was not standing directly above them.

"He can't see you," Lyman whispered. "Stay still."

What was his father doing home? Had he been fired again? From a part-time, cash-under-the-table job? It didn't matter. All that mattered was that he *was* home.

"*Lyman!* Yo, buddy! Where you hiding?"

Yo, buddy? His father never called him buddy. That false cheerfulness was more troubling to Lyman than anger.

"Come on out, pal! Police officer is here to see you!"

Lyman and Hatchet exchanged a look, and he saw her leg muscles tense as she glanced at the sea, considering a dive. It was a treacherous drop, jagged rocks waiting below, a greater likelihood of broken legs or a broken back than a successful entry into bone-chilling water, and yet she was considering it. He'd known that she was in trouble, but until this moment, he hadn't appreciated her desperation.

"If you stay here, I can make them go away," he whispered. "Do not jump! You'll die. I'll get them to go inside. When we're in, run back to the house fast. Okay? *Run.*"

For a long moment, she searched his eyes, assessing how much she could trust him. He saw her weighing her options: a nearly suicidal leap or believing that Lyman would do what he'd promised.

"Do not move," he said, and he scrambled up from the ledge, trying to leave her no choice.

"Lyman!"

"I'm coming!" Lyman yelled as he reached the top of the cliff and hoisted himself over.

Back at ground level, he could see across the yard to his house, where his father stood on the porch steps with a smaller, leaner man in a black windbreaker. Deputy Sterling Pike. Their landlord. This brought fresh terror, because he also owned the old Purcell house. Owned the Ledge, period, all four houses on it. All of them had been empty until he'd rented to Corey that spring. He never came by, and yet here he was, and did that mean he wanted to look around his properties?

Lyman jogged across the yard, through the pines, and up to the porch.

"Where the heck you been?" his dad asked, forcing himself to edit his usual profanity.

"I was fishing from the rocks. I came as soon as I heard you. I thought you'd be at work."

Corey Rankin forced a grin, then sighed at Sterling Pike, giving him the best *These darned kids* sitcom-father face that he could muster.

"I need to be back at work, but the deputy apparently wants to talk to you."

To him? Lyman felt bile rise in his throat. A cop wanted to talk to him. This could mean only one thing: Dar had reported the bloody money. She'd noticed, and she'd called the police.

"How are you, son?" Sterling Pike asked. He had a warm voice but his eyes held the chilled distance of someone who expected to be lied to.

"Fine."

"Fine, *sir,*" his father corrected. Lyman tried to remember when he'd heard his father address anyone as *sir*. He could think of maybe three times, and all of them had involved conversations with police.

"You can call me Sterling. If you live on my island, you're my friend."

Lyman thought that if you had to tell someone you were his friend, you probably weren't telling the truth.

"I'm working on an investigation that I'm sure you've heard about." Sterling glanced at Lyman with those chilled eyes. "The homicides on the yacht? Are you aware of those, son?"

Homicides on the yacht. The words seemed to ricochet through Lyman's brain. He'd asked Hatchet what she had done, and he knew it might be bad, but killing someone? No. He didn't believe that.

Did he?

"Answer the man, Lyman!" his father snapped.

"Uh, no. I mean, I'm not aware of…I saw all the helicopters, but I didn't know what they were doing."

"Damn, boy, don't you talk to anyone?" his father said. "Been the only thing people have been speaking of. Where have you been?"

Hiding from you, Lyman thought. *Same as always.* "I didn't know anyone had been…killed," he said.

"Hell yes, they were!" Corey said, dark eyes brightening. "Fifteen men! Dead bodies all over the place."

"That's not entirely correct," Sterling Pike said, an undertone of contempt in his voice. "Seven people were killed. It is a tragedy, but it seems to have taken on some extra color that we don't need."

"Seven, huh?" Corey Rankin said. "Larry Toland told me fifteen. That's Larry for you. Same way he quotes his prices, just take reality and double it."

He laughed loudly. Sterling managed a thin smile. Lyman took the opportunity to peer at the cliff above Hatchet's hiding spot. He didn't see her.

"The people who were killed," he said, "were they cut or chopped up or—"

Both his father and Sterling Pike turned to him, wide-eyed.

"Chopped up?" his father echoed. "Shit, maybe it's better if you *don't* go around talking to people. Chopped up." He shook his head.

Lyman wet his lips. Tried again. "Well, how did—"

"They were shot, of course!" Corey snapped, as if this were obvious. "A regular killin' spree, rich people's blood all over the place." Then, to Sterling: "I still don't know what you're doing at my door, though, asking for my son. We didn't hear anything. Pulling me off the job the way you did, it's cash out of my pocket. Can't pay you if I don't get paid myself."

"I have a few simple questions. Is that all right?" Sterling Pike looked at Lyman as he said it. He was a tall man who seemed to lean forward at all times, looming over you.

"May I get a glass of water?" Lyman asked.

"You don't need any damn water," his father said.

"He can have his water," Sterling said.

"Thanks." Lyman opened the front door, hoping against hope that both men would follow him into the house.

They did.

Lyman went to the sink and got a glass of water and drank about half of it hurriedly, which was hard because his heart was pounding and his stomach was in knots. He wiped his mouth with the back of his hand and then turned to face the deputy.

"Have you met a man named Israel Pike?" Sterling asked. "Same name as me, but don't think I'm here out of family interest. He's not family."

"Thought he was your nephew," Corey said, and Sterling Pike's stare was so cold that Corey lifted a hand in apology. Lyman realized that his father was truly afraid of this man, and not just because he was a cop.

"Have you heard of Israel Pike, son?" Sterling repeated.

"He has the rowboat."

"That's right. Have you talked to him?"

Lyman shook his head. Sterling looked at Corey Rankin. He shook his head too.

"Haven't said a word to the man. Know he's a killer, though."

Sterling didn't respond to that. He turned his attention back to Lyman. "Has he ever been around the property?"

"I mean, we can see all the boats from here."

"Sure. But has he come near you?"

Lyman frowned and his father straightened up.

"What are you getting at?" Corey asked.

"Has he come near you, son?" Sterling said, not looking away from Lyman.

"No. I only know who he is from people talking. He's got a real boat but doesn't use it, and I think he killed someone. Is that true?"

"That's true," Sterling said. "He killed my brother, matter of fact. I watched it happen."

Nobody knew how to respond to that.

"Why are you asking my boy about Israel Pike?" Corey Rankin said at last.

"We executed a search warrant on his property today," Sterling said, "and some photographs were found. Lyman, have you ever seen Israel Pike with a camera?"

"Lots of times. He's a photographer. Dar, at the store, told me that he still uses film."

He wished he hadn't said anything about Dar. She was the one who'd seen Lyman buying socks with bloody money. He did not want the cop to go talk to Dar.

"Has he ever taken pictures of you?" Sterling asked.

"What in the hell does that mean?" Corey Rankin bellowed. He looked at Lyman. "You let him take pictures of you? What the—"

"No!" Lyman blurted out, and now his attention was fully on the two men in the room with him, Hatchet forgotten. "I never let him take any pictures. What are you talking about?"

Sterling opened the folder in his hands, removed a photograph, and held it up. It was black-and-white and showed Lyman running the rip. The tide was high and the rocks were barely visible and it looked as if he were running right across the waves.

Lyman's first thought was that he wanted a copy of it.

"He took that?" Corey Rankin said. "He took that picture of my boy?"

His voice held a familiar darkness, a tone that warned someone might bleed soon.

"Yes. He seems to have quite a collection. Your son is in only one photograph, but I'm speaking with all the families. I want to be sure you're aware of the situation."

Lyman stared at the photograph. A murderer had taken *his* picture?

"Quite a collection?" His father echoed Sterling Pike's phrase. "What does that mean? He's some kind of short-eyes pervert?"

"I did not say that. I'm just trying to determine who was aware of the photography and who wasn't."

"Well, my boy damn sure wasn't," Corey said. "Did you arrest the son of a bitch?"

"Not yet," Sterling said, slipping the photograph back in the folder. Lyman was both glad to see it go and a little disappointed. While it was creepy to know that a murderer had taken a picture of him, it had also been a really good picture.

"Why not?" Corey Rankin asked, and Lyman looked away from the closed folder in Sterling's hands and saw Hatchet appear at the top of the cliff.

Lyman's lungs locked tight. He was the only one facing the window, the only one who could see Hatchet, and yet she seemed so exposed that he was certain she'd be caught. She broke into an awkward, limping run, heading for the Purcell house. It was clear that the effort was painful; she seemed to shudder each time she pushed off her left foot.

Then she fell.

She dropped hard and fast, barely getting her hands out to break the fall, and once she hit the ground, she twisted and reached for her left foot in obvious agony.

Lyman did the only thing he could think of to keep the attention directed away from the windows: He dropped the water glass. Let it shatter on the dirty linoleum floor in a loud burst and jingle, shards scattering.

"The hell is the matter with you!" his father shouted, and Sterling said, "Hey, take it easy."

Lyman knelt and began to gather the shards of the broken glass. His hands were shaking.

"It's all right," Sterling said, kneeling to help him. Corey Rankin didn't bother to join them.

"Did I put a scare into you?" Sterling said. "I'm sorry. There's nothing to be afraid of. Israel is not going to hurt you."

There was plenty to be afraid of, and Israel Pike was the least of it as far as Lyman was concerned. His mind was still on Hatchet's fall. He had told her to run back fast. He shouldn't have done that. She was wearing clumsy boots and her feet were hurt.

He stood up, glass cupped in his palms, and looked out the window. The empty yard and the sea beyond were all that he could see. She had made it back to the house.

Sterling put a large, bony hand on Lyman's shoulder. His grip was too strong to be reassuring.

"I didn't come here to scare you. I just wanted to be sure that you had the chance to share anything that maybe *did* concern you. Is there anything?"

Lyman looked into those winter-sky eyes, swallowed, and shook his head.

"All right," Sterling said, stepping back. "No need for anyone to be scared. All the same, while this is being sorted out, probably be wise to keep a closer eye on your boy, Rankin."

His voice had shifted, a crisp contempt sliding in again.

"It's hard to work and watch him at the same time. Would've been easier if his mother hadn't run off."

Lyman saw Sterling's eyes narrow and his mouth tighten at the corners. The deputy did not like Lyman's father. Not a bit.

"You're working for Larry Toland this week? I know Larry a lot of years now. He's got some boys who help him out in the summertime. A bit older than Lyman, but not much. I could speak to Larry about that. Why don't we all go talk to Larry together."

Lyman thought of Hatchet alone in the Purcell house and blurted out, "I don't want to do that."

"You'll damn well do what you're told, not what you want to," his father said.

"It's not a punishment, son," Sterling Pike said. "Not at all. I want all our island families to stay close together until this is behind us. Maybe Israel is no problem at all. I'll find out. Until then, we all need to keep an eye on each other. I suspect we can find a place for Lyman that's not so lonesome."

And just like that, Lyman was forced to abandon Hatchet without a word.

22

The bartender at Rock Harbor Brewing recommended an IPA called Storm Surge. She poured Israel one pint, then a second, and he was well into his third when Salazar finally walked in.

He saw her clock the beer in his hand, and the anger in her eyes became authentic. She didn't need any help with the acting this time. Didn't need to pretend she knew how to smoke a friggin' cigarette, coughing on it like a teenager while real cops searched Israel's house.

"Hello, Mr. Pike," she said, her voice cold and loud.

"Lieutenant."

She sat down beside him. The bartender drifted by. "What can I get you?"

"His tab," Salazar said. "My friend here is late for a meeting."

The bartender looked from one to the other, nodded, and turned back to the register. Israel drained the last of his beer in a long, delicious swallow. There was a high and tight sensation in the back of his skull, and he felt a pleasant distance from the reality of the room. All this from three pints, he thought with amazement. In the old days, he'd have needed a twelve-pack for a buzz like this. Tolerance really was a thing. Who knew?

"There are some folks in from out of state," Salazar said loudly, speaking to him but for the bar. "Going to need to talk to you. You in shape for that?"

"Fine shape."

"Yeah?" The authentic anger still burned in her eyes. Good. Let her be angry. She hadn't sat out on that island alone with no phone and no lights waiting to see what the next day would bring. She hadn't faced down a television camera, hadn't listened to Rachel Martin say *her* name on national radio. She hadn't rowed out to the *Mereo*.

She damn sure hadn't counted the dead.

"One hundred percent," he said carefully. No slurring.

"Then let's go." She dropped a twenty on the bar. "That cover it?"

He held out his hand with thumb and index finger barely separated. She tossed a five down, made a show of looking disgusted with him. Maybe it wasn't a show. Hard to tell.

Her car was outside, a Ford Explorer with the signature spotlight of the police cruiser mounted above the driver's mirror. She opened the passenger door, making him come to her. He hated her right then. It had all been her idea. She'd found *him,* not the other way around. And now she got to perp-walk him in front of an audience like Sterling had?

"I'll walk," he said. "Where's the big meeting?"

She said, "Do not fuck around," in a low voice.

He got in the car.

She didn't say a word until they were out of downtown. Only after she'd banged a left on Maverick Street and passed Sherman's bookstore did she speak. "What in the hell were you thinking? It *is* a parole violation, damn it."

"You ever heard of someone being sent back to prison for drinking a beer, Salazar?"

"Yes."

"Really?"

"Yes."

"Oh." He had not. He remembered the paperwork, of course, the stipulations on his freedom after fifteen years in a cell, but he had not imagined that meant he couldn't have three beers. Imagine that—you could serve your sentence, be released, ostensibly a free man, and they could send you back into a cell for drinking a beer. The more he learned about the American criminal justice system, the less he liked it. This was, of course, how Salazar had appealed to him from the beginning. Finding the weakness, prodding the wound, hitting it with high voltage.

"You can't be stupid," she said, her hands tight on the steering wheel. "Israel, you cannot afford to be—"

"They're searching *my* house and saying *my* name on the news, Jenn! You think I don't have a sense of my exposure here?"

She checked the mirror. "Keep quiet in my police vehicle, would you, Mr. Pike?"

Saying it as if she thought there was a microphone on. As if she was worried about having him in her car. Worried about everything. She made another left, looping them around and back toward town, then pulled up in front of the Knox County Courthouse.

"Let's take a walk."

He got out. "This is your best idea for a meeting spot? In front of the friggin' courthouse?"

"To warn you about the risk of violating parole? Yes, I think this will do just—"

"Stop it," he said, suddenly so weary he felt as if he couldn't take another step. "I need to talk. Do you not understand that? Please."

This seemed to unsettle her. She walked on in silence. Put her sunglasses on.

"I understand that," she said finally.

"I don't think you do. You're holding all the cards, and I've got police searching my home and TV news reporters banging on the door!" he half shouted, then managed to get himself in check. His stride felt unsteady; why had he had those beers? *To turn the volume down. Because the volume is scaring me right now. It is terrifying me.*

"You've got to see it through a wider lens," Salazar said softly. "I know—I can *imagine*, at least—what this feels like. But I'm telling you, Sterling is not the lead on this investigation. Not anywhere close to it."

"Your task force is running the show? Internal affairs sure is invisible, then."

She hesitated, then said, "There are FBI agents in town who don't know his name and don't care to learn it. They're sidelining him, all right? He's picking on you because he doesn't have anything real to do."

"The search warrant was real. The pictures they took, those were real."

They passed the courthouse and kept walking. The sidewalk was empty. The tourists and reporters and FBI agents were all down by the water, facing Salvation Point Island, where the action was. Israel remembered that courthouse, though. It was where he'd been sentenced to prison.

"What's the story with the pictures?" Salazar asked softly.

"The only part of me that's not a lie."

She glanced at him, waiting for more.

"You gave me a cover story," he said, "but it only works because there's some truth in the lie. Tell them I'm a photographer, you said. Well, I *am*. I mean, I want to be. I spent a lot of time in prison remembering that island and..."

He paused, searching for the right words.

"That island was healthy once," he said. "And those kids, they don't know that it isn't now, that another generation handed them this hate-filled, corrupt, selfish place. But if anyone can save it again, make it clean again, it won't be you and me. It'll be them. We can try to help, that's all." He knew that he wasn't making sense, wasn't explaining it right, and he wished he hadn't had the beers.

"The past wasn't all a lie, and the future isn't all hopeless," he went on. "That's the way people on that island feel now, like they're in one camp or the other. Either everything was bad or everything will be bad, right? Like a friggin' choose-your-own-depression story. Everyone looks past the beauty. The hope. I wanted to make art out of that because, believe it or not, I am more than an ex-con with grudges."

"I know that."

"Do you?"

She looked at him with a hurt that he appreciated.

"I want to be good at it," he said. "I think that I could be."

"Why do you only take pictures of kids?" she said.

"I don't. I had built that display from only the kids. That was the problem. It was a stupid choice. If Sterling goes in there and finds fifty portraits of old fishermen staring at sunsets, he doesn't give a damn. Instead, like a fool, I loaded him up with ammunition. I took those pictures because I find them hopeful, for one, but also because I needed my cover for the pictures you *told* me to take. That wasn't the easiest task."

They walked in silence for a block.

"I shouldn't have let you do the prints," she said. "Digital and we could have just destroyed—"

"Digital and I needed to be out there with electricity, risking surveillance and building a record of communication with a cop. You know what I'm doing and why. I don't know a damn thing other than the marching orders you gave me. I'm not asking you to disclose the whole game, but you *owe* me this one. Did I take the pictures that are missing from that yacht?" His voice was hoarse.

"No," she said. "You did not take them. I don't think they even matter. There were framed photographs taken off the wall, probably by the owner, probably months ago. A footnote in the report, but an excuse for Sterling to sweat you."

He felt as if his lungs opened a fraction. "Have you told anyone about me?"

"No."

"Nobody? Not even on your task force?"

She looked away. "No, Israel. But I'm not sure how much longer I can preserve that."

His lungs sealed right back up. "Not sure? Salazar, if people on that island find out I've been working with the police, they'll kill me."

"I'm doing what I can."

"What you can."

She snapped around to face him. "Seven people were murdered! This one is getting out of my control, don't you see that?"

He had needed her confidence; to feel her fear instead was awful. "When I said I would help—" he began, but already she was shaking her head.

"I don't need a refresher on our terms. I'm telling you that the world has changed."

"Do you know what happened to the women?" he asked.

Her bootheels clapping on the pavement was the only answer. He was not surprised and yet he was still infuriated. He knew that she could not share everything with her own informant but right now he needed her to share *something*. He had none of the leverage and all of the risk.

You will be a star player in those stories, Caruso had said.

"You know a guy named J. R. Caruso?" Israel asked.

"No. Who's that?"

"Says he's a private investigator. Showed up on the island on a private jet with military pilots, said he represented one of the victim's families, but wouldn't say which one, then told me the search warrant was coming and offered his help."

They had reached an intersection and had to wait for the light to change.

"His help doing what?" Salazar said.

"Coming up with a story."

"What kind of story?"

"Anything that ends it fast."

"*It* meaning—"

"The investigation. He did a whole lot of talking about Jack Ruby and Lee Harvey Oswald."

She stared at him.

"That was my reaction too," he said. "Guy's offering to help me by comparing this to the Kennedy assassination, I kid you not. He asked about Sterling, you, and my parole."

"Shit. What did you tell him?"

"Didn't tell him anything. Got off the plane and walked home, and sure enough, there you were, warrant in hand." He looked at the street, saw that they'd missed a chance to cross. He reached out and hit the pedestrian button as traffic flowed by them. "Military pilots. Who the hell are they here for?"

"How do you know they were military?"

"Saw the uniforms."

"Air force?"

"I think so."

"But you're not sure. Could've been National Guard or something."

"Yeah, that makes me feel better. I'm either Jack Ruby or Lee Harvey Oswald and people are trying to scare me using either the U.S. Air Force or the National Guard."

They were facing Route 1, a line of traffic backing up on it, tourists driving up the coast and locals driving home from work. The harbor was visible to the left. Israel had one ferry he could catch and twenty minutes to catch it and then he'd be back on the island, alone. He'd thought he was very good at being alone but it no longer seemed so appealing.

"Who benefits?" he said.

"What?"

"Two Senate candidates died out there. Rivals. Who stands to benefit?"

"I don't know. I'm out of my depth there."

He couldn't help but think of Caruso, who had seemed so deeply connected.

"Salazar," he said, "find out who those women were. Their real names, who brought them in, who took them out."

"They were your contacts. I never had the chance to say a word to either of them."

"Screw that," he said emphatically. "They were supposed to be *your* sources. I spoke to them in pursuit of *your* investigation."

"And if you want help finding them, we can begin that right now, but it means you sitting down with more police than me. Because I don't know what the hell happened out there."

"Do any of your other informants have more?"

"I don't have any other informants."

He felt as if the sidewalk were moving beneath him now. He put his hand on the pole with the pedestrian-crossing button, tried to focus on the cool of the metal, tried to pull the coolness of the steel into his spine and his mind. Traffic buzzed down Route 1. Salazar stayed silent.

"What you have," he managed finally, "is me. That's it. That's the sum total of what you can produce here?"

"I'll get more."

"What do you *have*?"

She was staring at the horizon as if waiting for someone to appear in the distance.

"I've got you," she said. "That's it."

23

He felt as if he were being numbed from the inside out, a strange detachment filling him like nitrous oxide. The light finally changed. He wasn't sure he could walk across the street, but when Salazar moved, he fell into step beside her.

"Don't give up on me now," she said. "Do not get scared, damn it."

"Don't get scared? I'm all alone out there, working with a cop against other cops, and I'm the only person who was—"

"Keep your voice down."

She could hold her head like a hawk when she was angry, seeming to look at you from the side of her eye and from someplace high, high above. It was a beautiful and frightening confidence. He remembered how it had felt the first time he saw it, when he was still in prison and she found and understood him. He remembered those moments and he remembered that she had told him more than she should have and that he had trusted her this far.

He wet his lips and asked the question that would either save or sink him.

"Do you have a ballistics report?"

She frowned. "What?"

"A ballistics report. Do you know what kinds of guns were used?"

"Why are you asking this?"

They'd reached a stretch of train tracks that led down to the waterfront. Israel stopped on the scattered cinders and faced her.

"Because the guns may be a problem for us," he said, and here it was, the thing that he hadn't told her because he hadn't had the chance. The thing he had been trying not to think about since he'd seen the first body.

And the seventh.

"What do you mean, a problem?" Jenn Salazar asked.

"I might know where they came from."

"What?"

He forced himself to keep looking at her. "I was worried about the women. They weren't talking to me, but they were in trouble, I could see that, and—"

"Israel…" She bent toward him, her hands clasped in front of her chest as if she were offering a prayer. Maybe she was.

"I didn't see the harm," he said.

The words were almost inaudible and yet they rocked her back like a slap. She turned in a slow half-pirouette, one hand rising to the bill of her state police baseball cap. Stood looking down the railroad tracks, her back to him. When she finally spoke, her voice was soft.

"Where did you get guns?"

"They were my father's."

She bowed her head. He saw her back rise and fall, heard her exhale. The fear she breathed out seemed to seep right into him, fill his belly with ice.

"I was afraid for them," he said. "It was just the two of them, and I didn't know what kind of situation they were heading into. They were scared, and they were alone, and—"

"You armed them," she said.

Israel stared at her, trying to think of a way to explain it. To tell her how it had felt, talking to them and seeing their fear and being met by their silence. How his promises that he knew a good cop made them laugh aloud, as if he were foolish beyond hope. How it had felt when the one who called herself Marie said that if he was really interested in their safety, he'd give them a weapon.

"You *armed them*," Salazar repeated, as if the three words were incomprehensible.

"I thought…for protection…I didn't think they'd use them. I never imagined that."

"You gave them guns and you didn't tell me."

"When could I tell you? In the police station? When you showed up at my house with Sterling? I've got no phone, no way to tell you anything unless we meet, and by the time I went on that yacht in the morning…well, it was too late then."

"Yes," she said. "It was too late then."

Salazar took the sunglasses off. Her dark eyes held none of the hawk's glare now. They were the eyes of a deer standing on a highway median surrounded by speeding cars.

"If anyone in law enforcement had those guns," she said, "you'd be in jail now."

"Figured that."

"When you went out in the morning, you didn't see them?"

"I saw a lot of dead people but no weapons."

She ran both palms over her eyes, then steepled her fingers over her mouth like a child trying to stay quiet, or calm, or both.

"Could they have done it?" she asked. "Could they have actually done it? *Seven men?*"

Israel gazed down the tracks to the cold sea beyond.

"Someone did."

"Maybe they were witnesses. We don't know."

"I'm not a witness and I'm not the killer. But you can't prove that. I can't prove it."

She shook her head, and he felt as if he stood centered in the crosshairs of a rifle scope.

"Can you keep me clean?" he asked.

"I don't know." She met his eyes. "I'll try. But now? I don't know."

It was his turn to nod. They had been sharing secrets and silence since the beginning, and he had understood the risk and understood the reward. They both had. He'd known that if he was caught helping her, he would be killed. He had believed in Jenn Salazar. He still did. It was like she'd said when they'd started walking, though: The world had changed.

Part Two

BEST-LAID PLANS

24

The first time Jenn Salazar came to see Israel Pike in prison, she said that she was there to talk about his father's boat.

"Why not sell it?" Salazar had asked. "It's impractical as an investment. Is it about legacy?"

They were alone in a visitation room. Salazar was in a blue uniform. Israel was in an orange one.

"I don't see why my inheritance matters to a major crimes detective," he said.

"Do you not?" she asked, and her voice was the calmest challenge he'd ever heard.

That was the first time he'd felt afraid of her. Not because he was in any sort of legal jeopardy, but because of the way she threw the question back at him, her eyes darkening, jaw tightening, voice as steady as a brick wall in the wind.

Do you not?

"Where are you from?" he asked.

"Rockland."

"I mean originally. That accent isn't Mainer."

"I think you mean the absence of an accent."

"Want to answer the question?"

"I'm from Florida. I live in Maine now. The badge and the gun are given to me by the State of Maine. Does that help?"

He watched her, wondering how in the hell she'd found her way to Salvation Point Island and a long-dormant boat. "You looking to buy a lobster boat? Give up the police life, settle down to do some fishing?"

"You're evading, Mr. Pike. Why are you evading?"

He'd gone silent then. Not quite nonresponsive, but close, offering only curt, clipped answers. *I've got nothing to tell you. It's my money*—that kind of thing. She watched him for a long time and then stood and left without another word and he went to his cell and sat on the cold floor with his back against the bunk and wondered who was talking to her and what they might have said.

He did not sleep that night.

Three weeks passed before she returned. He considered refusing to see her or demanding an explanation for her visit, but already he thought he might understand. It was the way she'd looked when she'd said, *Do you not?* Her body had told the truth in that moment. Her body had shown the depth of her rage, the *personal* interest she had in these questions. She had tried to tamp down that rage, and she'd almost succeeded. Almost. He remembered the dark spark in her eyes and the shiver of clenched muscle in her jaw, so he went back to the visitation room to sit across from her once more. She wasn't in uniform this time. Wore an old leather jacket over a T-shirt and no makeup and looked as if she hadn't slept in several days.

"You're spending a lot of money," she said, "to keep a boat idle."

"The hell is the matter with you, coming back to do this again? You got nobody out there who needs police help?"

The wrong thing to say. Her face changed and he saw it and she saw him see it. That was the first time, he thought, that they began to communicate. To understand each other. Not with words but with a single exchanged beat of action and reaction, a nonverbal call-and-response that told each of them something about the other.

"I intend to help people," she said. "Don't you worry about that."

"I'm glad to hear it. Not sure how coming here accomplishes anything, though."

"I'm a curious woman," she said. "The Lost Zone is closed. Not much need for a big, fast boat out there anymore. Why are you keeping it?"

"I'm not really under deadline pressure in here."

"Bullshit. You've planned carefully for that boat."

"I'll get out eventually. Be good to have it ready."

"Five more years."

"Like I said, eventually."

"Would you want it to be sooner?"

He did not answer that. He could feel her stare.

"Why did you kill him?" she asked.

"Kill who?" he said. He had no idea why he picked this ridiculous response other than some vestige of the false hardness you learned in prison, the way you never gave a straight answer, never trusted a soul. As if refusing to trust were a tough-guy thing when the reality was the polar opposite.

"Why?" she asked again.

"It was a bad day."

"That's the reason? A bad day?"

"Sure."

"I don't think it was."

"What do you know about it?"

Her obsidian eyes were fixed on his when she said, "What would you say if I told you that I had been on that boat?"

And then he knew.

Then he understood her.

He felt at once adrift and trapped, unable to turn away from her eyes. He wasn't sure how long she let the silence ride. It felt like a lifetime.

"You did a good thing," she said at last. "But you didn't solve the problem. Follow me?"

"I can't do anything about that," he said. "Not from in here."

"Probably not," Salazar agreed. "But Pike? You don't have to be in here much longer."

His hands were clenched, fingernails leaving half-moon imprints on the heels of his palms.

You did a good thing, she had said. This woman who had been on his father's boat.

"I was fourteen," she told him then.

He felt a chilled prickle from inside his skull go straight down his back, as if spiders were skittering along his spine and snakes were flicking tongues in his brain. His skin went cold, his blood hot; his knuckles ached from the sustained tension in his hands.

"What do you want from me?" he asked. What more could she possibly want beyond what he had already done? He had taken his father's life; he had given his own over to this awful place. No more could be asked of him.

"To help me burn it down," Salazar answered.

"Burn what down?"

"The island. All of them."

"All of *who*?"

"The people he worked with. He didn't do it alone. You have to know that. You know your uncle, certainly."

The flat disclosure unsettled him, made him feel as if he'd done nothing. That wasn't right. He'd given up everything.

"I can't kill them all for you," he said.

She smiled at him then. It was a terrible smile, her lips parting like a trapdoor above an endless darkness. And it was the first time in years that Israel Pike had not felt alone. Someone shared his secrets now.

"We won't go that way," she told him. "Not again."

He didn't answer. Still hearing, *You did a good thing,* still hearing, *I was fourteen.* He couldn't draw a breath. Felt squeezed in a way he had not since his first week in a cell.

Jenn Salazar leaned close, her hair falling forward, her voice low when she said, "If you tell me to leave now, I will leave and I will never come back. I promise."

He believed her. So all he had to do was say it. Tell her to go. Leave the past in the past.

He wet his lips, didn't speak. She watched him with that side-eye gaze that was already becoming familiar, a hawk or an eagle or an osprey, some bird that waited in the wind currents until the moment was right, then descended with shrieking speed and shocking violence.

"Salvation Point," she said. "What a name for that place."

"Don't blame the place. The island was there before the evil."

"How do you know?" she asked.

He thought about the things he could tell her—that his grandfather had been a good man; that his father hadn't committed a crime until they closed the Lost Zone and turned a thousand square miles of lucrative fishing ground into barren territory; that the first crime had not been as bad as the second and the second had not been as bad as the third. That he honestly believed if you removed the second mortgage and added health insurance into the family dynamic, everything would have been very different. He wanted to tell her all of these things.

But...

I was fourteen, she had said.

"It's a bad place now," he said at last, and that admission was enough for her. She was pleased with him. It was the first time he had pleased her, and he knew that he wanted to earn that response again.

"I'll say it one last time," Jenn Salazar said. "I might be able to get you out of here early."

Freedom was an awesome lure, and yet he thought that he should swim on by it, conscious of the hook that was buried inside.

Five years left, though. More than eighteen hundred mornings waking up in a cell.

"I hear you're taking photography classes," Salazar said. "Hear you're pretty talented."

Israel nodded.

"I can use that skill. Someone who knows the island and is known on the island with a camera in hand? I think that would help a great deal."

He was already shaking his head. "You want an informant, look elsewhere."

"I don't want an informant. I want an honest man who lives on that island."

"I just sit out there being honest. Nothing more."

"Maybe a little more."

"There we go."

"It's about doing the right thing," she said. "I think that matters to you. I think doing the right thing is one of the reasons you're here."

"Tell you what," he said, "let's put me to use somewhere else. Pick a spot that isn't Salvation Point Island and make me the same offer about getting out of here early."

She shook her head.

"Then I won't do it."

"Why not?"

"Because I don't trust the people on that island."

She smiled again. That trapdoor of a smile.

"Good news," she said. "Neither do I."

25

The parole board quietly fast-tracked his release.

He was assigned to the Maine State Prison store in South Thomaston. A transition job; days in the shop, nights in the cell. The shop sold goods made by woodworkers in the prison, from simple cutting boards to ornate ships in bottles to furniture. Israel loved the woodworking shop because the smells and sounds reminded him of his grandfather's boatyard. The only things missing were cigar smoke and stories of sailors.

The store where the woodworking goods were sold stood on the main street in town, right on Route 1, with the shop on the east side of the road, and the storage room and loading dock on the west. Tourists loved the place—coasters, clocks, Adirondack chairs, all carved by real live prisoners, how quaint! The prison store was only ten minutes from Salazar's house, and she came around there frequently, chatted with the inmates. They all knew her by the time Israel showed up. Nobody was surprised when she came in and told the warden who ran the place that she wanted to buy lunch for Israel Pike and discuss his future. She gave them all these little prerelease pep talks.

The conversation was different with Israel.

"You'll need to trust me," she said. "That means you'll need to understand my story. There aren't many people who know it. Not on the street, not in the station. This matters, okay?"

"Okay."

She had been born in Florida, somewhere around Miami; she

149

wasn't sure where because it hadn't been in a hospital and everyone who had been present at her birth was gone. Her father had abandoned her mother at the news of the pregnancy. A grandmother did most of the raising of the baby, although Salazar wasn't certain she had actually been a blood relative. Her mother left, the grandmother died, and an aunt had stepped in. They spoke primarily Spanish in her home. Sometimes Salazar went to school; sometimes she didn't. Then her aunt died and it was just her and the husband, a man she referred to as her stepfather simply to make things easier. Her stepfather worked on the docks in Miami, and he began to have more friends over, later nights, extra beers. She thought about running away. Didn't. Where would she go?

She was fourteen years old when one of her stepfather's friends gave her the doctored cocktail that left her unconscious, still fourteen when she woke up alone in the back of a locked U-Haul truck in the snow, still fourteen when a stranger put a needle in her arm in the parking lot of a commercial wharf that stank of diesel and dead fish, still fourteen when she woke up on a cot in a stone cellar with her hand cuffed to an iron ring set into the wall. A man came into the cellar, fumbled with a hypodermic needle, and injected more drugs into her bloodstream. Then he took her out to a boat and put her belowdecks in a cramped V berth. She'd pretended to be unconscious, watched him move through slitted eyes.

"I don't think," she told Israel Pike two decades later, "that your father was really good with science. The drug dosage seemed to be a problem for him."

Your father.

First time she'd said that.

He would never forget hearing those words as long as he lived.

The man left the boat, assuming she was unconscious, and after waiting long enough to be sure he was gone, she made her way up to the deck. The boat was at anchor, and the dinghy he'd used to transport her from the house to the boat was gone. There was a bleached-gray rock island visible some two hundred yards away. Maybe three hundred. A long swim, but what was the alternative? She tried it.

"I wasn't prepared for how cold that water was," she said. "I'd lived in Florida my whole life, and I could not imagine how cold an ocean could get."

But she'd made it all the way to the bleached-gray rock, salt water searing her throat, cold crushing her lungs. She'd made it.

And there onshore waited another man. Kind and compassionate, this one. He took her out of the water and into his house and gave her blankets and broth and listened to her story, which she offered in broken English; Spanish was her first language. He asked her what she wanted him to do.

"Take me to the police," she said.

Her savior nodded, said of course that was what he would do. And he did.

The cop at the station was tall and had eyes like arctic ice and told her to call him Sterling.

Israel's fingers curled into fists. "Sterling."

"Yes."

"You're sure," he said.

"I am sure."

"Then why isn't he in prison with me?"

"Because there is a difference between my memory and prosecutable evidence. Let me finish my story, then we'll talk about what I plan to do."

The tall cop named Sterling brought in a young man in a suit who gave her a Sprite and a KitKat and began to ask questions. He did not give her his name. His questions weren't about what had happened to her or at whose hand.

"He asked if I was on drugs," Salazar told Israel, her voice cold and toneless. "Did I sell drugs? Did I work for men who sold drugs? If the police tested my blood, would they find drugs in it? It was a combination of intimidation and gaslighting. They tried to make me question my own memory."

Eventually, the man in the suit and the cop named Sterling gave her some pills—medicine to keep her from getting sick, they said, after all that time in the cold water—and then they left her in a locked room with her empty Sprite and the KitKat wrapper, and when they came back, the man from the boat was with them. The one who'd put the needle in her arm and left her.

"They called him Charlie," Salazar told Israel that day on the loading dock. "No last name, but I remembered Charlie. He said he was my uncle and that I was a runaway. He had some papers with him. I don't know what was on the papers. It didn't seem to matter then. I've always wondered, though. What in the hell did he walk in there with?"

She told Israel the story on a bright spring morning when the air was clean and crisp, and yet he felt like a man suffocating in ever-thickening smoke. A family from South Carolina walked out of the prison showroom store wearing headbands with lobster claws that bobbed in the air and made them all laugh as they walked to their Audi. Salazar went silent until they were gone, and Israel clenched and unclenched his hands in a slow, methodical rhythm, synchronized with his breaths. A trick he had learned in prison for times when the anger rose.

"I was in a fog by then," Salazar said. "Shock, of course, but also the pills hitting. The *medicine* they'd given me. It was as if they were in one room and I was in another, behind glass. The last thing the man in the suit told me was to stay off drugs. I remember that. Then I was walking out of the police station and your father was promising that he'd take me home if I wasn't any trouble. If I behaved, he'd take me home. Just behave. I tried to."

Israel closed his eyes, wiped his mouth.

"Then what happened?" he said, eyes still shut.

Charlie Pike had taken her onto his boat and brought her out to another one, a cargo ship of some kind, a ghost freighter with an engine that shuddered the deck and fogged the air with fumes. Three more men had waited on that one, maybe four. Salazar wasn't sure because she hadn't been conscious for most of her trip aboard it.

Her next stop had been a wharf in Canada. She'd been put on a truck there, and she had no longer been alone. There were other girls now.

Fourteen years old when she'd escaped her captors; fourteen years old when she'd been returned to them.

She was sixteen the second time she got away from her captors. That had been in Calgary, where a stranger named Bernardo Thomas had fed her oatmeal with a spoon and smashed the muzzle of a shotgun into the teeth of the man who eventually arrived looking for her, claiming to be her stepfather.

Bernardo Thomas had taken her to a shelter run by the Jesuits. The police had come and gone a few times, attempting to interview her. She hadn't told them anything. They weren't surprised. They'd met a few like her before.

"You wondering why I didn't tell them the whole story?" she'd asked Israel as they leaned against the loading dock in South Thomaston, Italian sandwiches from the market up the street resting untouched between them. Lunch break.

Israel shook his head.

"Why not?" Salazar asked.

"Because I understand it. You'd already tried. They'd already failed you once. You made a risk assessment based on experience."

"Risk assessment based on experience. I like that. Yeah. I made the risk assessment. I hadn't seen a place resembling home in almost two years, and the only man who'd treated me like a human was the same man who reminded me daily that he'd kill me if I left or caused trouble, and the only time I'd tried to tell the truth before, it had done no good. So you know what I told them? I told them that I did too many drugs. Because I remembered that guy in the suit, on the day I made that swim through the cold water, telling me to stay away from drugs while your father walked me out the door. The next time I talked to a cop, I said that's what my trouble was, drugs. It worked better."

She'd stayed in the shelter for a while, then gone into foster care. Her foster mother was a teacher, her foster father a stonemason. They'd had a daughter of their own who was killed by a drunk driver when she was fourteen. Their last name was Ross, and they told her she could go by any name she liked. She kept her own. She didn't want to pretend she was someone else. She tweaked the name, that was all. Jennifer became Jenn with two *n*'s. She liked the way it looked written down.

"Better balance," she said. "And I didn't feel like a Jennifer anymore. It had no edge."

She had an edge—years of overwhelming trauma that she sought to burn and inhale, taking what she wanted from it, destroying the rest. And she did want something from it, she told him. Purpose. To be a protector, the one thing she'd never had.

Her foster family moved to Pennsylvania. She went to a counselor. She went to school. She made it through college, then the police academy, then moved to take a job in Florida. She wanted to see the palm trees again, feel warm breezes. She'd intended to stay in Florida, but at night when she was alone, she remembered the cold-water swim somewhere off the coast of Maine. She remembered the island.

"You ready for the fucked-up thing?" she asked, tearing at the bread of her uneaten sandwich. "I had a really positive memory of the island itself. Because there had been a moment when I first arrived when it felt like escape. Rescue."

"Salvation," he said. "Lived up to the name. For a minute, anyhow."

"When I came out of that water shaking from the cold onto those rocks that tore my skin? I remember thinking it was the most beautiful place I'd ever seen."

"What made you decide to come back?"

"A calendar photo."

"You're serious."

"Yes. A probation officer I knew had visited Bar Harbor. Came back in love with the place, hung this wall calendar, and I thought, *I know the place.* She was joking about the Mainer accents too. I remembered your father's accent. The way he couldn't pronounce his own fucking name. Like, who gives a kid a name with an *r* in it if no one can say the *r?*"

"Cholly Pike," Israel said, and Jenn Salazar laughed without humor.

"There ya go."

"So you came back looking for him?"

She shook her head. "I came back, strange as it may sound, because of the positive memory, not the negative. I came back because I was struggling down in Florida. I was struggling with myself, you know, and for whatever sad, warped reason, I remembered the way I felt coming out of that water onto the rock. Everything in that place was *mean,* it was designed to *hurt,* the freezing water and the hard sharp rock were pure pain, and yet that day, it felt so good. Because I'd *made* it. Escape. Survival. I remember the way the air tasted. Remember the way the blanket felt on my skin when the one kind man, the one honest man, put it around my shoulders. It was rough, like a horse blanket, but it was the best feeling I'd ever had in my life."

She ripped off a piece of bread and tossed it in the gutter, and they watched as a gull claimed it. Israel's break time was up, but his bosses weren't going to say anything to him when he was with a cop. Getting his warnings, they thought. His parolee pep talk.

"My first job up here was in Brunswick. I liked it. Liked the people. On my own time, I went out to the islands. There are so many of them! More than a hundred inhabited islands in Maine; that blew my mind. I kept looking for the right one. I was actually on Salvation Point five, maybe six times without remembering it, without knowing for sure. They look alike, these islands. I liked Salvation Point. I met good people out there."

"How did you find my father?" he asked, the last word leaving his lips like an offering, something she needed to hear him say. She did not react, though.

"Newspaper. There was a murder on Vinalhaven a few years back, and the reporter mentioned that it was the first homicide on a Maine island since Charlie Pike was killed by his son on Salvation Point, and there was a picture of your father. I knew him right away."

"Yet you didn't assume I was like him. Why not?"

"Because you hated him," Jenn Salazar said, fixing her eyes on his.

"How'd you know that?"

"It's what everyone told me. They all liked your father, of course." He nodded.

"Except for the woman at the market," she added.

"Dar."

"That's her. She told me not to worry about you coming back and causing problems. Said people gave you too little credit and your father too much credit. I was curious about that."

"She knew him," Israel said, "and she knew me. We're family, of a sort. Our grandmothers were sisters. Whatever kind of cousin that makes her."

"She told me you got sideways because of drinking, drugs."

He nodded. "Those things were real."

"What wasn't real?" Salazar said. "Because you've got secrets, my friend. I saw that in your face the first time I visited."

He paused.

"Think about what I've confided in you," she said. "Really think about it, Pike."

He thought about that, and then, for the first time in his life, he told the truth about killing his father.

26

The stories people told about Israel's struggles with drinking and drugging weren't lies or character assassination. They were real enough, he assured Salazar.

"What wasn't real—or what the rest of the world didn't understand—was the point of that last summer on the island. Everyone thought my father was trying to use it to fix me. Save me. They were half right."

"Were you giving him a last chance?"

"Trying to. I thought if I reminded him of how he'd learned to fish…if he remembered my grandfather, maybe he could find the thing that was there and had been corrupted and—"

He stopped, unable to find the words to clarify what he believed everyone should understand: That you shouldn't bury the past and you shouldn't idealize it, that either approach was poison. You had to consider the past with clear eyes and a calm heart.

You had to hope the man you hated could become something closer to one you loved.

"You wanted to reboot him," Salazar said. "Cleanse him of his sins, send him back out a new man."

Had it been that pure and that foolish?

"I guess it was something along those lines," Israel said.

"And instead you killed him."

A Dodge diesel roared by, leaving an acrid fog of exhaust in its wake. Salazar waited on Israel. He pictured his father sitting in the skiff at the wharf, looking at Israel with contempt. Every man on the pier that day had seen the contempt, and none of them had understood it. Charlie Pike wasn't disappointed in his son for failing to do the right thing; he was disgusted with him for thinking the right thing mattered. For thinking small.

Cute—that was the word he'd used. Israel had a real cute notion of the ways of the world.

"If you were trying to save him," Salazar said, "then you knew he was in deep."

"Sure. I knew where my drugs came from. He didn't take them, and I was supposed to be impressed by that, evidently. But smuggling them, selling them? Well, that was supporting your family. His favorite phrase: *You've gotta support your family.* All the rich people putting their estates up, knocking down a fisherman's old house to build a summer home, he told me they weren't supporting their families. Trust-fund babies, every single one of them, he claimed. Never mind the jobs they had, the work they'd done. He dismissed it all as inherited, unearned wealth. I suspect a few folks with summer homes are good fathers. Pretty damn sure of it. Money and morality might not be close friends, but they are not mutually exclusive either. But my old man wouldn't believe it. All that was good on that island was either gone from it or fading fast. You did what you had to do to keep the right kind of people on the island. A big deal to him was protecting the 'right kind of people.' His kind of people. If you had to break the law to protect them, well, that, Salazar, is called *supporting your family.*"

"He told you that."

"Several times, including the day I killed him."

She watched him in silence.

"I confronted him that day, challenged him, gave him an ultimatum. He was..." Israel choked on a sad laugh, remembering. "He was shocked. First that I would threaten to turn him in to the police, but on a deeper level, what he saw as a *moral* level, he was genuinely shocked because I didn't *get* it. I didn't understand that life was binary, and you have to choose: either make money to preserve your way of life, or surrender it. In his mind, everyone involved in crime was an immoral asshole except him. Gangster's logic—they're all dirty, so why *not* take their money?"

"You knew he was running drugs when you came out for the summer," she said.

"Drugs and guns."

"But you didn't know about—"

"Human beings? Girls? Children?"

She held his gaze.

"No. He told me that day, no more than three hours before I killed him. It was his example of all that I didn't understand."

"Explain that."

"The families didn't care enough to protect their girls. Families like theirs, my father said, never would. People who'd let a girl be taken, who'd trade her for money or drugs? Fuck 'em. They'd already ruined the girl."

"He said these things." Her voice was devoid of emotion, a clipped staccato.

"He said them." Israel wiped his mouth with the back of his hand. "And then *I* said that I was going to turn him in. He said, 'Bullshit, you will.' I said, 'We'll see.'"

He paused, looking at the pavement but seeing the open ocean alongside his beloved island, smelling the salt and the sea and the sweat, remembering how each swell had felt beneath the skiff.

"We got back to the wharf, and he sat there in the skiff, refusing to get out because I think by then he believed I would go to the police. He started in on the way my grandfather would've viewed this, the way those generations who *supported their families* would've felt about me. The other men there were looking at me and seeing one thing, then looking at him and seeing the other..."

He lost his words. Rage twitched in him like a dreaming dog's paws. He closed his eyes again. "I wasn't stupid enough to want to kill him in front of all those people. I wanted to shut him up. That was all. Just shut him the hell up."

Silence. The gull swooped in and tottered up, eyeing the bread. Curious but cautious. Israel moved out of the way so it had a clear path. They watched it claim the bread and take flight.

"The amazing thing about that day," Israel said, "was how many people saw it and heard it and didn't understand it. Some went to their graves believing I'd murdered an innocent man because he called me out on my lack of accountability."

"You let that happen, though. You chose that rather than telling the truth. You lied."

"I did not lie. I chose not to talk. There's a difference."

"Is there?"

He looked at the prison store, where tourists wandered in and out buying quaint handmade goods from inmates.

"It's what I chose," he said.

Salazar didn't press him. She sat in a silence that felt thoughtful rather than judgmental.

"There are girls being trafficked through that island," she said at length. "I know it. I try to help each one, but that's no different than what you did. The system has to be brought down for it to mean anything. So I need to know everyone who's involved."

"Then why don't you bring in more cops?"

Her face showed her disappointment in him. It was a *You know better* look that reminded him of his grandfather.

"You think your uncle is the only person in law enforcement

who looked the other way out there? You think the islanders will start talking to strangers with badges? All you friggin' people have a phrase for anyone who hasn't lived on the right rock for the last century: *From away.* I've come from away, Pike. It's a hard place to start."

"Take down Sterling, then. Start with him and keep knocking the dominoes down."

She shook her head. "I'll take one bad man down and leave— what, ten? Twenty? I want them all."

"You can't take them all down."

"Sure, I can. It's not that big of an island."

He loved the way she said that.

"It's more than the island," he said. "The system that you've described, it's so much bigger than that island."

"You're right. It involves Florida, New York, Jersey, Quebec, Calgary. Get the girls far from home, get them helpless, ideally get them to a place where there's a language barrier to boot."

"So Salvation Point doesn't matter. It's a link in the chain."

"The heart is a link in the chain. What happens when you stop the heart?"

He thought about that.

"You remember Sterling," he said, "and you remember my father. You have not named the man in the suit, the one who came in and asked you about drugs. Do you know who he is?"

"Not yet."

"Ideas?"

She was quiet. "Working on them," she said at last. "A couple are still local. One is poised for bigger things."

"What's that mean?"

She looked at him as if weighing whether to place a bet that she could not afford to lose. "One of them is running for the Senate," she said. "A man named Paul Gardner."

"Holy shit."

"Yes," Jenn Salazar said. "Holy shit."

Israel tried not to look afraid. "How many people from SPI do you think are involved now?" he asked.

"Maybe three, maybe thirteen. I'm not sure yet. This is where I could use some help."

He was sure she was looking at him when he said, "They police their own on that island. Anyone finds out that I'm coming after Sterling—"

"They won't."

"Anyone does," he pushed on firmly, "and I'm dead. You understand that?"

"Yes."

He took a breath. "What do I need to do?"

She stood and dusted her uniform pants off. Put on her sunglasses.

"I want to see any girl who passes through that island who doesn't fit. You find her for me, and I'll find out who she is and where she's from. I will get her away from whoever she is with, and I will find out who brought her there."

Alone? he wanted to ask. *You are going to do that alone, Lieutenant Salazar?* But he said nothing because she was here already, she had found him, and she had done that alone. She had gotten off his father's boat and fought through cold water to a sharp rock, and after they'd put her back on that boat, she had survived everything else that came her way and then she had returned to the rock with a gun and a badge.

Alone.

"How many people will know I'm working with you?" he asked.

"None."

"Bullshit."

"Hand to God. It is an internal affairs task force, because police and the attorney general's office are targets. What that means?

Nobody trusts anyone else. If I cultivate a relationship with an informant who delivers quality intel, I won't be questioned."

He was already thinking about the methods of communication, the risks. "I won't use a phone," he said. "And I won't use a computer. If I do this, I talk to you and you alone. In person."

"I can work with that."

27

The next time they met, he was a free man, and she was focused on his uncle.

"You think he's small-time," Salazar said, "and you're wrong. It might have started with bribes and handshake deals, looking the other way with one man while putting the handcuffs on another, but that was long ago."

They were in Camden for this conversation, sitting at a table outside a bar called Lucky Betty's, a fun, funky place in a converted old service station on the town's main street, uphill from the village green and the harbor below, one of those postcard shots of New England. Salazar always picked places where tourists bustled through and two strangers wouldn't stand out.

"Reviewing his arrest records over the years is like identifying the moves in a chess game," she said. "He stays on Salvation Point, but his police authority isn't limited to one island. He's got a half a dozen in the mix, the sort of burden that would've been split among several officers in a different generation. Manpower gets depleted, and most cops don't want to work there—pulling overtime hours but not getting paid for it, dealing with isolated communities who have their own brand of internal policing—and Sterling Pike magnanimously offers to take on yet another island. Each year, he'll make some intriguing arrests, but he seems to deliver for the DA's office on only half the potential prosecutions. The rest fall through the cracks. Over the years, he's formed some interesting alliances with prosecutors and judges. None of them seem to like him much, but they work with him. I suspect they don't feel they have much choice."

"Why not?"

"Because he's very good at stockpiling ammunition. Here's an example: Ten years ago, he arrested a woman for operating a boat while intoxicated off Salvation Point. She was a twenty-three-year-old law clerk for a fifty-year-old Knox County judge. The boat she was in was registered to the judge, who was in his underwear in the cabin below deck, and his wife was back at home, oblivious to this little pleasure cruise. There are half a dozen witnesses who saw the judge on the boat, but his presence did not make Sterling's probable-cause affidavit. Later, Sterling said he'd failed to calibrate his Breathalyzer properly, and the charge against the clerk was quietly dropped. Think he's got a friend in the courtroom now? That's one camp of his targets—power brokers. Another camp? The violent."

"What do you mean?"

"Sterling has an eye for cruelty. He's happy to prosecute a garden-variety fuckup, someone who throws a punch in anger. But anyone with a darker streak, anyone who *enjoys* the violence? He'll cultivate that."

"To what end?"

"Control," she said simply. "If you live on an island, and you're afraid of vigilante law *and* the real law, what options do you have other than going along?"

And you want me to go back to this place? he thought.

"Your uncle understands power dynamics," Salazar said. "He understands how to keep his head down. Why do you think he stays on that island? You believe he has any real affection for the place?"

Israel shook his head. "No. His family's gone, the community is drying up around him, he's got nothing but bitterness for what's left. And, apparently, he has power. That would suit him. He wouldn't abdicate the throne. He likes punching down far too much for that."

"Do you ever talk to your cousins?" Salazar asked.

"I haven't spoken to them since I was maybe eight years old. I hardly remember their mothers. They looked the same to me. Beautiful but cold. Both were blond-haired and blue-eyed and both hated winter, which is a bit of a problem if you're living in Maine. I don't think my grandmother got on well with either of them. The marriages fell apart fast, and the kids moved with their mothers. Sterling stayed. The boys would come back to visit in the summers. Briefly. Not surprisingly, neither of them dropped me a letter when I was in prison."

Salazar nodded. "One son graduated from law school at Notre Dame, the other got an MBA from Penn. One ex-wife lives in Savannah, the other in Ojai."

"I don't know Ojai."

"Town Californians like to pretend is wilderness. More yoga mats than hunting rifles."

"Got it."

"Supposed to be a lovely and restorative place. Not a cheap one."

Israel nodded, sipped his seltzer water. Salazar had a Modelo Especial.

"One of his exes remarried, the other didn't," Salazar said. "Neither works. Both live in beautiful homes with no mortgages. Neither son carries any student loan debt despite going to pricey private schools."

"You can't believe Sterling made *that* much money hustling people on the islands," he said.

"I said it started with hustling. That's a long time ago, and he's got more cards in his hand now. You tell me, is there any cash to be made in the drug trade? You used to be a buyer."

He hated to hear that, but it was true. "There's money," he acknowledged. "Particularly Down East, in those remote regions. You're paying four, five times per gram what you'd pay in the city. Supply and demand, it's that simple."

"There you go. And what about weapons trafficking? What about human trafficking? Once you've claimed a trafficking corridor, how fast do you think you could grow?"

He exhaled and sat back, looking down the street toward the bucolic harbor.

"Sterling is in all of that?"

"Yes," she said. "He's in all of that. He owns a piece of a network, essentially. From the locations to the mules to the local law. He provides access, and he provides protection, and that's serious value to big-league players in any one of the syndicates I mentioned and probably more."

"Then why haven't you already busted him? If you know all this, it should be—"

"There's damaging evidence and then there's knockout evidence," she said. "Do I know enough to hurt him? Yes. Could I absolutely win in the courtroom on his turf? I don't think so. I could get him fired, maybe get him some prison time, but more than that? Not yet. I'll get there, though. But I'm not like you, Pike. I'm not obsessed with taking down one man. I want all of them, anyone who played a role, the whole network, up and down the coast."

"I'm not obsessed with taking one down. That one is personal to me, that's all."

"They're all personal to me," Salazar said.

Israel thought of the island he'd known as a boy and then thought of the scope of crimes that Salazar had outlined, the sheer volume, the money.

"Why does Sterling stay there?" he asked.

"Because he's practically invisible. When was the last time a federal agent set foot on Salvation Point?"

"I don't know if one ever has."

"Do you think one could arrive without being noticed?"

"No chance."

"There ya go." She drained her beer, set it aside. "He's invisible, he's protected, and he's the law. A man like him gets off on that kind of power. Only thing I *don't* understand is why he keeps buying up the island."

Israel cocked his head. "Buying what?"

"Land. Houses. Businesses. Your uncle owns half the island by now, rents some of it, but not much. The rest decays around him. He doesn't invest a dime in maintenance, doesn't seem to give a damn what happens to any of it, yet he continues to acquire. Why?"

She wasn't expecting an answer, and Israel didn't have one. The bartender approached the table with another cold Modelo in hand and swapped Salazar's empty for the fresh one. Israel sat in silence until they were alone again.

"You want me to watch him?" he said. "That's my role?"

"That's your role. I'll take anything I can get, of course, but what I'm most interested in are the women," she said. "The girls. Because you will see some. I am sure of that."

"He saw you when you were a teenager," Israel said. "That's long ago, sure, but how are you so confident that he doesn't recognize you now, or won't remember you at some point?"

"Because I was utterly inconsequential to him," Salazar said. "Inconsequential and not unique. There were many girls like me who passed through over the years, and he didn't see us as human beings, Pike. He saw cargo."

Her jaw clenched and she looked away and neither of them spoke for a time.

"All right," he said at length. "I will go back home, and I will do what I can."

He'd returned to the island the next day. He had lived in darkness and he had rowed his boat and he had taken his pictures and watched everyone, listened to everything. Searching for anyone who fit the profile Salazar had outlined.

Only two women had.

They appeared at the beginning of the summer and moved into one of Sterling's numerous rental properties, a bleak studio with a galley kitchen in a building with a small widow's walk. Below their apartment was what was once a welder's shop, although it had been vacant for many years. They kept to themselves. When Israel asked questions, the replies were terse. He received first names only: Jacqueline and Marie. They had worker's visas, they told him, and they were on the island for the summer, looking for seasonal work. Problem with that was, you needed to have a job to get that visa; the government didn't hand them out first, to his knowledge. Seasonal employees from overseas were common in Maine. They usually worked unholy hours at restaurants or lobster shacks or motels and left in September. They didn't stay in an apartment above an abandoned welder's shop looking out to sea.

His arrangement with Salazar was that they met in person in Rockland each Monday. Different venues, agreed upon beforehand, a calendar of meetings that could seem like chance encounters. On the Monday after Jacqueline and Marie arrived, he met Salazar on the long breakwater to the lighthouse in Rockland Harbor, handed her photographs of the women, and explained what they'd told him.

"Ask them to talk to me," she said. "Don't use my name, though. Not yet. Just tell them there's a cop they can trust if they're in trouble. Press a little. See how they react."

He pressed a little. Jacqueline and Marie shut down. Started to avoid him. They stayed in the apartment or on the widow's walk for most of the day. They watched the sea as if they were waiting for something to come from it. They didn't search for any work, didn't take the ferry to the mainland, didn't interact with anyone except Sterling, who stopped by once, stayed exactly nine minutes, and left, and Corey Rankin, a world-class ne'er-do-well who lived out on Little Herring Ledge. Rankin brought the women groceries. Stayed less time than Sterling had. The women seemed to hate him.

Israel went back not long after Rankin's visit. Asked them was everything all right, were they in any trouble, was anyone hassling them.

"Just you," Marie had said, but she did not seem to mind Israel. She smiled with her mouth but never her eyes. The other one, Jacqueline, did not smile at all. They were of a similar age and look, dark-haired and dark-eyed and petite, Marie maybe two inches taller than Jacqueline and probably a few years younger. She had a single tattoo on the inside of her left wrist, a word in script, *Respirer,* which she told him was French for "breathe."

"What does that mean to you?" he asked.

"A reminder that I'm still able to do it," she said.

"What brought you to Salvation Point?" Israel had asked then, the fifth or maybe sixth time he'd tried, and she rolled her eyes and looked disappointed in him for pursuing it yet again.

"It's none of my business," Israel began, and Marie laughed.

"You're right," she said with that accent they both had.

He should have dropped it, but Salazar had told him to press a little, so he did. "It's none of my business, what you're doing here, but if you're in any trouble, I know a cop you can trust."

The laugh Marie gave him this time was not as warm as the first one.

"Get the fuck out of here," she said. "Go row, row, row your boat."

The one who said her name was Jacqueline watched him with something between fear and curiosity.

He left.

That night, Sterling had come back to see them. Fourteen minutes this time. Israel waited for him to come by his house, expecting they had told him about Israel's overture. Things stayed quiet. The next two days, Jacqueline and Marie continued to watch the water. He knew better than to try again. He'd risked enough.

But he was certain that they were afraid. He had spent enough time watching fear in the human body to see it. That was being in prison—watching for fear, hiding your own, and staying the hell away from the truly fearless, who tended to be the truly insane. Jacqueline and Marie were waiting on something, and they were afraid of it. He knew this.

And so he went back, against his better judgment. Tried one last time. Marie told him to go row his boat again, Jacqueline stayed quiet again, and he gave up, was done, was walking away, when Marie spoke to his back.

"If you're really so worried about our safety, give us guns, not cops."

The mistake he made was looking back. A single glance.

She wasn't joking. She wanted a weapon, and she was afraid. He looked at her and he looked at Jacqueline and he left without another word and went home and sat in the gathering dusk and then returned in full dark with two guns in a backpack.

"What's this?" Marie said.

"Proof that you can trust me."

"This is how you show that?"

"Yes. So when I say you can also trust the cop I want to introduce you to, remember that I did this first."

He left them with the guns. He saw them the next afternoon. He was on the water; they were on the little widow's-walk balcony of the old apartment. He waved; they waved back. That night, he went to the apartment. The door was unlocked, the place as empty as if they'd never existed. They were gone.

Gone with his guns.

The next morning he sighted the drifting yacht.

Went out to investigate.

That was the sum total of his experience as an informant for Jenn Salazar. Two women were missing, seven men were dead, and his father's guns were lost.

Hell of a job.

Today, on the ferry back to Salvation Point, knowing all of this and knowing that Salazar was in danger of losing control of the confidential nature of her own investigation, he wondered: Would he change anything if he could?

Even now, he wasn't sure.

Sometimes it was worth putting your neck in the noose. Salazar had been fourteen years old when she was brought aboard his father's boat. She hadn't made that choice.

Why should Charlie Pike's only son be allowed to make his?

Part Three

THE CARUSO DOCTRINE

28

Lyman Rankin's bad day was getting worse.

The only thing worse than leaving Hatchet behind that afternoon was being sent to work with the boys Larry Toland had hired.

Lyman had moved to Little Herring in spring, which was the worst time to be a new kid. In the summer, you could ease into things. Fall or winter, you still had enough time to find a friend or two, at least. But spring? The other kids all had their own alliances and grievances by then.

This problem was exponentially greater on Salvation Point. The kids on the island weren't awful. Not by any means. But they all knew each other *so well*. It wasn't that there weren't *many* new kids—there had never been a new kid, period. His class was a fifth-sixth split, and even with the two grades combined, there were only nine kids. Five girls, four boys. Seven families. Everyone had known everyone else forever. Worse, their parents knew Corey Rankin. Whatever chance Lyman had of coming in clean and making his own reputation, the way he had in Framingham, did not exist on SPI. After two days, he heard the first under-the-breath reference to "the drunk's kid." Compounding the problem was his remote existence on the Ledge. He couldn't participate in pickup games or afternoons on the rocks and water, couldn't do anything spontaneous, his life governed by the tides. If his father was sober, he would bring Lyman to SPI and back in their dinghy. That was a big *if*, though. Lyman had missed a lot of days that semester because his father was too hungover to take him, and the tides trapped him on the Ledge.

It had been a lonely, miserable spring. On a normal summer day, he would have been excited about the chance to work with some of the island kids, seeing the opportunity to forge a friendship before school resumed. Today, though, when all he wanted to do was get over to the Purcell house and see Hatchet and explain that the police were not looking for her and hadn't seen her, he was the last one to show up for a job the other kids had been working on all day.

Perfect.

The job was at a sprawling summerhouse on the southwestern shore of the island. Larry Toland ran a painting and drywall business, which meant working a lot of hours in a short season for exterior jobs, so he needed each one ready to go before the last was done. The men hung drywall and painted; the kids cleaned and prepped. After talking with Sterling, Toland sent Lyman to join two other boys, Danny Graves and Evan Morris, sanding and pressure-washing the back deck of the house.

Lyman was the youngest, and the oldest, Evan, was a mean-spirited fourteen-year-old. As soon as the adults were gone, Evan announced that he was in charge of the pressure washer, which he promptly used to spray Lyman in the back. It hit hard, a blast that would leave a bruise, but Lyman didn't give him the satisfaction of crying out in pain. A benefit of being Corey Rankin's son was the ability to absorb punishment without reaction.

Just work until quitting time, then you can get back to her and explain, he told himself.

It was a beautiful day, the kind of day that brought tourists surging up from Massachusetts and New York and Connecticut. A lot of lobsters would be sold on the coast of Maine today. Lobsters and clam chowder and ice cream and beers and brightly colored drinks. Lyman wouldn't mind being a tourist for a day. Let alone a summer person. Who owned this house, he wondered, and why didn't they appreciate it enough to take care of it themselves? It was a perfect summer day and they weren't even in their perfect summerhouse. What a waste.

The house was built onto the high rocks above the water, the deck supported by long, angled beams so that it seemed to float above the sea. The tide was going out, exposing more of the rocks, everything smelling fresh and clean. If Lyman owned this house, he would never miss a sunrise or a sunset. He would sleep on this deck in nice weather. Maybe in bad weather.

He worked a sanding block over the porch railing, the cloud of fine dust rising in the air, the gray grime vanishing. The process reminded him of cleaning the floors and trim in Dwayne Purcell's house, and that made him think of Hatchet. What was she doing? How bad had she been hurt when she fell? As the hours wore on and he didn't show up, would she begin to think that he had betrayed her?

He was lost in these questions when Evan Morris shot him with the pressure washer again. This time, he had dialed the nozzle closer to the jet setting, and it scorched a red line across the back of Lyman's calf.

"*Ow!*" Lyman shouted. He could absorb punishment, but he hadn't been expecting this one, and it hurt.

"Don't be a jerk, Evan," Danny Graves said. Danny was a quiet, redheaded kid who struggled with reading but could solve any math problem. Danny didn't say enough to Lyman to feel like a friend, really, but at least he never said anything mean.

"Oh, I'm sorry, Graves, did you want to be cooled off instead of Rankin?" Evan turned the pressure washer on Danny, laced a quick, cruel blast over his back.

"You're a dick!" Danny snapped, but he didn't turn, and Lyman saw that he was blinking away tears. Evan had all the advantages of a bully: size, strength, and a weapon. It was better to keep your head down.

"Speaking of dicks," Evan said, "I heard your mother loves them, Rankin."

Lyman rolled his eyes and followed Danny's lead, ignoring Evan and continuing to work. The "your mama" jokes were a lot less painful than the pressure washer.

"No, I'm serious," Evan said. "I heard the first time you and your dad lived out in that shit-pile on the Ledge, he was shacked up with a whore."

Lyman kept sanding, trying to focus on the task, trying not to wonder who had told Evan Morris that Lyman's mother had once lived in the house on the Ledge. It had been for such a short time, so long ago. How did everyone on an island know everything about your past?

"I heard," Evan went on, "that he was pimping her out, trading her for money or, more likely, drugs. Is that true, Rankin? Did your dad pimp your mother out for drugs? Or maybe a six-pack? Was she not very good? Did he pimp her for Allen's Brandy?"

Lyman was so distracted that he ran the sanding block in his right hand across the index finger of his left hand. He bit his lip and kept his head down, watching the red rash fill with bright beads of blood.

"Answer me, Rankin! Or else—" Evan shot a blast from the pressure washer past Lyman's ear. This time the water had a high whine, and when it touched the cedar railing, bits of wood exploded into splinters. The jet setting.

Danny Graves whirled. "What are you doing? That thing can break *brick*, Evan! You're going to ruin the wood and get us all in trouble!"

Evan Morris's pimple-pocked face split into a sneer and he

lifted the pressure-washer wand, brandished it like a machine gun. "Don't test me, Danny."

"It was a cop who brought him down here, dumbass! Did you not even see that?"

"I did see that. Why were you with a cop, Rankin? Is your dad pimping *you* out now? That's child abuse. You should tell a friend. I'm listening."

Danny Graves muttered an oath under his breath and turned away. Lyman kept sanding, although the nice, clean work was now marred by drops of blood. The silence frustrated Evan, who returned to his previous tactic: insulting Lyman's mother.

"So what I heard was, Rankin's mom, she'd go from place to place, you know, wherever some fisherman needed a BJ, and then she'd do her thing."

He fired the pressure washer in staccato bursts while he made grunting noises in the same rhythm: *Ugh, ugh, ugh, ugh.*

"Then the fisherman, who probably had, like, five STDs and wasn't wearing a rubber, he'd get closer and closer…"

Ugghh, ugghh, ugghh.

Lyman's hand was squeezing the sanding block so hard, his elbow ached. He knew he would lose a fight with Evan Morris, lose it badly. He needed to remember that and not take the bait. Keep his head down, like Danny.

"And then Lyman's mom would *really* go to town, you know, just sucking her brains out, and then the fisherman would go— *ugghhh!*" At this, Evan Morris leaned back, depressed the trigger of the pressure washer, and sent a high, arcing stream of glittering water off the deck, and Lyman, who knew better, who really and truly did know better, whirled, threw the sanding block, and pegged Evan in the side of the face. It was nothing but a glancing blow, but Evan dropped the pressure washer and glared at Lyman with delighted fury, hands bunching into fists.

"Oh, you stupid little shit," he said, and Lyman was balling up his own hands when Danny Graves spoke.

"What is that?"

Evan and Lyman ignored him. Evan was crossing the deck, his fists rising to shoulder level, his lip curled in a sadistic grin. Lyman stood his ground, knowing that he would lose this fight but also knowing that he could hurt Evan in the process. Make him earn it, at least. He never fought back against his father. It would feel so good to finally do some hitting.

"What is that?"

This time, Danny screamed the question loudly enough that both Evan and Lyman looked at him despite themselves. Danny was pointing in the direction that Evan had fired the last blast of water. Lyman followed his finger down to the shore below where the receding tide had exposed more of the rock, and then he saw it too.

There was a body in the water. As the waves rushed in, long dark hair swirled. When the water pulled back out, the body turned, and a human arm was clearly visible, an arm with an extended hand, like someone reaching out for rescue.

Another wave washed in, the body shifted in the churn, and then a dead woman's face rolled skyward, her unblinking eyes staring directly into the sun, a single strand of rockweed draped across her ghost-pale skin.

It was Hatchet.

Lyman screamed and ran for the deck railing. Looked down at Hatchet and...

It wasn't Hatchet.

Was it? In the churn of water, it was so hard to tell.

Evan Morris, the resident bully of Salvation Point Island, bent at the waist and threw up on the deck he'd been hired to wash.

Lyman ignored him and ran to get help.

29

Israel was on the ferry back from Rockland when he saw the police boats.

He'd been so lost in his memories of Salazar that even though he should have noticed the activity off the northern shore of Salvation Point, he hadn't. Only after the passengers in the stern began to crowd toward him in the bow did he follow their stares.

There were three Maine Marine Patrol boats in the horseshoe-shaped cove on the north side of the island. A few summer estates were perched high above them, but down low there was no water access, only jagged rock. It was a rough, mean coastline even by Maine standards. One of the boats was a dive boat with three divers in full dry suits in the stern, one coming out, two going in.

"You think they'll find another one?" someone behind him said, and Israel turned and stared into the sunburned face of a stranger wearing an Acadia National Park baseball cap and a Bar Harbor T-shirt.

"Find another what?" Israel asked, thinking about his father's guns.

"Body," the man said. Then, reacting to Israel's face, he clarified, apparently believing he'd been misunderstood. "Corpse. They found a woman's corpse. A fisherman did, I think. We saw it on Twitter while we were waiting for the ferry."

"They found a dead woman out here?" Israel said. "Today?"

"I think so. Like I said, it was Twitter. Who knows?"

"Shit," Israel said, wondering how in the hell Salazar had not known, then realizing that she probably knew now but had no way to reach him. The strategic silence, that designed disconnect that had seemed so smart, kept coming back to bite him.

"Yep," the sunburned man said. "Eight dead now."

"What's that?"

"The yacht. You heard about *that,* didn't you?"

"She came from the yacht?"

"I mean the total. Seven on the yacht, one washed up from swimming, eight dead since we came up from Virginia. Crazy!"

"Crazy," Israel agreed numbly. "You say she was swimming?"

"Went out too far, didn't respect the current. It's cold water here, even in the summer." The tourist laughed. "My wife wanted quiet on this trip. I wanted to go to Vegas, she wanted quiet, so we came up to Maine, and look at it now. Man plans, God laughs, right?"

"Right," Israel said and stepped away, wishing he had a cigarette or something. Maybe this was what he was missing out on by not having a cell phone. Most people had something to put up between themselves and the world.

He had nothing.

The ferry turned as if to shield its passengers from the scene and followed the channel to the pier. Passengers shuffled to the stern, waiting to disembark. Israel's breath came in short, sharp gusts. He put his hands on the rail and remembered the bars on his cell. He took his hands off the rail and put them in his pockets. Stood there while the ferry docked and the rest of the passengers exited. Only when he was the last one on the boat did he move for the gangplank. There was a news crew filming on the pier, interviewing Brian Wickenden, a gregarious lobsterman from Port Hope who probably provided great color commentary for the viewers but knew nothing about the murders on the *Mereo.* Israel was grateful for him because he commanded the reporter's interest and allowed Israel to walk by unnoticed.

Walk on home, then. That was the only place to go, right?

But he had to verify that what the sunburned man on the ferry had said was the truth, and he wasn't going to be able to do that from home. Not in any depth, at least. There would be an update on NPR, sure, but they were cautious at NPR. The good people of Salvation Point didn't maintain the same journalistic standards. Inside Dar's market, gossip was currency, and there might be some truth within the gossip.

There would also, of course, be a crowd of curious people with questions for him.

He looked down the dusty road toward his home and then back at the market. Took a breath and crossed the gravel parking lot and pulled open the door.

Nobody turned to look at him. They were all watching the single TV that was mounted just below the ceiling, ten faces tilted up toward the screen like flowers seeking the sun. Dar leaned against the counter, back to the door, remote control in her hand.

"This is the scene in Penobscot Bay, where state police and the Maine Marine Patrol continue to search the waters off Salvation Point, using a combination of side-scan sonar technology and human divers," a woman's voice narrated. "They are searching in the area where the body of an unidentified female victim was discovered by some local teens who were cleaning a deck at a waterfront home."

Unidentified female victim. Israel's skull felt pressurized, his legs numb.

"We have breaking news in that case," the voice continued. "Live at the scene in Rockland, we go to Annie Hutchison."

The screen shifted to show an attractive blond woman standing beside the Rockland ferry terminal looking just the right amount of windblown. She was wearing a rain jacket with the network logo even though the sun was shining.

"Thank you, Holly," Annie Hutchison said. "Sources with the

police and the state medical examiner's office tell me that an autopsy will be performed and an official cause of death announced, but all signs currently point to drowning."

All signs? What were the signs, Israel wondered, other than that they'd pulled her from the water? And wasn't that only one sign?

"No other information has been released, and police remain tight-lipped about this situation because the woman has not been identified. Although there is no official connection, it is important to remember that this discovery was made near the place where just days ago seven murder victims, including Senate candidates Richard Hosmer and Paul Gardner, were found aboard a luxury yacht. No one is suggesting a link between the two events at this time, but it is safe to say that plenty of locals are talking about the possibility because this is an extraordinary event for a community of this size."

Israel felt as if the beer that had been purged from his bloodstream was back at full strength, making everything slow and distant. He looked at the cooler. Six-packs and cases and—hello, old friends!— a few tallboy PBRs. He pulled open the door, felt the cold blast of air in his face. Reached for a PBR.

"Authorities are asking for help in identifying the drowning victim. She was found wearing a two-piece black swimsuit with no identification on her person."

Here it begins, he thought, *the female body as spectacle. Dead body? Oh, well, we can still make that work. Maybe it's even better that way. Grabs the audience's attention.*

He pulled the PBR out, let the cooler door swing shut, heard the soft sigh of the seal sucking tight and felt as if it were his own brain closing out the potential of good judgment. He was withdrawing into a primal place, feel and react, a sensory memory that conjured his first nights in prison, his first fights. *Do not think of tomorrow or of yesterday.*

Be here now.

A mantra for mindfulness, civilians thought, but *Be here now* was a fighter's philosophy too. Act and react. Do not think beyond this moment, this space, this opponent. Worrying about other people could get you badly hurt, even killed.

"According to information released by the Maine State Police, the drowning victim was five feet, three inches tall, approximately a hundred and five pounds, with brown hair, brown eyes, and a dark complexion. She is believed to be somewhere between eighteen and twenty-five years of age. The only identifying mark on her body was a tattoo on the inside of her left wrist, a single word that only adds to this tragedy."

The frost on the beer can seemed to seep into Israel's blood.

"What was the word, Annie?" Holly the newscaster asked.

"The word was *respirer,*" Annie Hutchison said gravely. "It's a French word meaning 'to breathe.'"

"'To breathe,'" Holly said. "Oh my goodness. Reporting live from Rockland, that's our own Annie Hutchison."

Israel opened the cooler door and replaced the unopened beer. He still wanted it, but not as badly as he wanted to get the hell out of here, get into fresh air. He felt the way he had on his first night in prison, sure that he would have a heart attack or a mental breakdown, unsure only of which would come first.

Dar muted the TV as the broadcast shifted to the weather.

A woman at the lunch counter said, "That tattoo, how's *that* for irony? You got one word tattooed on your body, and it's something you can't do at the end."

It is not something, Israel thought, *it is the only thing.* The only promise any human being had was a finite number of breaths. You just didn't know the number.

A man at the counter said, "She came from that boat. Probably was there partying with the rich guys. Jumped overboard, like Natalie Portman, remember her?"

"Wood," Israel said. They all turned.

"Israel," Dar said. "When'd you sneak in?"

He looked at the people seated at the lunch counter, wondering if they could see the panic that felt so obvious to him. You had to learn to hide that early in prison, and it wasn't easy.

Israel said, "Her name was Natalie Wood."

"Yes!" The woman who'd called the tattoo ironic slapped her palm on the counter, then pointed at Israel as if he'd won a contest. "That's it. Shit, what a way to go, right? Riding around on a multimillion-dollar boat, then right into the drink."

Israel walked toward the door.

"Hey—did you need anything?" Dar called after him.

"No," he said. "I'm good."

The group at the lunch counter were talking again before he reached the door. Only difference now was volume—they spoke in hushed voices.

"Was that the guy the police were talking to?"

"Yeah, I think so.

"One who had all the photographs?"

"That's right."

He opened the door and stepped out into the sun and squinted into it; he started to lift a hand to shield his eyes, then lowered it.

In one of the photographs he'd taken, the woman who called herself Marie had been sitting on a tall rock on the shore of Salvation Point at sunset, reaching up to shield her eyes from the sun so she could keep looking west, toward the mainland. He'd loved the way she'd shielded her eyes and refused to turn away from the harsh light. It was the way you looked at a sunset when it was almost spring and the warm days had been gone for a long time. The way you looked at a sunset when you were very young or very old.

He had given that photograph to Salazar. The police who'd searched his house and the boatyard might have found a negative, though. Had he destroyed those? He thought so, but he wanted to be more confident about that.

Respirer. He remembered the curling script of the tattoo, exposed when the sleeve of her raincoat slid up her forearm as she extended her hand to him.

Waited for him to place the gun in her palm.

Keeping her safe. You were keeping her safe, that was the idea, it was only the two of them and you knew trouble was coming, you could see it in their eyes, their bodies, the way they watched the water, you knew that trouble was—

"Israel!"

He whirled, hands rising and clenching. Dar Trenchard gazed back at him. She lifted her own hands, palms out.

"Easy," she said.

"Sorry, sorry."

"No, I get that." She stepped closer, making sure they were alone. "Side door of my house is unlocked. Why don't you go over there, get some rest, have a beer, soda, whatever."

He was confused by the offer. "I'm fine, Dar. I'm heading home, that's all."

"I wouldn't do that."

"Excuse me?"

"They're waiting for you up there."

"The reporters? I can handle them."

"Not reporters." She looked back at her market again, verifying that they weren't being watched. "Oz and some others."

Oz. Matt Osgood, father of Melody, whose picture Israel had taken. Sterling had gone on his merry trek around the island, spreading the word that a recently returned convicted killer had been taking pictures of their children. Protecting and serving.

"I guess they don't trust Sterling to handle it," Israel said. "Don't blame them."

He laughed. Dar didn't. She watched him closely, bright blue eyes shining with sorrow.

"I'll be fine," he said. "I'll talk them down."

"No," she said. "You won't. They're stirred up. Island justice. You know the kind."

He did. Island justice had existed on Salvation Point for as long as the place had been settled. The islanders policed their own. A wild wind of rage rose in his chest and he wanted to walk right down to his house and wade on into the fight. It would feel good to hit someone today. It might feel even better to be hit.

"Israel?" Dar said, voice sharp, as if she'd read his thoughts. "Go wait in my house."

"It was sick," Israel said, rubbing his jaw. "The way Sterling looked at innocent pictures was *sick*, Dar. The way all the cops looked at them."

"Even Salazar?"

He didn't like the direct question about Salazar. He gave Dar a raised eyebrow. "You think she's different because she's a woman?"

"No. I think she's different, period."

He tried to look skeptical. "A bighearted cop ain't gonna help me, Dar."

He didn't even sound like himself. Was she clocking that change in tone, scrutinizing him, searching for the lie? No. The paranoia was pushing into his brain, that was all.

"Wait it out," she said. "Tell the truth and wait it out."

"What I've been doing."

"Don't change." She looked back at her market. "I'm a couple hours from closing. Go to my house, okay? And when I'm done, we'll talk. You could use a friend, is my guess."

He exhaled, nodded. "All right. Thanks."

She walked back into the market. Israel clenched and unclenched his hands, looking up at the big old sea captain's house that needed so many repairs Dar couldn't afford to make, and then he turned from it and walked up the road to where the righteous mob waited. He knew island justice better than anyone waiting on him did. He'd administered it once already, and he'd returned to dole it out again.

How's that going, buddy? a voice that resembled his father's whispered.

I killed you, Israel thought. *I finished it.*

Only one of those things was true, though. He saw that clearly now. The old man might win yet.

Israel walked on, alone. His house was off the northeasternmost lane on the island, built below the crest of a hill to provide shelter from the howling winds. He had to walk over that crest to see whether they were still waiting for him.

They were.

Matt Osgood was standing there with an aluminum bat, Darian Miskewycz pacing beside him, his broad chest pressing against his T-shirt, all the muscles bunched with adrenaline and rage, and the third man was one Israel knew only as Hoss. He was Oz's sternman, a well-known oxy addict, and he had not come by his nickname ironically—he stood six and a half feet and weighed probably two hundred fifty pounds.

They could kill me, Israel realized as he stood on the rocky crest of the hill, the wind fanning his hooded jacket out behind him like a duster. His palms were slick and his heartbeat was a metallic echo in his skull, like the soft kiss of a hi-hat cymbal. He felt like he had on many nights in prison, and he felt more like himself because of that.

"Hello, boys," Israel Pike said. "Sorry I kept you waiting."

He walked on down the hill.

30

The three men waited for him, two of them watching Oz, who was tapping the porch railing with the aluminum bat. It was a Little League bat, smaller than standard. That wasn't good news; the lighter the bat, the harder you could swing it with one hand. Israel would've preferred to see a weapon that required a windup. That bought you time.

Israel had no weapons except his fists and his work boots. His first drug dealer had sold him on the importance of a heavy boot, ideally steel-toed. *If anyone gets you down—and they will, soon enough— you're going to need a kick that counts,* he'd advised.

Israel shrugged out of his hoodie as he walked down the hill, let the wind peel it off his body. He wanted to be unencumbered. He was taller than any of them except Hoss, leaner than all of them, faster. They had all been in fights, but he wasn't sure how many of them had been in fights that counted. He knew none of them had been attacked in a prison shower by a lifer with a shiv made out of a broken metal broom handle.

Three on one, though. He would have to be very fast. The downside to wearing heavy boots was compromised foot speed; the upside was the one kick that counted.

"Why you looking for me, Oz?"

He crossed the patchy lawn where clumps of rough grass fought their way up from thin soil. The three of them walked to meet him, fanning out. Israel stood, hands at his sides, palms flat. Oz stopped, but Hoss and Darian orbited Israel. He could smell their body odor, the sourness of their overheated anger. Darian moved warily, the way a man walked around an unfamiliar dog. Israel wasn't unfamiliar to him, though. Their fathers had fished together, their families had gathered for holiday meals. The last of those gatherings had been for a Super Bowl party at the boatyard, the first win of Belichick's career in New England, the February after the Twin Towers fell, back in the days when the worst things seemed farthest from home.

"The police told me," Oz said.

"Told you what?" Israel said. "That I'm a photographer? Nobody gathered that from watching me carry a camera around every damn day? Needed Sterling's detective work?"

Oz started tapping the Little League bat against his cupped palm. It contacted his wedding ring each time, the rhythmic clang of a distant bell buoy.

"You're gonna need a friggin' *bulletproof* explanation of what the hell you've been doing if you want to stay on this island," Darian said from behind Israel.

If he wanted to stay.

"I'm a photographer. There's not a soul on this island hasn't seen me with a camera in my hands. And nobody said one word, ever, because—"

"Nobody knew you were taking pictures of their kids like a pedophile!" Oz shouted.

So there it was. The obvious assumption, and yet it still cut through Israel's soul, hearing it said out loud. If these ignorant bastards only knew...

"Anyone who's concerned is more than welcome to look at the pictures," he said. "If they could do that with a clean mind, they'd ask me for prints, because I take beautiful pictures."

"I don't think you need to worry about anyone else's mind," Darian threw in. He was still circling. Hoss had come to a stop and was standing behind Israel. He had to choose which man to focus on, the biggest one or the one with the bat in his hands. Israel watched Oz. He would make the first move.

"People are being lied to and believing the lies," Israel said.

"Sterling was lying when he told me that you have pictures of other men's daughters?" Oz shot back.

Every woman on the planet was another man's daughter, yet most men thought about that only when they wanted to, not when they needed to.

"I am not ashamed of those pictures," Israel said. "I know the spirit of them."

The bat hit the wedding band over and over. *Ting, ting, ting.* Almost a soothing sound. Slow and steady, running at a quarter of the speed of Israel's pounding pulse.

"If you're trying to convince folks that you didn't get fucked up in the head in prison," Oz said, "this ain't the way to go about it."

"I don't feel a need to convince anyone of that. Why would I?"

"Because you killed a man and went to prison and came back to fish from a rowboat like a sociopath and now we find out you've been taking pictures of children!"

"Got me pretty well figured out. Killer, convict, creep. That sum it all up?"

Oz looked sideways and down, as if a snake had moved in the grass near his foot. Hoss was standing so close to Israel that his shadow had overtaken Israel's, as if only one man stood before Oz now. Hoss was the greatest concern, and not only because of his size; he had the bearing of a man who wasn't entirely sure if he cared to keep on living. Israel felt that rising from him like steam.

The thing you feared most about yourself was impossible to miss in another person.

The bat swung into Oz's palm one more time—*ting*—and then he gripped it and held it, his forearm muscles tightening.

"Explain it, Pike. Why you been following my daughter?"

"I haven't been."

Oz's eyes widened. "No? Police were lying to me, then?"

"If they said that I followed her, then yeah, they were."

"You take pictures of her?"

"One," Israel said. "It's a good one. You'd like it."

Hoss knocked into Israel, bumped him forward. It didn't take much effort, but Israel was pleased to note that Hoss still leaned in to do it, with no appreciation for the need to keep your shoulders and feet aligned for balance. Good.

"You'd like it," Israel said, keeping his eyes on Oz. "Your wife would too. It's that kind of picture. Don't let Sterling or anyone else tell you different."

"I'd *like* it." Oz barked a laugh and looked from Hoss to Darian, who'd stopped moving and already had his hands curled into fists. "The balls on this prick."

"Have you seen it?" Israel asked. "Did they show it to you or just tell you that I'd taken one?"

"Shut your mouth," Oz said, and there was the answer. He hadn't seen the picture and thought he didn't need to see it. He'd been told there was a picture of his daughter taken by a killer, and what more did you need to understand?

"Put the bat away," Israel said.

"I should put it up your ass, you sick fuck."

"First place you'd think to use it is my ass, and *I'm* the sick fuck?"

Oz's eyes brightened with rage. "I don't know whether they'll get you for those killings on the yacht or not. Seems like you did a pretty good job out there. Let's see what you can do when you don't have a gun, when people are ready for you."

"You know I didn't kill them. You also know you haven't seen the picture. You're just looking for an excuse."

"To what?"

"To let your own illness win," Israel said. "Your own evil."

Oz's bright eyes went dark and then Israel knew it would begin and figured he might as well start it. When people came at you in packs, wasting time never favored the prey.

He feinted at Oz's face with his left hand, then watched as Oz did the dumbest thing he could've done—he ducked and swung the bat simultaneously. The duck cost him his balance and made the swing more of a stab. Israel grabbed the bat with his right hand and yanked it down and forward. Oz compounded his mistake by trying to hang on to the bat. Israel twisted and drove upward and hammered his left fist into Oz's descending face, heard the nose break. He whirled away, letting Oz fall into Hoss's legs as he ripped the bat away from him.

He turned as Hoss charged. Israel feinted with his head and shoulders, and Hoss raised his forearms to take the impact of the bat, which was ideal when Israel hit him in the ankle.

Hoss dropped, howling.

Two of them down now, and the only weapon was in Israel's hands. Island justice indeed. Overconfident and off-balance, both of them.

There are three, not two. You've lost sight of—

Darian struck him from behind, clawing at the bat. Israel rolled with the tackle, ducking his chin and spilling Darian over his back. Three down now. Israel swung the bat from his knees, hit Darian in the tailbone, and almost instantly was blasted from the left. Oz was back up.

Two down, one up. Had to keep track.

He jabbed Oz in the solar plexus with the bat, then rotated it over and clipped him in the temple. He could win this thing. All he had to do was—

Hoss kicked him in the head, and the sky swirled and blood filled his nose and mouth.

He'd lost track again. It was difficult with three. He ducked Hoss's second kick more from luck than skill, rolled across the rocky ground, rose to his knees, and swung the bat without pausing to look. Felt it connect with bone. Heard it. That distant bell buoy was coming closer now, louder, clanging in heavy seas. Blood was in his mouth. He needed to get to his feet. Needed to stay fast.

He got up just in time to go down harder, driven into the ground by Darian's tackle. Or was that Oz? Hands scrabbled for control of the bat. He released it and rolled onto his back. Watched Oz's face come into focus as he pursued the bat, bending over for it, lowering his face once more.

You don't learn, do you, Oz?

Israel hammered the heel of his heavy boot into Oz's face. Oz howled, spewing red spray, and Israel reached out and got his hand on the bat and drew it in and enjoyed that small victory in the fraction of a second before Hoss kicked him in the back of the head.

With steel-toed boots.

Israel knew it instantly, felt it as his head snapped sideways and white-hot pain lanced through his cheek and up to his ear.

Please kick again, he thought, *kick again or I might die right here in my own yard under a bright sun.*

Hoss obliged, winding up and driving his foot at Israel's face like a placekicker going for the game-winning field goal. It was the worst mistake he could have made. There was no need for Hoss to take his foot off the ground, no need to risk his balance when Darian was coming at Israel from the other direction. Once Darian had knocked him down, Hoss could do a Russian folk dance on Israel's spine. Instead, Hoss went for the wild kick to match his wild eyes, and Israel was able to catch the back of his foot, although he had to take the impact of the kick to do it. The bell buoy clanged a gale-force warning inside his skull and he saw red and black but he kept hold of that boot and twisted right to left, dragging Hoss forward and upending him, and then Hoss was down beside Oz and the bat was in Israel's hands again and he thought, *I'm gonna win, I'm gonna take all three of them.*

Darian kicked him in the stomach.

He had moved faster than Israel had believed he could, and that was how you lost fights. How you died. You could never under-estimate your opponent, and Israel had.

He tried to roll away, but he didn't have enough breath in his lungs and the pain was slowing him and so was the bat. He was committing their sins, putting too much value in the weapon. The only thing that mattered was speed, and he no longer had it. Darian kicked him again, this time in the neck. Spit flew from Israel's bloody lips and he saw Hoss scramble to his feet and whirl with enraged eyes and Israel knew that he could not stop it now. He was down and crawling in the dirt and Hoss was coming at him and Darian was picking up the bat and even Oz was rising. Three up, one down. The end was coming, and he'd done enough damage making them earn it that they would not show restraint.

Jenn Salazar said, "Stop moving."

Israel twisted his head and saw her standing there in uniform, right hand resting on her duty weapon. It was still holstered but her hand was on it and her badge was bright in the sun.

Everyone stopped. For a moment, it was silent except for the sound of ragged breathing. Then Oz said, "He broke my friggin' nose!" in a voice so high, it was nearly a squeal.

"Saw that," Salazar said. "Tell me, who brought the bat?"

Oz spat blood. Glared at her. "He's a pedophile. A killer and a pedophile. You need to get his ass off our island."

"Wish you'd let the police handle police business."

"It'd be nice if you did! He should be back in a cell!"

"You wanna press charges?" she asked.

Oz stared at her, breathing through his mouth, his nose pulped against his face.

"I can arrest him," Salazar said in a neutral tone. "Not for all the things you're accusing him of—those sound like crimes that require a bit of evidence—but for assault and battery? Disorderly conduct? Check and check."

Oz smiled with bloody lips, nodded. "Lock him up."

"Sure. Only thing you've got to do is promise me that you'll explain in court how it happened. Tell the prosecutor how Pike attacked the three of you down here. Maybe he lured you onto his property? But the bat is his, and he attacked the three of you, right?"

Oz's smile faded. Salazar got out a notebook, flipped it open, clicked a pen.

"He did beat the hell out of you. He had all three of you down at one point. I got no problem telling people that I saw that. I just need you to do the same."

Oz spat blood again. Looked at Hoss and Darian. Israel was still on his back on the ground.

"If I arrest him," Salazar said, "you've got to back me on it. Deal?"

"I'm not wastin' days in a courtroom for this prick. They'll send him back where he belongs soon enough. The real cops are coming for him."

"I'm relieved to hear it," Salazar said.

Oz glanced at her with contempt, then locked eyes with Israel, said, "I'll be seeing you," and turned and limped away. The others followed, a labored march up the shallow hill, their path marked by spilled blood.

31

When they were gone, Salazar knelt beside Israel in the dust and evaluated his injuries.

"Men are such fools," she said. "You get in trouble and you've got to lash out at the world, got to spread the pain. How in the hell did you think you were *helping* anything, coming down here to fight them?"

"Got a right to walk in my own house, is all that it is." The dizziness faded. He could see the rocks and dirt trying to absorb his blood, drink it in.

"You knew they were waiting for you. Dar told me that. She said you knew and still you came."

"My house," he repeated, as if her observation about men being fools needed further validation.

"Can you stand?" she asked.

He nodded, and the bell buoy clanged. No more nodding.

Salazar put her hands under his arms and helped him up. He staggered, fell into her, and she held him upright. It was the first time they'd ever touched beyond a handshake. She was warm and strong against him, and his blood was dripping onto her uniform shirt.

"*Respirer,*" he said.

"What?"

"Her tattoo. 'Breathe' is what it meant." Speaking made him dizzy.

"Let's get you inside."

She guided him forward. She had her arm around his waist and he had an arm around her shoulders and he thought that from far away, they might look like a romantic couple, tourists visiting the quaint Maine coast. All you needed to do was remove the badge and the uniform and the blood.

His legs had steadied by the time they reached the porch and he got up the steps without trouble and then opened the front door and saw that while Oz and Darian and Hoss were waiting for him, they'd let themselves in. There were broken dishes on the floor, smashed cabinets, shattered lamps, baseball-bat-size holes in the plaster.

"Holy shit," Salazar said. "I need to arrest those assholes. I really do."

"No." He took another step. She released him, and he missed her supporting strength. He walked to the counter and found his water bottle and dumped some of its contents onto a dish towel and set to work wiping the blood off his face. He leaned against the counter but stayed on his feet. He didn't want to sit yet. Wanted to be sure he was capable of staying upright.

"Good timing," he said to her, speaking around the wet towel. "Thanks."

"I should arrest them." She was still looking around the house, surveying the damage.

"They'll say they didn't do it. To prove they did, you'll have to get an evidence tech out here. I've had enough police in my house today."

"They might've killed you."

"Didn't, though. Like I said, thanks."

She faced him, eyes grim. "Listen, I only risked coming here because I needed to tell you that—"

"They're dead. I know. I saw the divers when I was coming back on the ferry."

Salazar eased down onto a kitchen chair, leaned forward, braced her elbows on her knees. She looked exhausted. He had never seen her like this.

"Only one is confirmed," she said.

"They'll find them both. Or maybe they won't. But they were both down there."

Salazar didn't argue.

"That was Marie, with the tattoo," he said. "I remember the tattoo."

Salazar didn't say a word. She sat with her head down, her back curved, as if she were resisting some relentless pressure from above.

"You know cause of death yet?" he asked.

"There were no wounds. She probably drowned."

Israel closed his eyes. He could picture the young woman's face. So, so young. Little more than a child. He could see her slim arm with the scripted tattoo as she reached out for the gun. He remembered how her too-young face hardened when she closed her fingers around the grip of the Colt revolver they called the Judge, the one loaded with .22-caliber long rifle shells. She had looked too calm. The other one, Jacqueline, had taken the Smith & Wesson .38.

"They're both dead, Salazar," he said. The last word pulled at his lips, reopened the cuts. He licked blood off.

"Maybe not."

"Yes, they are. They arrived together and they died together and they were the last ones left who could vouch for me in any way, and somehow I can't bring myself to care about that right now."

"Jacqueline could be safe. They might not be looking for her."

He shook his head. "They sent divers in. That's not something you always do when you find a drowning victim, right? You're the cop, you tell me."

"No," she said, sounding as if he'd broken her spirit, as if he were the cop and she were the informant. "You don't look for a second drowning victim unless you have reason to believe there is one."

Israel touched his lip, felt the blood slick as oil on his fingertip. "You think Paul Gardner was corrupt," he said.

"Been working to prove it, and I can't. Not yet."

"I'm just thinking out loud." He paused, rubbing the blood between his thumb and index finger. "Does my uncle have an alibi for the night of those murders?"

"Yes," she said. "That much I know."

"It's legit?"

She nodded, looking crestfallen. "He was on the mainland with about fifty witnesses. A police union meeting."

Israel barked out a laugh. A police union meeting. Wasn't that beautiful? Meanwhile, Israel had no witnesses, no alibi, and a prior conviction.

"Maybe Caruso knows something," he said. "Maybe if you talk to him—"

"There is no Caruso. Not one who's a licensed private investigator, at least."

Israel lowered his hand. "What?"

"I checked him out. If the guy who talked to you is licensed in any state, if he's a member of any PI association, if he's got a gun permit, if he's *real,* then he gave you a fake name. There is no private investigator in this country named J. R. Caruso."

"I wouldn't be surprised if he's not licensed," Israel said slowly. "But he was pretty damn specific about his background. Said he'd been a cop, had been in the military, had gone to—"

She was already shaking her head. "Not under that name. And the plane is a problem."

"What do you mean?"

"I checked the tail numbers on every plane in and out of the airstrip on SPI today. There were no jets. You sure it wasn't a prop plane?"

"Am I sure...yes, Salazar. I know a jet from a prop plane."

She was looking at him with a squint, but what was behind it? Doubt? Skepticism?

"It was a jet," he said firmly.

"Then it wasn't on this island."

"The hell does that mean? I didn't hallucinate it. They can hide tail numbers, I'm sure."

"No," she said. "They can't."

"Well, it was there, damn it! I sat in it!"

She turned her palms up, helpless.

"Try again," he said. "Look harder."

"I don't know how I'm supposed to do that," she said. "But if you see that guy again, stay clear."

The man had arrived in a jet that somehow had gone unreported, and the pilots had worn military uniforms.

"Sure," Israel said. "I'll stay clear."

The sun was going down, and it suddenly felt very cold.

32

Corey Rankin took Lyman home when the police were done interviewing the three boys who'd found the dead woman, and once they got to the house, he was almost kind, behavior that fit him like a stranger's suit, making them both uncomfortable.

He kept asking Lyman to describe the dead woman. Asking him what she looked like, how old she was, what color hair she had, things that Lyman did not want to re-create for anyone, not the police, not his father, not anyone ever.

Because she'd looked like Hatchet. Wasn't her, but could have been.

"Dark skin?" his father asked, and Lyman shook his head.

"White?"

"I guess."

"What do you mean, you guess! She was white or she wasn't!"

"She was gray," Lyman said.

That quieted his father for a minute. Out of distraction, not compassion. He was drumming his fingers on the table, eyes distant, as if he were trying to picture the dead woman for himself, as if he wanted that awful image. Lyman would have been happy to give it to him. Let *him* carry that memory for the rest of his life.

"Sterling was down there?" his father asked, cracking open a beer. "Saw her up close?"

"Yes."

"You talked to him?"

"Not much. He got us away pretty fast."

"Who else was down there?"

It was the fourth time he'd asked this, like it was a party he hadn't been invited to.

"Mr. Toland and some other people. Evan's dad came down to get him. They made me go wait on the porch for you."

"Uh-huh." More drinking, more drumming fingers. "Now Sterling trusts jackasses like Oz and Darian to clean it up. Ain't that beautiful. I'm in it until the shit hits the fan, and then I'm told to sit."

"What are you talking about? Oz and Darian weren't there."

Lyman's father looked at him as if he'd forgotten his son existed for a moment. "Sterling gets under my skin is all."

"I'm sorry."

"There's an asshole like him in any town in the world. Now, listen: What you saw down there, don't let it linger in your mind. If you let it linger, you'll get nightmares, and then you'll get all fucked in the head. Better to forget it."

Lyman nodded and said he would forget it.

"I didn't see much of her anyhow," he lied. He just wanted the conversation to stop.

"Good," Corey said. "That's not shit for a kid to see." He finished his beer, opened another. "I'll make us some supper."

While he set about burning grilled cheese sandwiches and opening a bag of Cool Ranch Doritos and a third beer, Lyman went out on the porch.

"Don't go running off!" Corey hollered. "Not tonight!"

"I won't," Lyman called back. He stood on the porch staring at the dense, dark pines that crowded together and obscured the Purcell house, hoping that Hatchet could hear him or see him. Hoping she knew he had not abandoned her.

"Supper's up!" Corey bellowed, and Lyman retreated into the house for the gourmet meal that awaited. His father ate in silence, eyes distant. There was a thin sheen of sweat on his forehead. He chewed nervously.

"Sterling's a prick," he muttered. "Acting like he's the king of the island instead of a friggin' deputy sheriff. I guess he is the king, though. Damn close, anyhow."

Lyman didn't respond to this. All he knew about Sterling Pike was that when they'd been evicted from their last place in Framingham, his father had done two things: fill up the car's tank using a stolen credit card and call Sterling. One day later, after sleeping in the cold car, they were back in the house on the Ledge. Sterling Pike had spoken to his father in a low voice, asking was there paper on him in Massachusetts, which Lyman understood meant was there a cop waiting to arrest him down there, and Corey had acknowledged that that was the case, and Sterling had still handed over the keys to his little house on the Ledge. It wasn't what a cop should do, and when you were in the kind of trouble that Corey Rankin was in, a cop seemed like the last person you would want to call, but that's what he'd done.

"He's gonna own it all, and for nothing," Corey said. "Absolutely nothing."

"Own what?" Lyman asked.

"Forget it. I'm talking out loud is all." Corey rolled his neck, cracked his knuckles. "Wanna throw some darts?"

"Sure."

Corey picked his beer back up. It was already empty. He always drank fast but tonight he was sprinting. He stood, said, "I've got to find something for this friggin' headache first," and went up the stairs.

Lyman ate a Dorito, wondering why his father seemed so nervous. It was Lyman who'd found the dead woman, not his dad. It was Lyman who had all the secrets. Lyman who'd lied to the police.

The last one troubled him the most. He was an honest kid.

Always had been. He'd been lied to so much in his life, he couldn't bear doing it to others.

His father didn't come back downstairs. The dart game appeared to be forgotten. Lyman picked up his book, ate another chip, and looked out the window into the gathering dusk. He stared in the direction of the Purcell house. What was she doing in there? Did she know that he would come back as soon as he could?

He knew what it was like to be left alone, waiting and wondering if your only ally in the world was going to return. He made a silent vow to her that he would be back. He would not leave her alone.

33

The sun eased down and Salazar stayed in Israel's house. He was surprised she was willing to linger, after all these months of sub-rosa meetings and prolonged silences, but he appreciated it. After the past few days of feeling the squeeze from all directions— police, press, neighbors, and a man named Caruso who evidently didn't exist and flew on a plane without tail numbers—the simple act of sharing space with someone who knew his reality, knew his heart, was an enormous comfort.

His head and ribs throbbed, and he felt a dull nausea, and he tasted blood in the back of his throat, but he had felt pain many times before and knew how to live with it. Live within it, almost.

"You should get checked for a concussion," Salazar said. She was leaning back in a kitchen chair with her feet propped on another, and she kept looking from him to the door, and her hand stayed near her gun.

"I don't have a concussion," he said. "And they're not going to come back."

"Not sure I agree."

"Trust me. They all went home to nurse their wounds." He paused. "And tell the story. Their version of it, anyhow. They're on the back deck at Oz's house or maybe sitting around the bar at the Fish House and they've got an audience." He'd watched it happen before. Tempers flared, folks gathered, and then one of two things occurred—a quiet cool voice would prevail and a tenuous truce would return, or the majority of the islanders would side with the aggrieved. He'd never seen vigilante violence escalate to killing, but there had been a few people chased off Salvation Point when he was a kid. Or *frozen out* was a better way to put it.

"I can take you in," Salazar said.

"I don't need a hospital."

"I don't mean that. I'm talking about protective custody."

"A cell. That sounds great."

"Protective custody might not be the worst thing, Pike."

He dabbed his lips with the damp towel, then squeezed it out.

"You know who my first visitor in prison was?" he asked.

She shook her head.

"Sterling. He came by to wish me well. He had two people sit in on the visit with us. One was a CO. The other was an inmate serving life without parole. Sterling was flanked by two guys, one with a badge and one without, both of them on the inside and both working with him. When you talk about protective custody, understand why my trust isn't sky-high."

She stared at him. "Why didn't you ever tell me that story?"

He dabbed at his face again, removed the towel, studied his own blood. "Because you told me about being on my father's boat first. After that, Sterling's intimidation tour didn't seem so important."

She pulled one knee up against her chest, hugged it to her with an arm. It was the most relaxed posture he'd ever seen her in—usually she stood as if she needed to show you that she could hurt you.

"Was that the first time you understood his reach?" she asked.

"It clarified his reach. I'd had a sense of it before—everyone knew he was a fixer, that he took bribes and he held grudges and he amassed as much power over the powerless as possible. Dirty-cop shit. I hated him for that mostly because my grandparents were so ashamed, so hurt. I can't say I worried about any betrayal of the badge or anything. I didn't spend much time wondering how far his reach extended; I just wished my grandparents could sleep easier."

She was silent, looking deeply troubled. He poured more water on the towel, put it back to his face. He wanted to cover his eyes with it, wanted to block out the memory of that hand closing around the grip of his father's gun.

Respirer.

"It's a lot worse than bribes," she said.

"I know that now. Hell, if I didn't before prison, I knew pretty quickly once I was there. The fighting I did inside, I had to do because of someone on the outside."

"You think he was trying to have you killed."

"No. Maybe? Only thing I'm sure of is that he was testing me. He didn't know how much my father had told me, so the beatings were his version of threat assessment. After enough time went by and I didn't talk—or die—I think he lost interest. I was no longer an issue. He knew where I was, after all. I wasn't a hard man to find. Just hard to kill."

"Why didn't you talk?" she asked. "You knew things about a corrupt cop."

"No," he said. "I had only a sense of the corrupt cop. That is very different. And after a while…"

When he didn't finish, she raised her eyebrows and pushed her chin forward, asking the question without any words. *Say it already,* her face told him. *Just say it.*

"After a while, I liked the fighting," he told her and licked more of his blood off his lips. "A lot of bad men tried to kill me, or at least hurt me. I came to enjoy spoiling their plans."

"You broke a man's leg in three places."

"That's right."

"You enjoyed that?"

"He was doing life for rape."

"You enjoyed that?" she repeated.

Israel looked at the blood on the towel and remembered the way the man had smiled as he approached him holding a jagged piece of an aluminum mop handle. He remembered the way the man had howled as Israel trapped and cracked his knee, the way he'd looked heavenward for help just before Israel lifted his heel and then snapped it down on his fibula, a bone that was as slender as the mop handle.

"I didn't hate it," he said.

Salazar looked at the floor. He wished he hadn't said it. Looking at her bowed head, he thought that things were generally better when he said less. He thought of the women who'd called themselves Jacqueline and Marie, how Marie had dismissed his offer to introduce them to a cop they could trust and challenged him to produce a gun.

What had she seen in him that made her think that was worth asking? Had she been surprised when he'd delivered, or had he simply met expectations?

Either way, she was dead now.

"Have you seen the ballistics report?" he asked. "They've got to have that by now, right? At least know the caliber of the weapon that killed them all?"

"They have it, but I haven't seen it."

"Thought you had rank."

"I have rank on Sterling if you believe in a traditional chain of command, and of course he doesn't. But rank on this case? Don't kid yourself. A couple of Senate candidates get murdered, and state police are nothing but foot soldiers for the FBI."

"Can you get the report?"

"I'll need a reason. A compelling one." Still not looking at him.

"Tell them that you interviewed me. You'll need to be honest about that, anyhow; those three assholes will be telling everyone on the island how you kept them from giving me the punishment they thought I needed. So, you came by, you broke up the fight, and you asked me did I have a gun. And I said no, same answer I gave Sterling. But then I told you—or maybe you asked, I don't know— I *admitted* that my father had guns hidden in the house and I knew where they were. It's enough to make you suspicious, right? Then you'd pass that information along."

She wouldn't meet his eyes, stared at the old kitchen floor as if it were a work of art. "What if I pass that along, and they say, *Yep, those are the ones. Thanks, Salazar, you cracked it. We've got him now?*"

He squeezed the towel out in the sink, watched his blood run down the drain.

"If that's the truth," he said, "we're going to get there sooner or later. Is there a gain to waiting?"

"I don't know. We have to communicate, though. The off-the-grid shit, the silence, can't continue." She withdrew a cell phone from her pocket and placed it on the table. "What was safer once is riskier now." She set a plastic card the size of a driver's license down beside the phone. "The phone's clean. Bought it at a gas station on my way out here. It's powered up but not activated. The card will tell you how to activate it, load it with minutes, all that. You have my number. When you get the phone activated, send me a text from it. Say whatever you want, make it sound like you're talking to an old friend and have the wrong number, whatever. I know you can't keep it charged out here but if you're not using it much, the battery should be good for a couple of days."

He looked at the phone but didn't pick it up. She ran her hand through her hair, pulled her knee up to her chest again. He'd never seen her so vulnerable. There was an awful camaraderie to that. She looked the way he felt—squeezed on all sides and trying to hold it together without betraying a hint of the pressure.

"You came out here to give me a phone?" he said.

"No. I came here to tell you something you needed to hear from me."

"I appreciate that, even if the guy on the ferry beat you to it."

"I didn't come to tell you about Marie," she said, and finally she raised her head and faced him again. "I was already on my way when I learned that."

"So what did you learn?"

"It's not about what I learned. It's about what I always knew."

He waited.

She'd been sitting in that curled-up posture, knee hugged to her body. Now she unfolded and sat tall, shoulders back, chin lifted, everything the familiar *Fuck around and find out* bearing she'd brought to those first prison visits. Everything except her eyes. The hard light was gone from them, that gleam of preternatural confidence, the eyes of a hunting guide you would follow deep into the darkest woods.

"There is no task force," Jenn Salazar said.

34

For a moment there was no sound save the dripping of water and blood into the basin of the old sink.

"They disbanded the task force?" Israel managed at last. "Who made that call?"

"No one disbanded anything. It didn't exist. Never did."

"What?"

"I wanted to build one." She swallowed but did not take her eyes off his.

"Wanted to."

"Yes."

"But…"

"When I found you in prison, I told you nothing but the truth. My story is real. I know what happened on this island, I know what is still happening on this island, and I know that your uncle is something beyond evil. I came here to burn him down. Him and everyone who was ever aligned with him. I needed help doing that. I wanted yours."

"So the lie is—what? There's no officially designated task force?" He asked this with a degree of hopefulness because it sounded bureaucratic, the type of problem that would bother Salazar and the detectives around her but wouldn't really matter in the end.

"There's no one else."

"I'm the only informant. You said that. You…" He stopped talking, finally grasping the point she thought was obvious.

"There is no one looking over my shoulder," she said. "There's not another cop on the planet who's even aware of what I'm trying to do out here. What I have done. I am alone. Well, not alone. I have you. I needed someone on the island, someone who fit there and always had. I fully intended to build a task force, to make it everything that I pretended it already was. But I couldn't just walk into my captain's office and say that I wanted to open an investigation of another police department. I had to show why, had to present evidence of what existed out here, and from there I would build the response it deserved. Then the yacht happened."

The yacht happened. Seven dead men.

"So if you seek protection for your informant," Israel said slowly, "you are going to have to explain the investigation itself. No one above or even around you knows that it exists."

"That's right."

"When they served those warrants today, I kept telling myself that at least I was protected. That Sterling couldn't push it beyond the island, not really. At some point, the state police would step in."

She held his gaze but didn't say anything.

The betrayal of Salazar's disclosure was something too big to comprehend at once. It was like being in the middle of the ocean and finding out that there was no fuel in the tank and a hurricane was on the way. Once you'd had a destination and now you were rudderless in a storm.

"I moved back to this place," he said, "knowing what reception was waiting for me and knowing the risks…I did that for you. Because I trusted you."

"I know."

He looked away. Her eyes were too familiar and had been too trusted and he no longer wanted to see them. "You were using me."

"I was hoping to deliver on all of it. With you."

"Do not say *with*. That implies a partnership. You weren't working *with* me. I was working *for* you. And now I'm in the fucking gallows because of you."

"We will fix that. I'll get help. All I need to do is come clean. That had to start here, with you."

"Come clean," he echoed, and laughed bitterly.

"Yes. I'll go to my boss—one of them, the one I trust the most—and I'll tell him the truth. What I was doing, what you were doing, what we know and what we don't."

Israel took a breath, felt the air sting his lacerated lips. "What would happen to you?"

"I'd lose my job, of course. I think we're well past the point where a consequence of that nature seems significant, though. Maybe I'd be charged with something too. I've recruited informants before but I've never hid one. In ordinary times, I think the state would protect its own if possible. These are not ordinary times."

If you didn't know her well, you wouldn't have detected the faint tremble of her jaw.

"Tell them what we know and what we don't know," Israel said. "That's your plan."

"That's what has to be done."

"We don't know a damn thing."

"We know that Sterling has been—"

"About the yacht," he said. "The threat to me isn't Sterling's history, it's a mass murder that I have somehow become a suspect in. Don't tell me about Sterling. Tell me one solitary thing that we know about the *Mereo,* where two Senate candidates and five other people were killed."

Silence.

"Exactly," he said. "Explaining what I was doing for you doesn't help me. Not at all."

"It is the right thing to do, though."

"That's what you told me last time. When I was still in prison, remember that?"

She looked away.

"And you got me out," he said. "You said you could do that, and you did. You had to tell someone about me."

"You're known as my informant, only I claimed it was for drug trafficking. We've had homicides related to interstate drug trafficking over the years, and I said that I wanted an informant who'd been inside and was going back to that world."

"Back to that world? So in other words, you claimed that you expected me to return to heroin and pills? An addict who's likely to relapse and just might talk to police?"

She shifted, uneasy. "It was the best narrative with you. The cleanest."

The cleanest narrative—that Israel Pike hadn't changed, would never change. He thought of Caruso telling him that the world was in the process of building a narrative, and Israel could help shape it or watch while it was shaped for him. He'd had no idea that was already taking place courtesy of the one woman on earth he trusted.

"I intended to change gears quickly. Once I had proof that there was human trafficking going on out here, I'd be able to deliver on everything that I'd pretended I had in play," Salazar said. "Without proof, though? I was making some massive accusations, and I..."

She took a shallow breath. "I was going to have to reveal some things about my life that I hold close. I am not scared of revealing those things; they are not my fault, not my flaws. But I don't share them easily. What I imagined, Israel, was sharing them in a way that counted. Do you understand that? I imagined saying that I had all the evidence needed to bring Sterling and everyone around him down. Then and only then would I share my own story."

Her face was so bereft that he wanted to touch her cheek with a kind hand, lift her chin gently so she was looking him in the eye, and tell her that he understood. He also wanted to smack her in the mouth and tell her to get out of his house. He thought that he could hate her; he knew that he could love her.

Tick, tick, tick. Blood and water dripped and drained.

He said, "You thought you had time to put it all together."

"Yeah."

"You weren't counting on seven people being murdered."

"No."

"But they were murdered. And I'm in the crosshairs now."

"I will testify for you," she said.

"Testify to *what?*"

"Everything that I did. Everything that I asked you to do."

"You're missing the point, damn it. What were you doing the night they died on the *Mereo?*"

"Working."

"On the mainland?"

"Yes."

"Then you don't know *anything* about that night. Who was on the yacht, who did what, where they went. You don't know where I was or what I did."

"I know you didn't murder anyone."

"But you can't testify to that. You can say that you don't *think* I murdered anyone, but you can't prove that I didn't."

"No."

"Then you're not able to testify to a damn thing that matters. I'm still twisting in the wind, all alone."

"I'll fix it," she said.

"Get out," he said.

She didn't move.

"Get the fuck out of my house," he said, each word cool and

clipped. "I need to think without your voice in my ear. I've had enough of that, and I'm paying for it."

She winced.

Israel let the silence expand until finally she nodded, stood, and slid the chair back up to the table. "I came out here because I had no other choice. It's the only way I could tell you."

He hated the tone of apology in her voice. It wasn't the woman he knew. The woman he'd trusted.

"What do you want me to do?" she asked.

"I don't know."

"We've got to make a choice."

"Not tonight," he said. "I've earned the right to think for a few hours." He couldn't look at her.

"I'll fix it," she said again. "I mean that. It had to start with me telling you the truth."

He didn't respond. Didn't look up. Heard the opening and closing of the door and never took his eyes off the bloody towel in his aching hands.

35

Lyman was sitting at the table trying unsuccessfully to stop thinking of Hatchet and to focus on the words in his battered paperback of *Cujo* when his father's shadow fell over the page. Lyman hadn't heard him return to the kitchen. Corey always walked around the house as if he were in a stomping contest, so Lyman was surprised—and scared—to see him standing there, staring down at him. He'd taken off his sweatshirt and wore only a sleeveless T-shirt now, the muscles showing along his sunburned arms. His stare was cold and empty and disconcertingly sober.

"Hey," Lyman said, and his voice came out small and high.

"Hey," his father mimicked, going even higher, the voice of a scared girl, a baby.

Lyman looked around the kitchen, thinking, *What did I do?* But there wasn't anything wrong in the kitchen. No chores had been ignored, no money stolen, no water poured into a vodka bottle to dilute it. Mistakes he had made before and would not make again. So what was putting that look in his father's eyes?

"Is everything okay?"

"Is everything okay?" Still with the high voice, saying *Ith* instead of *Is,* giving Lyman a lisp that he did not have. Then he dropped lower, back to his own voice, his own *mean* voice, and said, "No, everything is not okay. I've got a little sicko as a son, and that, buddy boy, is *not* okay."

"What are you talking about?"

His father looked away from him and stared at the floor as if there were something of great importance there. His sandy hair was thinning on top, and Lyman could see red skin and freckles on his scalp. He was getting old, hollowing out. But still strong. Still fast and still strong.

"What in the hell were you doing with your mother's things?" he said.

Oh no. The tub from under the bed. How had he noticed? Lyman stared at him, stunned, and then he got it: The pills. There had been pills hidden with the old clothes.

"You are one sick kid, taking that stuff," his father said in a low voice. "*Sick*. Bras and panties, your *mother's* bras and panties."

"No," Lyman said. "No, no, it is nothing like that, jeez, stop it, just *stop it*!"

An almost hopeful light showed in his father's eyes. "Yeah? Then where are they? You took the whole friggin' tub out, where is it?"

The tub was with Hatchet. He could not explain that, and he wasn't a good enough liar to come up with another explanation quickly.

"*Where?*" Corey Rankin thundered, and now he was tugging his belt off, then coiling the thick leather band in his fist.

Lyman looked at the door. His father caught the glance.

"Oh, you'd better not even *think* about running."

Lyman could do better than think about it. Right now, standing where he was, he could make it through the door before his father caught him. Corey Rankin was fast, but not fast enough. If Lyman made it to the yard, he'd be safe. Gone.

The problem was where to go. Because his father was sober, and that meant he would keep looking, and eventually he'd go to the Purcell place, where Hatchet was hiding.

Lyman turned away from the door.

"You are going to tell me"—Corey Rankin paused to punctuate the command with a snap of the belt off the table, a whip-crack sound—"what in the hell you did. And you are going to tell me the truth. Because, boy? If you tell me one lie, even *one* lie, they're going to pull your body out of that ocean. I'll kill your ass. My son or not, I'll kill you."

"I burned it."

His father stood still. Cocked his head. Searched Lyman's face to see if it was a lie. "Burned it?"

Lyman nodded.

"You're bullshitting me."

"I'm not."

"You burned it."

"Yes. I set it on fire and I threw it down in the quarry. Put a rock in to sink it so I'd never have to see it again. It's down there."

His father frowned, unsure if he believed the tale. "Why in the hell would you do that?"

Lyman thought about what to say. What Corey Rankin would want to hear. He thought about it, and just when his father stepped closer, seeming convinced he'd caught his son in a lie, Lyman found the right answer.

"Because it was all that was left of my mom, and...well, fuck her," he said.

Corey stopped moving. Lowered his hand, let the belt dangle. "Yeah?"

Lyman nodded fiercely, the tears hot on his cheeks. "She left me with *you,*" he whispered, looking his father dead in the eye. "So...fuck...her. If there's anything else in this house that belonged to her, I'll burn that too."

His father laughed. Barked it out like he couldn't help himself. "How about that," he said.

Lyman saw his father believing the lie and he understood

something then, a revelation: It wasn't hard to sell a lie if it was what you felt. What you felt was maybe more important than the truth. More authentic.

"Give me something else that belongs to her," he said in a trembling whisper, "and you can watch me burn it."

Lyman could see a hideous pride in his father's eyes.

"Well, you got some sand after all," Corey muttered. "I'll be damned."

For a moment, Lyman thought it was over. He had not run, and he had sold the lie, and it was over.

Then his father hit him in the face with the belt.

The first strike came so fast that Lyman never even got a hand up. The leather strap whipped across his cheek and sliced the bridge of his nose and then he was ducking and covering his face as his father snapped the belt back down, catching him with the buckle this time, hitting Lyman's ear and the back of his head, hitting *hard*.

Lyman fell to the kitchen floor. He was only three feet from the door, could wrench it open and run, but…he wouldn't do that to her. No. He would not.

So he covered his head with his arms and curled up tight on the floor, trying to make himself as small a target as possible, and he stayed down there and took it. Across the back, primarily, the back and the butt and a couple more shots at his head that his arms mostly absorbed.

Finally, Corey Rankin tossed the belt on the floor beside Lyman. There was the sound of the refrigerator door opening and the crack and hiss of a beer can.

"You got some sand," his father said again, sounding like a dad who'd watched his son round the bases with a surprise home run at a Little League game. "But you'll never talk to me like that. You want to burn that bitch's shit, I'll hand you the matches. Happy to do it. But you mind your tone when you talk to your father, boy. You mind your tone."

The front door opened and smacked shut and a chair scraped across the boards as he settled in on the porch with his beer, muttering about pills, how he'd needed those pills.

It was over now. Lyman was bleeding from the slice on the bridge of his nose, there were painful welts swelling along his back, and his ear throbbed, but it was over, he had not run, and Hatchet was safe for tonight.

36

It took Israel a couple hours to put the house back in order, or as close to it as he could come. He moved numbly, his body racked by pain, his mind ravaged by shock.

No task force.

No one but Salazar knew anything that he had been trying to achieve on the island.

I'll fix it, she had said.

Sure.

It would be that easy.

His head ached and his lips throbbed and his ribs and back protested at any quick movement. He'd taken worse beatings, though. Wouldn't that disappoint Oz and Darian and Hoss, to know that their little intimidation visit wouldn't have stood out in a prison yard.

Yeah, sure, tough guy, he thought. *You're still tasting your own blood. Keep telling yourself it's nothing.*

He filled two garbage bags with the remnants of lamps and vases and dishes that his Salvation Point pals had left in their wake. The sun was down and the only light was from a pair of flickering kerosene lamps. They soothed him. Funny how flame could seem to warm a cold house even when you couldn't feel its heat. After all these centuries, people still built new homes with fireplaces and woodstoves, bought electric replicas of fireplaces, left images of crackling wood fires on their TV screens. Everyone was primal at heart, wanted nothing more than a safe den and a warm fire.

He picked up the cell phone that Salazar had left him.

It was clean, she had promised. Then again, trusting Salazar had led him into this mess.

No task force.

He read the activation instructions on the card and used his pocketknife to scrape clear the foil that covered the PIN. Blew the dust of it clean and studied the code and the phone and wondered how fast a fake could be put together. It would take some time. But Salazar's specialty was working with undercover informants. She might have more phones than a Verizon dealer in her trunk.

"I can't give up on her now." He said this aloud, said it firmly. Tried to let the sound of his own voice convince him.

He shifted his weight to his right hip, a motion that lanced pain through his ribs, and pulled the two halves of J. R. Caruso's business card from his back pocket. Put them on the table and pressed them together. The number was visible.

The tail number on the plane had been visible too. Salazar had said she couldn't find any record of it, but Salazar had also said she worked with a task force and that higher-ups in the state police were intent on investigating Sterling Pike.

He looked at the card for a long time in the flickering light from the kerosene lamp and then he activated the cell phone and sent a text to Caruso. He typed it fast and hit Send without pausing, sure that if he overthought it, he'd hold off. He couldn't keep holding off, couldn't stay passive. The sharks were circling and he was bleeding.

This is Pike, he wrote. I'm going for a boat ride tomorrow morning. You should come.

The response was almost immediate.

You're a wise man—it's a great day to get on the water. But I'll bring the boat to you. Sunrise work?

Israel held the phone for a moment without responding. He

was half hoping that Salazar would call and chastise him for not trusting her. Half hoping that she'd explain his suspicions away. The phone made no sound, though. The only message was the one from Caruso. If Salazar had given him a compromised phone, she was willing to play the long game.

He finally answered Caruso's message.

Not sunrise—7 a.m. Let the locals clear out of our way.

He hardly had time to put the phone on the table before it chimed again.

Done. See you at 7.

Israel shoved the phone aside and went to the window and looked out at the darkness.

He had trusted Salazar, and he had never trusted Caruso. The latter felt more natural. He knew how to talk to a man who was guaranteed to lie to him, a man who entered the conversation with an absence of morality and a clear agenda. Caruso simply needed to see Israel as a partner and not a pawn. That would take a little convincing. Caruso thought he had all the leverage. Or maybe it was time for Israel to embrace the reality of his role. Be a pawn— same as he had been with Salazar—only this time, be one knowingly. Worry only about himself. It was always easier to navigate the world when you were alone. There was no salvation in this misnamed place, and only a fool would return to it with hope.

Be gone now.

There was a mantra he could believe in.

37

Lyman's father went to work alone the next morning. Before he left, he came upstairs and stood in the doorway to Lyman's room, staring down at him.

"Stay home today. Don't even think about crossing the rip, you understand? You've got that welt on your face and the cut on your ear, and I don't need people getting the wrong idea."

The wrong idea. Lyman wanted to ask him how the truth could be wrong, but he knew better than to do that. The truth was usually trouble for his father.

Lyman nodded, waited until he heard his father leave the house, then slid out from under the covers, dressed, and hurried down the stairs and outside. It was early but hot. Too hot. It had that creeping, thick stickiness that came on when the wind stopped, even though the wind never really stopped on an island. It was the sort of air that suggested a thunderstorm on the way.

He went through the trees and down the rocks to the Purcell house. The plywood rested over the door, and everything was still and silent save for the sound of the surf, the low thump and boom of inbound waves, the soft churn of receding water.

He knocked. "Hatchet?"

Nothing.

"Hatchet?" Louder this time.

"Yes, Lye-man." Her voice was faint.

He pushed the plywood away from the doorframe, expecting to

see her standing there to the side, hatchet in hand, but she was on the couch.

"I'm sorry I couldn't come to see you last night," he said. "My dad was home and I was afraid..."

He stopped talking when he got close enough to see her face. One dark eye regarded him from beneath a curl of raven-colored hair, the other eye hidden, pressed against the couch. Beads of sweat on her forehead, her olive skin now the color of dirty snow.

"What's wrong?" he said. "Hatchet, are you sick?"

"The foot is a problem," she said.

He saw then that she had removed the gauze wrap over her left foot and the wound was bare again. The cuts along the side and the ball of her foot had reopened—if they'd ever closed—and the flesh on either side was an unsettling shade of white tinged with blue-green. Dead skin. Dead skin that went deep, not just a surface layer. The blood that oozed from the center of the cuts was yellowish.

"Infection," she said very simply, calmly. "It will be bad soon."

"It looks bad now!"

She looked up at him. "Yes," she said. "But it will be worse."

Only then did she register his face, his own wounds.

"Come here," she commanded.

He stepped closer. She touched his face, moving her fingertips with the exquisite gentleness of someone who knew pain.

"Who did this?" she asked.

"It's not a big deal. Not like your foot."

"Who?" she demanded.

He looked away. "My dad."

Her fingertips traced the welt on his cheek, then moved to his ear, through his hair, found the knot the belt buckle had left. He heard her draw in a breath. Not dramatically, but with a quality of resignation. Then she lowered her hand.

"Why?" she asked.

Lyman shrugged, made a gesture like a man lifting a bottle to his lips.

"The police who came yesterday," she said, "what did they ask?"

"Nothing about you. He wanted to know about a man named Israel Pike."

Her face changed—she knew this name, but she didn't seem scared. Just curious.

"You know him?" Lyman said.

"Not well."

"But you do? You know someone on Salvation Point?" He was alarmed by this because somehow it made her feel less like a secret.

"I need help with my foot, Lye-man," she said, ignoring his question.

He reached for the bottle of hydrogen peroxide. She was already shaking her head.

"Something...more," she said. She sounded tired. "Or better."

He didn't know what was better, but he did know that he didn't have any more. He'd emptied the first-aid arsenal in his house.

"I'll have to buy some," he said.

She misread the hesitation in his voice, said, "I will give you more money," as if that solved it. But the problem wasn't the money, it was making the trip down to Dar's in direct defiance of his father.

Looking at her foot, though, he saw a bigger problem. It was a ghastly wound, and now he was aware of a faint, sickly odor, like the kind that came from a lobster or crab shell left on the rocks in the sun.

"The tide is right," he said. "I can cross now."

She didn't understand.

"I'll go get medicine," he said.

He touched his ear, felt the swollen bruise, and thought that his own injury was a gift. It would explain the questions that he would have to ask at Dar's market.

38

It was still low tide, so he was able to make the run without getting wet, but he'd have to hurry at the market because the water was coming in. Dar's was busy, several people seated at the counter finishing breakfast and a couple of people buying groceries. He slipped into the rear of the market, stopped by the cooler for a bottle of water and two bottles of Orangina, then moved on to where the first-aid supplies were kept.

He put two bottles of hydrogen peroxide in his basket, then studied the rest: travel-size packets of Benadryl and Advil and Pepto-Bismol. He steeled himself and went up to the cash register.

Dar was at the far end of the lunch counter peering at the TV from behind the group clustered around it, but when she saw Lyman, she came down to him.

"Good morning, Captain. Gonna have a blow tonight, don't you think? Nothing better than a summer gale, am I right?" She started to smile and then took a close look at Lyman's face and the smile faded fast. "What happened, kiddo?"

Lyman touched his cheek absently. "I was playing on the rocks," he said. "Clumsy."

Dar's kindly eyes went sorrowful. She didn't say anything, just gave him a look that said she knew darn well that was a lie and she was disappointed by it.

"It's not bad," Lyman pressed on, "but I got a pretty good cut on my ear." As Dar's eyes went to his ear, Lyman wished he'd not drawn attention to the bloody scab, so he added, "And a bad one on my foot. That's the only real problem."

"On your foot."

"Yeah. So, uh, I was wondering what you had that I could put on that to stop infection. Do you have anything? It's pretty bad."

"May I see it?" Dar asked, and Lyman went rigid, a cold knot forming in his belly.

"Uh...I don't want to do that."

"Be good if I could have a look, see if it's bad enough that you need a doctor."

"It's not that bad. I just need something to put on it."

Dar cocked her head, studied the welt on Lyman's cheek and the crusted cut on his ear. Her voice was low and soft when she said, "Captain, is this about the socks?"

Lyman didn't follow the question.

"You shouldn't have done that," Dar said. "And I should've stopped you. A joke like that, it's poking the bear, kiddo."

Lyman remembered then, the story he'd fabricated about the socks that said IF YOU CAN READ THIS and BRING ME MORE WINE on the bottoms of the feet. He'd said he was going to give them to his father as a joke. He wasn't a good liar. You had to remember the lies you told. He didn't enjoy this and never wanted to be good at it.

"It wasn't the socks," he said. "I never even gave him those."

Dar looked unconvinced.

"Lyman, I've seen plenty of kids get busted up on the rocks. *I've* been busted up on the rocks. Those marks didn't come from playing on the rocks, did they? Tell me the truth."

Lyman hated to look into the face of a woman who was so kind and lie.

"I'm fine," he said. "Really. I'm fine. I just need something for the cut. So it doesn't get infected."

Dar looked at him, sighed, then straightened and turned to the rack of supplies behind the counter. She took an antibiotic ointment off one shelf, a box of bandages off another, then something called saline wound wash. She put them down on the counter, never saying a word.

Lyman thought, *More, or better.*

"You don't have anything stronger?" he almost whispered.

Dar was quiet for a moment. Then she said, "It's really that bad?"

"Yes." Lyman was almost crying now, both from the stress of his mission for Hatchet and the emotional weight of lying to Dar. "On the foot, it's really bad."

"And you won't let me see that?"

Lyman shook his head. He was determined not to cry in front of Dar, but she could see he was fighting tears, and that must have helped, because she said, "Wait here," left the cash register, and walked through the swinging doors that led to the kitchen and the storeroom. While she was gone, Lyman took a breath and tried to compose himself, wiping at his eyes with the back of his hand.

Dar returned from the storeroom, set a small orange bottle down on the counter, and slid it across to him, her expression grave. "If it's *really* bad, you take one of these, then come back and find me and we'll go to a doctor together. They're just old antibiotics, won't hurt anything, but I'm no damn doctor. I shouldn't be doing this."

"I don't need a doctor, and thank you, Dar, *thank you.*" Lyman closed his hand tight around the bottle.

"Use the saline wash first." Dar bagged up the supplies. "It won't get better on its own, Lyman. And I'm not talking about the cut or the infection. I'm talking about the bigger problem. You follow?"

"Yes," he said, handing her several bills.

"Okay, then." Dar rang up the sale, gave him his change. "If you know it won't get better on its own, then you know you're going to need some help. I am here if you need me."

Lyman took the bag and put the pill bottle in it and said, "Thank you." Dar nodded with that distant sad expression, her eyes on him all the way to the door.

On his way back to the Purcell house, he stopped twice to make sure no one was following him. No one was, but he felt like he'd started trouble back there, as if he'd walked across a trip wire and set something dangerous in motion.

It was the lying, he thought. Not just about his own injuries, but about Hatchet. Yesterday, a police officer told him that seven people had been killed—*murdered!*—on a boat, and Lyman Rankin might not know how all that fit together with Hatchet and the woman whose body had drifted into the rocks, but he absolutely knew things that the police didn't, and that wasn't right. A good kid, an honest kid, would tell the police what he knew. A good kid wouldn't look a nice woman like Dar in the eye and make up a story.

You told yourself that it was okay to keep one secret, but then the one secret turned into a bunch of secrets, and suddenly you weren't just keeping them, you were lying about them.

He could go back and talk to Dar and have her call the police, someone other than Sterling, and maybe they could *help* Hatchet. They could do a better job than him, at least, a twelve-year-old kid taking bloodstained money and telling lies.

When he pictured it, though, all he thought of was the betrayal Hatchet would feel when a cop came to the door instead of Lyman Rankin, how she would know immediately what had happened. He thought of that, and he thought of the way her face looked when she'd said, *They will kill,* and he broke into a jog.

The prolonged exchange with Dar had delayed him, and the tide was coming in, rising over the riprap, some of the rock bridge across the strait hidden by water. Dark clouds massed to the southwest, promising a storm. Lyman eyed the rip. He'd have to be careful, but he could make it—and he'd better. Getting stuck on the island with his bag of supplies was not an option.

He made it across, but not without soaking his shoes, and there was one point where the water tugged at him so fiercely, it almost knocked him over. He kept his balance, but it all felt more perilous now, like it was only a matter of time before he fell and fell hard.

39

Caruso arrived on time and alone, piloting a Mako 24 with an open console and twin Mercury 200s on the stern.

"Morning, Mr. Pike."

"Let's ride," Israel said. "Give it another fifteen minutes and a news crew will probably show up."

Caruso studied him. "Wasn't a news crew that did that to your face. Who came for you?"

"Like you don't know." Israel stepped off the dock and into the boat, trying not to show the way the long stride hurt him.

"If I'd sent someone for you, they wouldn't have stopped with a schoolyard beating."

Israel turned and looked at him. Saw how serious the man was.

"Let's ride," he said again, and untied one of the mooring lines.

Caruso started the engines, backed away from the dock, turned into the wind, and headed southwest, where low clouds were building. A pressure change was blowing in, one that would scour the island with wind and rain. Israel sat in the stern, his hand wrapped around one of the chrome rod holders. It was a nice fishing boat and it was registered in Maine and he wondered how Caruso had acquired it so easily. For a man with a private jet, a recreational boat was probably not hard to come by.

Caruso was still wearing the expensive boots. They had no place on a boat, but he stood with easy balance and operated the wheel and throttle with a light, confident hand. He was familiar with the sea. He also seemed like a man who had money but didn't care for it or at least didn't care about it. He wanted the action. This would be important to consider.

"Where are you from, Caruso?" Israel said, speaking over the sound of the outboards.

"All over. Military brat."

"What about your father?"

"My father is relevant to you, Mr. Pike?"

"Sure. You can learn a lot about the son if you understand the father. You know that I killed mine."

"I do." Caruso gave him the half-amused look again.

"I expect you think you learned something about me from that. Tell me something about your old man, then. We're supposed to be trading information, right?"

"I don't remember *trading* being the operative term." Caruso navigated expertly between the brightly colored buoys that made a maze out of the sea, then redirected them northeast. "I'm not hiding anything, so I'll tell you this much before Google does— my *old man,* as you term him, was a soldier and a scholar. Drafted into Vietnam, lost his left leg below the knee, came home, got a prosthetic, got a couple degrees, then went to work for a think tank."

"What did he think about at this particular tank?" Israel asked.

"How to avoid unnecessary armed conflict. The Stimson Doctrine, shit like that."

Israel didn't know anything about the Stimson Doctrine. "What did he take away from it?"

Caruso shot him that look again, the one that said Israel entertained him just enough to be endured. "The Caruso Doctrine, if I had to distill it, comes down to this: Successful deterrence is all about the mind of the deterree, not the deterrer."

"Clarify."

"The enemy must believe you have both the capacity and the

will to deliver on anything you threaten—and that threat should be untenable to them."

"Do you think he was right?"

"Oh, I *know* he was right."

Interesting guiding philosophy for a man who'd jetted out to a remote island to negotiate with—or threaten?—Israel Pike.

The Mako spanked across the low swells. They were now beyond the colored buoys, out in the Lost Zone, where no fishermen had cause to venture. Caruso went on along his northeasterly course, nothing but gray-blue water in every direction and, in the distance, the silhouette of a Europe-bound freighter. The Mako, so large at the dock, seemed very small now. Finally, Caruso throttled back, and the volume of the engines lowered as he kept only enough power to face the boat into the swells.

"Private enough for you?" Israel asked.

"Closer to it than before, anyhow. Mind if I pat you down?"

"Yes."

"Only way we're talking."

Israel took a breath and then stood and spread his arms. Caruso moved into the stern and ran his hands briskly and efficiently over Israel's body. It was a professional search, but it conjured memories from prison, and Israel had to concentrate on the horizon line to keep from letting his anger show. He had not been touched by a guard in nearly three months and in some ways he had preferred the closed fists and stomping heels of yesterday. At least the island men had shown an understanding that they had to take it from him.

"Turn around," Caruso said.

Israel turned around. A thorough man, Caruso started at the skull, removing Israel's baseball cap before running deft hands over his spine and down the backs of his thighs, then tugged Israel's jeans up away from his boots and ran his index fingers between Israel's calf and the leather. Satisfied, he straightened.

"All good."

"Do I get to do the same to you?" Israel asked.

"No. But I've got a gun in a spine holster, a knife clipped in my pocket, and no recorders or cameras." Caruso sat down behind the wheel and swiveled to face the stern. "Didn't expect to hear from you last night. I assume the beating you took opened your mind, but I assure you, I had nothing to do with that."

He was sincere, and Israel nodded. "I know it. I also know that you're not going to tell me who you're working for."

"No, sir, I'm not."

The swells lifted and dropped them. The sea was calm but the air was uneasy, too warm, too still. There would be rain this afternoon, a good storm.

Israel took a breath and said, "Is Sterling protected?"

"Not by me."

"You mentioned him yesterday."

"That's right. I said he might make trouble for you."

"I was surprised you knew of him. I mean, he's not a household name outside of Salvation Point."

Rise and dip, rise and dip. Silence.

"Your uncle is trouble for you, but I play in a very different world," Caruso said eventually. "And he was never on that yacht. So if you've got a hard-on for Sterling, you're out of luck bringing him down on this one. I could sell you as the murder suspect far easier than I could sell your uncle."

It was the first disclosure he'd made that intimated he knew anything about what had occurred on the *Mereo*.

"I don't give a shit who you're protecting and why," Israel said. "I care only about keeping myself out of it."

"Wise words."

"But I need to know who you *don't* care about protecting. Who can be sacrificed."

"Why?"

"Because if I threaten the wrong family," Israel said, "that's a good way to die."

Caruso pointed at Israel, then tapped his own temple. "I keep saying it, Pike—you're smarter than you seem."

"Thanks. Now tell me."

"I fear you're overestimating your value."

"I liked that line you said about your father's doctrine," Israel said. "About the way deterrence works, and the way it doesn't. I'm not smart enough to quote it back at you, but the way I heard it, it boiled down to the risk of miscalculating an opponent."

Caruso's smile was authentic this time. "You're something, Pike. You really are."

Israel didn't respond.

"Know any Latin?" Caruso asked.

"Nope."

"Try these on: *Ex injuria jus non oritur* and *Ex factis jus oritur.*"

"A mouthful. Put it in English."

"The first one means, basically, that an illegal act cannot create a legal claim. If you gain something by illegal means, the court shall not recognize it. The second camp, *Ex factis jus oritur,* means that out of facts, the law arises. If illegal acts are facts, well"—he spread his hands—"the law has to adjust for them. If a country seizes a territory, you've got to accept the reality of the world, which is that it now belongs to them."

"Your education cost more than your boots. Impressive."

"I think you're in the second camp," Caruso said.

"Why?"

"Because that island lost its law a long time ago, and you know it."

"We've got Sterling," Israel said. "What more do you need?"

He was waiting for the amused expression, but Caruso didn't give it. He was all business.

"Sterling should've been promoted off the island years ago, or fired from it, or forced to retire. He stays, though. Why? Because he's leveraging his authority into properties. People get off that dump of an island, they sell to him, and sell cheap. That's standard graft, though; even the Rhode Island Mob would yawn at that. Nothing special. But Sterling doesn't sell the properties. I find that curious. He sees value in something that nobody else does. Why?"

The boat got broadside to a swell, and Caruso adjusted the wheel to keep them steady. As he did it, he gestured at the sea.

"You know where we are?"

"The Lost Zone."

"Valuable fishery once. Could be again."

"Only temporarily," Israel said. "A few more degrees of ocean warming and it won't be."

"You're right, of course, but you're a horizon thinker. There is still a lot of money to be made out here in the short term."

Israel acknowledged that with a nod.

"Do you think," Caruso said, "that a Senate candidate who pledged to open the Lost Zone up again could win?"

It was the last question Israel had expected.

"One senator doesn't make that call."

"No," Caruso agreed. "It would take more. An appeal and a sympathetic Supreme Court. If a candidate could promise those things, could he win?"

"Maybe. What's one fishing island in Maine worth, though?"

"This might be the only true swing seat in the next election, the talking heads tell me. The balance of power in the United States for at least the next two years."

The balance of power in the United States? Salvation Point was an island with a year-round population of 153—well, 154, now that Israel had returned—and the Lost Zone was an expanse of cold water without bright buoys dotting its surface or nets scouring its depths. It couldn't matter that much.

Then again, he remembered the way the island had felt when he was a boy. He remembered that his grandfather owned a boatyard on the island because there was demand for such a thing. Remembered that there had once been a high school, restaurants, and eight ferries a day. If you could sell the restoration of Salvation Point and communities like it—even if the restoration was a lie—could you win? Did enough people want to return to the myth that badly?

Maybe.

Your uncle owns half the island by now, rents some of it, but not much, Salazar had said that afternoon at Lucky Betty's. *The rest decays around him. He doesn't invest a dime in maintenance, doesn't seem to give a damn what happens to any of it, yet he continues to acquire. Why?*

Because if Paul Gardner had been elected to the U.S. Senate and reopened the Lost Zone, Sterling would have made a fortune, that was why.

Israel took off his baseball cap, bent the bill in his hands, let the wind cool him. It was too damn hot. He needed those clouds to blow in, obscure the sun. It was so bright that his sweat-stained cap brim glittered like metal. He stared at it.

"Look at me, Pike," Caruso said, his voice suddenly sharp.

Israel looked at him, curious about the change in tone.

"You were in the can for years, then you got out and came back to a place you don't like so you could do penance for a crime you don't regret," Caruso said. "Odd choice. Know what it tells me?"

"No."

"That you're a man with no family and no friends. No home. You're adrift. So what do you have at risk except yourself?"

Israel put his hat back on and stared hard at Caruso. Caruso grinned at him.

"Not trying to sound harsh, chief. Just calling it as I see it. If you could leave this place with enough money to go put your feet up under a palm tree for the rest of your days, with professional assistance in disappearing from the media and every other asshole who wants a piece of you, what would you be leaving behind? What's the sacrifice?"

All the things Caruso cared about were different than the things Salazar cared about. How Salazar circled and watched and waited and schemed while Caruso acted.

"I knew the woman who was found dead in the rocks yesterday," he said.

Caruso straightened, then rolled his neck side to side, as if trying to shake off the response. "Does she matter to me?" he asked.

"We know she does," Israel said.

The wind gusted warm in their faces, then died down. Caruso was silent and motionless.

"All take and no give, Caruso."

"Lesson in leverage. Take notes."

"Here's a note: I'm the only person you've got who might be able to explain the whole thing."

"Don't bet on that."

"But I am," Israel said. "I'm betting it all on that."

"Tell me more about the woman. You seem to think she matters, tell me why you—"

"Oh, I *know* she matters. It's not a question of thinking, you smug son of a bitch. If she doesn't matter, I'm already dead."

Caruso looked so steady, it was eerie—he was like a church steeple standing amid ruins.

"*Ex factis jus oritur,* isn't that what you said earlier?" Israel asked. "I caught that one. Probably didn't pronounce it right, but I caught it all the same. Way I understood it is this: Power is power. If someone has claimed something important, you can't worry about *how* they got it. The point is that they have it now. Is that close enough?"

"Absolutely. But you've got nothing."

Israel had to show a capacity for harm. It was that simple. It was why Caruso was here—because some powerful people weren't sure if they should be scared of Israel Pike. To them, Israel was like an insect that you trapped under a jar because you weren't sure what kind of insect it was, and you wanted someone to tell you if you needed to fumigate the house, burn the bedding, tear up the carpets: *How dangerous is this creature? How fast does it breed?*

What's that you say? It's small and all alone?

Under the shoe it goes, then.

Crunch.

"Here's what I've got," he said. "Evidence that women—girls, *children*—have been trafficked through Salvation Point Island for years, and people on your yacht knew about it. This started when the Lost Zone was closed. I don't care if you think closing the Lost Zone was the best thing in the world or the worst. It does not matter. What matters to the family of anyone on that yacht is that I can prove the history and I can prove that they knew about it. And I can tell them about Marie and Jacqueline."

He stared at Caruso, his heart running like a winded horse. It was all bullshit, of course. He couldn't prove anything.

"Nice play," Caruso said softly.

Israel tried not to exhale, tried not to show his relief. The dark secrets of Salvation Point mattered. Senators and judges and sons of soldiers from think tanks all cared about his little island. That was good.

That was also terrifying.

"Thanks," Israel said. "I thought you'd like it. Now you need to be true to your word. The only thing that has come out of your mouth that I trusted was that you didn't care who killed the men on that yacht, you just needed to be able to sell a story about it. I'll do that. In exchange, I want to go missing."

"Missing."

"That's right. I don't care how the world sees it—maybe I overdosed, maybe I fell out of my boat, maybe I was murdered, I don't give a damn. I want to go missing, and your client is going to pay for it."

"I could make you go missing right now, for free. It's a big ocean."

"I'll bring you witnesses," Israel said.

"Witnesses."

"Yes. I'll need a day, maybe less. But I will hand over a story, complete with witnesses, and in exchange, you'll be ready to make Israel Pike disappear."

"Where do you want to go?"

"Somewhere warm," Israel said, "and not surrounded by water."

Caruso gazed at the oncoming clouds. "I can make that happen."

"Here's how you'll do it," Israel said. "I get money, I get access to this boat, I get access to your plane, and I get clean cars provided to me in five cities that I'll name later today."

"Why five?"

"Because I don't trust you."

Caruso gave a ghost of a smile. "How much money?"

"It won't be enough to make your client sweat, I can promise that. I'm a simple man."

"I'll have to discuss this. I can't authorize it out here right now."

"Fine. Take me home, and go call your client. Show me how I'm going to get out of this, and I'll show you a road map to whatever story you want to tell. Make me the villain, I don't care. Make me a dead villain—that might help us all. Just be prepared to demonstrate how I'm making it out, and bring me some money for the trip."

He stretched his legs out and crossed them at the ankles and tried to look confident. Caruso watched him with suspicion and a measure of intrigue.

"Take me home," Israel repeated.

Caruso turned back to the wheel.

They did not speak on the return trip. When they approached Israel's dock, the property was empty. No waiting cops. Not yet, anyhow.

Israel stepped off the Mako as Caruso went to tie the mooring line.

"No need to tie up," Israel said. "Get going. You'll hear from me. Be ready when you do."

"Okay, Pike. Make good choices."

"Only those."

Israel walked up from the dock to his yard and stood in the sun watching as the Mako departed. When it was out of sight, he sat down on the weathered deck boards, took his baseball cap off, and flexed the brim the way he had on the boat when he was trying to get his thoughts together, the only time Caruso had ever spoken sharply, breaking his cool character, demanding Israel's attention.

Look up, his voice had said, *give me your eyes.* It was a voice Israel knew from a dozen prison fights he'd survived and a hundred he'd witnessed, a voice that said *Look at me* only because the speaker didn't want you to look around and realize that the threat was really coming from another direction, that people were ganging up on you. There was always the one man out front sent to distract while the cowards swarmed in from behind.

He tilted the cap, searched. Found the glimmer of metal, then used his fingernail to guide a thin chip out of the band of the cap. It was no larger than a dime, flat and almost weightless, sticky on one side.

A bug or a tracker? Both? Holy shit, it was small. Impressive, really.

He put it back in the band of the cap, went inside, put the cap on the kitchen table, and removed his clothes and checked them. He found nothing on his shirt or in his jeans. Slick work on the hat, though. He remembered then how Caruso had checked his boots, ostensibly looking for a wire or maybe a knife.

He found another chip stuck to the Gore-Tex lining of the old Danners. So thin it was like aluminum foil.

You should trust no one, Pike. But you've got better odds with me than with most, Caruso had said.

Encouraging.

Part Four

THE PAIN BRAIN

40

Hatchet was still sitting on the old couch when Lyman returned from Salvation Point with the medical supplies.

"I got it," he whispered, easing the plywood sheet into place behind him. "Real medicine, antibiotics."

When he showed her the orange pill bottle, she seemed uncertain, almost distrustful. She took it and looked at it like there were bad memories inside. Rattled the pills, then popped the top, removed one, and inspected it.

"Whose are they?" she asked.

"Dar's," Lyman said, and after her blank face reminded him that the name meant nothing to her, he added, "She owns the market. She's a good person, a really good person."

And Lyman had looked into her eyes and lied today.

He set the bag down, pulled out the various bottles and bandages, and assembled it all in front of Hatchet. Her dark eyes tracked each addition. When he set the change down as the final piece, she pushed the bills back to him. "Keep."

"No. It's not my money." He sounded petulant, and she caught the tone.

"You can keep it," she said. "I don't care." She patted the cushion beneath which the rest of the bills were hidden, some of them stuck together with dried blood. "You keep it all."

"I don't want it!" He backed away, jammed his hands in his pockets, and paced. His feet were soaked and his beloved Salomon shoes squished and he kept thinking about how it might have gone if he'd been delayed longer. He probably could've waded across, but it would have been tricky, especially with the bag in his arms. If the tide came in too high, he'd have been stranded, forced to either beg for a ride from someone on Salvation Point or wait for his father and the inevitable whipping.

Or he could have been dragged right off those rocks and into the sea, a lost boy, a forgotten child, gone as if he'd never existed.

For what? For her? He didn't know her. Maybe she really was a murderer. She was hiding with a hell of a lot of money. That wasn't something a good person did.

Behind him, Hatchet shifted forward on the couch and set to work cleaning her foot. She was silent, methodical.

She said, "Thank you, Lye-man."

"*Lyman,*" he barked, lowering his hands to his sides, clenching his fists. "It's Lyman, not Lie-man, but that's what you've turned me into. The Lie Man. That's me, lying to everyone all the time because you won't tell me the truth. There were people murdered and a woman was drowned and I saw her face, I saw her dead body, and you *know what happened and won't tell me*!"

He hadn't meant to say any of this and certainly hadn't meant to shout it, but by the end he was almost screaming and his muscles were tight and trembling all the way from his clenched hands to his neck and there were hot tears in his eyes. He hated that, wiped them away with a balled fist.

Hatchet said, "Drowned."

Just that one word.

"Yes! I saw her, I had to look at her face, and that was bad enough. But the rest of the people were *murdered,* and there are police all around now and I lied to them, I lied to everyone, I got beat up by my dad to keep him from finding you, I went to get you medicine and told more lies, and you won't even tell me your stupid damn *name*! I could get into so much trouble, they could put me in jail, and you could, you could...*you could die*!"

"You saw this woman?"

"*That's* all you care about?"

"Tell me about her. Tell me now."

Her intensity frightened him.

"She was in a swimsuit and she floated in right below us, it was me and these other kids working on a deck, and one was picking on me and we were about to fight and—"

"What did she look like?"

He started to answer, then couldn't. She was watching him in a way no one had ever watched him before—as if he had a great and terrible superpower.

"Lye-man..."

"Like you," he managed. "She looked like you."

She began to cry then.

She wept without making much sound, curling into herself. When she dragged her injured foot across the ragged old couch cushion, fresh beads of blood appeared but she didn't react. She looked like a little girl, and it was scary.

Lyman crossed the room to her. He wasn't sure what to do to help. Hug her? No. She didn't like to be touched. But she was crying so hard and there was so much pain in her eyes and she was alone in this old house, alone except for Lyman Rankin, who had just shouted and cursed at her, who had just acted like his father, the worst of men.

He reached out, very tentatively, and took her hand. She didn't respond to the touch at first but she didn't pull away from it, either, and after a few seconds she squeezed his hand, and then squeezed even tighter as her body heaved with silent sobs.

"I'm sorry," Lyman whispered, but she didn't answer.

He couldn't guess how long she cried. He didn't speak anymore but he stayed there beside the couch and he held her hand. He had never seen anyone else cry like this, so hard and so long, but he himself had done it. In the early weeks after his mother left and on the worst nights with his father, Lyman Rankin had cried longer and harder than he'd ever have believed possible.

The way Hatchet was crying now.

There had been no one to hold his hand. He didn't know if it was worth much, but he thought that it was better than nothing. On those nights, he would've liked to have someone, anyone, hold his hand.

When the tears finally stopped, she went silent, still curled up tightly, seeming almost smaller than him. Her dark, shimmering eyes were fixed on the wall but seemed to see nothing at all. He wondered what she was imagining. Or who. He wanted to ask, but he knew better. She'd never tell him. She would never say a word about anything, and that was why it was so awful to tell these lies on her behalf. He was an accomplice who didn't understand the crime.

He was just about to tell her this, to try and explain his anger, when she lifted her head from the couch cushion and faced him.

"She was my sister," she said.

41

She told him all that he had wished to know, and by the time she was done, he wished he hadn't heard any of it.

The girl who had drowned was her younger sister, she said, and she had been kept by bad men. He did not like that word *kept*.

"Like a prisoner? A hostage?"

"Like that, yes." Her eyes were dry now but she still had a far-away look. For some reason, Lyman was certain that she wouldn't cry again. At least, not in front of him.

"Did they kidnap her?" he asked.

He saw a flicker of deliberation, as if she was reminding herself that he was a child. He knew that look, had seen it when he asked people questions about his mother. He hated that look, because it meant the adults were going to avoid telling him the truth.

"It's not fair," he said, "to ask me to help and not explain."

She thought for a long time and then said, "I will show you."

"Show me?"

She stood. Tested her foot, winced, then extended her hand to him. After a moment, he took it. He was sure that they'd walk for the front door together. Instead, she guided him to the right, down the hallway, and unbolted the door that led to the cellar.

He had never liked the cellar at Dwayne Purcell's house. It stank of old wet stone and felt like going down into a well. He'd ventured into the cellar only twice before, once to simply check it out and the second time in search of a bucket and rags to clean things upstairs. He hadn't found much, and the door had swung shut behind him and scared him, and then he ran for daylight like a little kid. After that, he'd kept the cellar door shut.

Now he followed Hatchet through it and down into the dark.

The stairs smelled of ancient trapped moisture, and the sea sounds seemed to boom up from within, as if the house were in danger of slipping off its foundation and sinking, but it was less scary this time because Hatchet was with him.

There was a flashlight on a shelf at the bottom of the stairs. She reached up as if she knew exactly where it waited. He was surprised she'd come down here at all, let alone spent enough time in the dank room to learn where the flashlights were.

The light was dim, the old batteries probably close to dead, and it couldn't illuminate the outer reaches of the room. Nothing was visible except for the stone floors and a few old paint cans. Not much maintenance was done at the Ledge. As far as Lyman knew, the only work that had been done on any of the four desolate houses that now belonged to Sterling Pike was when he and his father had covered the front door of this house with the sheet of plywood. The other buildings deteriorated, and if Sterling Pike had any interest in preserving them, he hadn't shown it. Lyman wondered what he was waiting on and why he wanted the sad old structures at all.

Hatchet walked to the back of the room. There was nothing there to see. A mildewed rug spattered with ancient stains from gasoline and oil cans and some old wooden shelves on the far wall, nothing on them but junk—forgotten tools and broken appliances and other things that should have found their way to the dump years ago.

She didn't go all the way to the shelves, though. She stepped around a shop vac and then bent and began pulling up the mildewed old rug.

"What are you—" Lyman didn't finish the question, because right then she lifted the rug up to reveal a steel door in the stone floor.

Everything else in the cellar was rough-edged, the stone blasted or broken with no attention to detail, but the edges along the door's frame were perfectly square and flush. The door itself was bare metal, heavy-looking, maybe two feet wide and three feet long, with a circular bolt that folded flat into the frame. He watched as Hatchet tugged it up from its notch, and he realized that it functioned as a handle.

He saw the strain in her face as she lifted it, but he didn't move to help. He felt a prickle along his spine and imagined something bursting out from the other side, some confined monster with sharp teeth and long claws.

A gust of fresh air blew up from below, smelling of the sea. He heard another one of those signature subterranean booms that had always seemed unique to the Purcell house, but this time it was louder and sharper, like you heard when you were sitting on the shore. In the faint light, he could barely make out the stone steps leading farther down. A second cellar?

"What is this?" Lyman said, and his voice echoed off the bare rock walls, sounding louder and higher and more fearful than he liked.

"I need to show," Hatchet said in a tone so plaintive, almost desperate, that it shut down Lyman's objections.

When she started down the steps, he followed.

They went down seven steps before she found another light. Lyman counted each step. He was holding his breath, although he didn't know why. The smell down here was fresh and clean. When the waves came in, you could feel the cool. There was a faint daylight glow at the base of these steps. The house was literally connected to the sea.

Hatchet reached the bottom and raised the flashlight higher, illuminating the room, and Lyman's held breath melted in his lungs like ice closed in a fist.

They were standing in a chamber that was empty except for

aluminum cots, six of them, squeezed in tight, like a barracks in an old war movie. The fabric covering the frames was olive green, and there were blankets on a few of the cots, their original color lost to filthy gray. At the far end of the room there was yet another set of steps. An iron handrail was bolted to the stone. Several rings were set in the stone near the cots, and short lengths of heavy chain hung from two of them. There were stains on the floor and on the cots. One stain was the color of old red barn paint and it covered most of the cot.

Innocence isn't lost in a blink, but it can feel that way.

Lyman Rankin said, "You and your sister were kept here."

Not a question.

She looked at him with appreciation and sorrow.

"Yes," she said. "Long ago. Your house was empty then."

He tried to imagine being kept in this place.

"How long did you stay here?" he asked.

"Not long," she said softly. "It was a…" She searched for the right word as the waves washed in and out, the hollow thump of the water arriving followed by the whisk-broom sound of it receding.

"Prison," Lyman said.

"No," she said, and then, "Yes. It was a prison. But I was not here long. I was taken other places."

Lyman chewed on his lip, thinking. "Were you with her?" he said softly.

"Sometimes. Sometimes in another place."

"With the same men?"

"Not always." She tilted her head, her face darkened, and she said, "Or maybe yes. All the same men. Different faces but not different men."

Lyman thought that he understood what she meant. He felt his stomach knot just imagining it. He didn't want to imagine too much of it. His father hardly let a day go by without referring to Lyman's *whore mother*. Yesterday, he'd nearly gotten in a fight with Evan Morris over that word. He understood the word, knew exactly the idea and the hurt and the hate wrapped up in it. And the fear. There was always some fear in it, he thought, although he didn't understand that as clearly. He knew only that when his father called his mother a whore, it was his father who was diminished, not his mother. When Evan talked about Lyman's mother, doing his sick thing with the pressure washer, there was something in his face that was so close to Lyman's father's, it was terrifying. Cruelty, yes, but also fear. They mocked the woman because they were afraid of the woman—or of something inside themselves—and they tried to hide that weakness with meanness.

How to explain to Hatchet that he understood? There was no way. He was a child and she did not believe that a child could understand…and maybe he didn't understand all of it, but that was fine, he didn't want to. He only wanted to show her that he understood enough.

"They hurt you," he said, choosing the word carefully, because he knew there were other words that would be appropriate but they were worse words, more dangerous words. And in the end, *hurt* was enough.

"Yes," Hatchet said, and that was all, and that was also enough. Neither of them wanted to talk about the specifics. Lyman walked to one of the iron rings set in the wall and lifted the short length of chain that dangled from it. He had to use two hands. He found the glint in the metal that had drawn his eye. The chain had been struck over and over with some sharp object.

"Did you find the hatchet here?" he asked.

"Yes. On the floor."

"Someone used it on this, I think. There's a chip in the blade."

She joined him, examined the chain with her fingertip, and he saw the horror of recognition cross her face. The chain had been hit many times, very hard, but it hadn't broken.

"It didn't work," he said.

"No."

He didn't want the touch of the chain in his hands any longer. He dropped it—it made a sound like a sack of coins falling on stone—and stepped away. Pointed down the stairs to the wet gravel and the teasing foam from the sea.

"This is how you got in?"

"Yes. When the tide is low, it is easy. When the tide is high…" She glanced at her feet. "Not easy."

"You came from the boat," he said. "The big one."

"Yes."

He had to face her for the next question. "Did you kill those people?"

"No," she said. No hesitation. No break of eye contact. "I did not. But they were bad people."

The next wave rode in. *Boom.* It washed out. *Whisk.* Lyman closed his eyes and breathed in the trace of clean water it left behind. She touched his cheek, swept his hair back along his forehead.

"I am sorry, Lye-man," she said.

"I'm sorry too."

"You only help," she said. "You are so good. Kind. You will be a good man."

The last sentence was the one that mattered. He'd needed to hear it, needed to be sure that she saw none of the sickness hiding in him that she'd seen in the men who'd brought her to places like this one. On many nights, he'd lain awake wondering if the thing that had ruined his father was genetic, whether that same cruelty and selfishness—the fundamental *badness*—lurked in Lyman, waiting to take over, to rot him from the inside out, a prisoner of his own blood, helpless against evil.

You will be a good man.

He held her hand tighter.

When they got back upstairs, neither of them seemed to know what to say. The effort of the steps had exhausted her, and she eased herself back down onto the couch. He watched her, then he crossed the room and took the bag from Dar's off the old, rickety coffee table and pulled out the two bottles of Orangina. Opened them one at a time, listening to that soft pop of the seal and the subsequent soft hiss of the fizz.

He handed her a bottle of Orangina, and she patted the mildewed cushion beside her. "Sit."

He sat and sipped the Orangina. "It helps," he said. "A little."

She didn't answer him but she drank the Orangina and they sat in silence together and he knew that her thoughts were troubled but at least she wasn't alone.

Like he'd said about the Orangina, it helped a little.

42

It might all have gone differently if not for the storm.

It came on at noon, and it came out of the southwest, sweeping off the mainland and over the bay and strafing the first island in its path—Salvation Point—and then moving over the strait and the riprap breakwater that was by then submerged beneath an angry sea. The western shore of Salvation Point caught it first, then the eastern shore, then the western shore of Little Herring Ledge, the storm passing over them in neat waves, like calculated aerial assaults.

It came at Dwayne Purcell's property on the northeastern corner of Little Herring Ledge from behind, so Lyman and Hatchet were unaware of the lightning that marked the leading edge of the storm. They could see the changing skies, the clouds going from pale gray to nickel-colored to the blue, black, and purple of bruises, shades that Lyman knew all too well. They could feel the pressure drop, the way the heavy air began to lighten and then stir, a coolness creeping into the day like a draft under a poorly sealed door in the winter. The clean smell of oncoming rain.

But they did not see the lightning. And Lyman was not concerned about the time. He was still processing the horrors that he'd seen in the basement, and he knew that his father would work until four on SPI, go to Dar's and have a beer or two and buy a case or two for home, then load up the dinghy and motor across the strait.

Plenty of time, then.

The storm also provided a fresh distraction because Hatchet

began to draw the clouds. Lyman kept a pad and pencil in the Purcell house, a good way to pass the hours he spent in hiding, and she picked them up without comment and started to sketch. With the single pencil, she could shade in a way that made you think there was a wide range of color. All shades of gray, sure, but still very different. She gave the clouds a texture so realistic that Lyman thought they would feel soft to the touch. He wanted to know who had taught her this, but he was afraid it was her sister, so if he asked, the sadness would overwhelm her again. While she was drawing, she seemed pulled out of herself entirely, as if she'd drifted up and out of the window and into the clouds, like one of the gulls she rendered so easily and beautifully.

He watched her darkening the sky with quick but careful strokes of the pencil, fascinated—and sure that he had plenty of time before his father got home.

Meanwhile, the lightning arrived ahead of the storm. Wicked tongues of lemon-colored light snaked over tossing waves. On Salvation Point, Larry Toland told his siding crew to pack up. Nobody was going up an aluminum ladder and getting his ass cooked on his insurance's tab.

It was time to call it a day.

That cut Corey Rankin loose early, and he did what he always did when gifted with spare time—he headed for the nearest drink. That was at Dar's market. It was quiet when he entered, and Dar was never particularly welcoming to Corey, so he decided to skip the beer at the counter and grab two cases to take home. If he hustled, he might beat the rain that was chasing that lightning. There was no one around when he set his two cases of PBR beside the register, and because he was alone, Dar embarked on a conversation that she might not have if people had been within earshot.

"Corey," she said, "I want to tell you something."

Corey Rankin looked up from the dirty five-dollar bills he was unfolding. "Yeah?"

Dar's eyes were flint chips. "The socks were my dumbass idea, not his. My bad joke."

"Socks?"

"The ones with the stupid crap about wine. I put him up to it, all right? Lyman wasn't going to tell you that, but he should have."

Corey Rankin stared at her, genuinely puzzled.

Dar said, "But I'm going to say this to you just one time, so you better listen sharp: If that child walks in here again with so much as a single bruise on him, you'll be going to jail. I won't be calling Sterling Pike to go hash it out with you either. It will be the state. You won't be able to bribe or bargain your way out of trouble."

Corey said, "Lyman was in here today."

"That's right."

Corey's fist tightened around the roll of fives. "He was talking to you about his homelife, was he? Well, that's nice. That sure is nice."

"He didn't want to say a word, but I made him. Because I saw what shape he was in, and I suspected I was to blame because of the socks."

"Because of the socks," Corey echoed.

"That's right."

Corey stared at the shopkeeper, rage and shame and confusion making his head throb. "Lemme see. Make sure I got it all straight. My boy was in here when he shouldn't have been, and you were minding his business instead of your own, and the next time the wiseass kid comes in here with a mouthful of bullshit, you'll send me to jail."

Dar repeated, "That's right," in a calm, even tone. Outside, the thunder ripped the sky. The store's screen door smacked in the wind. The overhead lights flickered but stayed on.

"You cocky old whore," Corey whispered. "You're trying to bait me. Trying to tease me into slapping your smart mouth because then I *will* go to jail, and that's just what you'd like to see, isn't it? You been judging me day after day while I come in here and pay you with my fuckin' money. Oh, you'll take the money too. Yes, you will. Judging me all the while."

Dar was silent.

"Baiting me," Corey said. "Knowing what'll happen to me if I hit a woman."

Dar placed her hands flat on the counter and leaned closer. "I know what happens when a man hits *me*," she said. "He doesn't do it again."

Corey snorted. Dar slid her right hand out from under the counter, and Corey looked down and saw the snub-nosed revolver she held.

"Go ahead, big man," Dar said. "Take the *bait*."

"You're a nasty bitch."

"You can say that again."

"My family's got nothing to do with you. The people on this friggin' island, they act like they're judge and jury, got no one to answer to."

"That's your worry, Corey? That you won't find a proper judge and jury? I think that's precisely what you're hiding from out on the Ledge. Am I wrong? If I were to look into warrants down in Massachusetts or Rhode Island, would I not find—"

"Shut up, damn it. I swear, I don't want to hit a woman, but—"

"But you would, and you have." Dar lifted the gun, held it steady, gazed at Corey. "Try it, you drunk piece of shit. Let's see how fast those hands move when they're not reaching for a beer."

The screen door smacked. Two men hurried into the store, ducking against the wind.

Corey pocketed his bills, grabbed the cases of PBR, then opened his hands and let the cases fall and smack off the old plank floor. Busted cans of beer hissed and foamed. "Oops. Guess you lost your money and your booze, Dar. Some days, shit happens."

"Big man. Look at yourself, throwing things around in my store like a child. Not throwing any real punches, though, because there's no other child in here to hit, and now there are men who'd see you attempt to hit a woman, although you'd get your tiny pecker shot off if you tried. You don't even *think* about going home to find a child to take it out on, you son of a bitch. You don't even think about it."

Her voice was rising, the gun still in her hand, and the two men who'd entered the store were staring. Corey Rankin left without a word, stepping over an arc of spraying beer and banging out the door and into the wind.

He had told the boy not to go to the island. He had told him plain as day. Only instruction he'd given the lazy little shit today was to keep his whining ass out of Dar's. To avoid making a fool out of Corey, drawing gossip and threats from some do-gooder bitch.

It was the first place the boy had gone.

Corey had time to think on that while he piloted his dinghy across the heaving strait, the rain just beginning to fall. A bit of wisdom from his own father came back to him then, an old joke that wasn't a joke at all: *What do you tell a woman with two black eyes? Nothing. You've already told her twice.*

He'd told the boy once.

Now he would tell him twice.

43

Israel Pike left his baseball cap on the table and removed the tracker from his boot with a knife and put it inside the band of the baseball cap alongside its partner. He didn't know if that would screw things up somehow, alerting Caruso that he had found them, but he had no other choice, because he had no other shoes. He picked up the cell phone that Salazar had left, less sure about this one. Part of him still trusted Salazar. Another part remembered her false task force.

If there was trouble, though...

He put the phone in his pocket. Outside the window, lightning flashed like a warning.

Before he left the house, he gathered all the change he had, stacked nine quarters together, and wrapped them in electric tape. Then he went outside and found an old hose that was coiled beneath a nonfunctioning spigot. Most of it was dry-rotted, but he found a solid stretch nearly a foot long. He cut it at both ends with his knife and then filled the hose with sand and gravel and used electric tape to cap the ends. He tested its heft. Enough weight and plenty of flex. He slid this into the cargo pocket of his pants, clipped his knife into the right-hand pocket above it, and dropped the roll of quarters into the left-hand pocket. Then he put on a pair of thin glove liners, the kind that allowed for maximum dexterity while keeping the fingertips covered. He walked out of the yard toward the road, then hesitated, turned, and went back to the house. Picked up the baseball cap with the tracking chips.

"Come on, Caruso," he said, and he put the cap on his head, left the house a second time, and walked down the road toward the boatyard.

The storm that had been promised by the morning's thick, warm air was coming in now, rain spitting, dark clouds crouched over the gray sea. Good. The worse the weather, the fewer the onlookers. The helicopters that had been omnipresent since the bodies were found on the *Mereo* were gone now; everyone who was chasing the story was chasing it somewhere else. Salvation Point offered only so much local color. At some point, it wasn't worth the effort or the fuel. The yacht was down in Rockland, or maybe Boston, who knew. The families of the dead men were scattered around the country. Salvation Point's fifteen minutes of fame were fading fast.

Crime scene tape flapped in the wind along the fence that bordered the boatyard. There had been no reason to hang it except to attract attention and stir gossip, but Sterling had made a point of ringing the entire property with tape. Israel skirted the fence and walked down the main pier with his head bowed against the rain, looking for Corey Rankin's dinghy. A yacht tender, that was the official name for Corey's style of boat. Ironic, if you were feeling dark-humored.

Rankin's boat was nowhere to be found. Sterling's Boston Whaler with the sheriff department's insignia was missing too.

Israel walked through the rain to the boatyard fence and unlocked the gate. The crime scene tape stretched enough to allow him to slip through without cutting it.

The rain was blowing harder now, needle-sharp on his neck. He walked down the pier and climbed onto his father's boat and went into the cockpit. Did the *N'ver Done* have another sail in it?

He put the key in the ignition and turned it.

Stutter, stutter, bark, bark, hum. A clatter, a churn, a fog of fumes.

All the magic of an ancient Caterpillar engine turning its single screw. The boat still fired after all these years, as good as its name promised.

How he had loved to watch his grandfather launch a new boat. The whole island had. It was a celebration, each new boat something that turned the fishing village into a place with loud dreams and soft prayers.

He walked to the stern and gazed down at the prop while the boat thrummed beneath him. He remembered the way Salazar had quizzed him on his need for a *big, fast boat* when he'd purchased it. Big and fast. Sure. He could make fifteen knots with a fair wind and following sea. The most sluggish of police boats would catch him without taxing its engines. He remembered the way the stern of the *Mereo* had looked on the day he'd boarded it to count the dead. You couldn't see the motors on that yacht. Couldn't see the props, certainly. Everything was so sleek and tucked down deep.

The greatest power always seemed to be sourced by invisible engines.

He returned to the pilothouse. It was enclosed, prepared for the cruel weather, and down below was a cramped V berth with two cots.

Salazar had woken up inside his father's boat when she was fourteen years old.

He had not descended into the berth compartment since he'd learned that, and he would not today.

The unique feature about his father's boat was its fuel capacity and range. It had been designed with one task in mind—to fish the farthest reaches of the Lost Zone. The boat had a range of roughly a thousand nautical miles. You had to keep going, keep fishing, keep hauling up money. You couldn't afford to stop. If you stopped, well...

He looked up at the weathered, mostly uninhabited buildings along the waterfront, once home to such charming chaos. A single boat was making its way toward the wharf, throwing a wake. Israel lifted a hand at the captain. The gesture was not returned.

Salvation Point. Welcome home.

He'd told Caruso he wanted to disappear to *somewhere warm and not surrounded by water.* It had been a bluff then. Kind of? It had been whatever move you called the frantic side-to-side scamper of a trapped creature.

That did not mean it had been a bad idea.

He went back to the cockpit and checked the fuel and pressure gauges. Everything looked good, ready to run, tanks full. All you needed was a destination. He shut down the engine, left the key in the ignition, took off his baseball cap with Caruso's trackers in it, and hooked it over the gearshift.

His phone rang.

It was so loud it felt aggressive, like a sonic weapon. He had not had a cell phone since he went to prison and he hadn't bothered to check the ringer setting on the phone Salazar gave him. He wasn't anticipating any calls. Now he fumbled it out of his pocket and stood staring at the display: Unknown number.

He hesitated. In the end, he made his decision based on the sound—answering was the easiest way to shut it up and make sure it didn't ring again.

"Hello."

"It's me," Jenn Salazar said.

"Okay."

A pause, then: "Are you on the move?"

Immediately, he thought that the phone had been a trap. She'd waited to call until the moment he'd boarded the boat? She was tracking him, no different than Caruso.

"What do you mean?" he asked.

"Sounds like a lot of wind. You on the water?"

"No. Standing by it, though. Can't hear me?"

"Barely. It's always a shitty signal at best out there. This weather isn't great."

"What's up?" Israel said.

"Ballistics," Salazar said.

"You got them?"

"Yeah." Her voice was low. "Two of the seven were killed with a twenty-two-caliber long Colt. Another was killed with a thirty-eight."

His breath left him as if it had been stolen. His guns.

"You there?" Salazar said.

"Yeah," he managed. "So they did it, then. They actually went out there and shot up the whole—"

"There's a big new question, though—the other four vics were dropped with nine-millimeter bullets. You didn't give either woman a nine, did you?"

"No." He was more puzzled than relieved.

"All right," Salazar said. "So we've got some help, and some fresh problems."

"Yes."

"I haven't mentioned you yet. Didn't have to. Just said I needed to know the bare minimum, bitched about being frozen out of the investigation, and that's what I got, the bare minimum. I don't have the full report, only the caliber of the killing guns."

Israel faced into the blowing rain. Scout-party rain, the real storm massing behind it.

"Who the hell had the nine?" he asked.

"No idea."

"Did they find it on the yacht?"

"No. They say there were no guns on the yacht, period."

"Think I can convince people that one of the three wasn't mine?"

Silence. Then she said, "We'll figure it out," in a voice that was far from reassuring.

"Sure."

"I think I've found your friend with the jet," Salazar said.

Israel straightened. "Who is he?"

"James Robert Knight. Had a maternal grandfather who was named Caruso."

No wonder he'd been so fluid with the lies. The family history was probably accurate. Israel was sure that the doctrine was.

"How'd you get to him?"

"Remembered what you'd told me about the Smithsonian, how that stood out among all the bona fides he threw at you. So I spent a lot of time researching graduates of its forensic anthropology program." She gave an empty laugh. "Could have saved that time and started with something easier—he's partnered up with the same group as Jay Nash, the security consultant who was killed on the *Mereo*. If I've got the right guy, that is. I'll need to show you a photo."

"Maternal grandfather named Caruso, the Smithsonian background, and worked with Nash? Has to be him. He wasn't bothering with much of an alias and I doubt he'll care that I found out. He thinks he's operating at a different altitude. I'm irrelevant."

"I agree, but I still need to confirm. What are you doing, where are you?"

He looked across the bow of his father's boat.

"Standing outside."

"Go back inside. Keep your head down today. I'll find my way out there. Be ready for news crews, though. There's a press conference taking shape for this afternoon. Enough people are aware of yesterday's search that you should brace for the possibility of being named a person of interest. Not a suspect. They won't use that word."

"Like that matters."

"It does."

"In a courtroom, maybe. Public opinion? No. This island? Absolutely not."

"I'm just telling you to be prepared."

"Sure," he said. "Prepared. Got it."

"This is why we have to talk. We can't wait this thing out. Not anymore. It's too big and moving too fast. I'm prepared to own it."

"You are."

"As much as I can."

There you go, Israel thought. *And since you're alibied for the night of the killings, and since you did not put a gun in anyone's hand, exactly how much can you own, Salazar?*

"Israel?"

"Yeah."

"I gotta go now. I'll be in touch. Take care, lay low, be smart. You'll see me soon."

"All right. And thanks, Salazar. For checking it out."

"I'm going to figure out how to keep you clean, Israel. I promise."

"I'll see you soon," he said.

"Copy that."

The phone went dead in his hand. He lowered it and looked at it as the rain spattered it. Thinking about what it would be like to be named a *person of interest* in a mass murder. Thinking that his father's guns had killed at least three people. Where had his father gotten the guns? Maybe they couldn't even trace them back to Israel. Nobody knew except for the dead women.

And, now, Salazar.

Are you on the move? she'd asked minutes after he'd set foot aboard his father's boat.

But she'd also spent the day running down the things he'd

asked her to help with—the ballistics report and Caruso. Was that an indicator of trustworthiness or the latest trick in her playbook?

He looked up at the old boatyard, saw the decaying bench where his grandfather used to sit in the evenings, and wished more than anything in the world that he knew a single living person whom he could trust without hesitation.

It wasn't that kind of world, though. Not anymore, not for him. He powered the phone off and left it in the pilothouse with the baseball cap, shielded from the rain, then climbed off the boat and walked up to Dar's.

People were running in and out of the market, hustling to beat the weather. Too late now. He went in and stood dripping water onto the floor and waited for Dar to finish ringing up the woman at the register. He held the door so the woman could step out, watched her duck her head and pull her hood up against the rain. Watched her give him a familiar, suspicious stare.

Then she was gone and it was just Israel and Dar.

Dar took one look at him, assessed the damage from the fight, and said, "It's worse to warn you, isn't it? Maybe if I'd kept my mouth shut, you'd have gone somewhere else. Once I told you that they were waiting on you, it was as good as done."

"Wasn't like that."

"My ass."

He crossed the room, shedding water with each step. "You've got those cell phones, the temporary kind, right?"

"Burners?"

"Call 'em what you want. May I buy one?"

She took one down from the rack behind the counter. It looked like the same thing Salazar had given him.

"You seen Sterling on the island today?" Israel asked as she rang the purchase up and he handed his card over.

"I have not."

"What about Corey Rankin? Where's he working now?"

Dar stopped and gazed at him with interest. "What do you want with Corey?"

"To chat with him."

"Was he with them, down there at your house?"

"No. Don't worry about that."

She put the phone in a bag. "Too busy beating on a child to beat on a man, I guess."

"What's that?"

"He was in here not twenty minutes ago, and I nearly took a shot at him. That boy, Lyman, he's good all the way through. His father is a first-class son of a bitch. Lyman came in all bruised up, wanting to buy medicine, and I should have called someone. But who do you call? Sterling?" She scoffed. "Corey's on Sterling's till, like half the island is. It's different times out here, Israel. There are moments when I think I ought to go."

"Where would you go?"

"That's just the trouble. That, and..." She gave him a cold smile. "I don't intend to let anyone run me off my own island."

"I know the feeling."

"And look what happened. I don't have your temper, at least. I can endure better. But I'll be damned if I enjoy it. Sterling treating the place like his private playground, buying up properties just to watch them collapse. Only man I've ever known who seems to want to live in a graveyard."

If Caruso—sorry, James Robert Knight—was correct, then it might not be a graveyard much longer.

"Where can I find Corey?" Israel asked.

Dar sighed and passed the phone over. "Corey was headed home, would be my guess. Got rained out of work and came to buy his beer."

"Thanks." Israel accepted the phone from her. "Does this thing have a charge to it or will I need to do that before I can use it?"

"It will have a bit of one, I think. Can't say how much." She appraised him. "What do you want with a shit heel like Corey Rankin, Israel?"

"A word is all."

"Uh-huh. Bear in mind that a word with a man like that is apt to make him punch down, not up."

"What does that mean?"

"Don't cause trouble for his boy. I have a soft spot for the children of asshole parents on this island. You know that."

He did.

"I'm offering Corey a lifeline," Israel said. "If he's smart, he'll take it."

But he could feel the weight of the rolled quarters in his pocket and the gravel-filled hose against his thigh.

"Same thing I said about you yesterday," Dar shot back.

He acknowledged that with a nod. "I've got a favor to ask, Dar."

She waited.

"May I borrow your boat for the afternoon?"

She had a dory with a covered cockpit, a sturdy little craft for making the crossing to the mainland. It was painted bloodred with crisp white trim and everyone on the island knew it—and trusted it.

"You're not going to tell me why, I take it?"

"I'll tell you why—because people on this island believe things about me that are not true, and they're using their fists and boots and baseball bats to make the point. The weather's bad, the water is rough, and after yesterday, rowing around in my skiff isn't going to be much fun. I'm hurting, Dar. I wouldn't ask you if I weren't."

She looked at the wall above his shoulder. Enough time passed that he was sure she wasn't going to agree to his request, but then she reached under the counter and retrieved a key on a rubber fob shaped like a buoy. She tossed it to him.

"Thank you," he said, and his voice was thick. She was the only person he knew who might grant him a favor. The only one left on the island who would even consider it.

"You were a good kid," she said. "That was a long time ago, but I always hope it lingers, you know? That the thing inside a good kid never goes away. That we can never take it away, at least. Because children have no power in this world, and that is one of the cruelest things I've observed about it."

"Thank you," he repeated, because he didn't know what else to say.

"Sure. Don't crack up my boat."

The market door opened, and three older men shuffled in together, grumbling about the weather, and Dar gave Israel a final warning glance and then went down to the lunch counter to tend to the newcomers.

Israel pulled up his hood and stepped back out into the rain.

44

The summer gale offered chilled wind, and the narrow strait between Salvation Point and Little Herring bucked with disgruntled seas, slowing Corey's return home and increasing his rage.

Lyman had gone to the island. The only thing he'd been told not to do, he'd done.

As if Corey didn't have enough to worry about. And what had that bullshit about the socks meant? The socks said something about wine. Corey would find out just what the little wiseass thought was so funny. What the hell did that back-talking little bastard do with his days? And where the hell did he spend them?

He'd better be home. He had just better have his ass planted in a kitchen chair.

But Lyman was not in the kitchen.

He wasn't in the house at all.

Corey fished in the cooler for a beer, found there were only three left, and thought about the two cases he'd dropped on the floor at Dar's. Son of a bitch. That was Lyman's fault. Now there were only three beers to get him through a long night after a hard damn day's work, all because of a boy who knew no more about respect than his mother had.

I'll tell him twice. Oh, yes, I will.

But where in the hell was he? The kid took off night after night and vanished, and usually Corey didn't care to hunt for him. It was storming, though. The rain was falling and the wind was rising behind it, and just where did the little shit hide out from this weather? There were only four houses on the island, and two of them were one good nor'easter away from becoming kindling. Dwayne Purcell's old place had held up all right, but it was also sealed tight.

Corey stepped onto the porch, scanning the yard, beer at his lips.

There wasn't a soul in sight. Nothing but the rocks and water, same as always on this forsaken spot. And the gulls, of course. Even in the storm, the damnable gulls were there, shrieking, rising, diving, swooping, and shrieking again. Corey would've liked to open up on them with a twelve-gauge, cleanse the sky. He tracked the flock as if he might take a shot, followed the rise, the dive...

And saw that there was an open window at Dwayne Purcell's house. It had been cranked open so that it jutted away from the siding, barely visible between the uppermost branches of a single withering pine. If not for the gulls and the wind that made the boughs sway, he might not have seen the open window.

But he did.

45

Lyman Rankin was cranking the window shut to keep out the blowing rain when his father kicked down the plywood sheet over the door.

Lyman had his back to the door, and there was an instant, a blissful half second, when he was able to believe that the storm had blown the plywood down. Then he heard his father's voice.

"You little fuckin' sneak."

Lyman whirled away from the window and looked first at his father and then at Hatchet—no, he looked *for* Hatchet, because she was gone.

She had moved with speed that he wouldn't have believed she still had, and when he saw her, he could tell that it had cost her in pain. She was scrambling around the corner, crawling, her feet the last things visible before she disappeared into the darkness of the hallway.

Running on him.

Leaving him alone with his father's wrath.

No different than his mother.

He felt a moment's betrayal over that, but then he turned to his father and saw Corey Rankin's cruel, narrowed eyes sunk in the hollow eye sockets above his melting, beer-fat jowls, and he thought, *Good. Stay gone, Hatchet.*

Because Lyman had seen his father's rage plenty of times, but this one was special. It would not be an open-palm session. Lyman could tell that already.

"How long you been breaking into houses?" Corey Rankin said, and his voice was low and clear, and that scared Lyman even worse. He realized, with terror that seized his lungs, that his father was sober.

That was very bad. He was a mean drunk, but if he wasn't drunk? Lyman hadn't encountered that level of anger many times. His mother had, though. He remembered those nights. The nights when she'd pushed open the door and told Lyman to run.

"I asked you a question," Corey said.

Behind him, the sky had gone black without need for a sunset, the bruised sky darkening and deepening until it seemed like full night. The wind raked the house in gusts. Rain strafed the shake shingles and spattered on the rotting doorframe that Corey Rankin had exposed like a bandage torn from a wound.

"A few weeks," Lyman whispered. There was nothing to gain by lying. The only thing worth lying about was the woman who had vanished from the couch. Lyman willed himself not to look to the right, where she hid in the hallway.

"A few weeks," Corey echoed, and stepped farther into the room. "Runnin' outta my house, breaking into a dead man's, and yet you've got the balls to go down to Dar's and tell your tales. Heard you and old Dar had quite the little laugh at my expense. Jokes about winos? Bought some cute little socks, even. I'm funny stuff to you, eh? Where are the jokes now, son? Tell me one. I'm all fuckin' ears."

Corey was looking around while he spoke, taking in the food on the kitchen counter and the grocery bags on the floor. He froze when he saw the plastic tub with the women's clothing.

"Burned it, you said. You damned liar."

When Corey Rankin turned back to his son, he had the look of a wolf fixing its gaze on prey. He walked toward Lyman with a slow, calm rage, a sickness in his eyes.

"Been coming down here to play dress-up? Miss your mommy that much but don't have a kind word for the father that gave you life. That bitch left, don't you remember? But you want her back, and I'm nothing but a joke to you. The best parts of you ran down my leg."

Lyman shifted to his left, toward the kitchen, and his father moved to head him off. He was four steps away, moving surefooted because he was sober. Lyman was fast, but his experience out-running his father came when the man was drunk. Now his father was closing in, blocking the kitchen escape to Lyman's left, and the old coffee table was blocking Lyman's straight path to the exit, which meant only the path to the right was open. He didn't want to run right, though.

Hatchet was over there somewhere.

Corey Rankin took another step and his fists rose. Lightning flashed on the other side of the gaping hole where the front door belonged, illuminating it like an emergency exit sign straight ahead. Lyman would have to be fast. Faster than he had ever been.

"Come here, son," his father said.

Lyman ran.

He knew that he couldn't clear the coffee table in a jump, it was too long, so he leaped onto it, thinking that he'd need to plant one foot and spring off the table, and then the hole in the wall where the door belonged, open and calling to him, would be there for the taking. Once he got outside, he could outrun his father. He just needed to make it there.

He planted a foot on the table, pushed off, heard one of its ancient legs snap beneath him, and stretched out like a desperate hurdler, the wide-open doorway waiting.

Corey Rankin snatched Lyman out of the air by grabbing one fistful of his T-shirt and one fistful of the seat of his pants. Lyman's momentum carried them both forward, but Corey didn't drop him. He held on and pivoted back and for one strangely glorious moment, Lyman had a sensory memory of being a very young child and playing airplane with his father. Corey Rankin had never once dropped his toddler son in those games.

Today, he threw him.

Lyman sailed back over the now-broken coffee table and the couch and into the wall. The impact smashed a hole in the drywall, which belched dust; it blew the air out of Lyman's lungs and shot a searing pain through his body from head to toe. He hit the floor in a crumpled, gasping heap.

"Made me do it," his father said. "Why did you make me do that, damn it? Thought it was all fun, didn't you? Bet you sure as shit aren't thinking that now."

Then he stepped toward Lyman, and there was the sound of a leather belt whisking through denim loops, the jingle of a buckle. Lyman curled into a ball and put his arms over his head. A familiar posture. Then he heard the belt buckle hit the floor. The sound came as a temporary relief: *He's giving me a pass. He feels bad about throwing me into the wall that hard, so he's done now, he won't hit me anymore.*

When he peered through his fingers, though, he saw that his father had knelt by the broken coffee table and was wrenching one of the legs off. He hadn't dropped the belt because he was done hitting; he had dropped the belt because it wasn't brutal enough.

Lyman closed his eyes and covered them and made himself as small and hard as he could, curled tight and braced for pain even while the stunned realization of *He might kill me, he really might kill me* floated through his brain. He heard the crack and rasp of wood as his father tore the leg loose, heard three steps as his father crossed the room, heard thunder hammering the heavens.

When the first blow came, Lyman cried out from a mixture of pain and relief. Relief because the blow was not a savage crack of wood on bone but rather a heavy, clumsy kick to his legs. No, not a kick. Something had dropped on his legs, and it stayed there, dead weight.

He pulled his hand back from his face, lifted his head, and saw his father slumped on top of him, Hatchet standing above him, her namesake tool in her hand.

46

Lyman pushed himself back, slipping out from beneath his father's bulk and into the corner of the room. Corey Rankin did not move. When the lightning flashed again, Lyman saw the blood dripping from his father's scalp in fat red drops that spattered on the scuffed floorboards. His first thought, crazy but clear, was *I worked so hard to clean that floor.*

Then he looked up at Hatchet.

She was staring at Corey with an expression torn between horror and hate.

"He is a bad man," she said. The hatchet was in her hand, held down against her leg. She twirled it once, twice, like a batter in the box readying for the next pitch. Corey Rankin was down and he wasn't getting up anytime soon. The way that blood was coming—no polite drops now; it was a steady, dark rivulet—he might not be getting up at all.

Hatchet looked at Lyman for the first time, her expression as wild as her body was still.

"Your father?" she said as if she didn't quite believe it. "He is your father?"

"Yes."

"He is a very bad man," she said. "You need to know this."

"I know it," Lyman whispered, but her eyes were so intense that he looked away and again saw the blood. How could so much blood appear in such a short time? He felt a surge of dizziness and lurched forward, thinking he was going to be sick. He gagged, a dry, racking heave, which triggered fresh pain in his shoulder. He saw more blood, this time on the floor beneath him, and realized that it was coming from his nose.

Hatchet spoke in a voice that was soft but somehow darker than the storm raging outside. "Be still. Let me see."

She stepped over Corey Rankin's body like he wasn't there at all, put the hatchet down, and came to Lyman's side. She knelt beside him, and her hair brushed his cheek and came away tipped with his blood. She touched the side of his face and then the back of his head and then along his spine and over his shoulder, probing with gentle but firm fingertips.

"Nothing broken," she said. "Very lucky."

She rose and stepped away and he could see his father clearly again, crumpled on the floor with his left cheek mashed against the boards, his lips pushed out as if he were whistling. The blood was framing his head now, forming a wide pool. Rain swept inside in gusting curtains, soaking the floor, and the wind shivered the house. All of the heat had gone out of the air. The storm was cold now.

Lyman sat up and turned his head and then froze, not from pain but from the sight of the wall. The drywall was punched inward, and the indentation showed the outline of his head and shoulder and one foot. It looked like something that should have been in a cartoon.

His father had done that to him. Had grabbed him and thrown him so hard that Lyman had almost gone through the wall.

Hatchet returned with a rain-dampened towel in each hand. She pressed one to Lyman's face and guided his hand up to hold it there, then turned to Lyman's unconscious father and gave him an appraising look before lowering the second wet towel to his head and wrapping it tightly around his skull. She did not handle him as gently as she'd handled Lyman.

She said, "I used the back."

It took Lyman a moment to understand that she meant the back of the hatchet. That she hadn't tried to split his father's skull wide open with the blade.

Lyman said, "Thank you."

Hatchet said, "I shouldn't have. He is very bad."

Lyman said, "I know."

Hatchet said, "I thought that he might kill you."

Lyman said, "Me too."

And then he finally started to cry.

She limped back to Lyman, eased down beside him, and held him while he cried.

"He is your father," she whispered, and the way she said it made Lyman think that it was a reminder for her, not him. It seemed that she could not get her head around the idea that a man who had a son would throw that son through a wall. She repeated it once more, four simple words that conveyed a great mystery, a great horror: *He is your father.*

"Did you kill him?" Lyman asked.

She stroked Lyman's hair, regarded the unmoving man with the blood-soaked towel wrapped around his skull, and whispered, "I don't know."

"He would've killed me," Lyman said.

"I was afraid that he might. I had to help."

"He would have," Lyman said. "He will. If not today, then soon. He hates me. I don't know why, but he hates me."

"He hated himself," she said. "Trust me."

"How would you know?"

"Because I know him."

"Bad people," Lyman said. "That's what you mean. You know other bad people."

"No," she said. "I know *him.*"

He looked at her, stunned. "You know my dad?"

She nodded.

"How?"

She didn't answer. Didn't move.

"How?" Lyman repeated, rising to his feet, the pain almost forgotten in the moment. "How do you know my dad?"

He'd never seen her look so uneasy. She closed her eyes, bit her lower lip, and then the answer to his question came not from her but from a man's voice in the direction of the doorway.

"He kept her prisoner. That's how she knew him."

Lyman and Hatchet turned toward the door at the same time, and the man that stood there with the storm at his back lifted up both hands, palms out.

"It's me, Jacqueline. Israel Pike. I am here to help."

47

Israel heard what he'd said and wanted to laugh. It sounded like that old joke about the most terrifying words being *I'm from the government and I'm here to help.* Israel Pike, here to help? Being associated with him hadn't gone well for anyone on Salvation Point Island in a long time.

He stepped farther into the house. Jacqueline picked a hatchet up from where it lay beside Corey Rankin's body, watching Israel warily.

"I put a gun in your hand last time," he said. "I'm sure as hell not worried about letting you have an ax now."

She rose slowly, keeping her eyes on him while she reached for the boy, Lyman Rankin, who shrank back toward her, looking at Israel with fear and distrust.

This was the way it had gone since he'd returned to the island. Fear and distrust. He was Israel Pike, and he was here to help, and no one believed it. *You kill one man and you pay for it the rest of your life,* he thought, and he wanted to laugh again. He felt high and dizzy, looking down at the body of the man he'd come to confront, the problem he'd thought he might solve. Corey Rankin's eyes were dull, and his curled lips were pressed between the floor and his teeth. It looked like the efforts of an amateur taxidermist on a rabid dog.

Israel might have done the same thing to him if things had gone differently. He could nurse any illusion of a plan that he liked but the reality was that he'd come out here with his gravel-filled hose and his taped roll of coins and he'd planned to beat this son of a bitch for as long as it took to learn something, anything, about the fate of Jacqueline and Marie. Now Corey was dead and Jacqueline had done it.

Israel stepped carefully around the gathering pool of blood, knelt, and put his gloved fingertips to the side of Corey's throat. No pulse. When he looked up, he saw the boy watching him with questioning eyes.

Israel shook his head.

"I had to," Jacqueline said.

They were the first words either of them had spoken since Israel entered. He had been at the Rankin house when he'd heard voices and what might have been a sob from the neighbor's home, a home that he'd thought was abandoned. He'd followed the sounds, unsure of what to expect but certainly not anticipating this.

"She had to do it," Lyman Rankin confirmed. "He was hurting me. I think he was going to kill me."

The boy said this last bit with heartbreaking calm and acceptance. Israel guessed that this wasn't the first time the child had thought that his father might kill him, but it was the first time he was sure he would.

Israel looked at the boy and felt a strange sense of the inevitable. The wind and rain were pushing at his back and it seemed almost as if the storm had whipped itself up out there on the cold sea for a single purpose: to deliver Israel Pike to this room, these people. He didn't like the feeling. He'd wanted to be alone and in control of whatever violence occurred, not blown in for the aftermath.

Being alone was so easy. There was almost nothing to fear when you were truly alone.

He wasn't alone anymore.

They watched him, silent, waiting. Jacqueline held the hatchet in one hand and the boy's hand in the other. The boy's nose dripped a thin, drying trail of blood and there was a sheen of dust across the rising bruise on his face.

Israel inventoried the room—the broken table, one of its legs resting near Corey's lifeless fingers, the drying blood on the boy's bruised face, the punched-in drywall above the couch.

"That's from me," Lyman Rankin said, following Israel's eyes to the wall. "He threw me."

Israel looked at the dust on the boy's bruised face, realized that it was from the drywall, and felt his blood thicken and slow in his veins. He could not look at Corey Rankin's corpse because he wasn't sure that he could keep himself from lifting his boot and stomping the dead man.

"She stopped him?" he asked, still looking at the dented wall, the broken outline of a son thrown by a father, like an image negative on a strip of film.

"Yes," Lyman said.

Israel let out a breath, stepped back from Corey's body, and tried to think. To process how quickly everything had changed. Behind him, the wind whipped rain in, puddling the floor with water, pinkening the rivulets of Corey Rankin's blood.

Inevitable, he thought again, *I am inevitable in this room, and so are they. We've been riding along on different storms but they were bound to collide. Here we are.*

He decided to shut out the weather as best he could. He needed to see this room and these people and nothing else. Needed to forget that there was a big open wild world out there, a place where he could disappear, alone.

When he moved to the door, Jacqueline stepped forward, hatchet in hand.

"I'm closing the door," he said, turning his back to her. "If you need to use that thing on me, now's the time."

He wrestled the cracked sheet of plywood into place across the doorframe, sealing out some of the storm. He felt strangely calm, serene even, the way he did in the instant after the first punch was thrown in a fight. You knew what was happening then; anticipation was gone. It was a time for response, that was all, and the simplicity of that was a relief no matter the stakes. The world got smaller in that moment after first blood was drawn. For an instant, at least, there was the sense that you might be able to control something.

He turned back to them. Jacqueline eyed him uneasily. She was dressed in baggy workout pants and a hoodie and her feet were bandaged. Her face was drawn and pale, as if she'd gone many weeks without seeing the sun. She hadn't trusted him before the murders on the *Mereo* and he didn't imagine that had changed, but the dynamics had. He could step outside and call the police. She would have to answer the officers' questions now, not him.

Call the police.

That was such an obvious choice.

Why had he closed the door when the obvious, no-brainer decision was to leave it open and walk through it? Instead, he'd sealed himself in here with them, rolling the rock over his own tomb.

So leave. Do it. Walk away.

Israel looked at Corey Rankin's corpse and then at the boy and then at the boy-shaped indentation in the wall. He lifted his hands and showed his palms, the universal gesture of *No harm here.*

"Jacqueline," he said, "I came here hoping that the man who is now dead on the floor might be…compelled to tell me what he knew about you and Marie. I never much cared for the man, and I care even less for his friends, so his current condition doesn't trouble me. It's going to be real trouble for all of us soon enough, but it isn't my concern now. Do you understand?"

"Yes," she said. She lowered the hatchet but didn't release her grip on it.

"She had to do it," the boy said again. The words seemed to be on a loop in his brain. Israel glanced at him.

"How bad are you hurt, son?"

"I'm okay. She stopped him before it got worse."

"I understand," Israel said and he tried to convey depth in that statement, tried to let the boy know that he was a man who actually *did* understand what it was like to be in a kill-or-be-killed situation.

"No, you don't," Lyman Rankin said.

Israel eased down into a crouch so he could look the boy in the eye.

"Do you know who I am?" he asked.

Lyman avoided his gaze, but he nodded.

"All right. Then you've probably heard that I was in prison for killing a man, haven't you?"

Another nod.

"That man was my father," Israel said. "Have you heard that?"

Lyman Rankin didn't speak, but he finally looked Israel in the eye.

"Trust me," Israel said, "I understand."

He thought that the kid would come unglued eventually— shock was a weak Band-Aid—but it would be a while before that happened. He was already hardened in a way that no child should be. He also seemed to have trust—real trust—in Jacqueline.

"How long have you been here?" Israel asked, turning to her.

"A few days."

"You came here from the *Mereo*?"

Nothing.

"Do you know about your sister?"

There was a beat of silence. She swallowed. "Yes."

"I'm sorry."

She started to give him the cold, impassive look again—then softened and nodded, and for a moment he could see the girl she had been at the start of whatever horrific journey had brought her to this place. He thought that she had probably been on this road for a while and that she didn't remember much of that girl anymore.

"Who hurt you?" Lyman asked, and it took Israel a second to realize the question was for him. After seeing what had happened in this room, it was easy for Israel to forget that he was beat to shit himself.

"Some of your father's friends," he said, watching the boy closely. Lyman Rankin did not seem surprised. He nodded as if that made sense—and as if it made Israel a little more trustworthy.

Israel looked from Jacqueline to the boy and down to the dead man.

"Tell it to me the way it happened," he said, "and I will see if I can help."

"You cannot help," Jacqueline said.

"All right. Then I'll go away and you can wait for Sterling to come lend a hand."

She knew Sterling's name. He saw that in both her face and the way her hand tensed on the hatchet.

"I have two options for us," he said. "I'm not sure that I like either of the options myself, so I won't waste my breath telling you that you should. But they might be better than what you've got right now. There were seven men killed on that yacht and some were killed with the guns I put in your and your sister's hands. There's another dead man on the floor in here, and you're holding the weapon that did that killing. It would be worth considering your options while it's just the three of us in here, Jacqueline."

She opened her hand and let the hatchet fall. It clattered onto the floor, the blade landing in blood. She put her arm around the boy and said, "I need to sit."

They went to the couch together. She kept her arm around the boy. He looked at her and said, softly, "Jacqueline?"

"That is my real name, yes. Jacqueline Picard. You choose what you want to call me, Lye-man."

The boy seemed to require time to think on this.

Israel said, "Who else did the shooting on the yacht? Did you have other guns?"

Jacqueline shook her head. "One of the men on the boat did."

"Which one?"

"I don't know his name. He came with the one we had the pictures of."

"Pictures?"

She met his eyes. "They were pictures to those men. They were tickets home for Marie and me."

Israel stepped over the dead man and sat in a kitchen chair. He took the gravel-filled hose and the roll of taped quarters out of his pockets and set them down on the table. Leaned forward and braced his forearms on his knees.

"Why don't you tell me what happened after I gave you the guns," he said. "And we will figure it out from there."

"We will not *figure it out*," she said, sounding weary and beaten. "It has gone too far to fix."

"Show him," the boy said suddenly. His voice seemed to startle Jacqueline as much as it did Israel. "Show him the room. It makes a difference."

She turned to him as if prepared to argue or dismiss the idea, then saw something in his face that gave her pause. They looked at each other in silence for a moment and then she gave a faint nod.

"Yes," she said. "It makes a difference."

48

Israel Pike had never believed in ghosts until he went into prison. Then there was a day when they moved him from one cell-block to another. The CO was escorting him down the long tiled hallway and Israel's mind was on the book he'd been reading, a thriller by Lori Roy that had provided a beautiful escape out of his world and into another, when they passed by an empty cell that drew his eye. Maybe it caught his attention simply because it was empty—prisons were overcrowded in Maine, like they were every-where in America—but once he looked inside, he felt a presence pass through the bars and brush against him, a physical sensation, undeniable, not aggressive but firm enough to knock him off stride. It was the incidental, brushing touch of a stranger hurrying past you on a sidewalk, only it left him cold, a dry-ice chill.

The CO, Brian Freeman, was a good guy, one of the rare ones, and he didn't complain about Israel's sudden stumble. He just followed Israel's gaze into the empty cell and said, "Did you know him?"

"Who?"

"Chizmar. Died in there last night. Friend of yours?"

Israel had never spoken to the man, but he found himself nod-ding. "Yeah," he said. "Friend of mine."

The cold lingered long after Chizmar's cell door was out of sight.

It was a memory that Israel wished he did not have and a story he'd never shared with anyone, but it came back to him in the room below the basement of the house on Little Herring Ledge. As he looked around the place, he was certain that someone had died here. Or a part of someone had, anyhow.

There were old, stained cots scattered across an uneven stone floor. There were ringbolts set in the stone walls beside the cots and others set in the floor, and there was a single piece of chain discarded carelessly in one corner. The low-ceilinged, cramped space seemed to be a part of the sea itself but held none of that freshness, none of that openness. You could hear the water and you could smell it, yet it was out of sight and held at bay by the walls, a promise withheld.

Israel looked at Jacqueline, this small, quiet woman with the dark eyes, and she gazed back at him defiantly with an awesome sad strength that said *Yes, it was that bad* and *No, it did not break me.*

"You are right, Lye-man," she said. "It does make a difference."

She sat down on one of the cots. The boy looked shocked, and Israel understood why—the simple act felt appalling, like dancing on a gravestone.

Jacqueline saw the boy's face and said, "It is fine. It is my room now."

She put out her hand, and Lyman Rankin, who'd been orphaned by her ax, crossed the stone floor, took her hand, and sat beside her. Dislodged dust hovered in the air around them. Water trickled through stone somewhere below. Jacqueline stared at the descending steps that led out of the room and off to…where? Someplace exposed to the sea. Israel wasn't sure. She knew, though. Her eyes promised that. It was as if she were waiting on someone to emerge.

"This place," she said, gesturing at the cell-like room around them, "was a stopover for me. One boat to the next. When I was taken from home, I was not on land again until New York, or maybe it was New Jersey. Close to the city, I know that."

"Where is home?"

She didn't seem to want to tell him.

"Generally," he said.

"Canada."

That left plenty of room, but Israel didn't care.

"An island," she added. "A better one than this."

"Okay."

"My grandmother lives there still. When my mother died, my stepfather took us off the island. That was…the beginning of the bad things."

She paused, gathered herself.

"My sister and I were both brought through this awful place to others. I was allowed to see her enough to be scared for her, and she was allowed the same. Because it was easier to control us that way. You understand?"

"If either of you ran, the other would be harmed."

"Yes. It went on that way for a while." She glanced at the boy.

"Lyman," Israel said, "maybe you could go—"

"I'm not afraid of the story," Lyman Rankin said. "It's not going to hurt me. I understand more than you think. I wish I didn't, but I do. And I'm not leaving her."

Israel saw the truth of it all in his young face—especially the last part.

"All right," he said. "Then we'll hear it together."

He turned back to Jacqueline.

"You'd been waiting for that yacht. I watched you, watched her. I took her picture. She was looking into the sunset. She didn't even put a hand up to shield her eyes."

He wasn't sure why he'd said that, and yet it seemed to make a difference to Jacqueline, put an almost-smile on her face, as if a memory had penetrated the grief.

"Yes," she said, "we were waiting. When it was done, we were going to go home. That was what they'd promised." She paused. "They were never going to let us do that, were they?"

"What the hell happened out there?"

He felt as if she were seeing the yacht's salon, that polished mahogany and the white carpet and the table set with all those crystal wineglasses. Bodies on the floor, blood on the carpet, on the walls, splashed across the shower stall.

"I will tell it once," she said, almost speaking to herself.

49

The man who put the murders into motion had made contact with Jacqueline five months earlier, in Fort Lauderdale. She had been in Florida for nearly a year then, and she saw less and less of her sister. They had been gone from home for nearly four years. Whenever she was alone, she sketched pictures of home—her island, her clean place.

She burned the pictures or tore them into shreds when she was done. They were her memories and she didn't want them to be tainted. The past was clean and the present was hell, and after three failed escape attempts with her sister, she saw no way out that wouldn't end her sister's life.

On several occasions, she considered suicide. Thoughts of Marie kept her alive.

"If I had been alone," she told Israel, "it would have been easy."

It was winter in Florida and Jacqueline hadn't seen Marie in weeks—not since they'd been granted a few hours in a shitty Miami motel for Christmas—when the man with the plan appeared.

He arrived with money and questions, and she thought he was a cop. She did not trust cops. He assured her that he was not in law enforcement. He was a private investigator, he said. Jacqueline Picard didn't believe him, but she was used to being lied to. This man was different, though. This man carried himself as if he had nothing to fear in the world, and when he made a promise, she found herself thinking it was believable only because most liars were afraid.

His name was Caruso.

Caruso offered her more money than she'd ever had to tell him everything she knew about one man. He showed her pictures of this man.

It was Paul Gardner.

The name meant nothing to Jacqueline. Not then. Later, of course, she would learn of his history and his ambitions. In the moment, he was merely a familiar and hated face.

Once upon a time, not so long ago but across enough trauma that it seemed to have happened to a different person, Jacqueline and Marie had been aboard a yacht that was owned by Paul Gardner's brother. She did not know the names of the two men and expected that any she'd heard were aliases, but she did remember the name of the boat.

Mereo.

She had wondered what it meant, just as Israel Pike would later wonder about it while he sat in a police interview room explaining how he had gone aboard the yacht to count the dead.

She recalled being on the yacht for the better part of a summer. She didn't know what harbor they'd left or what harbor they'd returned to. She remembered the faces, remembered the bodies, the booze-and-cigar-tinged breath. The pain and the bruises. The laughter. Bleeding in a shower. Blue pills and white pills. The relentless rocking of the world belowdecks.

All of this, she could tell Caruso. But she didn't. What he'd offered in return was of no interest. Money? She didn't want money. She wanted her sister.

She wanted safe passage home.

She told Caruso this, and he listened and then left, and she would have thought he was gone for good if not for that strange, preternatural confidence, his fearlessness. She had worth to him beyond anything she'd known before. It was a terrible kind of value, but she felt it nevertheless—it was something like power. Not because he respected her or cared about her but because she had something that he could not simply take.

She had expected that he would hit her when she refused to tell him anything, had been prepared for violence and threats. He wasn't the beating kind, though. She thought that he believed such actions were beneath him, inefficient, the tools of simpler men. He'd left without a word.

The next day, a driver took Jacqueline to a resort hotel on the beach, a world apart from the motels she knew on the opposite side of I-95. She'd visited this hotel before, but never alone. This time, she was escorted to one of the familiar suites to find not another abuser, but her sister.

They were alone and they were together for the first time in so long. No men threatened them. No men hit them. No men visited at all.

Five days passed. Five exquisite empty days. No harm came to them. They were free to move, and the hotel staff delivered one delicious meal after the other.

On the sixth day, Caruso arrived.

He wanted to know if he had earned a conversation. He did not use the word *trust*—she thought again that he believed such tactics were beneath him, foolish—and on some level, she appreciated that. He was a man who saw the dark world and saw it clearly. He did not see the point in pretending otherwise. She had asked for time with her sister, and he had granted it. She had asked for safe passage home, and she believed he might grant that as well.

If only because she meant so little to him.

No, it was more than that—she suspected that he wanted her far away from all she knew in Florida because that was where he had found her. The farther away Jacqueline Picard was from Caruso, the safer he would feel when he was done with his task.

She did not yet understand the task.

That day, sitting on the private terrace of the Miami resort, Jacqueline and Marie Picard told Caruso what they remembered of the man in the photographs, Paul Gardner. Caruso recorded the conversation and asked minimal questions and then he left again. When he returned the following morning, Jacqueline's strange sensation of power grew.

"I told him we did not want any money. We wanted to go home," Jacqueline told Israel and Lyman. "I said this firmly. Those were my terms. I didn't expect him to agree; I had never been able to tell anyone my terms. But there was something about him that told me I could try. Not because he was kind but because I didn't matter to him, and that politician, Gardner, mattered deeply. So I said he could keep his money, but he had to see that we got home, back to our grandmother, to our island. He said he would need me to give him more than words for that to happen and then he showed us a camera so small that I could not believe it worked."

She held her index finger and thumb up with a fraction of an inch between them, indicating the minuscule size of this camera, and Israel thought of the tracking chips he had found in his hat and boots.

The sisters would go north, Caruso said. Back to the terrible island they both remembered, but they would not stay in the godforsaken basement where the sea hammered at the stone walls. He promised this. They would be together, and they would be safe. They would wait for the return of the yacht called the *Mereo*.

Then they would be taken to it.

"We would be wearing these cameras, he said, and if we did that, then we could go home when it was done. I thought I understood what he intended to record. You do too; I can see it in your face."

Israel Pike felt a flash of shame, as if the recognition of other men's evil meant that it lived in him somehow. Maybe it did. You arrived in this world with a corruptible soul. What mattered was whether you fought against that, and how long, and how hard.

Jacqueline was wrong about what Caruso wanted. He'd promised that no one aboard would touch them and even said they would have protection on the yacht, a bodyguard. When Marie pressed him as to what, exactly, *would* occur on the yacht, what the minuscule cameras were supposed to record, Caruso told her that the goal was to *refresh some memories*.

"I will always remember that phrase," Jacqueline said. "He told us that we would know some of the men on the boat, and he was curious if we could handle that. The word he used was *composure*. Could we keep our composure around these men."

A humorless smile haunted her face.

"I assured him that we could."

Less than twenty-four hours after that agreement in the Florida hotel room, Jacqueline and Marie had been flown north. They had never been on a plane, and since they had no identification, there was no way they could have boarded one if they'd wished to. That was no problem for Caruso—they flew private, on a jet. Their destination was a small airstrip in a place of rock and wind-whipped sea. There was little there besides a runway. A car waited. The car took them to a small harbor port that smelled almost like their home island, cold and clean.

Two men waited for them there. One was running the boat, and the other was a police officer, in uniform, bold and indifferent to the idea of any watchers.

His name was Sterling Pike.

50

He told us that it was his island," Jacqueline Picard said. "That if we had ideas of escape or looking for help or causing trouble, he would know, and he would stop it, and we would pay. He was very different from Caruso. More...familiar to what I had seen before."

Israel felt a pitiful disappointment, knowing that Caruso was allied with Sterling. He had never trusted the man, but he'd hoped that Caruso's contempt for the island deputy was legitimate. He thought of the way he'd doubted Salazar and favored Caruso and he felt sick with self-loathing.

It's my island, Sterling had told them.

Israel's bruised hands ached from clenching and unclenching.

"Who was the other man?" Israel asked.

Jacqueline hesitated and looked at Lyman Rankin.

"My father?" Lyman said, and Israel felt as if a snake had slithered into his chest and struck at his heart with venom-filled fangs. This child understood far too much of the world.

"Yes," Jacqueline said.

Lyman Rankin took the news without much reaction, but Israel knew he was folding the horror up and tucking it somewhere deep within him. Lyman would see Jacqueline's face in this moment again on sleepless nights and he would wonder about what was in his blood, in his heart, and whether it would surface despite him, fearing both his nurture and his nature. That was the legacy of a bad father.

Sterling Pike and Corey Rankin took the Picard sisters from the sleepy harbor town out to an island they both remembered, although neither of them knew its name until they were on it for the second time. Salvation Point.

"This time on the island was better than what we had known here before," Jacqueline said, indicating the room around them. "We did not see this place. You remember where we were, the apartment. It was like when we'd been in the hotel. Almost as if we were alone. But they were watching, of course. When you came by, at first we thought that you were one of them."

"I'm not."

"Marie didn't think you were. She said you felt like a different kind of man."

"What kind of man did she think I was?" It was a ridiculous question to ask in this moment, and yet Israel wanted to know, wanted to hear his nature contrasted with the likes of Sterling and Corey Rankin and Caruso. Wanted to hear *good* or *honest*.

"A dangerous one," she said without hesitation. "That was why she decided to ask you for the guns. It was a wild try. Who would bring weapons to strangers? You, who lived on this awful island and who spoke of police we should trust? It was so foolish to ask you for guns."

He gave a bitter laugh. "And yet I brought them."

"Yes," Jacqueline said. "We couldn't believe that. I did not care. The guns felt too small to change so much. But Marie said we had a chance now that we did not have before."

Israel didn't know how to feel about that, having seen the result. The guns had been small, but they'd changed plenty. "How'd you get the guns onto the boat?"

Jacqueline Picard met his eyes, her lips a tight line.

"The men waiting on the yacht," she said, "liked girls to have a certain look. Swimsuits beneath long raincoats. It would have been hard to get the guns on board without the raincoats. But this was what they liked."

I'm glad you killed them, Israel thought, a flash so sudden he nearly voiced it. She was watching him as if she'd heard the unspoken words. He looked away. "Nobody checked you for weapons?"

"No. We belonged to them. They didn't think there was anything about us that they did not understand."

We belonged to them.

He realized his hands were balled into fists again. He flattened his palms against his legs.

"Did Corey bring you to the *Mereo*?" Israel asked.

Lyman Rankin tensed at the sound of his father's name.

"Yes," Jacqueline said. She was keenly aware of the boy's reaction. Lyman's bearing showed that he knew exactly who his father was, knew it better than anyone in the room. It was true, no doubt, but that didn't make it any easier to see.

"Was Sterling along?" Israel asked.

"No. Corey was alone."

Israel pictured it, the long trip out across the cold water to the waiting yacht and all its power brokers.

"Why didn't you use the guns on him? Why did you go as far as the yacht?"

"His boat was useless," she said. "We needed a real boat. We were almost two hundred miles from home. I also believed that there was a chance that Caruso would see no purpose to betrayal."

A corrupt man but a pragmatic one. Her instincts about Caruso matched Israel's own.

"How did things go on the yacht?" Israel asked. "I saw the result, but…how did it come to pass?"

It happened quickly, she told him. Much quicker than she'd anticipated. Corey Rankin brought them out to the *Mereo* and left. They were not supposed to see him or Salvation Point

Island again. They were going to walk off the yacht in another port, Bar Harbor, Rockland, maybe somewhere south. Caruso had been clear about that. By the time it was done, he said, his team would be in total control.

His team, Jacqueline understood by then, was working for the other politician, the one who had been a judge, the rival for the Senate seat. Hosmer. The potential political power of the United States itself, according to Caruso, had all waited aboard the *Mereo* for two women of "a certain look" who'd been taken from their homes as children and trafficked up and down the Eastern Seaboard.

"Hang on," Israel said. "My uncle, Sterling, was working with Caruso. That means he was working with Hosmer?"

Jacqueline gave a little shrug. That didn't matter to her one way or the other. It was huge, though. Sterling's history was with Gardner, not Hosmer. It was Gardner, not Hosmer, who'd vowed to open up the Lost Zone.

"Sterling gave him up," Israel said. "His own boy, his ally, and Sterling gave him up. I wonder how much money they paid him."

Jacqueline Picard had no answer, of course.

"What happened when you got to the yacht?" Israel asked.

The Picard sisters were, in Caruso's planning, little more than a visual aid by the time they reached the *Mereo*. They were the living embodiment of the threat that hung over Gardner, proof that his secrets were no longer secret.

The Picard sisters stood in the salon where the champagne rested in the ice bucket and they listened while Hosmer told the others who they were and what they were prepared to say in court. He said that they also had photographs of their experiences with Gardner. That was a lie, Jacqueline thought, a bluff. Or maybe not. She was unaware of photographs or videos, but that didn't mean they did not exist.

Hosmer told Gardner to view the meeting as a gift. He would allow Gardner to end his campaign, to announce it as his own choice, and if that was done, then he would not bring the Picard sisters into the light. Jacqueline and Marie stood there while they spoke of them and around them and did not seem to see them. Jacqueline could feel her sister's anger like a living presence in the yacht's salon. But Paul Gardner looked at them and saw strangers.

"No recognition," Jacqueline said. "I think that was when Marie began to change. When her anger could not be stopped. He had hurt her, yet he did not even remember her."

She fixed a stare on Israel. "Gardner, he was a friend of yours, maybe? Everyone on this island seems to be his friend."

"We weren't especially close. He prosecuted me for murder, but he couldn't be troubled to show up in the courtroom to do it."

She studied him with fresh interest and then gave a small nod, as if this disclosure of a murder conviction wasn't surprising but something that suited him, like a man in a weathered cowboy hat telling you he'd grown up on a ranch.

For a time, the only sound was the sea working around the stone cellar while Israel waited for Jacqueline to gather her thoughts and finish the story. She took a breath, crossed her legs at the ankles. She moved her foot gingerly and with a wince.

"Gardner laughed at everyone," she said. "He laughed and he waved his hand, like this." She made a dismissive *Be gone* gesture, like someone brushing away a mosquito. "He said, 'Let your whores talk to the media. They have no credibility.'"

Israel's hands ached, and he had to release the clenched fists once more.

"Those were the last words of his life," Jacqueline Picard said. "When he said that, Marie shot him in the chest. She shot him and when he was down on the floor, he looked at her, and I believe he recognized her then. I believe he remembered her in the end."

She said this flatly, but Israel thought that it mattered a great deal to her.

"After that," she said, "it was chaos."

Israel thought of what he'd seen on the yacht.

"She didn't shoot all of them," he said.

"No," Jacqueline Picard said. "Not all of them. The man who was with Hosmer did most of the shooting."

"Jay Nash."

"He was a bodyguard. The one who was supposed to keep us safe. The gunfire started with another man, though. One who was on the yacht from the beginning. Maybe he was a bodyguard for Gardner. He wore a crewman's uniform. When my sister shot Paul Gardner, the man in the uniform came in from outside and fired at Marie. He missed. I think he hit another man. Or maybe he was aiming for Nash? I don't know. It was so hard to know. There were multiple guns being fired at once and all I wanted to do was get out of the way. To live. I remember the sounds and I remember the blood and I remember thinking that we had not been that close to home in a very long time."

"Your sister only shot once?" Israel asked.

She paused.

"Gardner's brother ran and hid." She looked impossibly sad when she said, "Marie followed him. He had hurt her too. She did not let him run away."

Israel remembered the way the man in the shower had looked when he'd found him. He had been shot point-blank in the head, at close range. No, Marie Picard had not let him run away.

"Do you know who killed the captain?" he asked. "The one in the pilothouse? When I found him, he had a radio in his hand as if he'd been calling for help. Or trying."

"Our bodyguard. Nash. He ran up there. He did not want any calls being made until he had time to think. That was what he said after it was done, after they were all dead—he needed time to think."

He'd bought time, all right. He'd had hours to think while the blood cooled.

"He came back down, and Marie came back up, and it was quiet again. There was a moment when he was looking around at all of the dead in the salon, and he had shot so many of them, and I could see that he was thinking of how it could be explained. There had been so much killing. He said we needed to build a story."

Nash had been Caruso's boy all the way. From the gunplay to the explanation without pause.

"That's why some were stripped down?" Israel said. "To create the story he wanted?"

"Yes."

"What was he hoping people would think?"

"I don't know. I only became sure that we were part of it." Her voice was as flat and dark as a calm sea at night. "I could see him building the story in his mind. I do not know all of the details of it, of course, the way he saw it, but I could see him realizing things. He put on gloves, and he removed some of their clothes. He moved some of the bodies. He found money in one of the staterooms. A lot of money…at least to me. Probably not much at all to them. He put the money into a bag and gave it to my sister and asked for her gun. Marie was in shock. She had not said a word. She took the money and gave him the gun. That was a mistake. That was when I knew. I understood him then."

Israel thought that he did too. Jay Nash, a Caruso disciple, had decided the killings needed to belong to the Picard sisters. He would have to convince the world of this.

"He was going to kill you," Israel said, "to blame you."

"There is the old saying that three can keep a secret if two of them are dead."

"Yes."

"He did not ask me for a gun," Jacqueline said, "because I had never held the gun in my hand. He did not know I had it. It was in my pocket, and I had never taken it out, not even in the worst of it. Shock? Fear? I don't know. But I saw the way he looked around that awful, bloody room, and the way he looked at me and my sister, and..." She took a breath. "I killed him."

There was a small muscle tremor along her cheek.

"All we wanted," she said, "was to go home."

For a long moment, no one spoke. Finally, Jacqueline broke the silence.

"Then we were alone with the dead men. There were no good choices then."

No, there would not have been. Not standing above the corpse of a man you'd shot, trapped on a yacht adrift in the North Atlantic.

"We could see this island," she said softly. "The terrible one. We knew the water would be cold, but it was the only place we could see. It seemed to be right there. So close. There would have been life jackets somewhere on the boat. I thought about that later. In that moment...I wanted to get away so badly, and the island looked so close."

Israel remembered where he'd seen the *Mereo* drifting beneath the rising sun. The women had been close, yes, but the water was cold, and the shore was punishing.

"You were in the water together?" he asked.

"Yes. For a while. Then Marie pulled ahead. I thought that was a good thing, because she would make it. I was going to drown. I was sure of that. The ocean was too cold and too strong. I was glad that she was out ahead."

"How did you make it?" Israel asked.

She gave a smile so sad he almost had to turn away. "Their

terrible money," she said. "The bag it was in was made to float. You can picture this?"

He nodded. "A dry bag. Sure."

"Marie would not leave it behind. She was determined to leave that ship with…something. I thought she would drown because of it. I took the bag from her." She paused, wiped at her jaw, and looked away. "But it floated. Their money stayed above water, and I was the one who had it then."

"Were you in here for a while?" Israel said. "Or did you start somewhere else and find your way to this house?"

"I was right here. In this room, mostly. It took me a long time to move. I'm not sure how much time passed before Lye-man arrived. Hours or days. It felt like forever, and it felt like nothing. My sister was gone. She was gone."

She stopped talking, clearly finished.

She was done telling stories.

Israel walked to the old stone steps that led out of the room. The water was descending with the receding tide, revealing more steps. They would lead right out to the horseshoe-shaped cove on the back of Little Herring Ledge, he realized. When the tide was right, you could transport things in and out with ease.

Things, or people.

When the tide was wrong, the door simply disappeared. He thought of his grandfather telling him stories of long-ago smugglers in his boatyard in a room that smelled of clean sawdust. His grandfather lowered his voice with dramatic flair when he reached the scary part of the story, then chuckled with bright eyes to let Israel know it was all a thing of the past. That he was safe.

In those days, Israel's father had been a fisherman, not a trafficker.

Israel turned to face Jacqueline Picard. "Back before all this happened, I told you that I could find a cop for you to trust."

He saw her hesitation.

"Would it matter if I told you that cop had been in this room? Been...through it, I mean. Like you."

That brought her up short.

"You believe that?" she asked.

"Yes," he said. "I believe it. She has lied to me about other things, but I don't think they were the wrong things to lie about. I do believe that she was in this room. The way you were."

She didn't offer a response right away, and he liked that. She was used to bad options and knew the risk of accepting the first hand that offered rescue.

"The best-case scenario," he said, "still involves you confessing to killing two men. One on the yacht, with a gun I gave you, and one here. I can vouch for the way the second one was killed, explain that you were protecting a child, but I'm not a man of credibility to police."

She gave the faintest of nods.

"The way things went on the yacht, though," he continued, "is more trouble. You won't be the only one who offers a version of how you got out there and what you were doing. It doesn't matter if you're the only one who *lived* it, that won't stop other people from saying how it happened. Especially Sterling and Caruso. The only reason they want to know the truth at all is so they can undermine it in the most efficient way."

She didn't say anything. Sat and watched him. The boy watched him too. Everyone waiting on Israel Pike as if he might have good ideas. His own idea earlier today had been to run and hide—with Caruso's help. To vanish.

He thought again of inevitability. Of fate. Why had he ever agreed to come back to this chunk of rock in the North Atlantic?

Because of this woman and this boy, he thought.

Because of innocents.

He rubbed his jaw and looked from them to the water and said, "The rest of the world thinks you're dead. They found your sister, and though they haven't found you, I don't think they're looking for you either. Not anywhere but the bottom of that ocean, anyhow."

She looked more intrigued than wary but still didn't speak.

"You said that home was two hundred miles away. You know that for a fact?"

"Yes."

"I've got a boat that could make it," he said, wondering just what kind of fool it took to voice these words. "If we could get you there, and the rest of the world thought you were dead...it might not be the worst of options."

She had eyes that didn't want to look hopeful but couldn't help themselves.

"All that might work," he said. "Likely would not, but *might*—if we were alone and talking only about the *Mereo*. But we are not."

Lyman Rankin, bless him, understood Israel's point immediately. He straightened, looked hard at Israel. "I've *been* keeping her a secret. You just started."

Israel damn near laughed. Probably would have if the kid hadn't been so fiercely serious.

"I trust that," he said gently. "But we'd still have to explain who killed your father."

He saw Jacqueline sag a little, and then he felt cruel for even mentioning the possibility of his boat, offering any illusion that escape was a possibility for her. What in the hell had he been thinking? He was about to apologize when Lyman Rankin pointed past Israel, at the steps that led to the water.

"No, we don't," he said. "Not if we get rid of him."

Israel Pike, who had killed his own father on Salvation Point Island, looked at Lyman Rankin, whose father's body rested on the floor above them, and thought, *There is no way I can do this.*

For some reason, though, he couldn't say the words aloud.

"Come here, kid," he said. "I want to talk to you alone."

51

Lyman liked Israel Pike. A strange response, considering he was a murderer, yet he seemed to be the kind of man Lyman had always wanted his father to be—he listened, he saw how others felt and *cared* how they felt, he considered things from different points of view, and, above all else, he was honest.

Well.

He was a version of honest, anyhow. The right one, Lyman thought. For a long time, Lyman hadn't believed there were degrees of honesty—it was black or white, hot or cold, truth or lie. He didn't feel that way anymore. He was pretty sure that Israel Pike didn't either.

Pike made him sit on the steps out of sight and earshot of Hatchet. He didn't care if her real name was Jacqueline; she was still Hatchet to him. His friend. His ally.

"How old are you?" Pike asked.

"Twelve."

"You should be a child still."

Lyman didn't know how to answer that.

"You aren't, though," Pike said. "You're not the kid you want to be, are you? Not anymore. I'm not going to talk to you like a child, then. These are big choices. I need to hear your opinion of them. You follow me?"

"Yes."

Pike's eyes tracked his as if they could see far deeper than the surface.

"Your father's body is upstairs," he said. "We both know the man's faults. I won't shine him up now just because he's dead. But I do need to know...did she have another choice?"

"What?"

"When she killed him," Pike said softly, "was it something she *had* to do?"

Lyman saw the living room in the storm again, saw his father exploding through the plywood sheet that covered the door, saw the look in his eyes when he'd ripped the leg off the overturned coffee table and advanced.

"Yes," he said. "She had to hit him hard. Because he wasn't going to stop."

Pike studied him.

"You trust her," he said.

"Yes."

"Why?"

"Because she just wants to go home," Lyman said. And then, as his throat tightened, "And because she fought for me. She didn't run. I was trying to take it, you know, so he wouldn't find her, but she...she didn't let me do that. Didn't let *him* do that. She put herself..." He couldn't finish. Wiped his face and repeated, "She just wants to go home."

"I know it."

"Will you let her?"

"It won't be for us to decide, kid. Not in the long run. The police won't stop. If it was only about what happened here, with your father, they would. I hate to say that, but they would. The people who died on that yacht, though?" He shook his head. "That shit doesn't stop. The police will follow her and they will find her."

"Maybe," Lyman said. "But if that happens, it shouldn't be here."

"What do you mean?"

Lyman pointed down at where the mildewed cots waited in

the stone room. "If the police find her now, after everything that happened, it shouldn't be in that room."

Pike exhaled and ran his hand over his face. His knuckles were laced with scars.

"I know," he said. "You are right about that."

Lyman imagined that Hatchet might make it. Disappear. It was what he wanted because it was what she wanted, but it also made him envision the world beyond Little Herring Ledge. Thinking of a world without Hatchet and his father, the twin forces that had squeezed him.

"Where will I go?" he asked.

It was a simple question that deserved a simple answer, but none came.

"I'm not sure," Pike said at last.

It was, at least, honest. Lyman nodded. Neither of them spoke for a moment.

"Even if we did it," Pike said at length, speaking slowly, as if he were puzzling on each possibility as he offered the words, "there's the scene upstairs. It's a mess. Wouldn't take a cop ten minutes to know a lot had happened in that room, and that's before the forensic folks get here, before they look for DNA. For blood. They'll find plenty of hers."

Lyman thought of her bloody footprints all around the house, of the Lyman-shaped dent in the wall, the blood on the couch, the clothes he'd brought from his own home, and he knew that he couldn't clean it all, not well enough. It simply could not be done.

"We could burn it down," he said.

"No utilities have been on in this house for years. No way an accidental fire starts."

"There's a bad storm," Lyman said. "A lot of lightning."

For a moment, he thought that Pike was going to laugh at him, although not in an unkind way.

"The lightning's passed and the rain's still coming. I appreciate your...creativity, though." Then, softer: "I appreciate your reasoning, is what I mean. Your heart."

Lyman looked away from Pike, wanting to offer more than heart, wanting desperately to offer a good idea. He wanted nothing in life more than to see Hatchet somewhere safe.

"It was my bad idea," Pike said. "I shouldn't have said it. I'm sorry."

Lyman turned back.

"*I* could burn it," he said. "And admit to it."

Pike stared at him.

"I really could," Lyman said. "That's the only lie I ever told that worked. I said I was mad about my mother leaving and mad about my father staying and so I burned things. And he believed me because it was mostly the truth. In all the ways that counted, it was the truth."

Israel Pike took a deep breath.

"I am a simple fool," he said. "Seven men are dead, some shot with my guns, there are people with more power than I've ever known circling like sharks, and I am listening to a child."

Listening. That was the only word that mattered to Lyman.

Lyman couldn't keep himself from asking a question.

"Why did you take my picture?"

Israel Pike was so flustered that Lyman regretted the question and was about to say so when Pike answered.

"There wasn't anything wrong about it. I'm sorry if Sterling made you think there was. I guess I'm sorry I took it. But there was no harm in it."

"I didn't mean it like that. I meant...well, I said what I meant. Why'd you take it?"

A long silence followed.

"Because you ran across those damn rocks as if gravity didn't exist," Israel Pike said at last. "Because you ran like you knew in your heart you were going to make it, no doubt, only courage. I haven't ever seen anybody run like that. Or at least, it's been a long time since I have."

Pike stopped talking, ran a hand across his mouth. "That doesn't make a bit of sense, I know."

"It does," Lyman said. "I think it does, anyhow."

Pike looked at him then and smiled. For a killer, he had the kindest smile.

"Come on," Pike said. "She's waiting on you." Then he stood and led Lyman back to the room where Hatchet waited. She looked at them with an unspoken question.

"You're hurting," Pike said to her. "How bad is it?"

"Getting better. Lye-man brought me some pills. They help."

"Not enough. You're in rough shape."

"So are you. So is he. We all share the pain brain."

Lyman smiled, and Pike looked puzzled.

"Can you move well enough to get on a boat?" he asked Jacqueline. "To stay upright and fight the boat if you need to?"

"Yes."

"Easy to say. Hell, do you even know how to run a boat?"

"I am from my own island," she said. "Do you not think an island girl knows how to use a boat? I may know better than you."

Israel Pike gave a wry grin.

"You might," he said. His chest rose and fell with a deep breath and he lifted a scarred hand and rubbed the back of his head, stroking his short-cropped hair as if it soothed him.

"It's the dumbest damned plan anyone's ever thought of in the history of this island," he said. "But you know something? It's not the worst of them. There's a difference between stupid and bad. Difference between the smart choice and the right choice too."

Lyman's throat was tight. He felt Hatchet's hand on his own and squeezed it.

"Couple things we all need to be clear on," Israel Pike said. "First, it's a dumb plan, and dumb plans usually don't work." He looked hard at Hatchet. "I've been in prison before. I'm not excited about returning, but I likely will. And you will too. You're smarter than me. Be smart enough to know that you *could* end up with your pick of lawyers, people who will believe you, who will make others believe you, and—"

Hatchet silenced him with the saddest smile Lyman had ever seen.

"Imagine if that happens," she said. "Imagine the life on the other side of that. Being the woman who shot one of those men. Can you see it? Can you picture that life?"

Pike nodded. "Yeah," he said, his voice low and rough. "I think that I can."

"They think I am at the bottom of the sea now," Hatchet said. "If there is even a chance of letting that be the end of it, I would like to take that chance."

Pike was quiet for a moment. Then he said, "The problem we aren't appreciating right now, in all the heat of it, the adrenaline, is that they've got to tell a story, and they're going to, and someone will take the fall. Caruso isn't lying about that."

Hatchet lifted the simple chain necklace from within her hoodie. She cupped the tiny pendant in her palm.

"I have the story," she said. "The true one."

Israel Pike understood her before Lyman did.

"That's the camera Caruso gave you?"

She nodded.

"Did it work?"

"I don't know. You have to connect it to a computer. But it did before. He made us test them."

Pike looked at the necklace as if it were too good to be true, fool's gold.

"You were in the water," he said. "It's got to be ruined."

"It worked in the water before," Hatchet said. "He made us test that too."

Silence. Israel Pike kept looking at the tiny pendant in the palm of her hand.

"If I trust one thing about Caruso," he said at last, "it's his technology. He's not setting up a senator with an old Kodak."

Hatchet released Lyman's hand, reached behind her neck, and unclasped the necklace. Held it out.

Israel Pike took it as if it were a heavy thing.

"If that camera actually recorded the whole deal…" He didn't finish the thought. He didn't need to. That's how big a question that was, and the answer would change lives.

Lyman looked at the necklace and remembered when he'd seen another like it.

"Your sister had one too," he said. "I saw it. I thought it was rockweed stuck to her, but it was a necklace like that."

He wished he hadn't said all of that, because it gave Hatchet an image she didn't need, but she merely nodded.

"Marie had one, yes."

"Who came for her?" Pike asked Lyman. "Who was the first cop down there?"

"Sterling."

That deflated Pike. He bounced the pendant in his palm.

"All right. So he's got one. That'll make him cocky. But if we've got one too…"

He looked up and a cold smile crossed his face.

"Imagine," he said, "if I'd stolen something from that yacht. Would take a dumb bastard to do that. The kind of impulsive man who's prone to poor choices. You both know the type. Everyone on this island knows that type."

The cold smile warmed like the rings on a stove burner.

"All right," Israel Pike said, "let's get you a boat."

Part Five

AMONG THE MISSING

52

I srael knew better than to move ahead with any of it, he really did, and yet here he was. Old crimes, new crimes, and the same damned island guiding him back to prison. A man who was born to be hanged would never drown, his grandfather used to say, a bastardized line from Shakespeare's *The Tempest*.

No, he told himself, looking at the earnest, hopeful face of young Lyman Rankin and the wary, dare-not-hope face of Jacqueline Picard, *there is no question of fate to it. Only decisions. If you've made yours, then think it through carefully and execute it swiftly.*

"I never knew this cellar," he said, "and I was never in the house. But I can about guarantee you that those steps lead down to a cove that's safe anchorage at low tide."

"Yes," Jacqueline said.

"Okay. The tide is our friend at the moment, but only if I hurry." He looked at Lyman Rankin. "I shouldn't leave you here."

The boy drew closer to Jacqueline. "Why not?"

"Because…" Because what, exactly? Because she was a killer? Well, so was Israel.

"All right, stay with her," he said. "When I come back, I'll be alone, and I'll have the boat. She'll take it and go. We'll give her a head start, and then we'll get help."

"Who is help?" Lyman asked.

"Dar for you, and the cop, Salazar, for me."

He lifted the necklace with the tiny pendant that Jacqueline Picard believed had recorded the truth out on the *Mereo*.

"This is a big chip," he said. "The last leverage either of us will have."

She nodded.

"You want to hold on to it until I'm back?"

She paused, then shook her head. "I trust you."

"Good." He pressed the pendant into her palm. "You should. But you also don't give up leverage like that. If I make it back, then you can leave it with me. Until then, don't let it go."

She looked at him with surprise—and, maybe, new understanding.

"When you're on the boat, I'll call Salazar," he said. "I'll give that camera to her. I won't tell her where you're headed, but it also won't take people around here a hell of a long time to notice that my boat is gone. Push it hard, all right? If you make it, pick a smart landing. Somewhere sheltered. You'll need to sink the boat."

She didn't say a word.

"When I bring the boat back, I'll bring some tools," he said. "We'll walk through it. It's harder than you'd think to sink a boat. Particularly one my grandfather built. But you'll need to do it."

He wished he could picture the place she had in mind, the privacy, the currents. He did not want to press her on that, though. It was better if he didn't know. He thought of the hours his grandfather had labored building that boat and then of the hours that women—children—had spent on it drugged or chained with Israel's father at the wheel, and he hoped that she succeeded in sinking it. The boat had been built with beauty and love and hope and had become corrupted, wretched. It was right to let her bring an end to it. Perfect.

Too perfect to ever work.

Jacqueline and Lyman watched him uneasily. He felt a need for some final words, something reassuring, or at least commanding, but none came to mind.

"I'll see you soon," he said, and then he walked up the stone steps, lifted the heavy trapdoor, and entered the house where the dead man waited on the floor. He didn't spare Corey Rankin's corpse so much as a glance.

The rain was still falling but no longer with punishing force. It was a fine, misting rain made cold by an unceasing southeasterly wind. He crossed the rocks and found the narrow footpath that led to the shore where Dar's boat waited, tied off to the rotting remains of what had once been Dwayne Purcell's dock. Purcell had been a friend of Israel's father, a drinking buddy, one of those old salts who liked to sit and talk about the ways things had been. Not with humor and nostalgia, but with hate. As if the passage of time were an insult, each new day an affront rather than a gift.

What a way to live.

Dar's dory started with the first crank. The sea was empty behind him. No police boats, no news helicopters. A solitude so vast that he could believe he was unseen and unwatched and thus that his return to the two waiting in the cellar was possible.

You had to believe it, even if it was crazy.

He engaged the prop and headed for Salvation Point.

53

The rain swept across the sea in sheets, making the surface look like hammered tin. Dark clouds lingered, dismissive of the wind. Israel stayed in the pilothouse, out of the weather, and stared at the burner phone he'd purchased, waiting for one precious bar of signal. He was most of the way across the strait from Little Herring before he was rewarded.

Salazar didn't answer. He called again. Got voice mail again. He was paying for his lack of trust. For his selfishness. He'd left her phone behind as he'd plotted to save himself. Now she didn't know the new number and wouldn't answer. Served him right.

He tried once more, thinking that he'd have to leave a voice mail. Salazar answered this time.

"Yes?" she sounded flat, unhappy, and distrustful—yet he'd never been happier to hear her voice.

"It's Israel."

"Where are you calling from?" Instantly on alert.

"The water."

"Whose phone is this? I've been trying to call the one I gave you."

"It's my phone." He didn't want to explain, so he said, "I wanted a backup, just in case."

"In case you couldn't trust me."

He let the wind answer that.

A few seconds passed before Salazar said, "Fair. But you've got bigger worries than me."

"I know it. I'm sorry. What I need is—"

"Hang on, damn it, let me finish, this is huge."

He hadn't even considered that *she* would have news.

"They're issuing an arrest warrant for you," Salazar said. "I've read the probable-cause affidavit. Your uncle wrote it."

He backed the throttle off, letting the seas buck the boat as he idled with Salvation Point ahead and Little Herring behind.

"On what evidence?" he said. "Did he plant something?"

"No. He didn't need to—because you gave him what he needed when you went down to fight those assholes at your house. Sterling leaned on Osgood, and now he's claiming you assaulted him. The PC has three witness statements. There is no mention of the homicide investigation. That was smart. Sterling knows he'd slow it down with that. Instead, he's pushing only the assault and battery. Keeping it clean."

"Oz came to my house to ambush me with two other guys and—"

"And now you've got to make it to a jury to explain that, because you took the bait. Meanwhile, the fresh charges will trigger a parole violation. Bail will be either denied or set prohibitively high. Best-case scenario, you find someone willing to put a lien on the boatyard. I'm not sure that will be enough, though, not with the violation."

He couldn't muster a response.

"I'm not going to let it happen," Salazar said. "I'm going to self-report. Otherwise, you're not safe. If you're locked up for a run-of-the-mill assault charge and a parole violation, there's no compelling need to argue for solitary confinement. That's why I was concerned that Sterling *didn't* name you as a person of interest in the *Mereo* murders. He can have someone take a run at you in jail. It's time to come clean. We both know it."

"Yes," he said. "We do. But I need a few hours."

"You don't have a few hours. Sterling's PC stipulates that he'll perform the arrest himself in his capacity as the island's deputy. Last I heard, the judge was signing it. Time is up."

"Then buy me an hour or two. I can give you the whole damn deal then, everything that everyone wants, I can put in your palm— literally."

"What are you talking about?"

He had to trust Salazar again, and he could do that, *would* do that, once Jacqueline Picard was on board his boat, northbound and gone. Not until then.

Why did he want so badly to help her run?

Because you know she's telling the truth, he thought. *Everything she said about that life waiting for her on the other side, it's as bad as or worse than you can imagine. If they let her make it to life on the other side, that is.*

Hearing about the arrest warrant waiting for him, he suspected they wouldn't. Jacqueline had disappeared once before, vanished from her home, but it had gone uninvestigated, her ongoing tragedy ignored. Why would anyone help her now? He thought of Marie accepting the gun with a cold brightness in her eyes, a look that said she'd seen enough of the justice system to believe she held her best chance in her own hand.

"I've got all of it," he said. "Who did it, when, and how. I've got it all and I can prove it."

"How?"

It was ten minutes from here to the boatyard, twenty back to Little Herring. Skirt the northern shore, away from any traffic. The storm would provide shelter. He'd anchor in the cove, get into that forsaken cellar, get Jacqueline out. An hour total. That was all he needed. One hour from now, he'd let Salazar take him into whatever protective custody she could arrange, stay alive while she searched that necklace camera and figured out what was on it.

If anything is on it. If it died in the water, you'll have nothing left to bargain with.

Except for the boy, of course. He could testify.

Israel wasn't sure he could let that happen. Put all of it on a child. Was it better to die in a prison shower room? Maybe.

"Israel?" Salazar said.

"I'm here. Listen, it needs to be you and only you. Come to Little Herring Ledge. No sooner than an hour. I'll have it all for you then."

"Little Herring?" she asked, puzzled.

"Only you. Promise me that. We've come too far alone to let anyone else in now."

"And look where we are."

"We're in amazing shape. You have no idea. I will give you everything you need to bring it home. The murders on the *Mereo,* the trafficking on Salvation Point, Sterling and Paul Gardner, J. R. Caruso or whatever his real name is, the whole damned show."

"You're serious."

"I am."

"How do you—"

"I do. That's all that matters right now. I *do* have it. I *will* give it to you. Come to Little Herring alone. From there...from there, you're in charge. I'll follow your marching orders, won't argue a damn bit. Won't need to. Because we'll have won."

Silence.

"One hour," she said at last.

"See you soon, Jenn."

He ended the call and powered off the phone.

54

The storm was his friend.

As others took shelter from it, Israel was granted the same within it. The wharf was quiet, no onlookers, certainly no camera crews. A few fishermen, but even they worked with their heads bowed against the driving rain. He avoided the main pier and brought the dory up behind the lobster boat, which helped shield him from the view of the fishermen, then tied off and cut the engine. Listened.

Silence save for the whistling wind and the rattle of loose chain link.

He stepped out of the dory and onto the ladder. The old rungs still held because his grandfather had run rebar beneath each rung, reinforcing it. A meticulous man, his grandfather.

The tide was coming in and he needed only a few rungs to climb up to the pier. He took them quickly, knowing that time was everything now; he was so close to the win, a win for all of them—him, Salazar, Jacqueline, every woman who'd passed through that horror of a house on Little Herring. All he had to do was get in the boat and go.

He was on board before he saw his own baseball cap hooked over the throttle and remembered Caruso's microchip trackers. Only a few hours ago, Israel had wanted to draw attention to this spot as a diversion while he went to Little Herring. Had he unwittingly set his own trap?

The rain popped off the pilothouse and puddled on the old pier. He picked up the hat as if it might bite him.

Maybe it already had.

If anyone came here and found that his father's boat was gone and Dar's dory beside it, there would be quick questions. If Sterling had a warrant in hand, Dar would tell the truth—the last she knew, Israel was on his way to Little Herring.

He needed more time. Minutes counted.

He put the hat on and ran up the wharf and splashed through the puddles and across the jagged asphalt to his grandfather's shop. A padlock secured the rusted hasp over the office door. The combination was the latitude of the first house a Pike family member had built on Salvation Point, nearly two centuries earlier. The old lock turned smoothly. Israel pushed the door open and the familiar smells smacked him like a rogue wave—sawdust and varnish, diesel and oil, paint and thinner. A million memories.

He cut through the office and pushed past the swinging door that led to the massive shed where once fishing boats for most of an island's fleet had been built. The space was emptied now, old jack stands and rollers pushed to the side, sheets of plywood leaning against the walls. In the back of the warehouse room, a single boat hull rested on enormous jack stands and keel blocks, positioned beneath a chain hoist. The hoist's last task had been to haul the guts out of a boat that was no longer seaworthy. The big engine had been turned to scrap, the rest left to rot. The gutted hull hovered above a deep mechanic's bay, the kind you'd see in an oil-change shop for cars, here providing easy access to the bottom of the boat.

Israel ran to it, found the ladder easily in the darkness, his movements born of memories, and crawled down into the bay. The smells of ancient oil leaks permeated the cool concrete. The boat hung above him, concealing him like a shroud. It would be a good place for a trapped man to make a final stand. Good enough that he hoped it might take his pursuers a while to determine that he wasn't actually hidden there.

He removed his cap with Caruso's tracking chips and dropped it in the farthest corner of the bay, hidden by the hull of the boat above, a place where any approaching man would risk gunfire coming from a protected position.

One hour.

All the time he needed to bring the whole thing to an end and walk safely away.

He recrossed the mechanic's bay and had his hands on the cold metal ladder when the harsh beam of a bright flashlight illuminated the office door and his uncle's voice called out, "Iz, come here."

55

Israel froze with his hands on the upper rung of the ladder, his head still below the surface of the floor. He thought about descending but didn't want to risk making a sound. His uncle spoke again, louder.

"Iz, don't fuck around. It's time to talk, old buddy."

Old buddy. What his grandfather had always called him, with affection, even when he was exasperated. Nothing like the cold cockiness of Sterling's echoing tone.

He thinks he's won. Has the warrant in hand and thinks that it is done.

On another day, Israel might have climbed up and walked to meet him. Salazar was still out there, ready to help, an ace in the hole that Sterling knew nothing of. If Israel were alone, the only one at risk, he might have given himself up without hesitation.

He was no longer alone, though. A woman and a boy waited for him across the dark water.

He slipped down the ladder with infinite caution, not making a sound. Crept to the closest corner of the mechanic's bay and pressed against the concrete wall.

Sterling's flashlight beam bobbed as it approached. He was pointing it in all directions, which was the only reassuring thing. The device was sensitive, but not so precise that he knew immediately to look toward the mechanic's bay. He knew only that Israel was inside the building.

Have to wait until he's behind the boat. When he walks behind the boat, you need to get back up the ladder in a hell of a hurry, because he'll check beneath, and you'll be down here like a lobster in a trap.

The light advanced. Sterling had stopped speaking. His footsteps were soft and sure, and Israel couldn't even hear him breathing. The light passed close to Israel, almost found him, but he was below it and shielded by the shadows of the hull of the boat above. Sterling would have to crouch down to see him, would have to get low.

Israel's fingers ached for the weight of a gun. It would be so easy. Wait for his uncle to duck below that old boat and peer down at him, wait to see that cocky grin, and then put a bullet right in the center of it.

He didn't have a gun, though. Sterling did.

The light shifted from left to right, drifting to the other end of the mechanic's bay and then beyond, into the farthest reaches of the shed. Israel strained to hear footfalls.

There, maybe?

Was that another?

He watched the light and he listened and finally he returned to the ladder. Wrapped his hands around the cold rungs and pulled himself up slowly. One step, two, three. Head almost level with the floor now. He paused there, drew in a silent breath, held it.

The flashlight passed by the mechanic's bay entirely, and he knew that Sterling was now at the back of the shed, making a careful circle of the building.

Israel pulled himself up the ladder and slipped off it and crept to his right.

In the boatyard's active years, there would have been so many places to hide. Not anymore. He stepped around the jack stand and stood beside it, seeking the shadows of the decaying boat as Sterling's flashlight beam pierced the darkness. Only one light, only one voice. That was the only good news—his uncle had come alone.

Israel scanned the room, searching for options. Not many. A

single stack of old pallets filled one corner of the warehouse space, tight against the wall. Not great, but the best of bad choices. He crept toward them as Sterling's flashlight beam swung from the office to the warehouse and began to pan across the space. He'd completed half of his circuit and was turning back. Israel ducked behind the only shelter—an eight-by-six sheet of plywood leaning against the wall. Others like it had been used to cover the broken windows. Someone had lazily placed this one here and forgotten it, but he appreciated the laziness now, because it left enough of a gap for him to slip between the wall and the wood.

"Come on, Iz," Sterling called, his voice loud and echoing in the high-ceilinged, empty room. "I've got a warrant, old buddy. Want to add a resistance charge to the list, I'm happy to provide it."

Outside, the storm was picking back up. The rain on the metal roof of the long warehouse sounded like hail.

Sterling's flashlight beam found the plywood sheet, lingered long enough for the hairs on the back of Israel's neck to rise, then moved on. The light fixed on the boat above the best hiding place in the room, the mechanic's bay.

Israel had vacated it with about thirty seconds to spare.

He eased out from behind the plywood and saw his uncle for the first time. Sterling stood in front of the boat on the jack stands, scrutinizing it. He had the flashlight in his left hand because there was a gun in his right. He lifted the gun and Israel saw a red dot appear on the wall of the mechanic's bay, searching for him.

Had Sterling come in here to kill?

It was a new notion, but not impossible. They were alone in here; his uncle could say it had gone down however he liked.

Israel's only weapon was his pocketknife. He drew it, felt along the back of the blade with his thumb. A knife at a gunfight. All he'd achieve with the knife was a justification of the shooting.

The rain on the metal roof was so loud that he'd get at least a few strides in before Sterling heard him. It was hard to hit a running target with a handgun. He doubted that Sterling put in a lot of range time. Israel would be able to make it to the door, make it outside.

And then?

Under the dock.

As a child, he'd played on the dock pilings, stepping from one of the X-shaped cross braces to the next and daydreaming of his grandfather's stories of sailors working high in the rigging of old schooners.

If he could make it under the dock, he'd have a chance. A short, cold swim into the rocks. As long as Sterling was alone, Israel thought he could escape in the water.

All he had to do was make it there.

It seemed an impossible hope, to make it that far without taking a bullet, until Sterling ducked under the hull of the boat and his flashlight beam angled skyward and Israel realized that he was descending the ladder into the mechanic's bay, slipping beneath the floor.

Move, Israel commanded his body, but it took him a moment longer than it should have. His body, it seemed, held a greater fear of a bullet than his brain did.

When he finally stepped away from the plywood, he felt as exposed as he ever had in his life. The empty room ahead of him sprawled out like Yankee Stadium.

He crossed it at a fast, quiet walk. His muscles were humming, the small of his back rippling, every nerve shouting at him to run, but running would have attracted attention that the swift, silent walk did not. He made it to the office door, eased through, and saw that Sterling had left the exterior door ajar.

Freedom.

He slipped out into the rain and only then did he allow himself to break into a run. It was dark and the rain was a shield of sound and the boat was just ahead. He could make it—would make it.

Did make it.

Was aboard the boat with a wild sense of victory before J. R. Caruso said, "Hello, Pike."

56

Caruso stood in the pilothouse, lost to the shadows, the only things clear about him his silhouette and the gun he pointed at Israel's chest.

"Ten points for ditching the hat and the boots," he said. "Most people wouldn't have noticed the trackers in either, let alone both."

Israel stood silent, caught.

"You know, I've been rooting for you," Caruso said. "You offered interesting possibilities. But things are moving faster than either of us would like now."

"Thought we had a bargain," Israel said. He kept both hands down against his legs, the folded knife cupped in his palm.

"Sterling has a better one. More plausible."

"You won't be able to sell me as the one responsible for what happened on that yacht," Israel said. "Not for the long term."

"We'll see, won't we? I'll see, anyhow. All I'm sure of, Pike? It's time for me to get off this fucking island. I hate this place."

"You're making a mistake," Israel said.

"Prove it." Caruso was looking beyond Israel, toward the boatyard, waiting for Sterling's appearance. Thunder ripped overhead, and the rain fell harder, as if reenergized.

"I'll let Jacqueline prove it," Israel said. He had not lifted his hands. His knife was still concealed in his right hand. It was closed, but his thumb rested on the raised knurl that flicked the blade open. He wanted Caruso's attention anywhere but on his hands.

"Lift your hands," Caruso said, as if reading his thoughts.

Israel ignored him again, said, "How'd you find them in Florida, anyhow? Jacqueline and Marie?"

He had Caruso's attention now. When Caruso edged forward, his eyes were on Israel's face, not his hands. His finger, however, remained on the trigger of his gun.

"You talked to them before they boarded the yacht," Caruso said. "You're not breaking any news."

"I talked to Jacqueline today."

"Not buying that."

"You'll want to be right about that one," Israel said.

A beam of light cut the darkness. Sterling, working his way back out of the building. A door banged open. Neither Israel nor Caruso glanced in that direction. They were focused on each other.

"If she's alive, where is she?" Caruso asked.

"Pick me instead of Sterling and find out."

"Too late in the game to bluff. You've had chances."

"We both have. You're about to regret one."

"Big words from a dead man."

"Shoot, then."

"We'll get to that."

"*He'll* get to it, you mean. You don't intend to do it yourself, but neither did Jay Nash on the *Mereo,* and he ended up killing several of them."

Caruso was silent. Interested.

"Nash rushed and he died," Israel said. "You're doing the same. You didn't give me enough time. I promised you witnesses, and instead you threw in with Sterling when he's the perfect one to go down for this—he's so much better than me, and you *know* that because you've thought the story through."

The knife was damp in his palm, rain soaking his fingers. He would need to be quick and he would need to be accurate. He thought that Caruso was likely a much better shot than Sterling.

He needed something to offer Caruso, to bait him with, buy time. The only bait he knew of waited in the dungeon below Dwayne Purcell's house, though.

He wasn't giving them up.

The enemy must believe you have both the capacity and the will to deliver on anything you threaten—and that threat should be untenable to them, Caruso had told him that morning.

Israel needed to make himself an untenable threat in a hurry.

Footsteps on gravel, splashes through puddles. Sterling running toward them. He'd clicked the flashlight off now, and there was no red dot visible from his gun. He took his marching orders from Caruso. That was important to understand. They'd both be ready to shoot but Israel needed to know whose finger was squeezing first.

"You're wasting it," Israel told Caruso as Sterling's boots hit the dock. "All I want is to *disappear*. You're wasting it all on a bet with Sterling. You dumb son of a bitch."

Caruso took a step forward, out of the shelter of the pilothouse, face intense, oblivious to the rain that raked him.

"You don't have anything," Caruso said. "Just good guesses."

"It's a big bet to be wrong on," Israel said, thinking that he'd act when Sterling reached the boat. Caruso would glance at him. Break focus for one instant. That would be enough time.

It would have to be.

Sterling reached the end of the dock. He stood above them, breathing hard.

"Hi, Iz," he said. "You're under arrest."

A red dot bloomed in the center of Israel's chest, the flickering light of Sterling's infrared sight.

"Give Caruso a moment, see if he agrees with you," Israel said. "He's not done thinking. It's not your island yet, Sterling."

"Yes, it is."

"It's a dead place now," Israel said, looking at Sterling despite himself. "You want to own it that badly? All of the evil you've carried through this place, it's worth it to you for this empty island?"

His uncle gazed at him through the rain with what seemed to be genuine disappointment.

"I love it more than anyone," he said. "Everyone else accepted its death. I did not. Most left. I stayed. This island has paid for my grandchildren's futures, Israel. The way it should have. I just found a different way to make a living out of the place."

"Blood money, you sick son of a bitch."

"It's always blood money. Someone always wins and someone always loses. I didn't accept the loss, is all."

"How much money did you get in exchange for setting up Gardner?"

"Didn't set up anyone. Told the truth about him. He set himself up."

"He was the one who wanted to open your beloved Lost Zone again. You bought up half the island betting on Gardner, only to sell him out in the end. Why?"

"Simple," Sterling said. "Because he was going to lose. Anyone could see that."

Israel almost laughed, even standing there in the rain with the red-dot scope on his chest.

"You adapt or you die, Iz," Sterling said. "How do you not see that? Your father saw it. Charlie wanted to be a simple friggin' fisherman, clean heart, clean hands, all that happy bullshit. Then hard times came and you know what? He saw the truth."

"What's the truth?"

"That nobody from away cares about this place or what happens to it. The world is always going to shit on us, and it takes some strength to survive here. A lot of people on this island need the strength and can't deliver it. I do it for them. I deliver."

Corrupt to the core, the man still thought he was a hero.

"You actually believe that," Israel said.

"Bet your ass I do," Sterling said, the gun steady in his hand. "Nobody's going to let you have a second chance to keep your home. I'm keeping it. And now I've got work left to do. Time to move along."

He was speaking to Caruso, not Israel. There was a hint of a question to it, that need for the final verdict. He would pull the trigger, but Caruso would make the call.

Israel looked at Caruso, who gazed back at him through the rain with indifferent eyes.

"The cameras were in small pendants," Israel said. "You're still missing one of them. I've got it."

There was a pause, then Sterling said, "Bullshit."

Caruso was still looking at Israel. Israel didn't speak. He just held eye contact and nodded one time.

Caruso fired so fast that Israel wasn't sure it had happened until the second shot was done. Two rounds released almost as one, and Israel never had time to duck, didn't even think of the knife in his hand, let alone attempt to use it.

Sterling's unfired pistol hit the deck before his body did. The gun bounced off the dock and into the bottom of the boat and he made a high sound of surprise or pain or both before he, too, fell. He didn't make it into the boat. His face clipped the gunwale with a sickening wet crack, like a board smacked flat against the water, and his body pinwheeled into the ocean. The splash wasn't loud over the drumming rain.

Israel looked at the water just in time to see Sterling's face vanish. He went fast, lips parted like he'd had one last thought.

"Give it to me," Caruso said, quiet and calm, as if nothing unusual had transpired. His eyes were already back on Israel.

At first Israel thought he meant Sterling's gun, which rested by Israel's feet. Caruso had no interest in the weapon, though.

"The necklace," Israel said, realizing that he'd succeeded—he had made himself an untenable threat. Temporarily.

"Yes. Give it to me."

"Good choice, Caruso. I knew you'd make it."

Israel stepped forward and reached into his pocket with his left hand, counting on how badly this man wanted this one thing, counting on him to follow Israel's left hand with his eyes.

He did. He was looking at Israel's left hand when Israel's right flashed out and up and first the knife blade was open and then it was in Caruso's throat.

There was a full moment after the man fell against him that Israel was sure the blood he was tasting was Caruso's. Even as Caruso dropped to his knees and reached to cover his bleeding throat with one hand and tried to raise his gun with the other, even as Israel stomped on the man's gun hand and heard bones snap like a loose sail in high wind, he was sure he was not hurt. It was only after he disarmed Caruso and stepped clear that he became aware of the blood running out of his own stomach.

Caruso had shot him just beneath the ribs.

Fast.

The man was awfully fucking fast.

Israel pressed his palm to the wound and looked at Caruso, dying in the bottom of the boat. Watched as the light of the living leaked from his eyes. Only when he was sure Caruso was dead did he drop his gun to the bottom of the boat, kneel unsteadily, and brace himself to examine his wound. The pressure of his hand against the hot dampness felt vital, the only thing between him and death. He had to see it, though.

He slid his hand back. Pain rode in as if to replace the blood that ran out. The bullet had entered below his ribs and exited through his back. The hole was clean, though. Did that mean something? He thought so. He'd been stabbed with a homemade knife once in nearly the same place. Was that his second year in prison or his third? Early enough that he'd thought he was going to die.

Didn't, though. Kept right on living, and that one looked worse than this does.

Of course, he had medical attention within minutes on that one.

He removed his belt and started to take his sweatshirt off, then thought better of it. No need for reaching or stretching. He fumbled Caruso's jacket off and then found the knife that had killed the man and used that to cut strips out of Caruso's linen shirt. It was a fine, clean shirt—or it had been. Now it was soaked with rain and blood and the muck from the bottom of the boat. Dirty. That was bad. No other option, though. He packed his wound with the linen, gasping at the pain, and then wrapped Caruso's jacket around his stomach, wrapped the belt around that, and took a moment to breathe and ready himself. Then he pulled the belt closed with all the force he could muster, cinched it so tight that the cool, dark night turned bright and hot and for a moment he was sure he was going to faint.

The light dimmed and the night returned. He got the belt buckled. The shirt patches, bunched jacket, and belt squeezed him tightly. A clean wound and plenty of pressure. Many men had survived worse.

He staggered into the pilothouse. Got the engine started and only then remembered that the boat was still tied to the dock. Shit. He fought his way to the bow and then the stern, casting off lines. The belt held the dressing against his wound. He would certainly live if he called for help now. With Caruso and Sterling dead, there wouldn't be much for Jacqueline Picard to fear, would there? She had more time than him.

He stood swaying and pictured her and the boy, Lyman Rankin, waiting for him down in that stone cellar, and he thought of Nash and Caruso and how many unknown people were massed behind them, and then he went back to the pilothouse and put the boat into gear. He started to sit, thought better of it. He had a vague notion that it was important to keep the blood flow going to his legs. You didn't want to elevate the legs when you had a chest or stomach wound. Where had he learned that? Some distant memory of some paramedic shouting while Israel lay beneath him on the concrete prison floor.

He steered with his left hand and held himself up with his right, and he motored away from Salvation Point and into the night.

The *N'ver Done* ran steadily, bow into the wind.

57

Lyman sat in the cold dark with Hatchet and the only warm thing in the room was her hand in his. Once, they heard a boat engine, but it faded as quickly as it had appeared. Someone passing by the Ledge without pause. Lyman was used to that sound.

"You will be fine," Hatchet said.

Lyman nodded.

"Safe," she said.

He nodded again. He was having trouble looking at her. He kept his eyes on the floor. The floor looked dry until you sat down, and then unseen moisture leached up out of it. That couldn't be good for a house. He remembered how the door had collapsed in the snow and how he'd come down with his father to put the plywood over it, the way the screw had torn through the rotted frame like it was a chain saw.

No purchase.

Nothing to hold on to.

"Lye-man?" Hatchet whispered, and she squeezed his hand until he finally looked her in the eye. "Thank you. For…all of your help."

"Sure," he said, blinking fast, swallowing hard, tears threatening. Where would he go? There was no one to take him. Maybe they'd let him stay with Dar, but what if they didn't?

What if they do? he thought then, and that seemed worse, not because of Dar but because it meant staying on the island. He thought of going back to school in the fall. Everyone would know about his father by then. But *what* would they know? Part of keeping the secret meant not telling the truth. So what would people know about Corey Rankin?

He didn't want to live on Little Herring Ledge or Salvation Point Island. Everything here had blown apart like a Fourth of July sparkler, with a slow warning glow at first and then a series of rapid, violent bursts. Nothing that was left could hold together. Lyman Rankin had lost his purchase on the world, on life.

"You need to take the money," he said.

Hatchet frowned at him, surprised and confused.

"The money upstairs."

"I don't want that money."

"You need to take it, though. It's a clue. That you were here."

She wasn't happy about the idea but she didn't argue.

"I'll get it," he said. "Wait here."

"Lye-man, don't—"

But he was already going.

He went up the stone steps and through the trapdoor and on through the real basement and up to the house. Opened the door and went down the hall and saw his father on the floor.

He stopped then. His father was dead and Lyman knew this but he was still afraid of him. If anyone could come back to life for one more savage swing, it was Corey Rankin.

You've got to do it, he told himself. *You've got to move past him. He's done hurting you. Prove it.*

He walked past his father, stepping carefully to avoid the dark pools of blood, and went into the kitchen. An old backpack was tucked in one of the cupboards. He had used it to sneak food and water out of his house and into this one. He found it and emptied it and walked back to the couch. It was dark in the room and his father's skin looked blue-white, his eyes sunken shadows, as if he were already nothing but a skeleton, a ghost.

Lyman put his back to his father and lifted the sagging couch cushion and felt below for the money. His fingers touched crisp bill edges. He pulled out the first two packets and put them into the backpack and then reached down and did it again.

He did this fifteen times before all of the money was in the backpack. At the very bottom, he found the bag that Hatchet had used to carry the money from the yacht. It was a nicer bag than his own, waterproof, designed to float if you got in trouble, and it had made the trip once already, so he put his own backpack inside this one and then zipped it shut.

He straightened and looked at his father one last time. The blood spread out all around him, a long trail that seemed determined to reach Lyman, to touch him. Of course it was already in him.

A soft engine sound shuddered through the room and then he heard Hatchet's voice from far below, faint and distant. "Lye-man?"

He stepped over his father for the last time and rushed back down to meet her.

By the time he reached the lowest level of the cellar, the motor noise was clear. They listened together as it grew louder, seeming to shape-shift, at first a window fan, then a lawn mower, and finally the throaty and undeniable noise of an outboard.

The motor choked off, and then there came a harsh crunch of a hull on crushed shells and granite, followed by the overloud waves of the boat's wake. Lyman thought that last rush of water after a boat ran ashore always seemed angry, as if the sea had lost something that belonged to it.

Hatchet took his hand.

A loud splash, then footsteps, and then a man's voice, so ragged it wasn't immediately familiar, called out, "It's me. Israel Pike."

A shadow moved at the base of the steps and Lyman pulled back to stand close to Hatchet as Israel Pike limped up to them. He was drenched in rain and sweat and holding his side as if he'd been struck by a cramp. Hatchet got to her feet and went to Pike and supported his weight as he eased down onto one of the cots.

He was hurt.

Badly hurt. A belt bound a balled-up black jacket to his side but there was blood all around it. Hatchet reached for the belt but Pike pushed her away. It wasn't with much force. He didn't seem to have much force.

"Your boat is here," he said. "Don't make that for nothing."

She didn't respond, stayed there kneeling beside him and looking him in the eyes.

"Sterling's dead," he said. "So's Caruso. You got a little more time to work with than we'd thought, maybe. Don't waste it, Jacqueline."

He looked down at himself then, as if the notion of extra time had reminded him of his own trouble.

"Let me help you," Hatchet said.

"I got help coming," he said. He cleared his throat and spat a stream of crimson onto the stone floor. "But you've got to be gone when it gets here. You know that."

Hatchet looked at Lyman and then back at Pike. She seemed uncertain now.

Lyman said, "Quiet."

Hatchet looked at him with surprise, but Lyman saw recognition on Israel Pike's face. Recognition, and defeat.

There was another boat approaching.

Then the defeat faded from Pike's lean face and something close to a smile replaced it.

"Salazar," he said. "She's punctual."

He tried to stand, didn't make it, and sat down heavily. Looked at Lyman.

"Go out there on the rocks, kid. Wave her in. She'll see my boat." Then, as an afterthought, "If it's anybody but one woman alone, yell as loud as you can, then run like hell."

58

There were dancing white orbs in Israel's peripheral vision, and he could no longer blink them away. He had given up trying around the same time he'd grounded the boat. He'd come in too hot and damaged the hull, but not so badly that the boat wouldn't run. He hadn't seen any other way to go about it. He knew he couldn't wade and didn't figure he had time—or strength—to make the long walk from the dock at Corey Rankin's house, then all the way down the stairs.

"The boat ran fine," he told Jacqueline Picard as they waited for Salazar. "Ran fast and steady. Made me happy. There's an old loran navigation system, if you know how to use it."

He wanted to clear his mouth of blood again but he didn't like the look of what he'd spat onto the floor, how it seemed dark and bright all at once, so he swallowed, worked his tongue around his lips, and said, "You really know where you're going?"

Her dark eyes were fixed on the belt that held Caruso's jacket to his ribs.

"Yes," she said. "I do."

"It's a big ocean out there."

Her eyes flicked up to meet his. "I can handle it."

He supposed they'd have to find out.

"When you get there," he said, "you'll need to cut it loose. But first you've got to hurt it. It seems like it should be the easiest thing in the world, to sink a boat, but it's not."

He was talking too much and his words were slurring. He stopped, took a breath, and said, "Can you figure out how to do that?"

"I can sink that boat."

He was interested by how damn confident she was in this. He was interested in a lot about her but the time for asking questions was fading fast. He settled for one more.

"How do you feel about your island?"

He thought she wouldn't follow that one, but she did.

"I love my island," she said without hesitation. "I never wished to leave."

He nodded. Thought about telling her that had been true of him with this place once and that he hoped it could be again, but that wouldn't be the right thing to say—not to her, and not in this room. She'd seen the Sterling Pike era here. The Charlie Pike era. She hadn't seen the Josiah Pike era. Different worlds on Salvation Point.

Or had they been? He knew only what he'd been told. You couldn't go backward, regardless. Had to figure out how to go forward. Sterling had been wrong, saying that you didn't get a second chance with your home, that you had to keep it or lose it, everything zero-sum. The whole nature of time said that you *couldn't* keep it. You visited it, that was all. So how did you preserve what you loved about your home? Tell the right stories and help people find their footing whenever you could. Understand that you were temporary. Understand that being temporary wasn't a tragedy.

He didn't think that he'd said any of this aloud, that all of it was in his own head, but Jacqueline said, "What?" and leaned close.

"Never mind," he said, and then a beam of white light angled up the stairs and pinned their shadows onto the wall behind them. He lifted J. R. Caruso's gun. Damn near pulled the trigger, too, because the light made him think of Sterling at the shipyard, but it wasn't Sterling.

It was Jenn Salazar, with Lyman Rankin at her heels.

"Holy shit, Israel" was all she said when she saw him. She came toward him then as if the gun in his hand weren't real. He had to lift it toward her to make her stop.

"What are you doing?" she said.

"What I promised. Promised you and promised her. She leaves first. Then you get what you want."

Salazar looked at Jacqueline Picard. Jacqueline didn't move. They studied each other as if they'd met before. They hadn't. Right? He was almost sure of that, but it was getting harder to be sure of things. He blinked, tried to clear the white orbs from his vision. Failed again.

"You were here," Jacqueline said. "That is what he told me. That you were in this room, like I was. Like my sister was."

"Yes." Salazar's voice was faint and the sea was loud. Or was that the sea? So damn hard to tell. All the background noise was loud and the voices were soft. Israel cleared his throat, spat. Salazar looked at the blood that he sprayed onto the floor and started toward him again. He lifted the gun again. He wished she would stop making him lift the damn gun. It was heavy.

"She's taking my boat," he said, "and she's leaving. Nobody's stopping her. Not even you."

"She's not taking your boat."

"The hell she isn't. Don't test me, Salazar. Do not—"

"They'll be looking for your boat soon, probably with helicopters. They won't be looking for mine. She'll take that one. It's a chance, at least."

For a moment, he was stunned. Then he looked back at Jacqueline and saw the calm way she was regarding Salazar. He looked around the stone room where they had each spent time, and he understood.

"You're letting her try."

"Yes," Salazar said. "But we need to hurry."

Israel started to rise, and Jacqueline reached for his free hand. He thought it was to help him up. Only after he felt the soft weight of the necklace chain did he even remember the camera. The one that told the truth, if it had recorded anything and if the water hadn't ruined it.

He looked from the pendant to Jacqueline.

"I hope it worked," she said.

"Me too."

He stood. The room reeled, and Salazar caught him before he fell.

"Sit down!"

"Not in here," he said. "I will not stay in this place."

She didn't argue with that. She helped him down the stone steps and out into the clean night. The rain had stopped, and two boats waited.

59

Lyman watched the cop named Salazar help Hatchet into the boat. It was a state police boat. He thought that was smart. Not many people would stop a police boat. She had a better chance of making it in that one than Israel Pike's lobster boat, for sure. He'd run it hard aground. The tide was coming in, though, helping to ease it off the rocks. It wasn't yet high tide, but close. The rip would be almost underwater now, Salvation Point sealed off for another night.

Pike sat on a flat rock beside Lyman with the gun in his hand while Salazar showed Hatchet the instrument console, talking her through the controls. Hatchet had limped badly on the way out but stood with confidence in the boat, with easy, natural balance. She nodded in quick, short motions, tilting her head left and right, like a gull.

Lyman started to smile at that and then realized that he was crying.

Pike heard him and turned.

"Come here, kid."

Lyman wiped his face and shook his head.

"Come on," Pike said. "Lyman. It'll be all right. We're going to…" He either lost his train of thought then or didn't have a plan to share. And how could he? Hatchet's plan made sense because Hatchet had a goal: home. Lyman didn't have a home.

Without a destination, it was hard to make a good plan.

"We'll figure it out," Pike said.

Hatchet heard them talking and looked away from Salazar, searching the shore.

"Lye-man," she called.

"I'm fine!" he shouted back, but he couldn't keep the tears out of his voice.

"Come here," she said. "Where I can see you."

Lyman shook his head.

"Say goodbye, kid," Israel Pike said, his voice sad and gentle. "You did a hell of a thing for her. She's got to see it through now. Tell her goodbye. You'll regret it if you don't."

Lyman couldn't take it anymore. Couldn't stay here and say goodbye.

He ran.

It was what he knew to do.

He ran away from the Purcell house and up toward his own as Israel Pike and Hatchet called his name. Broke through the trees and kept running, then pulled up short, gasping. Why was he running for his own house? What was there for him?

Behind him, he heard the outboard motors on the police boat come to life.

She was leaving.

He began to run again. Away from both the Purcell house and his own house, running into the rain and wind, toward the rip, the long breakwater that bridged the sea between the Ledge and Salvation Point. Usually, he felt a giddy sense of freedom in this stretch, running on the rocks of Little Herring Ledge in the wind. Not tonight.

He could see the outline of the boat that was taking Hatchet away from this place. She was just a silhouette because the console lights were dim. The boat was pulling away from the cove, running parallel to the rip. It would reach the midpoint, the deepest water, and then angle out to the open sea and take her north, take her away, make her disappear.

He realized then that Israel Pike had been right. Lyman would regret not saying goodbye. Hatchet had to go, there was no other option for her, and saying goodbye—and doing it right—was the one thing he could control. He'd fled from that. He would regret it.

Maybe he would see her again. *Never impossible,* she had told him when he asked if she might have known his mother, if they might even be family somehow, if there was any chance he was not completely alone in this world. He could see her again, somehow, somewhere.

But if he didn't...

He pushed through the pines, searching for the lights of the boat, and a branch caught his bag. It was the first time he'd even thought of it. He was still wearing the pack with all of the money. Her money, from the terrible men on the terrible boat.

He freed it from the branch and scrambled up a sloped boulder that gave him a clearer view of the sea. The police boat was running parallel to the rip. The tide was high but not all the way in. If he hurried, he could shout to her. If he was fast enough, he might even be able to throw her the money.

He ran.

He ran toward the rip with an easy stride, still fast, but not full out. He searched for her as he ran, wondering if she could see him or if she was looking straight ahead. She was at the wheel with her back to him, a shadow within shadows.

He was fast enough to get within earshot, but the problem was the tide. It was nearly to high tide, the water covering large segments of the rock. He knew from experience that the rock would be there just a few inches beneath the surface, but you couldn't see the rock. You had to trust that your foot would find it, and you had to be willing to get a little wet, to take the risk of losing traction. If you lost traction and slipped on those rocks with a rising tide? That was a good way to say the big goodbye.

The police boat banked alongside the breakwater, turning to face the open ocean. Fifty feet more and then it would pull away and head for the northern sea and her unnamed island. Her home. She might be able to hear him if he shouted from here, but it was no sure thing, not in this wind and rain.

He looked out at the rip, which was now nothing more than a few jutting islands of hostile rock in the gloom. Down below, though, flat stones waited. He knew that. His feet knew it.

Lyman began to sprint.

He thought he would have five dry stones before he found water. He found six, and that last one, the surprise gift, gave him added confidence as his left foot splashed through the water onto the seventh stone, and he accelerated. His ribs and shoulder hurt but his legs were strong and his feet were solid. Eight stones, nine, ten, eleven. The water was deep enough now that it added drag, pulling his feet down, making his ankles throb. He splashed on. Twelve stones, thirteen, fourteen, fifteen. The water over his ankles now, forcing him to engage his upper body as he hoisted his feet up from below, the water trying to suck them back down as if enraged that he was even attempting to escape it.

Twenty. Splashing and thrashing now but still moving forward. High knees, churning ahead. Twenty-five. Thirty.

He glanced to his right and saw the boat approaching the high pile of rock that stayed dry even at peak tide. The highest point on the rip. Perfect place to wave goodbye, but he'd waited too long. He would need wings to reach the heights now. Impossible.

He almost stopped running as that word—*impossible*—filled his mind and heart. It was not fair, all the things that were impossible and all those that were not. His mother had abandoned him to a cruel man, and that should have been impossible, yet it had happened. His father had thrown him into a wall and then come to kill him, and that should have been impossible, yet it had happened. It could not be only the bad things that were possible. If those things had happened, then why should it be impossible that a boy could fly?

He ran for the high, dry rocks.

A wave rolled in from the boat's wake and slapped all the way up against his thighs, almost toppled him, but his feet held on to the stone as if they belonged to it, and then the wave surged past, and he felt faster, lighter, and still fully connected. The rip was a runway, and Lyman Rankin was a jet.

He looked to his right again. The boat was directly below him, bow pointed toward the northern sea. Shadows moved. He thought that Hatchet had turned to face him, but he couldn't be sure.

Then her voice found him in the darkness, one word that sounded like two: *"Lye-man."*

She had looked back for him. She had found him in the night.

He looked down at her as the boat rolled in a swell.

"Goodbye," Lyman shouted into the rain and the wind.

And then he jumped.

60

Israel watched the kid jump and heard Salazar take a sharp breath, anticipating disaster.

She hadn't seen Lyman Rankin run before, though. Hadn't watched him defy gravity.

There was an instant, at the apex of his leap, when the boat seemed to be both too far away and rolling in the wrong direction. An instant when the boy seemed certain to hit the water at best and smack right off the gunwale at worst, the way Sterling had before he sank.

He cleared the gunwale, though. Landed on his heels in the stern and skidded forward and should have fallen, painfully, but Jacqueline Picard caught him like a dancer with a familiar partner, hooking one arm around him and pivoting to absorb his momentum while she drew him tight.

Salazar exhaled.

"Damn it," she said. "She's got to bring him back now."

Israel didn't say anything. Out on the police boat, the two shadows that were the woman and the boy conferred. The boat turned to face north again. The motors throttled up.

"What's she doing?" Salazar said. "She can't take him! That's not... I can't ignore that! I've got to tell someone about the damn kid!"

"You can ignore it." Israel was still tasting blood, but his mouth wasn't full of it the way it had been. Was that good or bad?

"No, I can't. He's a child."

"So were you. You were fourteen years old when you were put

on that boat." He pointed at where the *N'ver Done* was grinding off the rocks.

Salazar hesitated. "It's not our option. His father might be a piece of shit, but he'll look for the kid."

"No, he won't. He's dead."

She turned and stared at him.

"He's upstairs in Purcell's old house," Israel said. "He's been dead for a few hours. I had bigger things to worry about."

The wind whipped her hair over her face, and she pushed it back and peered at him as if now he would make more sense.

"Man, did you see that kid run?" Israel said. "Did you see it?"

"I saw it." She came closer to him, knelt by him. "We need to get you out of here in a hurry."

"I'm fine."

"Pike, you're anything but fine."

"You got the necklace?" he asked.

"No. She gave it to you."

Oh, yes, she had. He fumbled for it in his pocket, only to have Salazar take it gently from his hand. He'd been holding it the entire time.

"Keep that safe," he said. "It's everything you need, if it worked."

"What do you mean?"

"It's a camera," he said. "She had it on board the *Mereo*."

Salazar stared at him, then put the necklace carefully into the pocket of her windbreaker and zipped it shut.

"We've got a lot to catch up on," she said. "But we'll do that in the hospital."

"Nope."

"Pike, it's not a matter of—"

He grabbed her arm with all the strength he could muster. It wasn't much. She stopped talking and looked into his eyes. He had always been fascinated by her eyes. Could fall right through them if he let himself. He couldn't let himself tonight. Not until he'd talked.

"You got something to record with?" he asked.

"In the hospital, sure."

"Stop it. I don't have the energy to argue, and you're going to need the recording."

"I'll get plenty of chances." But she was looking away.

"Sure. Don't miss this one, though. Jenn?" He waited until she met his eyes again. "Do not miss this one."

She looked at him for a long moment and then pulled her phone from her pocket and opened a voice-recording app. Showed it to him to prove that it was running.

"All right," he said. "Thank you. I'm going to tell it like it happened. You got questions, they should probably wait."

She hesitated, then nodded.

Israel Pike, a killer and an honest man, looked from the recorder to the sky, where stars were fighting their way out, and said, "I killed Corey Rankin on Little Herring Ledge. I confronted him about the crimes he'd committed with my uncle, Sterling Pike, and we fought. He lost."

He took a breath. His chest and back hurt. He couldn't feel the wound anymore. The pain had moved on, as if tired of the entry point and hungry for someplace new.

"I was afraid for his kid too. Being alone in a place like this with a man like that. Ask Dar Trenchard about Corey Rankin as a father. She'll tell you."

"Where was the boy when you killed his father?" Salazar asked.

Israel looked away from the sky, refocused on her.

"I never saw him," he said. "I hope he ran away. That's all you can do with a father like that. Run fast, run far, and don't look back."

Salazar watched him in the dim light from her phone. Her hair was damp and glistening now, and her eyes held a matching liquid shine. He waited for her to turn off the recorder and call him an asshole and tell him to play it by the book. To tell the truth.

She didn't.

"Corey Rankin had a necklace," Israel said. "Told me he'd taken it off a dead woman's neck. Woman had drowned. Her name was Jacqueline. Her sister—Marie—drowned with her. Marie was found by other people, not Corey. Sterling took the necklace from her body. According to Corey, the necklaces have cameras that will show what happened aboard the *Mereo* on the night when all those men were murdered."

It felt good, telling the last lies of his life. They were not bad lies. It was good to tell them out here under the clean night sky and beside the sea and in the wind and the rain. It was an almost holy experience. He would let the lies leave him, and then he would be done with them.

Out on the North Atlantic, the tiny lights of the police boat were fading into blackness.

Go fast and stay smart, Israel thought—for them, and for himself.

"All I know," he said aloud, "is what I heard from three men: Sterling Pike, Corey Rankin, and J. R. Caruso. I will tell you what they told me."

And so he did. He told Jacqueline Picard's story as well as he could imagine it being heard from three of the many men who'd abused her and her sister for so long. He spent extra time on Caruso. He wanted to make sure he got the doctrine right. None of the justifications made any sense without the doctrine.

He wanted to try to make sense of these men. What they had done, what they had believed.

The wind warmed as he spoke, counterintuitive in the deepening night. The stars multiplied and brightened. His mind stayed clear. He talked until he was sure that he'd told it all or at least told enough of it to count. Enough for it to be verified in some way that mattered.

"Okay," Salazar said softly. "That's enough, Israel. It's time to stop."

He had argued with her before but he did not argue now. He watched her stop recording and save the file and then saw her switch to the phone's keypad and dial a nine and a one.

"No signal here," he said. "You'll need the radio."

As she went for the radio on her belt, he reached out and stilled her hand.

"Hey," he said.

"What?"

"Did you see that kid jump?"

"Yes. Of course." She unclipped the radio and moved it to her opposite hand so she could hold on to his. That was nice. He thought about telling her so, but he didn't. He wanted to get his point across first.

"That was beautiful," he said. "When the kid jumped."

She didn't answer him. She was talking into the radio. Israel could feel the sea beneath him, which should have been troubling because he was on land, but instead it felt soothing, reminding him of days in the first skiff he'd had as a boy. He could feel the sea and he could smell the sawdust of his grandfather's shop. The sawdust overwhelmed the smell of the blood, and he was grateful for that. He closed his eyes and breathed in the scent of shaved cedar and felt the swaying sea beneath him, holding him effortlessly and even tenderly, intimately, which was amazing, because he was so small and the sea was so vast and yet it knew him.

He rocked within the waves and smelled the sawdust and when he heard Salazar's voice calling his name, he smiled, recalling the way Lyman Rankin had run and the way he had jumped, how he had faced gravity and refused it.

"That was beautiful," he said again. "When he jumped, Jenn, it was beautiful."

He knew that she agreed, even though he couldn't hear her response, couldn't hear anything now because the warm waves were all around him, shaken by a cedar-scented breeze. That was fine. He did not need her response. Didn't need anyone's response.

His story was told.

61

The day was born out of black night and into gray fog and Lyman Rankin and Hatchet sank the police boat in the red light of dawn.

She hadn't sat once. She'd stood at the wheel throughout the night, her eyes on the sea, the navigation system, or Lyman. He'd stood with her until the steady motion of the boat and the thrum of the engines lulled him to sleep, and then he'd slept leaning against her, his head bobbing with the boat. When he woke, it was still full dark and there was nothing around them but the sea. The fuel gauge on the center console showed an eighth of a tank.

That had dropped to a sixteenth of a tank—he knew because he counted the individual lines—when the predawn light welcomed them into the fog. Hatchet hadn't touched the throttle. They were running at maybe three-quarter speed. Not full out, wasting gas, but as fast as she could push it without burning too much fuel.

She knew boats.

The fog filled with rose and golden hues as the fuel gauge went down to empty. The motors kept purring.

"We're going to run out of gas," Lyman told her.

She didn't answer. Just squeezed his arm once and then returned both hands to the wheel.

Minutes passed. Miles? It was hard to know, or even guess. He heard gulls in the fog but couldn't see them. The fuel gauge was clearly indicating that they were below the E now, running on less than empty. How was that possible? How could engines run on a dry tank? Maybe the gauge wasn't accurate, or maybe the hoses between the tank and the motors held more fuel than he knew.

Either way, they were still plowing ahead.

Not for long, though. They would come to a stop soon. Then what?

He had been staring at the fuel gauge with such deep focus that he became aware of the island not from seeing it but hearing it, a subtle shift in sound that he realized was the distant boom of waves breaking on rock. He had not heard that sound all night because they'd been so alone in the darkness that there was nothing to interrupt the water.

He sat up straight, forgetting the fuel gauge, and looked ahead.

The fog was still there, but so was an island. High rock walls leading to sloping green fields. A few trees visible. A barn. Another barn, maybe two, or was one a house? He couldn't make it out in the mist, but it seemed like there had to be a home among the buildings.

The boat kept driving ahead, running on empty as the sun rose and the morning mist thinned like a curtain pulling back to reveal a stage.

A house with two barns. He was sure of that now. There were weathered wooden steps leading down from the yard to the rocky shore, and between the cliff and the first barn there was a garden protected by a fence. All of it coming into clear view, which meant that the boat was too. He was afraid of being seen after so long alone and he turned to say as much.

Hatchet was smiling, though. It was so faint that you had to know her well to recognize the hope that was in her face, but Lyman Rankin knew her well by now.

He stood silently beside her as the motors sputtered, choked, and finally died. The tide took care of the rest, washing them in toward the rocks as the sun warmed their backs. As soon as they were in the rocks, where the water jostled them but could no longer knock them off course or pull them backward, Hatchet left the wheel and limped into the stern. She knelt and unscrewed a drain plug from the transom and pulled it free, then moved to a valve on the port side and removed it, then did the same on the starboard side. She tossed the parts into the sea. Water began to fill the boat.

She pointed at a high, flat rock beside the boat.

"Help me, Lye-man," Hatchet said, and so he did, climbing onto the rock and then guiding her up out of the boat.

"Now we push," she said. They shoved the boat from the bow, spinning it, and pushed it clear of the rocks and toward a small cove with deeper water. The boat was tilted toward the sky now, the bow high, the stern low. Hatchet watched it closely while Lyman looked up at the farm above them.

Someone was crossing the yard.

It was a woman. Walking with her head tilted to the side, curious. She had gray hair tied back and up in a loose tangle and wore a flannel shirt with the sleeves rolled up her forearms. No jacket. It was a cold morning, but you could warm up fast, working in the sun. Lyman watched the woman open a gate and advance toward them in the golden light, and he wondered if Hatchet knew her, if the woman might even be her grandmother, the one she'd waited so long to return to. He started to ask, then decided not to.

Time would tell.

Hatchet put out her hand, Lyman took it, and they helped each other across the rocks and toward the shore.

ACKNOWLEDGMENTS

While writing this novel and meeting Lyman Rankin, I found myself thinking frequently about authors who wrote of and for kids in terrible situations. Thanks to Gary Paulsen, Jerry Spinelli, Angie Thomas, Walter Dean Myers, Gary Schmidt, and so many other writers of books for young people who told the truth and never truckled, to paraphrase Stephen King's paraphrase of Frank Norris. A special tip of the hatchet to Mr. Paulsen, whom we lost while I was writing this book. If you want to know how books can save lives, read his memoir *Gone to the Woods*.

The American Library Association website (ala.org) is filled with wonderful resources for children and adults, and the Child Welfare Information Gateway (childwelfare.gov) has resources about abuse-and-trafficking prevention and intervention organizations.

As for *this* book—

Richard Pine is a peerless agent and advocate and an even better man, and he saved the book at a moment when his mind could have been anywhere but on my pages. I can't say enough about Richard's work on this book and his unflagging support across the years. His colleagues at InkWell Management maintain his high standard.

My editor, Josh Kendall, deserves more thanks on this one than I can put into words, but that's probably okay by Josh, as he has waded through enough of my words. It is special to work with someone who is not only an excellent editor but also a dear friend.

Working with a publishing team like the one I'm blessed with at

ACKNOWLEDGMENTS

Hachette Book Group, Little, Brown and Company, and Mulholland Books is a privilege. Michael Pietsch, Bruce Nichols, and Craig Young give me the time to get the books right and the support to get them out to readers. Sabrina Callahan, Liv Ryan, Karen Landry, Tracy Roe, and so many more make that latter step happen.

Angela Cheng Caplan and Allison Binder have been tremendous advocates in the worlds of television and film as well as great creative partners. Gideon Pine consistently offers insight and enthusiasm when I need it most.

Tom Bernardo, Bob Hammel, and Pete Yonkman are among the brave souls who continue to step forward to read rough drafts. I thank them in typos.

My wife, Christine, deserves the dedication on every book.

ABOUT THE AUTHOR

Michael Koryta is the *New York Times* bestselling author of eighteen novels, including *Those Who Wish Me Dead,* which has been adapted into a film starring Angelina Jolie and directed by Taylor Sheridan. His previous novels were *New York Times* notable books and national bestsellers and have won numerous awards, including the Los Angeles Times Book Prize. Koryta is a former private investigator and newspaper reporter. He lives in Bloomington, Indiana, and Camden, Maine.